For my parents, who always applaud
For my sister, who first made me realize I could
For my brother, who never fails to exalt the art
For my beautiful wife, my hero, and unwavering champion

And for all just trying to find their own way through the darkness

A PERSONAL NOTE
FROM A.G. MOCK

THE LITTLE WOODS you are about to enter are real. The nearby wooded enclave called the Beechnut is also real. As is the small, idyllic neighborhood nestled innocently at their beckoning edge.

I find it worth sharing that nearly all who spent their childhood here have not only moved away, but moved *very far* away. Cast like grains of salt across the earth, the places where most of my friends now call home are invariably thousands of miles from the Little Woods. For me, I couldn't seem to get far enough away. In my own exodus, I chose to traverse an entire ocean to live and work in the United Kingdom. (Amazingly, I later came to learn that one of my closest friends from the neighborhood had made precisely the same migration.)

So, the names of the wooded enclaves and mystical childhood landmarks in this story will likely have eroded from use in the real world, as the very few who had ascribed them have long ago drifted far, far away.

The result is that only a very small handful of people today actually know about the Little Woods you are about to enter, as well as its real location. For those individuals, the memory of that dark and pervasive wood will undoubtedly elicit a convoluted mix of intense emotions, from affectionate sentiment to gut-wrenching anxiety.

I am one of them.

After reading this book, I hope you will be, too.

While the following story is fully a work of fiction, some of the incidents portrayed within are *inspired* by events which actually took place, in some form or other, in or around 1977.

I will leave it to you to decide which.

This novel, and the two that follow in the *New Apocrypha* trilogy, are therefore borne from a troubling and lifelong lack of understanding as to why so many tragedies befell what, by outward appearances, seemed a genuinely paradisiacal place to grow up. From chronic, debilitating illness to premature deaths, alleged arson to suicide, our tightly-knit community experienced an onslaught of tragedies far exceeding statistical probability for a neighborhood of such minuscule size.

So, if you were to ask me if Evil actually exists—a nebulous, invisible but ubiquitous force able to exert influence upon, and change forever, the lives of those who encounter it—I ask you, new friend, to read on.

Perhaps the story about to unfold will resound in your soul as deeply as it does mine. If I've done my job well, the next time you go for a trek in the woods you might just hesitate, if only for the briefest moment, as your soul conjures an echo of our time together in the pages that follow.

And please remember, any resemblance to persons living or dead is a matter of coincidence as all characters and events portrayed herein are of my own tortured imagination. They are not mere aliases fabricated to protect the innocent . . . . Or the others.

So now it's time!

Come with me, and we'll head into the darkness together.

After all, you're not afraid to come play in the woods, are you . . . ?

Spookily Yours,

AG Mock

THE LITTLE WOODS

BOOK ONE OF THE NEW APOCRYPHA

EPOCH

EpochThrillers.com
AGMock.com

A.G. MOCK

First paperback edition, Epoch Thrillers, 2021.

Library of Congress Control Number: 2021902170

ISBN: 978-1-7362919-0-0 ┊ paperback
ISBN: 978-1-7362919-1-7 ┊ e-book

Published by Epoch Thrillers in St. Petersburg, FL, United States
Epoch Thrillers and its raven imprint are trademarks of Epoch Thrillers

EPOCH THRILLERS
EpochThrillers.com
AGMock.com

ET 10 9 8 7 6 5 4 3 2 1 First Edition

It's indescribable how darkness brings
on the feelings which come in the night;
how everything changes and becomes
more ominous somehow.

Normality takes on a different guise
as we hide beneath the covers.

To protect ourselves.

From the things out there....

D EEP, DEEP WITHIN the primeval woods the boys would one day call the Little Woods, beyond the warm yellow glow of summer's evening and the color of the wild flowers, a Presence cast its shadow across the darkness which already lived there.

It moved through this sanctum of silence and artificial night as nothing did besides, into the bleakest depths where the air pulls crisp and cold at the lungs and the lichen and moss prosper.

As it moved it grew, enveloping the forest in gloom as the scant rogue flowers there fell before its path, laying in withered remains like funereal displays of the poor.

Around this Presence came a wind. Brushing the leaves on the trees, it compelled their branches into enchanting, ever-increasing motion. With this dance came a sound, like the eerie, distant whispering of countless discordant flutes. As the Presence seized its new realm, this whistling of the trees grew. And from it—through it—the Presence seemed to speak.

"This," *in the swaying of the trees,* "is where I shall be. This is where I shall wait."

The declaration rumbled like thunder, undulating in echoes across the wood's canopy and becoming stronger as it dared to move beyond, high into the dusk sky.

Could it have been heard, it would have been dismissed as imagination.

When it was heard, it was.

"This is where I shall feed."

This Presence was Evil.

It was looking for a home . . . .

One

1995

I
N THE NOISE of voices speaking half-conversations into a dozen telephones and myriad papers rustling in frenzied hands, Ian sat at his desk staring vacantly at the boxy, blue–grey screen of his computer monitor.

The cursor blinked back at him with equal vacuity.

He let out a long, calculated breath and rocked his chair onto its rear legs, scratching at the left side of his head and unconsciously running his finger along an indistinct scar there, just above his temple at the edge of his thick mat of hair.

Waiting on the Parker account was really pissing him off now.

He'd spent endless days, and more nights of his spare time than he wished to consider, strategizing the precisely perfect print marketing campaign for the fast-rising Parker Realty Group. With new offices popping up across the various boroughs of the city almost faster than one could keep track, Parker had the potential to become a major advertising account for the *Manhattan Bulletin*. As the newspaper's VP of Sales, Ian was sure his investment of time and, yes, even emotional buy-in, was about to pay off: sometimes you can just feel it. He was also counting on landing the account for his team to meet revenue budget this quarter. He wanted them to get their bonuses, and right now this was the only way he could see that happening.

But then came the fax transmission from Aaron Parker himself, the group's namesake. It simply read:

May look to the Times after all. Maybe try next year – AP

Most people would say Ian was reasonably easygoing. But that single line fax had him about ready to pitch a fit. Hours and hours of effort lost;

more in person meetings, lunches and drinks than he cared to consider. Oh, and don't forget the ingratiating ass kissing. There had been plenty of that. Now, with a meager one line fax, Ian's budget was out the window. Just like that.

Fuck.

He closed his eyes, hard, and could feel the blood coursing unnaturally through his eyelids. It was a threatening sensation he'd had before and was aware of the significance of it.

Okay kid, breathe . . . find your happy place, man.

He'd committed long ago that he wouldn't take his job, or anything much for that matter, too seriously. No way he wanted to end up like his father. Year after year, Ian had watched him bring all the stress and burden home with him. Every night. Chasing the money so hard and taking his work so deeply to heart that one day that heart had nearly decided that enough was enough.

But the whole Parker thing was pushing him too far.

He slammed his mug on his desk and the remnant sludge of cold black coffee splashed up, out, and over his keyboard.

"Goddammit!"

Brilliant, Cockerton. Nice job.

Sticky rivulets ran down between the keys before he could grab something to wipe it off. So instead, he sat there and simply watched.

Time to rethink strategy.

He grunted and swiveled his chair a one-eighty.

"Hey Felipe. Let's grab a cool one. Down the Major League."

Felipe gestured for Ian to keep his voice down as he pressed his ear tighter to the dirty receiver of his tan-colored desk phone. He was unconsciously wrapping its spiraled cord between his fingers as he listened intently to the other end, intermittently peppering monosyllabic comments into a conversation only he could hear.

"Yeah—yeah, well," he answered in spurts. "Yes, that's right. Yeah—uh huh. Yes. Mmm, yeah. Yes . . . bye."

Felipe Menendez held the receiver at arm's length, stared at it for a single judicious moment. Then slammed it into its cradle—hard—grimacing as he bit his lip.

At least I'm not the only one having a shitty morning, Ian thought. Then immediately felt bad about thinking it. Then laughed out loud anyway.

Menendez shook his head, rolled his eyes and sort of laughed along with him. But his was a pitchy, nervous sound like that of a child in trouble. "I hope the Old Man hung up before I slammed the phone down—"

Jeremy Jones, a.k.a. 'The Old Man,' was the paper's CEO and President. Responsible for both the Bulletin's editorial content and overall revenue stream, Jones oversaw the journalists, the ad sales reps, accounting, photography and design. All of it. The whole kit and caboodle, as they say. Not nearly as ancient as the nickname would suggest, the Old Man was a good manager. But like most in this industry, he was tough. No pussy-footing around when it came to telling his senior managers exactly what he was thinking. Ian, as head of the *Bulletin's* advertising sales operations, often envied Jones' style, wishing he could be so blunt. But alas, the advertising department was different. Ian's team (not his staff, nor his employees, but his *team*) were ultimately an insecure bunch; it just wouldn't do to take the same hard-knock approach. Things had to be handled somewhat more gingerly to get the best results from these earnest, hard-working, but somewhat fragile egos who all had something to prove. And also a little something to make them each, well—convoluted —for want of a better word.

You play to your crowd, Ian thought and smiled inwardly, amusing himself over sudden images of some of their various quirks.

"I think I heard a click," he replied to Menendez as he came back to the moment, but shrugged as he said it and raised his pitch at the end. Just enough to impart that perfectly subtle element of doubt. So it was actually delivered more like: *I think I heard a click?*

And by the time those six words made their way to his vulnerable ears, Felipe had mutated their conveyance to: *I didn't hear him hang up yet. So yes, you slammed the phone down on your hard-ass boss and now you're toast and your career is in ruins. So you might as well pack your bags.*

Amazing how the slightest change of pitch or tone could indelibly alter the meaning of a few simple words.

Of course Ian did hear the click as Jones had hung up on the other end. He'd heard it loud and clear, in fact. But he wasn't about to tell Menendez that. This was too easy. And straight-up fun.

"Oh shit. You're shitting me, right Cockerton?"

Ian shrugged noncommittally.

Menendez bit his lip. "Awww, son of a—" He cracked his number two pencil into the same number of pieces and threw them across the room where they narrowly missed a part-time receptionist named Sally, who scowled madly if a little too overly dramatic. Felipe snarled whimsically back, and both smirked.

"So, whaddya say? Ian coaxed. "Forget about it? Over a quick beer. And the Yankees–Pittsburgh game."

Menendez pored over the work lying on his desk. Papers galore were scattered among pens, cigarette stubs, expense vouchers, and Lord knows what else. His PC barely squinted out from between manila envelopes, folders, memos.

"I don't know, man. Jones wasn't very happy about that report I submitted on the Hoskins case."

Ian leaned back in his chair, clasped his hands behind his head and became statuesque still. He stared at his friend and said nothing.

Menendez plopped down in his swivel chair and rustled through some of the clutter on his desk. When he looked up and recognized the cue he swiveled to face Ian, folded his hands in front of him and stared back just as blankly. Silent and motionless.

Game on.

A solid minute passed.

Maybe another.

Perhaps an eternity of minutes.

It was a stupid thing they did: just staring dumbly at each other. No movement. No eye blinks. No twitches. Statues in a moment. Sometimes a colleague would inadvertently stumble into this connected nothingness and upon receiving no acknowledgment from either colleague, move on with a head shake and a mutter, usually about how unprofessional it was. Sophomoric. Downright ridiculous.

Then abruptly, as though the freeze had never occurred, "You're right," Menendez blurted out. His voice was as loud as the silence had been deafening just moments before. "Balls to it. I'll take another look at the Hoskins case when I get back. Let's go."

II

The Major League was a sports bar around the corner. It wasn't one of those trendy new Hi-Tech-Sports-Themed-with-Multi-Tiered-TV-Screens-Everywhere-and-MTV-Blaring-from-Every-Speaker kinda bars that were springing up all over New York these days. The Major League was old school. The real deal.

Thank God.

A guy called Tony Lamont ran it, an Italian–American who'd taken over the bar from his father in sixty-four and hadn't changed much since. A huge expanse of scuffed and dated linoleum bar ran the full length of the single open room, and only two boxy Zenith TVs—one at each end of the bar—played the game of the day. Unless there were two games of equal interest to Tony, in which case each one played and usually competed audibly for your attention as Tony had the annoying habit of keeping the volume up on both of them at the same time. It made Ian feel a little schizo. He'd said so to Lamont once, laughing as he dramatically covered his ears. But Tony told him if he didn't like it, Ian could just go drink somewhere else.

It wasn't said aggressively, just sorta matter-of-factly.

That's how Tony was. He didn't cater to his customers. There were too many for him anyhow, he'd often said. So instead, he let his customers choose him. The games on the Zeniths were therefore the games Tony wanted to watch. If you didn't like it, or asked for something else, well then, I'm afraid, that was just your tough luck out.

Now that's not to say Tony Lamont was a hard man, or didn't care about the people who paid his living. It was like this: if you decided to give his public house your patronage, then great. If you liked it and wanted to come back again, then better still. And if you really liked it and became a regular, well, then, let's just say Tony had no family of his own, and that's what you became. His family. And you were treated accordingly. Which, as we can all attest, is sometimes pleasant. And sometimes not so much.

Ian and Felipe *were* regulars. And when they walked into the bar this lunchtime, they were greeted with a warm and boisterous, Italian-accented, '*Halloooo!*'

Felipe laid his 35mm Canon on the bar. "Hiya, Tone." He held out an open hand and Lamont was already there with a capped glass bottle of beer, condensation dripping enticingly down its brown glass side. Ian held his hand out and Tony provided the same to him. Then the bar owner lifted his own bottle, tipping it toward the boys.

"Cheers, my friends."

"Cheers," Ian and Felipe responded in discordant harmony as they lifted theirs and the three bottles clinked.

"Tone. The game on yet?" Ian took a swig. On the TV, a fatherly businessman was holding up a shaver and famously proclaiming that he liked it so much, he bought the company.

"No. Not yet. But soon."

Tony stepped out of the way to provide evidence to his statement. On the dusty flickering screen a sophisticated blonde was espousing the qualities of her slim cigarette as she inhaled with a look of climactic joy, then sensually wisped the smoke from her plump, red lips. Ian puckered his own lips and espoused *her* qualities. He blew a loud and emphatic kiss toward the TV and elbowed Felipe so hard he nearly knocked the beer from his friend's hand.

"Look at that, will ya?"

"That chick? Man, you get too excited Cockerton. She's way too false. And too—" Felipe surveyed the bar to make sure none were within earshot: "Too blonde."

"You can never be too blonde."

"I agree with Felipe." Tony leaned down, propping his elbows on the bar between them as he continued to polish a glass. "She is too blonde, my friend. That's your trouble Ian. You go for those phony types. You should find yourself a nice, dark Italian girl. One who knows how to cook her mama's pasta. That's what you need."

Felipe laughed and voiced his concurrence.

"Yeah, yeah. So you always tell me, Tone."

"Well, you always ask, my friend. So I tell you. And you need my advice. It will get you far, that I promise you."

"That's just the problem," Ian muttered as the barman turned to serve another. "I don't ask."

The barman turned around, slowly, placing his hand to his ear. "I didn't hear you, my friend?"

Ian's eyes were saucers. "Uh—nothing, Tony." But there it was again, that mischievous, pivotal pitch. So his words had actually come out like, *Uh—nothing, Tony?* Only this time Ian hadn't intended the betraying rise in tone. Nope, that was all nerves.

He cleared his throat.

"Just appreciative of your sage advice, Tone."

Lamont considered this glaringly obvious recant for a moment, cocking his head to one side. Ian could virtually see the cogs turning as Lamont considered his next move. Would he be kicked out of the bar today? Banned for a week? For life? You just never knew with Tony Lamont.

"No problem," Tony answered (except it actually did sound a lot more like *'noah probalem'*) and returned to serving an anonymous customer Ian hadn't seen around the Major League before. But then again, ten million people in the city, you're bound to bump into a new face or two. Even at your local hangout.

Ian spun on his stool and squared up to Menendez. "Oh yeah! That's *one!*" He thrust his index finger in Menendez's face.

Felipe shrugged. "Man, you've got nineteen more to go before you beat my record, son."

For weeks they'd had a running bet on how many times in a single sitting Tony Lamont would say 'no problem' without them unduly prompting him. Felipe was in the lead, and had been for nearly two weeks, which meant a free beer from Ian every visit until the record was broken and there was a changing of the guard, as it were. Like the Parker account, this, too, was pissing off Ian in a big kind of way.

"Still a whole game to go, my friend." For some reason, Ian acted out a lame impression of Groucho Marx flicking his cigar.

Felipe was confused, but didn't like to ask. So he simply laughed instead, not really with Ian, but at him. Sometimes, Felipe thought, that was just the best way.

The roar of the crowd crackled weakly from the two Zeniths' crusty speakers as some West End musical chick finished the national anthem. Before she'd even completed the word 'brave,' twenty thousand people were applauding wildly. Whether this was in response to her performance or anticipation of the game, Ian couldn't decide. It was more exciting to believe that it was in baited anticipation, so that's what he convinced himself as the Pittsburgh Pirates trotted onto the field at Yankee Stadium.

"Sweetness," he said aloud, probably without realizing it.

"You must be joking," Felipe returned, as only a true New York Yankees fan would. "Pirates? Those guys couldn't steal milk from their mamas. Never seen a sorrier bunch . . . ."

His words trailed away as the Yankees threw the first pitch: a low fast ball, just below the batter's knee. It was met with a beautifully firm *crack* of the bat and the ball rocketed in a crisp, level flight over the pitcher's head. It gained height as it soared over the shortstop, passed above the outfielders, who reached desperately but fruitlessly, then arched and dropped into the stands where a throng of fans scrambled to catch it. After an uncertain moment, one middle-aged man appeared from the melee and held the ball high in the air, met with a low muttered chorus of disappointment.

Home run.

"Yes! *Homer!*" Ian exclaimed as he beat his hands furiously against the bar. "Sweetness!"

Felipe Menendez's gaze was stone-like. His eyes bore calmly into Ian's face and ripped out his friend's tongue. If only he could.

"Already? I don't believe it," Tony said disconsolately as he shook his head. "Just don't believe it . . . ."

"I know," Menendez said and extended his hands to the bar owner who in turn took them and patted them. Theirs was a remorse that could only be dealt them by the Pirates.

The Pittsburgh Pirates, for God's sake.

The two bowed their heads in silence while Ian, always one to be sensitive to his friends (that, and the fact that he was indeed sitting in a city bar in the heart of Yankees territory) got up from his barstool, looked around at the variously disappointed New York faces, and of course . . . started to dance. And scream. And shout, and laugh.

"Homer homer *homer!*" he chanted, the grin on his face so wide he looked almost insane. He wouldn't have believed it if he hadn't seen it with his own eyes. Lewis, the batter, was rounding the bases and about to take home plate.

The stadium—well, perhaps a tenth of it, anyway—went wild.

Pirates 1. Yankees 0.

"Did you see that, Menendez? Did you *see* that?"

"Yeah, yeah, Cockerton. I saw it."

Then a voice, loud and unfamiliar, bellowed from the shadows at the back of the barroom. "Hey you. *Pirate Boy.*" The intonation of the voice was flat, but deep. And somehow inexplicably malicious.

Ian turned to find the source of the voice: a large, burly man in a corner booth, sporting a camo jacket and a matted dark beard . . . the anonymous man Tony had been serving just a moment earlier.

Anonymous was silent for a moment. Then he rose from his booth and calmly, but oh-so clearly, instructed Ian to shut the fuck up. "Shut the fuck up right now, PIRATE BOY."

Everything and everyone in the bar fell silent. Except for the two dusty televisions which, oblivious to the drama about to unfold in a small saloon on 42nd and 3rd, were crackling with a tinny organ melody as a cartoon Yankees pitcher threw a strike across the stadium's Jumbotron, then winked to the crowd as the rally text 'Let's Go Yankees!' spun across the giant screen.

It was a disturbingly surreal backdrop to Anonymous pulling out a .38 magnum from his waistband and aiming it squarely at Ian.

Ian's gut loosened as his chest tightened, pulling his body internally in two different directions at once. His lungs constricted, the ribs pressing down upon them. Prickles spread down his spine.

Anonymous took a step forward and the barrel of the revolver was now so close that Ian felt he was staring down the mouth of a cannon. It was unreal.

This is fucking unreal, Ian thought, rebuffing what his eyes were seeing.

Except it wasn't.

"N-now look. Buddy," he stuttered, trying hard not to stumble over the words as they forced through his lips on the barest wisps of air. He swallowed. A hard, dry effort. "Look. I meant no offense—"

Anonymous did not move. Except the tip of his index finger which tightened on the trigger. While it may have been imperceptible to everyone else in the bar, to Ian it was a terrifyingly tangible motion.

The .38's cylinder softly clicked along its natural clockwise rotation and the hammer pulled back, locking into firing position.

"Fucking outsider bastard scum," Anonymous calmly said in an almost soothing, eerie monotone. Then he shouted it at the top of his voice, *"Fucking bastard scum!"*

Menendez, hands up and palms out in the accepted gesture of non-confrontation, eased cautiously off his barstool. "Look, I think we can—" he calmly began until Anonymous spun the revolver toward him so swiftly it was astonishing.

"Fuck off Tex-Mex. You're another'un. Fucking bastard outsider scum! Now sit back down. Sit back down *right now* before I blow your Spick ass all the way back to Tijuana where it belongs."

Menendez backed slowly up onto his barstool.

Anonymous returned his attention to Ian but did not alter the .38's aim upon Menendez. "Now, Pirate Boy. Tell me one good reason why I shouldn't blow your friend's cock off." Without breaking eye contact with Ian, he quite accurately lowered the revolver's barrel just the perfect number of degrees so that it was now aimed squarely at Felipe's crotch. It was a move that reeked of extreme familiarity with aiming this weapon at a human target at close range; almost muscle memory. "*TELL ME!*"

"Wait!" Ian pleaded. "You've got no argument with him. It's me that's pissed you off. Point that damned thing at me!"

Anonymous shrugged, his mouth pulling into something like a twisted mimic of a smile. "How sweet. Sticking up for your faggot boyfriend. But I do have something against him. Against all o' you. Fucking faggots. Fucking weirdos. Bringing this country down. THE LOT OF YA. Outsider shits and freaks . . . ." His voice had broken to a disturbing crescendo and then flattened just as abruptly as he returned the gun's aim upon Ian.

Silence.

Except for the baseball game which played on. Something in the recesses of Ian's mind told him the Yankees had just scored a homer of their own, and with the bases loaded. And just like that, the Pirates had lost their advantage.

Sitting at the end of the bar on his own, an elderly man began to hyperventilate. His face was dirty and unshaven, hair and clothes ruffled and filthy. What no one knew was that the elderly man had scraped together whatever he could, just to pay for that single beer he was about to nurse for the next three hours. Equally, what no passersby on the street knew—nearly all who had refused him their pocket change—was that a two dollar beer would keep the elderly man out of the searing summer heat and provide, for a few hours anyway, the meekest sense of social belonging. It would allow him to watch a baseball game alongside a handful of fellow human beings. Which meant, for at least that period of time, the elderly man wasn't homeless; wasn't an outcast; wasn't a pariah. For the next few hours, the elderly man was just a regular guy. Watching a baseball game. And just like everyone else in about every way.

Except that he wasn't.

Right now, everyone else in the bar was silent. Statuesque.

Except the elderly man.

Coming unbalanced atop his barstool, he was clutching alarmingly at his chest as his breath escaped his mouth in shallow, rapid bursts. Shrill, hissing whimpers issued between these as he urgently sucked the air right back in again.

It was the excuse Anonymous needed.

He spun toward the sound and pulled his index finger.

Twice.

The first shot exploded the old man's chest, throwing him from the barstool as his insides came out. Despite the shot's deafening thunder, it was the sound the hollow-point made as it shattered the old man's ribs that Ian would never forget.

The revolver's barrel unwavering, its second round removed half of the elderly man's face as he had already begun sliding from the stool. Lifeless, his body slumped to the dirty tile floor and in the centrally cooled air, a small plume of steam rose from the man's insides.

Soft moans and wails filled the bar where, only minutes before, the men there had been laughing and swearing, reveling in the venue's inherent machismo. Now, all of that had vanished to insignificance as the murmur of stifled cries lent an odious, unnatural quality to the barroom's new vulnerability.

Frozen, his palms still held high in the air, Ian peered from the corner of his eye to see that even Menendez was weeping silently. And Ian screamed. "Jesus! He was only scared!"

Anonymous pivoted and the .38 magnum was again pointing back at Ian's forehead. This time, it was held a little less steadily, the smoking barrel swaying in the smallest, wavering ellipses. Ian could smell the gunmetal and sulfur scent of it, wafting foreign amidst the more familiar odors of stale beer and sweat. Then came the stink of the old man's ruptured organs, reeking like liquid iron.

Ian doubled over and retched. No liquid came with the reflex, but the acid taste of bile rose into his throat.

Anonymous required no further aggression. His index finger pulled back upon the .38's trigger a third time and an explosion seemed to rupture Ian's skull. It was an echoing *BOOM—boom—boom,* the unbearable percussion of a turntable's needle dropping onto a vinyl record at maximum volume and bouncing erratically across the tracks.

The world faded to grey as Ian collapsed—

—And behind him, Tony Lamont was reeling from the recoil of the 12-gauge sawn-off shotgun he'd just drawn from beneath the bar.

Anonymous' face dissolved, evaporating its features as the shotgun's flash of light and concussive sound filled the room. His body buckled unnaturally as it pitched backward, arms windmilling wildly as his index finger completed its pull upon the .38's trigger.

The shot went wide and embedded into a far wall as Anonymous, or what was left of him, crashed through a table and the revolver skidded across the floor, spinning.

The vile liquid of Ian's stomach finally released itself as his eyes, and his consciousness, shut to the nightmare scene.

†††

The car is in the road, on a hill, Hamburger Hill they used to call it? It's an old Ford. Oh! His parents had one like that. But this one is a crumpled mess. Ian steps (floats) closer to it and sees the people.

How could this have happened?

The front passenger seat extends well beyond where the windshield once was. The steering wheel is cocked and twisted, the driver's torso spread against it as if in rest. The man could be mistaken for asleep, if not for the spherical white bone poking through his skin.

Twenty yards from the car, the woman lays on the road. Her torso is folded backward.

At first, the sound of the sirens are a whisper in the distance. They grow louder. And louder. A kind of inharmonious whistling as their shrieking tones combine; a binaural calliope which raises the skin on the back of Ian's neck. Their lights illuminate the night sky, washing the backdrop of trees in a mixing, moving glow of blue and red. They grow brighter and brighter until they crest the top of the hill.

As the light within the man and woman grows dimmer and dimmer, then is extinguished altogether.

IV

The voice in Ian's ear was muffled, barely distinguishable. It sounded like it could be saying his name, but he wasn't certain. It was coming to him in discordant, binaural tones blaring through (behind) a static ringing. He began to lift his head from the floor when a thick pain lodged at the top of his skull, dull and throbbing, as if someone had thumped him with a sledgehammer.

Gonna be one hell of a headache, he warned himself, though he wasn't entirely certain why he felt this way.

Or even where he was.

He opened his eyes to the nauseating wash of swimming red and blue lights from the emergency service vehicles.

"Wha—" he started, but speaking made the blunt thud in his skull even worse. Then came the stench of his own vomit and he began to remember. He was lifting his head from the pool of it when he felt someone tugging on his shoulders, trying to help him off the floor.

"Jesus, buddy. Some afternoon." Menendez said, straddled over him and pulling him up. The words came to Ian faint and muffled as though underwater. They grew more clear once the ringing in his ears had risen to a crescendo then softened. "But you're gonna be okay. Let's just take you to those nice people over there . . . ."

Menendez positioned Ian's arm around his neck and carefully walked his friend around the dead man—Anonymous, Ian realized—laying virtually faceless upon the remnants of a splintered wooden table.

Ian's stomach contracted and pulled.

Outside, paramedics were frantically sliding gurneys out of ambulances and rushing into the bar, laden with cases of equipment.

"Gun shock," Menendez said to one of them, as if he had the slightest clue what he was talking about. It only made him sound doltish. "He was only like a foot away when the shotgun discharged. I thought he was—"

"We'll take it from here," the medic interrupted with objective disinterest and carefully placed Ian upon a gurney. Two more responders seemed to descend upon him from out of nowhere, and now all three surrounded the gurney, each picking or prodding or appraising, as Ian lay there dazed and motionless.

Vultures descending upon a carcass, Felipe couldn't help but think as the image seemed to change before his eyes like something out of an old Roadrunner cartoon. He almost grinned, then instantly reprimanded himself. *C'mon Felipe. These are caring people. What a shit job they had to do. Especially in this fucking city.*

He didn't know how long he stood there like that, or when he stepped away from the flurry of activity. But when Felipe Menendez opened his eyes again, the cartoon scene was gone and he was back inside the bar.

Half a dozen men and women in black shiny CORONER jackets were hunched over the remains of what had, just minutes earlier, been Anonymous and the elderly man. Behind the bar, a handful of cops were fervently interviewing Tony Lamont. The proprietor's eyes were streaming, his face contorted, mouth unnaturally stretching with every word, the way a toddler's does when it's on the verge of a meltdown. It was clear Lamont was trying his best to answer their questions, but also trying desperately not to lose his composure.

It wasn't working.

Tony broke down sobbing and buried his head in his hands, dropping to his knees while the cops looked on with barely disguised derision.

Felipe had obviously never seen the unflappable bar owner this way, and it was this realization, more than any other, that made him feel weak and suddenly very unsteady himself. He reached for his camera bag and noticed his hands were cold and trembling. As though not his own but merely on loan, his fingers were thick and slow as he fumbled through its contents. It was odd and slightly unnerving, the way it feels the first time you drive an unfamiliar car.

Meanwhile, unaware he was being watched, one of the cops with Tony rolled his eyes and chuckled. He shook his head as Lamont continued trying to lift himself from his knees but couldn't. Another cop mouthed the word, 'PUSSY,' and all of his buddies smirked and had to lower their gazes to keep from busting into full-blown laughter.

Vultures may be a little unfair, Felipe thought. *Unfair, but accurate.*

He pulled his 35mm Canon from his camera bag and reeled off some shots for the newspaper.

Fuck the Hoskins story. Jones is going to love these.

V

That night, in his modest studio apartment overlooking north Central Park West, Ian paced the hardwood floors in aimless circles. There was an unexpected sense of comfort in the way his sock-laden feet made their gently muted *phhuund sound* as they padded over the glossed hardwood floors. He hugged himself, repeatedly rubbing his upper arms to keep warm, despite the thermometer on the apartment's terrace reading 76°.

Across the avenue, amber evening light was slowly waning as his idyllic little piece of Central Park started to succumb to shades of grey. Once again, the silhouette of his 108th Street apartment building was beginning its nightly trek into the northern edge of the park. Soon it would fully envelope the Blockhouse and choke off all daylight from the iconic rocky stronghold. And there the park's woodland, which by day offered such wonderfully innocent respite to a haggard city's people, would begin spawning the stuff of nightmares for untold victims, unfortunate—or witless—enough to be lulled into the glow of cool evening enchantment. For human predators, not monsters, stalked those wooded glades by night, transforming their beauty into a dangerous, bête noire.

Maybe they are monsters, Ian reconsidered, and a tingle passed through his body, starting between his shoulder blades and working down his back. How could such a presence of peace and enjoyment devolve into such a tyrannical horror after the sun had cast its daily farewell?

The park stared back at him and had no answer; only smirked.

... The sound whistled through the branches of the trees....

It wasn't long after he moved into the apartment that Ian realized he would spend most of his evenings out here on the terrace, where things could be nicest. It didn't really matter how big (or small) the studio apartment was. He essentially lived on this six-by-nine wrought iron balcony, safely twenty-five feet above the throngs and happenings of the street, for as much of the year as he could muster. It made him wish tha—

With a sudden jolt, the cordless phone on the small table next to him screamed to life, its shrill electronic ring so loud and foreign to the rest of the gentle twilight murmurs that Ian winced. He'd left the ringer on its loud setting because the phone was usually out here, and that was the only way it could be heard over the street noise. But tonight was oddly quiet, and it didn't help that his nerves were already frayed; or that he was standing just a foot away as it audibly exploded.

He caught his breath, picked up the receiver in trembling fingers and pulled the antenna from its sheath, extending it fully. "HELLO." His greeting was terse. He didn't really care.

"Ian. It's Felipe. How are you ... I mean really?"

Ian paused before lying: "Fine, I'm okay. How're you?"

There was zero hesitation from Felipe.

"Great, I mean, we got a great story down there. And you should see the pics—"

"Yeah. Great," Ian replied in scantily disguised indifference.

Two men dead, a friend questioned by the cops—cops from the same precinct accused of beating the shit out of a vigilante in midtown just two weeks earlier—but at least the *Bulletin* would have tomorrow's exclusive front page. And that's what mattered. Right?

"Brilliant," he added listlessly.

Felipe didn't pick up what he was laying down. "Yeah man. Isn't it! And hey, you're sure you're okay. Right?"

Ian didn't want to answer again. So he said nothing.

Menendez ignored the silence.

"Oh yeah, and the Old Man says we can have tomorrow off. How about that?" Felipe chuckled nervously as he debated in his own mind whether or not to say what was lingering there. He decided he'd just say it: "Any other hangouts we can get a great story tomorrow lunchtime?"

When the comment was met with a *click* from Ian's end, Menendez knew he'd taken it a step too far. He softly placed the phone in its cradle with a frown.

Despite all the outward bravado, Felipe had come home that afternoon and sobbed alone as he rocked back and forth on his bed, the day's horrific events playing over and over again in his mind. And when his beautiful wife, Luisa, had come home from work, Felipe cried again as she cradled him in her arms.

He was sure Ian would know he was only joking on the phone.

Well, sort of joking.

He'd go to Cockerton's in the morning, then get some bran muffins and freshly squeezed juice from their favorite deli near Times Square. And everything would be alright again . . . .

Across town, Ian shivered on the terrace and switched off the cordless handset. He placed it on the metal table, where tiny droplets of condensation were already beginning to form in the swiftly cooling night air. Hearing Felipe's voice had revived the nightmare at the bar in a tidal wave of emotion.

Anonymous. The revolver barrel in his face, big as a cannon. The elderly man wheezing . . . his torso splintering.

Then from nowhere:

The car on the road. The crumpled mess.

Ian railed against the horrifying image, pushing the disjointed scene away before it was allowed to fully take hold of him.

But those people, why do I feel like I should know those people?

He stepped inside and reached for the Scotch.

It would help. For now.

He poured more fingers than normal, over precisely three cubes of ice (always three) and settled deep into the soft cushions of his futon as the sounds of the evening outside washed over him. Lifting the tumbler to his lips, again and again, soon only the discolored cubes of ice remained.

Then he closed his eyes.

It wasn't more than two hours later when he awoke from the same hazy dream he had experienced at the bar. Its lingering sensation—an uneasy feeling, more than anything—caused him to tentatively scan the studio apartment. He'd left the French doors open to the terrace and the summer's night breeze was wafting in through the curtains to reveal in spurts both the glare of the lights and the sounds of the traffic and passersby below. The mix was soothingly tangible against the angst of the uncertain dream which, along with the sounds and the lights, commingled upon his waking state in ebbs and flows as the curtains billowed open, gently fell back upon the doors, then wafted open once more.

. . . The car . . . .

Another fragment of the unsettling dream, filling him with a sense of despair that made his stomach heavy.

Ian stepped onto the terrace and picked the cordless phone from its cradle. He switched it back on and dialed the Eight-One-Four area code before pausing to look at his watch.

9:32pm.

Hesitation. That old feeling of impotent vulnerability.

Then the rest of the dream which flooded his senses in a deluge, the frayed images—

The hill . . . the man pressed into the steering wheel . . . the contorted woman on the road . . . .

—and feelings joining in a way that, while still not making sense, were suddenly all too real.

He punched in the rest of his brother's number. It rang only twice before it was answered.

"Hello?" A soft, rounded female accent greeted him. It was Bryan's wife, Rebecca.

Ian forced an unnatural smile as he spoke, knowing the physical act would change the tone of his voice; perhaps hide his concern a little more effectively than he felt able to do otherwise.

"Rebecca, it's Ian."

A moment of silence as the name registered. Then: "Ian! Oh my God, how are you? It's been such a long time."

"I know, I know. And I'm sorry. I've just been so busy. At work. You know."

"Yeah, tell me about it."

"Hmmm. Yeah. Hey Bec, is Bryan there?"

"Yeah, sure hun. Hang on a mo'." Muffled by a hand over the receiver, Rebecca called out his brother's name. "He's coming now, Ian. I'll talk to you later, okay?"

Ian's reply dwindled away as he heard her speaking over him in the background, telling his brother who it was just before Bryan picked up.

"Little brother, how the hell are ya?" Bryan asked genuinely.

"Okay. I'm alright. How 'bout you?" Truth was, Ian wasn't interested in eliciting an actual response. He was too anxious to get to the meat of the conversation. But he knew he'd have to take it slow at first. No need to upset his brother, or the man's entire family, without being certain of this whole thing. He'd just scout around for some info that might confirm or rebuff his worry.

Meanwhile, Bryan had been answering his question and Ian hadn't heard a single word of it.

"Good," Ian interjected randomly at what felt like an appropriate break, and breathed a bit easier when it seemed to fit. "Hey listen, how are Mom and Dad?"

At last, he'd been able to cut to the reason for the call.

It was an eternity before Bryan answered, the line clicking silently as the sound of the live electronics connected them across the three-hundred-odd miles of phone line.

Ian hadn't spoken to his father for nearly four years. His mother, sometimes, when she was alone. But his father, never. Not since the argument. Not since Ian had left for New York. Harold Cockerton (everyone called him 'Hare,' like those oversized rabbits) wasn't so keen on his youngest son's plans to leave home for the Big Apple. Hare knew only too well what kind of things went on in the city, and had no intention of seeing Ian fall into those same traps. Hare Cockerton himself lived in New York for a spell as a young man, before eventually coming back to settle into adulthood in the same small Pennsylvanian town where he'd grown up. And he was scared witless about Ian going. About losing him. Besides, the boy had done nothing but odd jobs after college, none of which he stuck to for more than six months at a time. And now at twenty-six the boy planned to not only leave town, but go to a dirty, crowded, mean city like New York. And get a job. And supposedly a career. 'Yes. And a good one,' Ian had confidently asserted. But Hare Cockerton didn't like the idea of it. Not one bit. He was sure Ian would be better off staying home and getting an entry level job at the mill. He'd see what he could rustle up.

". . . What makes you ask?" Bryan's voice finally closed the gap and as the silence evaporated, so did the memory.

Ian shook his head to separate, sort and understand the muddle of thoughts trying to confuse him.

. . . The car. . . .

"Look Bryan," he snapped. "Stop messing with me. I need to know. So just tell me. Now. Are they okay? Are they safe?"

Silence. A breath.

"Bryan! Fucking *tell me.*"

"Alright already . . . they're fine. Just fine. Why? What's with the sudden interest, Ian?" A hint of that old protective tone was beginning to creep into his tone.

"Are you sure, Bryan?"

"Jesus, Ian. Yeah I'm sure. You're starting to scare me a little, here. I think the question is, are you okay?"

Ian thought about answering truthfully.

And nearly did.

God, how it would have been comforting to tell his big brother the whole story: the bar, the psycho, the .38, the blood, the weird dream. Just to have someone believe him. It was all so crazy. For someone to simply hear him, to tell him it was all going to be all right would mean everything right now.

"I'm fine," Ian finally replied. "Just a strange thing happened to me today. Nothing big . . . ."

He paused.

"But it made me think of Mom and Dad."

"Hmmm," Bryan said and then paused a good couple of moments himself. "You're sure—"

"I'm sure. I Promise," Ian affirmed. What Bryan could not see was the slow, negative shake of Ian's head as the words had come out of his mouth. A manifestation of his sub-conscious mind, Ian himself was not even aware of the gesture. "And you're telling me straight about the Aged Parents?"

"Dead straight," Bryan assured him. "In fact, they just left. Like an hour ago. They were over here to see the kids. I mean, it's been at least three full days since they last saw them."

He chuckled awkwardly and cleared his throat.

"I end up getting the overdose of attention to make up for what they can't give you. It's great."

For a fleeting moment he almost prompted Ian to give them a call, but his better judgment decided against it. He'd rather just keep the peace. And then he completely ignored his own advice:

"Ian, why don't you call the old man a—"

"I'm not calling him Bry. He should've called me years ago. When I first came out here. Even if only to see that I was alright."

"You know he wanted to. And you know he cared," Bryan said more sternly.

"Do I?"

"Hell yeah." His tone softened. "He had me telling him everything you were up to, every time you and me talked or wrote. He was just too damn stubborn to pick up the phone. Manly pride. Where the hell do you think you get it from?"

Safely hidden within the blindness of the telephone, Ian allowed himself a slight smile. He was happy they weren't speaking in person. He wasn't quite ready to surrender. Not just yet anyway.

"Yeah, yeah, yeah. Tell me another one, Bry. Next you'll be saying he misses me."

"Honestly. There's no pleasing you sometimes. There really isn't."

The conversation continued for another ten minutes as they pivoted to talking about sports, and what the kids were up to, and other catch-up type nothingness. And for a short while, Ian actually forgot about the bar. And the dream.

His brother always had a way of doing that for him.

Ian took a quick minute to also chat cordially with Rebecca before hanging up, telling her to give the kids a kiss from their Uncle Ian, then called it a night. He hadn't noticed the chill as he talked, but now, as he looked out over the park and the darkness there, he felt the feeling of cold creeping back over him. Again he embraced himself, rubbing his hands over his thickly knit sweater before stepping back inside and gently pulling the French doors closed behind him.

The sounds of the busy street below disappeared as he nestled back into the futon. And like the remainder of the Scotch, the slumber which came was warm and soothingly encompassing.

At first.

In the receptivity of deepest sleep, Ian's mind opened and dream and reality mixed together. They ebbed and flowed as Ian's subconscious searched for something, someone, a forgotten face he hadn't even known he'd forgotten.

Someone from his childhood.

... There's a tree ... the face is a friend ... and there's woods ... ?

Ian rolled uneasily in the slumber, his pillow pulled tightly to his chest. The lines of his forehead folded into deep furrows as the scene morphed. Now he was watching a car, on Hamburger Hill.

... The husband and wife are on the front bench seat of the car. They are laughing and smiling as they climb toward the crest of the hill. Until the woman's smile skews instantly into the shape of a scream ...

A boy suddenly appeared beside the road.

... as the tractor trailer is a behemoth heading towards them ...

The boy was—

... and crosses the center line, the husband tugging hard on the steering wheel, his foot planted against the brake pedal. The car's tail slides, careening first to one side, then the other. The pungent stench of blistering tire rubber is the last sensation the couple experience before the truck and car ...

—a childhood pal, one Ian had long ago forgotten. Despite the nightmare dreamscape playing out behind this boy, Ian smiled at the fond remembrance of him.

... come together, metals blending, the woman thrown from the soft, comfortable glow of the car's cabin ...

As swiftly as it had come, Ian's smile evaporated.

... and a serrated sheet of metal slices so easily through the soft flesh of the man's neck ...

And his mouth opened to a scream.

... as the boy along the roadside is enthralled, his face alight at the

violence and the chaos. He claps and bounces in giddy excitement as the car is swallowed up by the truck and they meld together, a single twisted mass of metal and rubber and glass and smoke, scraping across the blacktop. They come to a jarring rest in the thicket of brown grass along the verge . . .

Though Ian sucked air deep into his lungs, in his sleep he was frozen with fear; the scream would not expel.

. . . as the boy slowly turns and looks directly at Ian. Thin, bloodless lips curl into a distorted grin as the boy exposes the impossible awareness: a morose cognizance between he as dream figure, and Ian as dream maker. The boy knows Ian is watching him—

The jarring peal of the cordless phone wrenched Ian from the vision, his hands scrabbling reflexively for the handset. Trembling beyond capability, the phone slid from his grasp and he had to fumble blindly for it in the dark. It continued to ring, slightly muffled as it skirted under the futon where he lay.

He snatched it up with considerable effort as the trembling in his hands spread like a drowning wave through his entire body.

Before he even heard the voice on the other end of the line, tears of apprehension were already running down his face.

Thin and uncertain, the voice was Bryan's. It numbly said:

"Ian, I think you should come home."

VII

The note Ian left on the call buzzer box in the lobby would be waiting for his friend when Felipe came for breakfast. Felipe always came for breakfast, and the two always went to the same deli near Times Square where the Mexican would offer to pay for them both then conveniently forget that he did so by the end of the meal.

All the note said was that there were problems at home, and Ian would be taking more than just the one day off. He would need a few.

'Be sure to tell Jones,' it finished.

Felipe was concerned when he found the note, but not overly so.

At least he wouldn't have to pretend to buy breakfast today.

VIII

It was not an easy journey home, and Ian certainly could have made it a great deal easier. But despite the urgency, he wanted to do it this way. He *needed* to do it this way. He needed the time. Time to think; time to digest. Time to breathe.

It took twenty-two minutes to the Port Authority bus terminal in the center of the city. Despite Ian's insistence there was no hurry, the taxi driver zigged and zagged through midtown traffic, slicing minutes off the ride as he adeptly cleared untold numbers of yellow lights just before turning red. Ian initially thought the driver was trying to provide exceptional service by getting his fare to his destination ASAP. But then he realized the cabbie was merely trying to get rid of him as soon as possible. With that base charge, quicker trips mean more fares per shift, which means more money for Yosef (the Hungarian driver's name). The driver's genuine gratitude for a modest two-dollar tip made Ian realize just how different their worlds were.

It was then a little over an hour as he then waited at the terminal's below ground gate—*which would make a perfectly good dungeon, should its utilization ever change*, Ian thought—as any number of various night crawlers offered to carry his bags or slit his throat for a fiver, whichever he preferred. Tonight, the bags won the toss. They might not have only a day earlier, before blind, youthful bravado had been bested by the shockingly thin veneer of mortality.

Another hour and a bit crossing the city, and a small segment of urban New Jersey.

Four more hours as the Greyhound rolled ceaselessly on through the dead of night, eating mile after mile of Pennsylvania's desolate central corridor which is Interstate 80.

Twenty-five minutes for a quick bite and a desperately-needed slash when the bus driver pulled into a Love's truck stop, sliding the bus effortlessly into an elongated space alongside three other buses and at least six or seven tractor trailers, all enjoying the benefit of cozy sleeper cabs.

As the sun came up, there were two more hours which passed the slowest as golden morning light slowly revealed the landmarks of his youth.

Then six and two-thirds minutes while Ian waited to offload his bags from the bus. Not too bad considering his were first on, last off.

So all-in-all, and ten hours later, Ian was home.

IX

There were few people in the bus depot as he waited for Bryan. Its empty halls echoed with every footstep or self-conscious murmur. It was cold and unpalatable; not at all the grand terminal of bustling excitement it once would have been. The gloomy disparity only served to make him all the more nervous at being here.

It had been a very long time; and what shit circumstances.

Again.

Ian walked about the station, listening to the hypnotic sound of his steps as they padded slowly about the polished stone floor. To say he was exhausted after traveling all night would be an understatement, and the soft, firm rhythm of his leather soled boots sounded as a metronome to drown out the world, seducing him to the side of warm, soft sleep.

He did not allow himself to succumb.

Instead, he paced slowly up and down the cool marble hall, listening. Thinking. Remembering.

After several circuits around the concourse, he dropped back against a smooth stone column, the leather of his jacket smacking with a reassuring sound as it kissed the marble. The trip had given him some breathing space, a critically needed separation between his normal, daily life and . . .

and this. Yet the anxiety of his youth, which he recognized all too well, began to bubble and simmer as the weight of this new reality truly began to sink in. He could not accept it. This was not real. None of it.

How could it be . . . ?

While the journey had helped him center, it hadn't actually presented any clarity, or managed to answer anything at all. In fact, it hadn't changed a single damn thing.

Because his parents were dead. And here he was, waiting in the bus station for his brother to come pick him up and take him back to their childhood home.

The place where it had all changed. And where he'd committed he would never return.

Yet here he was.

This. Is. Not. Real.

He kept repeating the mantra, but it didn't change the facts. But then again, he hadn't expected that it would. *Who would possess such powers, other than God?* What he had expected, was that it would calm his nerves, turn off the burner beneath his simmering anxiety.

Somehow, it did the opposite, the falsehood of the statement burnishing the tension rather than assuaging it.

And yet, in so many ways, this actually was not real. Because this just didn't happen. Not in everyday life. Not to normal people. *Surely?* Things like this only took place somewhere 'out there,' in the place we don't see, to people we don't know, in a hypothetical circumstance that does not really exist.

So you see, this wasn't real life.

At the very least, it couldn't be *his* life. Could it?

. . . the car is imploding, metal and plastic slicing through the driver's flesh, firing the passenger from it's safe haven; a sickening explosion of ribs, and blood dissolving features . . . .

The disturbing images made Ian feel tangibly sick. But try as he might, he couldn't prevent their intrusion. Then again appeared:

. . . the boy . . . .

At first, the child was foreign to Ian, so long had it been since he'd consciously thought of him. But then came that warm, crooked smile, and he recognized the expression he had experienced at least a million times before, buck teeth and all.

The boy was Ian's dearest childhood friend, Matt Chauncey.

. . . behind Matt's smiling visage, the car collapses. The man behind the wheel is swallowed up and becomes indiscernible from the vehicle, the woman bounces off the blacktop and comes to rest, bent and contorted, at the end of a spray of her own blood that begins to pool on the warm tar beneath her . . . .

Ian silently retched as he grappled to understand why a long forgotten friend from his childhood was so disparately inserted into this brutal nightmare vision of his parents. Then came an array of fresh images: new, yet ancient; intimately familiar, yet distant. They rose from somewhere deep, in a place he had not accessed in a very, very long time, and were soothing and unsettling at once. It was a film which flickered beneath his conscious thought, enveloped by a haze so thick, he was unable to process little more than the feeling of it. Yet somehow, he was aware that this memory would soon be revealed. Frame by frame.

The one thing he does see, with absolute clarity, is that he and Matt are together.

. . . they are in a wood . . . .

A shrill, piercing screech ripped Ian from the memory and he was relieved to see that he was still in the bus depot, comforted by the growing number of people making their way to buses and trains. He pressed the palm of his hand against the cool marble pillar he was still leaning against, and that, too, provided grounding relief. Across the large hall, the shrieking sound was coming from a young boy in basketball shorts and a psychedelic *Fresh Prince* T-shirt who had discovered what happens when you kick-scrape your sneakers across a smooth, hard surface. The boy was reveling at the array of high-pitched, penetrating tones he could elicit as he dragged his foot across the polished stone floor in varying amounts of pressure and duration. He would then beam with sheer delight as each of the resulting skin-prickling screeches echoed impressively throughout the great, acoustical concourse.

Ian found himself deeply entranced as the boy shimmied this way and that, consumed only by his own, unique world; expertly playing the floor like an inharmonious instrument. He hadn't thought about those childhood days for a very, very long time, and now he was beginning to realize just how much he missed them.

Then the Sneaker Squeaker abruptly stopped.

Somehow, through the increasing hustle and bustle of the station, the boy met Ian's gaze from far across the great hall, seemingly aware of the intangible connection between them. At first the boy's countenance was guarded, the stare he returned resolute and uncharacteristically confident for the boy's young age. The firmness softened, however, when Ian gently smiled and waved. The boy waved back, rather enthusiastically, and Ian realized he was actually laughing out loud for the first time in days . . . .

Until it was no longer the Sneaker Squeaker's smile which broadened that face; no longer the boy in the *Fresh Prince* T-shirt waving back at him.

In less than a blink of an eye, the steadfast reality of the bus terminal had morphed, time bending to one quarter speed. It was now the crooked but affable smile of Matt Chauncey beaming at him from across the busying concourse. Matt was wearing jean shorts and a T-shirt featuring Arnold Horshack and the words *Ooh! Ooh! Ooh!* emblazoned across the top. Matt was waving wildly—first from within the bus terminal, then somehow, even more impossibly, from the edge of a large, open field. Behind him, the columns of the great hall had transformed into towering trees, the passersby suddenly the familiar faces of their childhood friends.

. . . everyone is here. Playing and running and rough-housing. Next to the woods. And then . . . something. A vast, twisted tree . . . .

The bright luster of Ian's memory began to change—

. . . something feels wrong . . . .

—the sheen of it darkening and quickly souring. Now it was another memory, one Ian had buried deep, deep in the recesses of his mind. It had been locked away, in a secret place, where the dark things waited; pushed from the light long ago because it had never been fully vanquished.

Ian's chest tightened over his ribs, his breathing shallowed.

. . . something pierces the darkness now: a scream, a cry . . .

. . . pain, a boy's fright . . .

. . . but also laughter . . .

. . . chanting . . . .

Ian stood transfixed, mouth frozen in a soundless scream as time within the bus terminal ticked slower . . . *and slower* . . . as the great hall devolved into the dark place of his past. His eyes saw only inward as he sank beneath the murky waters of submerged consciousness. He therefore did not see the Sneaker Squeaker pick effortlessly through the syrupy movement of the growing throng of people, each an oblivious sloth to the malevolent distortion occurring around them. He did not see this same boy, who had somehow become his childhood friend, now transform into the T-shirt clad demon it was. Nor did Ian see how the abomination tilted its head curiously this way and that as it regarded so closely the grown man for whose benefit it had been summoned, and who now stood blind to the creature's very presence before him. Ian did not see the demon's unmitigated grin as it planted a cloven foot against the floor and, with just the right amount of pressure, dragged it hard and slow across the polished marble so that the motion released a perfect falsetto shriek, perverting the hall in great, abhorrent sound.

. . . the sound of the whistling through the trees . . . .

Broken, tired, and powerless against the darkness which for so many years he had internally battled, the sound enveloped Ian like flood waters and dragged him down to the furthest depths of his soul.

Back to the place where it all happened.

two
1977

THE WOODS WERE dark and deep. The sun, which shone so brightly upon the adjoining fields, soon dissipated and then was gone altogether as the woods thickened. Here the trees which flourished were domineering towers, only the mightiest earning the life-giving light above the competing canopy. By equal measure, the brush on the forest floor grew tighter and thornier, the ragged type of dense thicket which not only survives but thrives in scantest light. This was where the mushrooms grew. Where the dank air smelt thick with darkest greens, almost greys, as the moss and lichen prospered and the colors of the flowers were muted, waned, and then lost.

This was where the boys played, in the Little Woods, the bulk of their summer days. It was a private, tree filled haven for them, a secret world of their own creation. In the woods they were free—from parents, from teachers, from rules.

Free from the real world.

They played a game in the Little Woods, a tournament of sorts in which all the boys unquestionably participated. They called this game simply, 'War.' More than tradition, the game was a rite of passage, a deeply ingrained rubric upon their lives ascribed by some unknown, enigmatic force which beckoned them every summer.

And every summer they dutifully came.

None of them knew exactly how to describe the inexplicable pull the game had upon them, or who had first created it, or when the game had begun. They never wondered who had established the rules, or recruited the first teams. All they ever knew or thought was that the game had always just . . . been.

The first week of June the boys' minds would inevitably begin to wander from dreary classrooms and final exams to a summer full of fantastical, elevated adventures. It would also be this same time that each of the boys would stumble upon the realization that team selections for the War had begun . . . and were invariably occurring behind his back. This would then spur a feverish dance, as each of the boys chummed up to this boy or that, jockeying for a position on what they felt was the strongest team. None were aware that the maneuvers being orchestrated were the aggregate of thousands of years of finely honed survival instinct, represented in one neat little microcosm.

As their factions developed, so corresponding plans and tactics arose. Top secret strategies, replete with myriad unnecessary intricacies, would be found enthusiastically (if complicatedly) drawn across the last available pages of tattered, spiral-bound notebooks.

Of course it was only a matter of time before the best of these plans would be dismissed and thrown out for the 'dumb shit idea' it was, only to be unashamedly resurrected—and with the barest of tweaks—by the very boy who had pooh-poohed it in the first place. The fact that he would then boldly pass off the plagiarized plan as his own goes without saying.

So was the dynamic, as the boys vied for Alpha position, unknowingly establishing an inherent balance to the group as the team hierarchy inevitably fell neatly into place and the last of the year's school days fell neatly away.

And when that long-anticipated dismissal bell finally rang, its clanging peal officially announcing the start of three months of summer vacation, the boys would pour from the school in a human torrent. They'd sprint through the pale blue linoleum-tiled hallways, taking staircases two and three steps at a time, while woeful teachers looked impotently on. As they burst—and not a minute too soon—through the school's vast main entrance doors, they would delight in sliding headlong down the metal railings along the front steps. Even though Nate Franklin Jr. had broken off a tooth last year in the most resplendent, blood-gushing fashion.

They did this because . . . why not?

In what was then acknowledged as the single most glorious moment of the year, each boy would take a last labored step through the flimsy bi-fold doors of School Bus #33 and, in lifting a well-worn sneaker upon the bus's permanently mud-encrusted stair riser, step onto the bus . . . and into freedom.

One small step for boy. One giant leap for boyhood.

At last! Summer was here.

II

Bryan Cockerton was psyched for the game. Big time. It felt like his brother Ian, three years younger, finally had some kind of grasp of the strategies and tactics the War required. Too many seasons had passed with Bryan discovering Ian huddled in some thicket or bushes, crying his eyes out because a couple of the older kids had been a bit too rough with him. Or prancing about in the woods with Craig and Matt, giggling and laughing and taking none of the game seriously. Basically acting like the stupid little kids they were.

It really put a wild hair up his ass.

But this summer was gonna be different. He could feel it. This time, Bryan felt he might actually have a formidable player in his little brother who wasn't so little anymore.

The game of War commenced like clockwork on the first morning after school let out. As the sun crept above the horizon and most of the parents slipped joylessly off to work, the boys busied themselves packing brown bag lunches and waiting with keen anticipation for The March to come knocking on their door.

This year was no different.

As the two oldest boys from the neighborhood had moved away for college, Bryan and Ian now lived farthest from the woods, which meant this summer they were commissioned to lead The March.

From his bedroom above the garage, Ian peered through the brown and red plaid curtains and watched their mother pull steadily away in her faded yellow Pontiac. He waited patiently until she'd driven all the way to the end of the neighborhood's top street, turning right onto Route 60, before letting the curtain drop closed.

"She's gone!" he shouted excitedly down the hallway as he hopped on one foot and pulled a sneaker clumsily onto the other.

Downstairs in the kitchen, Bryan was scooping up the last two Mello Yello bottles from the fridge. Two brown paper bags atop the speckled Formica counter had already been stuffed with a perfectly assembled fluffer-nutter sandwich (a thin veneer of smooth, creamy peanut butter on one slice of spongy white bread, a decadently thick layer of Marshmallow Fluff on the other); a chocolate pudding pack; a trio of lunch cakes; and of course a PB&J—made by using hamburger buns because the fluffer-nutters had taken the last of the bread.

He dropped the first of the sodas into a paper sack and cringed as the heavy glass bottle flattened the hamburger bun PB&J. Grape jelly squirted from all sides and filled the air pockets and creases of the plastic wrap enveloping it.

OK then, he thought. *Guess that'll be Ian's.*

He more carefully slid the second bottle into his own bag, inching the sandwich to the side. "Ian!" he shouted up the stairs. "C'mon! Let's go!"

Ian bounded down the stairs and Bryan tossed him the paper sack as he rounded the corner. Pushing and shoving as they raced for the door, the boys burst from the house in a bout of laughter.

Heading down the top street and picking their way through the neighborhood, they knocked on door after door until all but one of their gang were in tow. The March then paraded in blissful ignorance toward the woods as a growing melange of boisterous insults, jibes, plans and laughs —and the grand dreams of youth—all grew to such a raucous buzz that not a single voice was discerned above any other. In what could then only be described as a collective Jungian unconsciousness, the indecipherable cacophony abruptly faded into silence. Instead of the sound of their own pubescent voices, the group focused only upon the cadence of their feet.

The satisfying *THWAAP* of sneakers against the warm, leathery blacktop became the only sound as sixteen rubber-soled shoes slapped in steady, rhythmic strides.

At the bottom of the hill, alongside a smattering of houses at the neighborhood's westernmost edge, a field of swaying corn marked the end of the neighborhood proper and the beginning of what they called the Wild Place. Twin ruts, the deep parallel gouges resultant of countless coarse-treaded tractor tires, started where the blacktop ended and cut across the field to form a primitive path. It wound through the corn and far into the distance until it vanished into the shadows beneath a thick cluster of trees.

Ian Cockerton stared down this track, his eyes transfixed on the receding line as the warm June breeze swayed the honeyed tips of immature corn on either side of the path. The stalks danced hypnotically in a pattern of repeating, cyclical waves across the field.

"Hey! Doofus!" Bryan shouted as he forced himself between his brother's thousand-yard stare and whatever it was out there that had so captivated his attention. "You with us, or what?"

Ian snapped out of the moment to find his older brother's face mere inches from his own. Without thinking about it he pushed him away, harder than he'd expected, and was suddenly wide-eyed as Bryan almost tumbled to the ground. Once he was aware his brother had caught his balance, he felt it safe to add for good measure:

"Jerk off, fat ass."

"OK. So that's the way you wanna play it," Bryan replied, squaring up to him again. "We'll see who's the fat ass when I reach those woods before you and ambush your skinny little ass!"

Bryan gestured toward the twin ponds, barely visible at the far end of the trail. The path there split into a distinct 'Y', just before the two reservoirs. One branch cut to the right, disappearing beneath the thick line of trees rising suddenly from the cornfield. The other struggled on in the opposite direction, thinned, then disappeared into the field's swollen edges, presumably from lack of use.

"You'd better be quick," Bryan added as he leaned into his stance, ready to run. "We're showing no mercy today, little boy." He dug his sneakers into the dirt and shot off, a greyhound after a rabbit. A slightly overweight greyhound, perhaps, but a greyhound nonetheless.

For a moment Ian hesitated, staring in the distance. He decided to let it go when he realized Bryan was already a good thirty yards down the dirt track, his heavy-footed strides pounding the packed dirt like a Clydesdale.

He took off after him.

It required a heavy sprint for the first twenty yards, but then he was able to settle into a good even pace, stretching his legs into a long, smooth stride. In just a matter of moments he was within spitting distance of Bryan.

A few more, and he was level with him.

Bryan cocked his head, scowled, and pulled out all the speed he could muster. Ian did the same, and clouds of dust billowed up from behind them both. For a spell they were neck-and-neck. Then Bryan pulled ahead. Then Ian. As the 'Y' in the trail grew closer, the twin ponds looming, the boys finally drew together, neither able to exceed the other's pace. Their arms and legs flailed at the air as both skidded to a stop and collapsed gracelessly onto the dusty trail.

Each boy pulled at his sides, stepping in tight circles and gasping for fresh air to replace the furnace heat in their lungs.

It was like this for a good minute or two before Ian was the first to (barely) speak.

"Dih—*bahhh*, dic—*bahh*." The sound emanated weakly between dry, heaving pants. "Dick—*bah*—bag!"

A hollow victory, but better than nothing.

"Di—tto," Bryan replied weakly and after such a long pause that even the minimalist impact of the feeble retort was lost. Then, as his labored breathing calmed: "Let me help you up."

He pulled himself to his feet and extended his hand to Ian, and both dusted off before continuing down the path as the rest of the gang soon caught up to them.

As The March made its way the last few minutes toward the tree line, some heads were lowered in repose, others held high in a defiant, unblinking stare. All said nothing, as they prepared to leave the sun behind and step into the beckoning shadows which all recognized as the gateway to the Little Woods.

If you were to look at this particular patch of woodland today you might not feel it was an especially distinctive sight. Just the typical pine, oak and beech of western Pennsylvania. But something close to a deeply seated reverence resonated within each one of the boys as they traded the bright heat of summer's light for the cool darkness beneath the trees. Perhaps it was an adrenaline-fueled blend of foreboding; perhaps a long-awaited anticipation of the game they were about to play.

Perhaps it was merely overactive imagination.

Whatever it was, the effect the Little Woods had on each of them that day would stay with them for a lifetime.

III

Matt Chauncey's apprehension of both the game of War and the Little Woods, while having no sentient foundation, was nonetheless very real to him. It was an anxiety that progressed over time, worsening as each summer approached. It crippled aspects of his interaction with the other boys to the point of becoming socially estranged from the group. He openly admitted he would no longer enter the woods alone—a fact he did not seem ashamed of, despite the fiercely cutting derision of the older boys in the gang.

Maybe Matt was just too stupid to realize how childish he appeared to everyone else. Or maybe he was only admitting what the other boys secretly felt.

Despite this palpable dread, still Matt came again and again, never once failing to take part in the boys' game of War in the woods. Even when every nerve in his body was screaming with electric fire not to join in. Now, whether he made any real contribution to the War once he was there was a matter of little debate. But you could never take away from him the fact that Matt showed up, despite his overwhelming inner mono-logue which desperately persuaded, at times even cajoled, him to stay home:

We can just stay right here, bud, Right? Eat PB&Js all day. Watch Tom & Jerry in our pajamas, he would convince himself. *That would be more fun. Right?*

And safer.

(In the years that followed, the few boys able to remember would look back and realize that Matt had, without a doubt, been the most courageous of them all.)

Then it finally happened. This year, Matt Chauncey hadn't joined in The March. When the troupe had knocked on his door—the manic banging of at least three of the boys echoing loud and hollow through the Chaunceys' house—the brusque announcement of their presence was met only by the bellowing barks of Ruby, the family's Irish Setter.

Ian Cockerton was Matt's best friend, perhaps his only real friend. So of course he knew him better than anyone. And it was no surprise to Ian when Matt didn't come to the door this time.

To be honest, none of the boys were very surprised. To be brutally honest, none were even much bothered. Most had expected it a long time ago. For Ian, the sudden realization that Matt might not actually join in the game this summer filled him with an oddly contradictory mix of both soothing relief and unexpectedly searing disappointment.

"Chauncey's finally ditching us—"

"—Pussy—"

"—Knew he'd wimp out—"

The overlapping sentiments had resounded from the gang as the boys stepped off the Chaunceys' front porch and trotted down the street in eager anticipation of the game.

Everyone was uniquely shocked when they found Matt alone at the edge of the woods, sat cross-legged beneath a pine tree and fiddling with some twigs while he waited for the rest of the gang.

It was only a matter of moments before that shock turned to the usual disdain as Ian, like everyone else, braced for Matt's feckless demeanor: the pathetic victim mentality from the boy who, for most of Ian's life, had been his tried-and-true best friend.

They weren't disappointed

The tree Matt was sitting under was at the outermost edge of the woods. Just two small steps and he would be right back in the bright yellow sunlit glow of the cornfield. But to Matt, sitting here in that patchy onset of the woods' shade was a victory. As Ian had expected, however, his head was hanging low, eyes darting about, hands nervously clenching and unclenching. The weirdest thing was the idiosyncratic way Matt's feet moved compared to the rest of his body language. In moments like these, Ian noticed they were always kicking and scuffing at the dirt, as if attempting to exude a casual, almost absentminded bravado.

Once, not that many summers earlier, this very portrayal of courage had actually convinced Ian that Matt was being honest when he'd said, with utmost stoic confidence, that he wasn't the least bit afraid to go play the game. In the Little Woods. With the others.

"Nope. Huh-uh. Not scared at all," Matt had proclaimed as he scuffed his feet against the brown and orange carpet in his bedroom while feigning a sudden, nonchalant interest in the condition of his cuticles. Then again, Ian had also believed Matt that very same summer when Matt had disclosed, again with that same absolute conviction, that he'd just seen Bigfoot taking a dip in the creek, down behind their neighborhood.

Ian had grown a little less gullible since then.

Despite their being the same age, Matt suddenly seemed to Ian nothing more than a frightened little kid, kicking pointlessly at pebbles in the dirt.

He guiltily pushed the thought aside as he offered to help Matt to his feet.

"Hey buddy. I'm glad to see you." Ian extended his hand. "C'mon. It's time to head in."

V

The Raker brothers (Jimi and Jack), Stewart 'Stu' Klatz, and a couple more of the older boys—friends of Bryan's, if that's what you wanted to call them—were first to race into the forest. Behind them, the rest of the boys followed the sound of their whooping shouts and hollers, weaving in and out beneath the trees and over thick brush.

"Right guys, let's break into two teams!"

At first the command was a disembodied voice, emanating from somewhere in the shadows. Then Jack, the elder of the two Raker boys, was revealed within a thin, shifting veneer of light.

"C'mon. We doin' this . . . or what!"

The words tapered into the distance, becoming lost with the boy who spoke them as Jack again darted away. Little more than a shade, he scrambled adeptly between rows of tall, dark trees until once again the shadows swallowed him and he was gone. All too familiar with where he was heading, the rest of the boys dutifully followed, picking their way through thickets and fallen branches as their eyes steadily adjusted to the increasing dark.

Another hundred yards or so passed until, one-by-one, they came upon a clearing and gathered together round the base of a colossal tree— the Father Oak, they called it—which dominated a cluster of lesser oaks, beech and other trees, all of which seemed to form a rough perimeter around it. A meticulous arrangement of rocks and stones had been placed between these outlying trees, linking them together like a dotted line. The attentive work of generations of kids long before them, it further accentuated the natural geometry of the circumference. At the center of the clearing was an oval of brushed dirt where several logs lay parallel to one another, arranged carefully as if church pews. They faced a single tree stump, three feet high, which stood alone beneath the Father Oak.

This was the place the boys saw in their minds when they thought of the Little Woods.

Jack jumped onto the stump and brushed his feet back and forth, adding to the decades of burnish. He surveyed the boys jostling before him, a General inspecting his loyal troops, and a chill ran up his spine as he took in the sight.

Then came the voice. It whispered sweetly: *It is time....*

There was a murmuring among the boys. At first low and soft, only a tentative few. But then a couple more. Louder, more determined. Until all of the boys were chanting, now shouting, in a fierce and unified chorus:

"PICK! PICK! PICK! PICK!"

Jack waved them silent and they fell obediently to a hush. Some shuffled anxiously in place. Others stared wide-eyed.

Several moments passed, the whispering of the trees the only sound as Jack studied the faces. The fear was palpable in some, the lust for the game in others.

He cleared his throat before speaking again, and the sound seemed to echo like a gunshot throughout the woods.

"Okay," he stated in the most authoritative of tones. "I'll take Stu."

The boys—all but Bryan—erupted into untamed cheering and hurrahs as Stu stepped forward to take his place next to Jack at the stump, high-fiving his team leader.

One of the tallest boys, Stu was also one of the best at the game. There was little doubt among any of the boys that this was due, in no small part, to the fact that Stu was the nastiest son-of-a-bitch among them. Bar none. A self-satisfied grin spread across Stu's face as he turned his gaze to Bryan. Then bent over with unabashed laughter.

It was all Bryan could do to contain his fury. As one of the two team captains this year, he'd approached Stu weeks ago. And surprisingly, Stu had agreed to be on his team. In fact, not only on the same team, but as co-captain. For Bryan, this was a no-brainer. Together, they agreed with self-assured righteousness, their team would be unstoppable, their victory ordained in the heavens. The two spit in their palms to seal the alliance and set about collaborating together for weeks. Admittedly, Bryan had done most of the heavy mental lifting as they formulated intricate plans, maps, strategies . . . essentially their team's entire battle plan.

Now it was painfully clear why.

Stu had offered little push-back. In fact, he had been so incredibly affable about every plan Bryan had put forth, that Bryan had been a little taken aback at the unanticipated level of cooperation.

It was a cunning move, the finest conspiratorial treachery.

Game on.

"In that case," Bryan said as he stepped resolutely into the oval clearing, snagging Jack's younger brother by the collar and all but dragging him to the stump with him. "I'll take Jimi."

Jack visibly winced. He knew he should have expected the retaliation, but contested the selection anyway.

"Shit, you can't do that Cockerton!"

"Sorry big Don." Jack's reaction was more satisfying than Bryan had expected it would be. "No vetoes. You know the rules. All's fair in love and war . . . . And all that jazz."

Jack needed to think. He paused as he contemplated his next move. He carefully scanned the faces. His younger brother Jimi had been a big part of his plans. Time to adjust strategy.

"Fine. Then Dan's with me."

Dannie Mercer—a.k.a. Big Dan—was a mutual friend of them both. He was big. Very big. And that was about it. He was slow as syrup and twice as stupid. But the strength he provided was a powerful bonus to whichever team he was on.

In short, no one messed with Big Dan.

"OK. Then I'll have Woody," Brian retaliated.

"Take him. See if I give a shit. But while you're at it," Jack declared, "you can take the three little douche-kateers there, too."

He gestured towards Ian, Craig and Matt. Apparently together they were some sort of pathetic package deal; the perpetually overlooked and underappreciated. Whether they liked it or not.

Ian *did not* like it.

In previous years, he'd dumbly accepted that the three together were perceived as having only the worth of a single, older player. But now he was pretty certain he could square up against just about any of the boys—as long as it was one-on-one—and come out of the deal faring pretty okay.

According to his books, anyway.

He was sick and tired of being lumped together as some kind of booby prize. He couldn't even say they were a contemptible pair, for that would require actual recognition of their existence. Nor could he say they were a pitiable alliance, for the very same reason.

Nope. They were simply invisible. The unseen booby prize.

And it sucked.

Bryan looked at him as if to say, *yeah I know, but just go with it this one last time* and signaled the three of them to join him.

V I

The teams chosen and, by his way of thinking, fates sealed, Jack draped his arms over Woody's and Stu's shoulders. He winked at Bryan with self-assured confidence before assuring that he'd see him, and his team, in hell. Then he was gone, scuttling through brush, in and out between trees, as Stu and Dan yipped like hyenas as they bounded closely behind him.

Bryan ignored the display and called his team together. *Six against three,* He considered. *Not bad odds.* "Right, now listen. Just over there," he poked his thumb over his right shoulder, "is our team's HQ. You know the story by now. One man has to sit and guard it at all times, especially when we get any prisoners to bring back."

Matt's expression revealed how much he truly doubted they'd be capturing anybody today.

"And I'll need a scout," Bryan continued. "Then of course, a couple o' you guys hafta come with me on infantry. We'll go looking for those bastards and I promise you, we'll find them."

He patted Jimi Raker on the back as he said this last part. The kid just might be the ace in the hole this year.

Jimi remained expressionless.

Matt shot his hand up and waved to get Bryan's attention. As he did, he made a series of noises something akin to Arnold from the popular sitcom, *Welcome Back, Kotter.*

"Dude. I'm right here." With just a minor stretch Bryan was able to slap Matt playfully on the cheek. "And we're not at school. Just say what you fucking wanna say."

"I'll do that job—"

"Infantry?" Bryan almost laughed. But knowing what was about to go down, and being stuck with this ragtag lot, and with Jack *et al* out there . . . somewhere . . . none of it was actually very funny.

Matt's face blanched.

"God no!" As if evading the inherent danger, he actually took a step backward as he said it. The way the teenage girls always do in the horror flicks when the knife-wielding maniac approaches them sooooo slowly. "Definitely not! I was talking about the first one. HQ guard. That's why I raised my hand."

This time Bryan did allow himself to laugh. Just a little.

"Fine. Matt, you're our man at home. Just do a good job and be sure to give the signal if you see any of Jack's lot inside of a hundred yards from here. Got it?"

Matt sighed with relief. "Yessir. Got it."

"Now who's gonna be our scouts?"

Craig nodded. So did Jimi Raker.

Bryan grimaced. What little mock confidence he'd been trying to muster immediately, unavoidably sloughed away. "What's with you Jimi— since when do you want pussy scout duty? You're infantry, through and through, man. You love that shit. Into the heat of battle. And all that."

Jimi said nothing, only shrugging his shoulders.

Bryan let out a loud breath.

Woody looked worried.

Matt hummed away to himself as he kicked indifferently at some leaves in the oval clearing.

"Huh-uh," Bryan said, shaking his head emphatically side to side. "No way Jimi, you're coming with me. You and Woody. I need you both. Out there. With me."

Jimi stared blankly into the tree canopy. His back now turned to Bryan, he shrugged in barest agreement.

"Hey, now, just wait a minute!" Ian interrupted. "Maybe I should be on infantry this time. If Jimi doesn't want it then fine, I'll do it."

Bryan shot him a look; the message was sharp, quick, and silent and conveyed Bryan's suspicion of Jimi, and that he needed to keep the younger Raker brother close.

Ian acquiesced with a reluctant nod and stepped down.

"Okay then guys. So Matt's our HQ sentry. Woody, Jimi and me are infantry. So Ian and Craig, that makes you our scouts. Now let's go for it! And remember," Bryan turned to Matt who was already off in his own little world. He dabbed his index finger into Matt's chest to ensure the kid was listening. "You give us a whistle if you see anything, even the faintest suspicion of anything. Right?"

Matt shrugged in agreement.

"And Ian," Bryan waved for his brother to come over to him. He leaned in and spoke quietly. "Keep an extra good eye out. Okay bro? I have a funny feeling, with Jimi you know. And, well, I just need you doubly alert."

He thumbed toward Matt who was now sitting on a rock, braiding dried leaves into a chain.

"OK," Ian assured. "But next time, I'm out there with you."

"Yeah, little bro. Next time . . . ."

VII

Bryan led Woody and Jimi north into the cool, dark heart of the Little

Woods. From his strategy sessions with Stu, he'd learned there was a stream up there, about a quarter mile from base camp, which was apparently Jack's favorite spot. He hoped to find them hanging out there —overly cocky and under prepared. So at least that was a plus to this whole team espionage fiasco.

At the base camp, Ian called Matt and Craig over.

"This is what I think we gotta do," he instructed as he picked up a stick and began to scratch a rudimentary map in the dirt. "Craig, you head west. I'm heading East. That way." He pointed about 90° from the direction Bryan and the guys had just taken. "Matt, you stay here, like we said, and just keep an eye on things."

Matt, pleased with his choice of soldiering, smiled triumphantly. He even puffed out his chest a little. "No problem, I just hope for their sake's they don't go trying to mess with me." He put an exclamation on it by grinding his fists together.

Craig openly sniggered, so Ian punched him hard, square in the chest. Craig hadn't expected it: he pursed his lips, quickly dabbing a hand to his mouth. "*Ubh*, you bade be bide by *dongue*."

Ian's attempt to prevent Matt from witnessing the derision was too late. Dejected, Matt stepped haughtily away.

"You guys can just screw off!" He disappeared through the brush adding, "Who needs you anyway!"

This time Craig straight up laughed, no hesitance about it. It came out as a big, whooping belly laugh. Ian tried not to do the same, but it was impossible. Together they guffawed for a good two or three minutes before they could finally catch their breath.

On the other side of the clearing Matt fought away the tears as he tried to zone out his two friends, and his feelings.

Sat cross-legged on a mossy outcropping, his back against a tree, he pulled a small bamboo flute from his pocket. A gift from one of his aunts who'd been to Africa or somewhere, he'd been carrying it with him everywhere these days. He raised it to his lips and rolled the end around his mouth to wet it. He couldn't play it, but knew this is what you did. He blew softly. Surprising even himself, it actually whistled to life. It was a discordant, shrill chord. But it was something.

Ian stopped laughing and cringed, uselessly covering his ears. He hated that stupid flute, and even the way Matt looked when he tried to play it. But he guessed it made Matt feel important.

Or maybe it just made him feel safe.

"Hey!" he shouted above the caterwauling of the instrument and peered around the tree. "You're gonna give the game away with that damned thing!"

Craig was still trying to contain himself, not very successfully, when both he and Ian struck out in their respective directions.

Leaving Matt alone at the camp.

VIII

Bryan, Jimi and Woody ran hard through the underbrush for a good ten minutes before stopping for a breather. The sound of water tripping over rocks announced the presence of the stream somewhere nearby. Otherwise, the only sound in the woods was that of the three boys panting as they caught their breath.

Bryan fell against a tree, its rough bark scraping his back as his T-shirt lifted out of his jeans.

"Well," he took another deep breath and considered if Jack's team might be close. "What do you think?"

He looked at his two teammates, raising an eyebrow.

Jimi flopped to the ground. "Dunno." He took a swig of water from his canteen. "Don't care."

Woody was already on the ground, but stood up to tower over Jimi. "Whaddya mean you don't know—you've always been with these guys out here. Where the hell do you go?"

Jimi stared at him defiantly.

"Now hold on," Bryan interjected. "Let's not get at each other. Not now that—"

"Come on Bry, he knows! He's just not saying so, that's all."

Jimi jumped up.

"Of course I know, you stupid dickbag. You really think they'll go to the same place, now I'm with you?"

He faced Woody so that the two were nose to nose.

That was more than enough for Woody's hair trigger. He cocked his arm all the way back behind his right ear, aimed roughly for Jimi's head—

Anywhere in that vicinity would do nicely, he thought.

—and threw the punch apparently before even he, himself, realized what he was doing.

Jimi had no time to flinch. Woody's fist landed squarely across his left cheekbone and he pinwheeled backwards, collapsing awkwardly to the dirt where he'd been sitting only moments earlier.

Woody stood frozen, his arm still outstretched, eyes wide and blinkless. The disbelief at what he'd just done was written all over his face. It would have been comical had it not been so real.

Bryan shook his head and slumped a little further down the tree he was leaning against. He already knew what was coming next. Jimi was a crazy sunuvabitch and there would be retribution.

A lot of it.

Jack and Co. were out there somewhere, maybe even watching all of this, waiting to take them down. And his own team were about to bash each others' brains in.

For a moment it dawned on him that maybe—just maybe—this was somehow all part of Jack's plan. Not only the overt espionage of using Stu against him, but also counting on Bryan to retaliate by picking Jimi for his team . . . and then methodically tearing the team apart from the inside.

He pondered the idea for a moment more before dismissing it. I mean, Jack just wasn't that bright.

Was he?

On the ground, Jimi smeared the back of his hand across his cheek and held it up to a patch of light, slowly rotating it until the thick swatch of red came into view.

Oh shit, Woody thought. *Oh shit a brick.*

Realizing what he'd just done, and what Jimi would likely do next, Woody assumed the classic boxer's stance: right fist pulled back to his ear, left raised defensively in front of his face. This time the pose was a conscious choice.

But Jimi didn't get up. He didn't try to bust Woody's head open like an overripe melon as he and Bryan expected would happen next. Instead, Jimi simply sat there in the dirt and presented his blood-covered hand in the same lackluster fashion that reminded Woody of the way they would present some mundane item to a roomful of lackadaisical classmates during Show-and-Tell back in grade school.

"Look what you did, you fucking idiot," Jimi informed him in an oddly dispassionate manner.

Puzzled, Woody held his stance, looking quizzically to Bryan for help. It was one of those, '*Is this a crazy trick?*' kinda looks.

Bryan shrugged noncommittally, so Woody maintained the pose, jostling in place and bouncing on his toes every once in a while, the way he'd seen fighters do on television. He continued this only for about a minute or so before realizing he was starting to look a bit silly, and relaxed his stance.

"Well," he said to Jimi matter-of-factly as he lowered his fists. "You were asking for it."

Jimi pulled himself up, brushed himself off, and pressed his hand against his cheek a few more times more until the bleeding slowed.

"You're right," he admitted, and Woody and Bryan had no reply.

Then he pointed past a thick cluster of trees at the top of a distant embankment; the one that must lead down to the stream.

"That's where they'll be. And Jack wouldn't in a million years think I'd tell you. So he'll be there."

Bryan grinned with sudden rejuvenation. "Well okay then! What have we got to lose?"

Woody shrugged his shoulders and capitulated.

"Right. I guess you're right. What have we got to lose."

And just like that, they were back on the hunt.

IX

After several minutes of unsuccessfully trying to skirt it, Ian found no way around and was now wading awkwardly through Dead Man's Swamp. A thick mixture of murky water, mud and stringy plant tendrils had already worked its way in and around his brand new basketball shoes, creating the frightful sensation of binding his feet.

It felt—and smelled—incredibly gross.

He'd known the swamp wasn't far from their base camp, but thought the route he took would pass wide north of it.

Not the case, he pointed out to no one but himself and carefully placed one foot in front of the other. *Move too fast, Cockerton, and you'll lose one, maybe even both, of those shoes.*

At first, the thick, swampy emulsion gave way to his steps easily enough. But the further across he wade, the more it flowed up and over the tops of his sneakers, seeping down into the shoes and creating a horrible *thwuck* sound as the vacuum it created sucked the mud back up. It felt the way he imagined a massive eel would feel, were it slithering into your sneakers, wrapping around your ankles, then snaking back out again.

God this is so fucking gross!

He waded several feet more before the murky water was up to his knees. He was halfway across when the dense water was nearly up to his thighs. And still a good thirty or more yards from the rim.

That's when it caught his attention.

He heard it at first, only turning in time to catch a glimpse. Around ten feet behind him, the mud opened up into a small circle, burped, then closed in upon itself again.

Ian stood motionless in the middle of the swamp, staring over his left shoulder. He watched and listened, intensely focused.

Twenty seconds passed.

The sounds of the forest murmured in his ear, but nothing more. He waited a few more seconds then began to move.

Cockerton ol' boy, you must've imagined it.

Cold, wet and up to his waist in sludge, Ian continued across the swamp, taking one labored step then another. He worked through the mud, ever-mindful that at any moment he could lose his sneakers beneath the grey-green murk. He tried to push the thought aside, but could feel the shoes threatening to pull from his feet with every step. It was already gonna be a long walk back home and he didn't much care for the thought of doing it shoeless.

Another ten yards passed.

The swamp was more shallow after the halfway mark, so it was thankfully below his knees again. But with the shallower depth came that thick, viscous composition.

At least the end is in sight. Almost there buddy, you can do thi—

His foot caught on something and twisted hard. Before he knew it he was falling, hands grasping at empty air. It happened so fast, the horizon seemed to rise up to meet his body in slow motion as another hole burped open in front of him. All he could think was how this hole had appeared so much closer now . . . .

Until the swamp was slapping him in the face.

Then the only thing he was aware of was the glutinous water covering his head, oozing into his eyes, forcing its way into his nose, his mouth; threatening to fill his throat. In less than a beat, his reality was profoundly altered as he sank below the surface.

One Mississippi . . . .

As it had done with his basketball shoes, the swamp sucked his body down.

Two Mississippi . . . .

The sensation of the heavy water was suddenly very real as it flowed over him, tugging him, a web of reeds and pulpy tendrils tangling around him.

Five Mississippi . . . I could die here—

Panic constricted his body like an electric rope that squeezed his chest and stiffened his limbs as the realization swept over him. He thrashed, stiff and rigid, and the action sucked him even further down. His face now pressed into the fine silt at the bottom of the muddy water as though something—or someone—were holding him there and shoving his face into the loam.

Twelve Mississippi . . . .

His lungs began to burn, his throat to convulse. Oblivious to his situation, they pleaded for him to please just open his mouth and take a breath—

I am going to die here.

—and then the image, the one from the old black and white film they'd watched in Matt's basement one rainy afternoon: the movie where the safari expedition stumbles into the jungle quicksand and the more the explorer struggles, the more he sinks, until only his pith helmet is left. At the time, Ian thought it stupid. He even condemned the hapless explorer to death for being such a simpleton, when the solution was so clear and obvious.

But now, as the oxygen evaporated from his brain and his thoughts began to fuzz and fade, he couldn't remember how the explorer had escaped.

If he had at all?

The monochrome movie scene began to swirl and swim, a colorless kaleidoscope. Now the safari explorer was a cartoon ranger: a little man, short and plump, with little round glasses. The Ranger floated in psychedelic, monotone space and gleefully beckoned Ian to follow him down . . . down . . . down . . . smaller and further away until he eventually blurred into nothing but a a flash of light.

Twenty-one Mississippi . . . now the whistling . . . .

Even though his mind knew a desperate attempt for life-giving oxygen would be his last, Ian no longer possessed the fortitude to prevent the instinctive, physical need to take a breath. His whole being went limp as he yielded to the epoxy of the swamp and began to suck in the water.

Then it happened. The thick silt and sludge and tendrils that had bound him began to loosen. Not completely, but enough for him to sense the slackened grip.

In one last weak and desperate effort he thrust himself up.

His face broke through the surface. Gasping and coughing, the vile swamp water propelled from his burning lungs as he clamored for air in a dizzy haze. He was bent over and trembling when another small hole burped open in the mud right in front of him.

Then another.

Then again, this one the nearest of them all.

Whatever it is, the fear in him whispered, *this time it will suck you down and you won't have the strength to get back up.*

So he started to run. The foot still anchored beneath the water, trapped by whatever it was that had felled him in the first place, stayed trapped while the rest of him lurched forward. With incredible torque, his body buckled violently to the left. His kneecap strained, could hold no more, then dislocated from the center of his leg with an unnatural, stomach-churning *POP.*

Ian screamed as the knee bulged under the skin from a place it should not be. The howl turned into a low, guttural moan as he dropped to one knee and instinctively tried to manipulate the other back into place.

It refused to move.

Wedged in its new, grotesque position, the mere sight of it made his stomach tighten. So he did something he never imagined he could: he cocked his arm back, squeezed his eyes closed, and struck the disjointed leg at an oblique angle with the open heel of his hand. The displaced patella shot back to the center of his leg, bone grinding against bone, and Ian cried under his breath.

Another burping bubble appeared in the mud.

This time Ian caught a glimpse of the golf ball sized rock as it whizzed past his head. It slammed into the swamp's oily surface, opening a hole in the sludge, then disappeared beneath.

And the realization dawned: *Jack and his infantry.*

Fresh panic tightened his chest like a cold fist driving through his ribcage and squeezing his heart. The oxygen-deprived vision of the cartoon ranger had been terrifying. Something deep inside told him what was about to go down would be worse.

Way worse. Fuckity fuck fuck FUCK!

Another rock flew by, this once slicing right in a wide arc before skipping across the water then slowly sinking.

Ian scanned the embankments of the swamp in harried, fleeting glances but saw no one. His breaths quickened as he pulled and twisted his leg, ignoring the searing pain from the effort to desperately free himself.

The foot would not loosen.

Groping beneath the surface blindly with both hands, he finally felt the culprit: a log—fat and heavy and convoluted—with a network of twisted offshoots that entangled his ankle and lower leg like a snare. He pushed with all his strength.

It did not budge.

Another rock whizzed past, heard rather than seen.

Out of options and resigned to his position in the swamp, Ian lowered his body back into the water and pressed against the log for support as he lay low and flat and as out of sight as possible. Thick oily water lapped over his chin and again filled his mouth, and he spat it out in gargling splutters as he struggled to keep his head above the water line.

Another rock. Another burp in the mud.

Several more, dangerously close.

Then . . . sudden nothingness.

Ian held his breath.

Hopefully the boys had run out of rocks. Or better yet, maybe they'd finally lost interest in this part of the game.

The thought had no sooner formed when came the next telltale *thwaaap*, this one followed by something new: a hollow, muted *thud* as the rock struck something.

Something beneath the water.

His log.

Shit! Their aim is getting better. A lot bett—

The blinding flash of light exploded across his vision. Then came the torturous, ice pick pain in his head. And a red flow that oozed warmly into his eye. He fingered the side of his forehead and was immediately sickened by the size of the gash there. The stone, or rock, or whatever the fuck it was, had torn the skin from his head so that a series of small, shredded flaps hung loosely from his temple.

Then it began to pulse—a loud, numb heartbeat on the side of his head, pumping a sheet of blood vigorously down his face.

He pinched the lacerated skin between the thumb and forefinger of one hand while the other raked the bottom of the swamp and awkwardly brought up a thick, gelatinous handful of silt. The pain as he smeared it across his temple was so intense he wanted to throw up, but could only emit a series of hacking, dry heaves. It was a crude poultice, but might help slow the flow of blood until the wound could thicken and clot on its own.

Ian wanted to go home now.

His knee felt sickeningly loose and grotesquely swollen and he was sure it no longer connected the upper and lower portions of his leg as it was meant to. He could barely believe that just minutes ago he'd been worried about losing his sneakers in the swamp. Now such an inane concern made him chuckle out loud, and the pain in his temple blossomed to an instant, excruciating crescendo.

He leaned back on trembling elbows, head barely above the water, and concentrated only on the steady, cyclical rhythm of his breathing. It took every last ounce of energy as he focused only upon pushing through the pain.

At least the boys will come now, he assured himself between shallow breaths. *They'll come, and they'll help. They'll help me home.*

Tears began to slide from beneath the lids of his tightly shut eyes; a moment later, he started to sob.

He didn't care.

The other boys could make fun of him all summer long for all he cared. He just wanted this to be over now; to be back in his bedroom, with his mom rubbing his chest and singing to him in her sweet, soft tones until all the nastiness went away.

He daubed at the tears with the back of his filthy hand and when he opened his eyes, found Jack and Stu clambering hurriedly down from a tree at the swamp's edge.

They're coming. It's going to be okay now.

Then came the sound, that shrill, jarring whistling which resonated so audibly around him he could actually feel the tight, distressing vibrations cycling through his chest. But this time it was accompanied by a smell: a rancid, indelible stench like sulfur that soured his mouth as though sucking on copper.

Simultaneously, horrifying images filled his vision. They were sporadic and disjointed and made no sense, but were as tangible as if happening right in front of him:

The Father Oak—a fire—fraying rope—the faceless screams of one of the boys—

The images jolted him into action. He tugged furiously at his leg, forcing his foot out of its slime-filled basketball sneaker. Then, in an adrenaline-fueled frenzy, he lurched into a stumbling run. He'd even managed a few paces before his torn ACL had other ideas. Behind the now grossly swollen kneecap his leg buckled and Ian pitched back into the water, his leg bent in a way it shouldn't be.

It didn't matter anymore.

The boys were already down from their perch, splashing wildly through the swamp. Rabid hyenas yowling and yipping, Jack and Stu bound frenetically through the murky water.

Their eyes empty and black . . . .

Three

THE BOY IN front of him (the Sneaker-Squeaker) looked both concerned and naturally interested. "You all right, mister?" he said in a cautious tone.

"Hmm. *What?*" Ian groggily opened his eyes, and his mind, to his surroundings as the intensity of the memory slowly vanished beneath the fabric of reality. Though the images quickly waned, the anxiety from decades past lingered like a mass in his chest. He stared emptily at the boy in front of him and for a moment, the great hall of the bus terminal rippled as though he were seeing it underwater. He instinctively reached for his temple before his mind could tell him the pain he felt there was a relic of almost twenty years prior.

"I said, are. You. OK?" The boy's question grew staccato and terse.

Ian nodded, and fought the remnant images. He could feel the grimace on his face, the furrowed brow lines across his forehead.

"Mmm, yeah. I'm alright."

The boy's expression revealed he wasn't convinced, but he shrugged his shoulders and walked away anyway.

"Hey," Ian called after him, after pulling a relieving breath of air. The boy turned but continued walking, half backwards. "Thanks."

The boy shrugged his shoulders once more and disappeared around the corner of the snack kiosk.

Ian looked at his watch: 9:27am. Ten full minutes had passed with his back to the marble column. It seemed like only seconds. But then again, could so easily have been hours. Perhaps years.

Bright sunshine suddenly streamed into the terminal as the vast entry doors opened and washed the grand hall in light. A silhouetted figure appeared in the opening and slowly stepped forward. Closer and closer the shadow figure approached Ian, who edged back against the column, bracing himself.

When the doors shut and the back light was extinguished, Ian's brother Bryan was standing at the far end of the bus terminal. Even from this distance the glossy veneer of Bryan's eyes, the numbness behind them they were trying unsuccessfully to hide, was evident.

The brothers held each other's gaze as they stepped toward one another, an impossible onslaught of thoughts and emotions passing unvoiced between them, a shared synapse of intense, silent feeling.

Then, without speaking, they simply embraced.

II

It was a quiet but strangely soothing ride home. For a while, neither man spoke more than a word or maybe two. Ian stared out of the Chevrolet Blazer's window and watched the summer storm clouds growing darker. Eventually, when the time to ask felt appropriate, he inquired as to how Rebecca and the kids were doing, all things considered.

"Okay. I guess," Bryan answered softly as he ran a nervous hand through his hair. "I guess we're doing alright. As you say, all things considered."

Bryan's lips trembled.

It was barely discernible. But Ian noticed and felt the need to breathe in . . . a long, steady intake to calm the ever-threatening angst which vibrated just beneath his conscious mind. As the sweet summer air filled his lungs, he measured the moments as the trees passed by in regular, even intervals and only allowed himself to exhale after he counted slowly to five.

The road thumped lightly below their wheels in a steady, almost hypnotic, rhythm, and Ian allowed himself the privilege of closing his eyes in the warm, secure comfort of the SUV.

He was safe.

For now.

He leaned back and enjoyed the soothing sensation as the breeze from the open window wisped through his hair. The air itself smelled sweet, almost cloy, and a moment later a spritz of moisture kissed his cheek. The feeling was real and appreciated more than anything he'd felt in a very, very long time.

He opened his eyes to the ensuing rain as the sound of it began to pelt against the Blazer's metal roof.

But all he saw was the Little Woods.

And the swamp.

And the boys sprinting wildly toward him . . . .

four

1977

YES! YES! DONNY shouted as he punched a clenched fist high into the air, jumping to the ground. "Got that little bastard. Got him good an' proper!"

"Which one of 'em is it?" Stu held an open hand above his glasses to block out the sun. "I can't tell which one it is . . . ."

Jack, too, squinted into the bright reflection coming off the water. "Well, I'll be—it's Cockerton's little brother!"

"Is it?" Stu smiled, barely believing their luck. First kill of the game, and it turns out to be Cockerton's little bro'. He high-fived Jack. "Nice one!"

"C'mon," Jack urged. "Let's get him before he takes off."

Ian sobbed as the vision of the faceless, screaming boy in the tree played over and again in his mind. He could hear every word of Jack and Stu's conversation as it echoed acoustically around the natural horse-shoe-shaped basin. And he now realized the boy he'd seen in that disturbing vision must have been himself.

He gingerly massaged his swollen knee while the tears rolled down his cheeks, making clean, parallel streaks against the caked mud on his face. The throbbing heat at the left side of his forehead was now as rhythmic as clockwork. The only saving grace of this macabre rhythm of pain was how it masked the thick, ballooning torment of his knee.

He didn't want to admit it to himself, but he was more than hurt. Now he was scared. Even at this distance he could see something in the two boys that somehow wasn't right; an empty darkness in their eyes. They had always been evil little sons-of-bitches, especially when it came to War. But when all was said and done, both teams always went back to the neighborhood together. One big gang. Tired and laughing and patting each other heartily on the back.

The sickening vision of the boy in the flaming tree told Ian it wasn't going to be like that today.

Jack and Stu were closing in on him now, making their way quickly through the swamp. They were both wearing military-style boots, not sneakers, and Ian laughed to himself at just how together these guys really were when it came to playing this game.

"Yo! Cockerton!" Jack shouted through cupped hands, overemphasizing his name's first syllable. "Yo *Cock*erton!"

He laughed aloud at his obvious joke and Stu joined in.

"*Cock*—erton!" they both screamed in shrill, unnatural voices.

Stu pulled madly at his crotch each time.

"We're gonna kill you, boy!"

Then Stu began howling. Actually howling. A guttural animal sound that came from somewhere dark, deep inside him.

Ian had never seen them like this before.

His chest tightened, breathing quickening as panic began to sweep through his body. His head filled with a thousand terrifying images, all of them swimming chaotically as they fought for dominance. It was a sudden, sickening melee of fears. He jerked his body forward, kicking madly at the water, trying to pull himself to his feet. Forget the dangling leg, there was a much greater danger out here.

And it was coming straight for him.

Ian forced himself up and stumbled into a clumsy one-legged hopping scramble as the two boys behind him increased their speed, splashing wildly through the swamp water. He could hear them gaining as he pushed himself onward as hard as he could, but everything seemed as if in slow motion. The horizon bobbed up and down in half time while the sound of thick water splashing into the air behind him echoed in decelerating rhythms with every teetering step. Even his temple pulsed in time to this slowing, measured beat as it released a stream of blood down the left side of his face and into his mouth with every step. Then he felt a claw digging into his right shoulder; another into his throat, and collapsed as everything started to fade to grey.

It hadn't taken long for them to catch up. Stu was first, and had thrown a broad, calloused hand over Ian's right shoulder. With his other he clasped Ian's throat. And with a single, violent tug, lurched him backward so that Ian's legs flailed in the air as he slammed onto his back into the water.

"Yes!" Jack screeched from further behind as he witnessed the takedown.

His fingers still firmly around Ian's throat, Stu straddled the younger Cockerton boy, pressing his face so close that his glasses smacked sharply against Ian's nose. His breath was hot and foul. It made Ian feel sick, but also kept him from passing out.

"Well, well, *well*. What have we got here then?" he asked as a drop of spit lingered on his lip, wavered, then dripped onto Ian's chin. "And just look at that lovely gash in your face, boy. I do believe you must be hurtin' some."

He smirked with wild eyes Ian had never before seen behind those rudimentary, black plastic-rimmed glasses.

When Jack finally caught up to them, his plodding strides splashed acrid swamp water into both of their faces. He grabbed Ian's hair and with one violent yank, wrenched his head to the side so he could inspect the gash in his temple, still sheeting with blood. "Huh! I did a pretty good job there, eh Ian?"

Ian closed his eyes tightly and said nothing.

"I *said*," Jack repeated, emphasizing the statement by jerking Ian's head back, harder. "I did a pretty good job. Now you'd better answer me this time—"

Ian's heart raced. He could feel it pumping insanely in his chest, a bomb about to explode. The thought of that happening was still swimming around in his brain as he heard his mouth utter of its own accord: "Yes."

"Good. Now we're getting somewhere."

Stu released his grip on Ian's throat and stood with each leg either side of Ian's waist. "What do we do with him?"

"You know, sometimes I think you haven't got any fucking brains in that skull of yours at all." Jack rapped his knuckles against Stu's forehead. "Or else you've scrambled them so damned much they just don't wanna work no more."

Stu was expressionless.

"For Chrissakes, we're taking him back to the Father Oak. We'll meet Dan somewhere, down that way. I told him to keep an eye on the Cockerton camp, y'know? They've got that pussy Matt Chauncey guarding it. Can you believe it?" He patted Stu on the back. "This is it my boy, we've just won ourselves a whole lot of fun."

The warm, enveloping greyness beckoned Ian once more as the pain throughout his body overwhelmed his senses and he found himself struggling to maintain consciousness. Seeing he was starting to fade, Jack yanked him back again and this time dunked his face into the murky water. Stu helped hold him there while Ian flailed and thrashed and the boys laughed.

Until the first air bubble surfaced.

"OK—guess we should let him up," Jack regretfully admitted as he released his grip. But Stu pressed down harder, a savage focus contorting his features. Two more bubbles broke the surface.

Ian's flailing weakened.

"I said let him go, man!" Jack punched Stu in the chest, forcing him to loosen his grip, and Ian surfaced, coughing and spluttering and expelling putrid brown liquid. Behind the sound of his own blood coursing through his ears, Ian could tell the boys were saying something, the same thing, over and over. But he could make out only slowed and thickly muffled voices. "Get up—get up—get UP—GET UP!"

The words became clear as the grey dissipated and the ringing in his ears subsided. They were tugging him by his wrists, pulling and half-dragging him through the water. Then Jack wrapped his arms around him in a bear hug that expelled the air from Ian's lungs as he was forced him to his feet. A lightning bolt of pain shot from Ian's right knee and ran all the way up his body where it lodged in his throbbing temple, the scorching agony cementing his return to cold, hard, consciousness.

"Walk!" Jack demanded. "I'm not carrying your sorry ass all the way back, you little shit."

Stu grinned and laughed in a short, erratic burst.

Ian lurched forward, managing a single half step before his leg crumpled. He instinctively threw his hands out to steady himself and unintentionally slapped Stu across the face.

Stu glowered. But said nothing. Instead, he scanned the area, found a twig and snapped it in half as he pulled it from the swamp.

"Big mistake if you think you can take me Cockerton," he said and the calm delivery of the assertion was far more frightening than the feral mania of moments before.

I'm NOT trying to take you!

Ian wanted so desperately to form the words but his mouth would not work. Earlier that day he was certain he could hold his own against any of the older boys this year.

But now....

Stu slowly circled the tip of the stick in a figure eight in front of Ian's face. And then, with no more consideration than one would give to inserting a key into a lock, drove it slowly into the raw, fleshy gash of Ian's temple. The skin bulged as the jagged tip plunged beneath the torn edges. Even when Ian stopped screaming, the twig remained hanging grotesquely from the side of his head.

II

"How far is it now?" Woody shouted after Jimi as they scrambled through the thick undergrowth.

"*Shut up,*" Bryan hissed under his breath.

Woody shrunk a little.

"It's over the ridge," Jimi whispered as he pointed. "There. About a hundred yards or so."

Bryan came to a stop. "Right. Hold on a minute then."

He tugged the back of Jimi's shirt.

"I say we get an action plan *now*. So we know what the hell we're doing. *Before* we stumble across them."

He paused. "If they are hiding up ther—"

The sentence was cut by a long, harrowing scream in the distance. An unseen bird took flight at the noise, wings flapping loudly at the otherwise quiet air.

Woody noticeably winced.

"Shit . . . ." Jimi said aloud for the three of them. "Seriously. What the hell was that?"

Rhetorical or not, neither answered.

Suddenly Bryan felt how cold it had actually become. It was always a bit cooler—and darker—back here, this far into the woods. But this felt nothing at all like summer. Instead, it felt a whole lot more like one of those autumn storms brewing up.

A storm much bigger than he liked to consider.

"This doesn't feel right—" Woody said aloud as if reading Bryan's thoughts, and the grave tone of his normally steadfast voice was in itself alarming.

"What do you mean?" Bryan asked, playing dumb to see if they really were on the same wavelength.

"Just what I said!" Woody's answer was uncharacteristically terse. "I don't like this. Something's not right . . . not the same as before." He turned to Jimi, the pitch of his voice rising, his words rushing together more swiftly. "Man, can't you *feel* it? And you know this place is haunted. Some kids were killed here, by their father I think, a long time ago. My uncle told me. He says the place is evil."

All three boys stood in silence as the words merged into the sounds of the woods, then wafted down upon them like feathers tossed into a breeze.

Then Jimi laughed. A loud staccato, hiccup of a sound. "Haunted. *Ha!* Don't be so fucking stupid, man. That's only a kids' tale." He shook his head dramatically. Perhaps a little too vehemently to be convincing, Bryan thought. "Dude, your uncle's just trying to spook ya."

"I don't know man," Bryan interjected. "Something *doesn't* feel right." He turned to Woody and shrugged. "But Haunted? You really believe that shit? I think it's just a storm coming in."

Jimi looked up at the blackening sky above the web-like canopy of leaves and branches.

"Yep. It's gonna be one motherfucker of a storm."

What few patches of blue were visible had begun to transform to a deep cast of bruise purple.

"So do we head back?" Bryan's question was to both.

"I don't know about Jimi," Woody answered. "But yeah, I say we head back to base."

Surprisingly, Jimi nodded in agreement.

"Alright then. I guess back it is."

No sooner had Bryan finished the sentence than something—a shadow—caught his eye in the brush just a few yards behind Jimi. He placed a finger to his lips and slowly indicated.

Woody peered into the darkness.

Jimi turned around to look. "*I don't see anything.*"

WAIT, Bryan mouthed silently, holding up an index finger.

He and Jimi stood transfixed on the thicket while Woody scanned the area, eyes darting wildly.

A twig snapped. The sound, crisp and clear, hung like an audible balloon in the lifeless air.

"*There,*" Bryan whispered. "*There—it's coming from those pines.*" He stepped cautiously over the uneven ground, picking his way stealthily toward the spot. Jimi followed.

The air began to move, growing into a slow, cold breeze.

"Do you see anything?" Jimi was circling round the cluster of trees.

Bryan shook his head in response.

Another sound. This time about ten yards from the same trees.

"*Over there!*" Bryan whisper-shouted, pointing feverishly at the shadow now plunging through the brush within yards of Jimi.

Jimi dropped defensively to one knee, spotting it at the same time. Crouching, he began to stalk low and slow toward the shape which was now motionless; nothing but a silhouette in the undergrowth.

Perhaps a boy. Perhaps a man crouching.

He cautiously pulled aside the thicket of weeds and brush, but still could discern nothing. Signaling to Bryan a dozen steps away, he rotated his open palms upward; raising his shoulders.

I don't know.

Bryan shook his head and mirrored the gesture back at him.

Then it moved. Jimi was certain of it. He rose from his crouching position and stood tall and steady.

"Hey! You!" he shouted between cupped hands.

It didn't answer.

"Hey, I said," Jimi repeated as he moved tentatively closer to the shape, now just feet away. He brushed aside the long dry tendrils of ivy hanging from the branches overhead. "You—in the bushes—I'm talking to *you.*"

No one answered.

"It's no use trying to hide in there. Acting like we can't see you. We already have, man, so give it up."

Silence.

"C'mon," Jimi insisted, growing less patient. "Who is it—*Jack?* Stu? . . . Dan?"

Surely not Big Dan – he just wasn't that stealthy.

Nothing.

The figure remained stationary and the only sound was the whistling of the growing wind through the trees. Jimi felt the hairs stand up on the back of his neck, a chill running down his spine like cold, dead fingers dragging down the center of his back.

"Come on guys. It's me, Jimi." He laughed nervously to himself as he persisted to try and persuade the figure to reveal itself.

Then almost too quickly to be seen, the figure shot from the brush and tore through the undergrowth, effortlessly dodging and twisting as it navigated noiselessly through the dense entanglement of trees and brush leading back toward the base camp.

"Only Stu can move like that—" Jimi exclaimed as he broke into a run. "C'mon!" He was already hurdling a clump of rotting logs when he shouted over his shoulder, beckoning Bryan and Woody to follow.

The boys ran full-out for several hundred yards, but could not gain on the shadow as it skirted deftly in and out between the trees. Becoming entangled more and more within thickets that had grown impossibly dense, Bryan was the first to let up, his chest wrenching with piercing heat as he slowed to a trot, then a walk.

"Look," he tried to call out as the other two charged ahead. He gulped in the damp air which was now so cold that it burnt his lungs "It's not Stu for Chrissakes. *Guys. It's not him!*"

Jimi and Woody stumbled to a clumsy stop and now all three were doubled over, grabbing the backs of their legs and panting as they caught short, rapid breaths.

What only moments before had been a breeze was now a fierce, howling wind. When it rose to a maddening crescendo—piercing the canopy far above with a shrill, frightful cry—Woody's expression of confusion, doubt and fear spoke for all three of the boys as they cast their eyes upward and saw the jet black nothingness which had begun to swallow the afternoon sky.

III

"Please no—" Matt was huddled tightly into a corner of the oval clearing, his back against one of the parallel laying logs, whimpering. *"Please!* I'll do anything. I promise!"

He placed an arm before him in a weak gesture of defense against Stu who was slowly closing in.

"I think I'll have as much fun with you as I had with your buddy over there." Stu nodded towards the younger Cockerton who was prostrate on the dirt floor, one hand holding a wounded knee, the other pressed to his bloodied face, his hair clotted with dirt and drying blood.

The sight of it all—Ian's red-stained shirt, the mud and layers of dark rust-colored blood—made Matt want to throw up. To him, Ian had become the embodiment of the *Creature from the Black Lagoon* and it scared him beyond understanding.

Sensing this, Stu's lips quivered with excitement. "Maybe I'll have even more fun," he said, finishing the thought as Matt sobbed in a fetal position at his feet.

IV

"If that wasn't Stu we were chasing, then what the hell do you reckon it was?" Jimi was shouting, stepping aggressively toward Bryan. "I mean, you seem to know everything, Bry, after all!"

"No. I really don't. And I don't know . . . what . . . that was."

"For fuck's sake, it was Stu!"

"No way." Bryan shook his head. "You saw how that thing ran. No chance."

"It was *Stu!*"

The pleading look in Jimi's eyes belied the angry certainty of his voice, the cracks beginning to show beneath his veneer of courage. He was getting cold. And frightened.

They all were.

"Look," Bryan pointed up. "Look at that. What do you think about *that?*" Through the leaves and branches high above them the sky was dark as night.

"It's a storm! That's all." Jimi's answer was unconvincing, perhaps even to himself. "It's a storm . . . ."

His conviction weakened with the very words which trailed away.

"There's no storm coming Jimi." Woody stated it plainly. Then after disappearing within a moment of deep thought: "Not a storm like you mean, anyways."

Neither Jimi nor Bryan knew exactly what Woody meant. And for that matter, Woody himself didn't really understand the comment which came out more by instinct than rationale. But they all felt it: something was wrong. Something that felt corrupted and rotten and like nothing they'd experienced before.

Now, all the boys had lived through many bouts of the intense, unpredictable weather so typical of western Pennsylvania. In the summertime it was hot. Stupid hot. And in the winter it was beyond what reasonable folks would call cold. At times the intensity was such that even the changeover seasons were often unsure what they were supposed to be. Snow in early May was never out of the question; neither was a seventy-degree afternoon just before Christmas. And there were so many severe thunderstorms that, already at their young age, the boys had become just about oblivious to them. Certainly nothing worth stopping the game of War for.

But this was not a typical summertime storm.

And deep down, they all knew it.

They walked in quiet rumination as they turned back for the base camp, finding themselves hurrying faster than expected through the dense undergrowth. Each was in his own world, focused only on one thing: getting back. No one even said a thing when Woody stumbled headlong into a blackberry thicket.

(Normally, this would have been a golden ticket for scornful mockery. Today it was just another thing that happened.)

"Shit!" Woody cursed and held out his arm for self-inspection. "I'm fucking covered in scratches."

He presented his arm to the other two.

"Just look at it!"

Jimi blankly nodded. Bryan pursed his lips and dispassionately threw Woody a bandana from his jeans pocket.

Woody swiped the blue paisley cloth up his forearm and in cleaning away the blood, revealed a web of myriad light pink lines running helter-skelter across his skin.

"Look at all that blood," he stated almost proudly as he held the bandana to eye level.

"It looks worse than it is. Just keep wiping it," Bryan replied as he poked Woody's arm at the greatest intersection of scratches and Woody responded with an unconvincing 'Ouch.' "See, just keep wiping. The blood's coming back already."

He poked at Woody again and Woody swatted his finger away.

"Well it will, if you're gonna poke at it, you friggin' idiot."

"Guys—Come on! Let's just get out of here." Jimi was indifferent to Woody's arm. All he wanted was to get back, and to get back now. He started walking again without bothering to wait for them, picking his way through the undergrowth and sweeping aside stinging branches with detached disregard. He ignored the pain as multiple striations raised across his own hands and forearms by the thorn-laden tendrils.

A few beats behind, Woody and Bryan followed Jimi's crude new path at a more careful, methodical pace. As the artificial night quickly descended below the treetops and absorbed what precious little light remained, they walked with arms outstretched, feeling their way through the dark.

As though summoned by this unnatural twilight, the rising wind cried even more loudly between the trees. It shrieked and wailed as clouds of leaves scattered through the air like flocks of birds, and brush scattered across the thickly matted forest floor. High above, unsettling creaks and moans snapped loudly as even the greatest of the trees pivoted in the wind, the weak and deadened wood sporadically giving way.

Then came the *craaaack* followed by something smacking the back of Bryan's head. He yelped—in surprise more than pain—as he ducked and swatted the air around him. A moment later the ground exploded and shook him to his knees as a plume of debris filled the air and choked out the woods' last remnant light. Concealing the massive bough which now filled the path where only moments before had been clear passage, a vast web of branches extended far in every direction, weaving up and over

Bryan, the fingers of a giant hand cupping a bewildered spider.

He covered his mouth and nose from the dust cloud and sputtered through tightly clenched fingers: *"Ar-e—yo-u—guys—okay?"*

His words went out into the veil of darkness, but no reply came back. He squinted to search the void which had only moments before been the Woods, but the darkness had become absolute. Reaching with extended arms, he probed the space around him and felt nothing but empty air and fingerling branches.

"Jimi?" he cried out. Only the wild whistling of the wind answered. Its shrill sound pierced an underlying, static rumble. "Woody?"

He crawled cautiously forward, hands searching the forest floor as he fought through the branches and limbs and fierce, pressing wind. Hoping to find anyone, anything, within reach.

"Woody . . . ? Jimi!" His pleas were desperate as the shrieking cry of the wind had grown to a frenzy, a binaural sound which danced through the air as Bryan edged forward on his hands and knees.

A minute passed, perhaps two, as he inched slowly and carefully forward. They felt like hours. When his left hand touched what surely must be the main bough which had fallen, he wrapped his arms around it as though giving it a hug. It was easily several feet thick. Holding tightly onto it and working his way along its length, he counted the heel-to-toe paces as he stepped nimbly between branches and sharpened points invisible in the dark.

Nine . . . Ten . . . Eleven . . . .

The bough was at least twelve feet long from the point where he'd made contact with it. Woody and Jimi had been no more than a pace or two in front. His mind raced as it realized the sum of the equation.

Oh God, please help us!

The wind whipped around him, between the trees and across the ground, plastering him sharply with dirt and debris and moisture. It wailed like the sound of a dozen eerie, discordant flutes all playing off key. Then something—a *whimper?*—impossibly heard above the din of sound. He shouted again, this time at the top of his lungs. But his own words were lost as soon as they left his lips.

Squinting hard, he probed the black curtain of the landscape but could make out only murky shapes against the inky background. Then a figure, little more than an area of deeper blackness, moved across what ineffectual field of vision remained. Was it large? Small? It was impossible to determine, or even how near.

"Guys . . . are you OK . . . ?"

But his only answer was the static rumble of the wind beneath that shrill, disturbing whistling.

They were gone. He knew it.

He could feel it.

His heart pounded beneath his ribs as if desperate to free itself from the cage.

The intervals between his breaths shortened.

His eyes darted frantically from side to side as cold, trembling panic began to take hold.

And Bryan began to run.

He turned in the direction he thought they'd been heading, nothing more than a guess, and aimed for an ashen break in the blackness. More than once he mistook a patch of thick brush for an opening between the trees and tore small ribbons of skin from his chest and arms. Still he ran, tracking only the penetrating whistling as its unnerving disharmony screwed and coiled around the treetops, commanding the air as if beckoning him.

Minutes were hours as time poured viscous like syrup. All movement became thick and slow against the quickening of his breaths, the hyperventilation saturating his brain with oxygen.

He had no idea how long he'd been scrambling through the brush when the intense flash of yellow and orange burst into the sky, flushing his dark-adapted eyes with blinding white specks. He squeezed them closed hard and when they reopened, the woods were bathed in an amber glow, the forest dancing macabrely in the light as flickering shadows stretched the trees to enormous, exaggerated heights.

I'm close . . .

The realization swept over him in a wave which doused the fiery panic that had taken control of his body. Half sobbing, he stumbled to a stop and consciously focused on slowing his labored breathing. Any curiosity about the great burst of light overcome by the single, inherent motivation to buffer his trembling nerves. Tears filled his eyes as his shirt flapped in tatters about his torso. At last, he was within reach of safety . . . and the others.

Bloodied and worn, he stumbled into the clearing and fell to his knees. When he raised his face, the heat of a bonfire warmed his cheeks as it raged in the center of the clearing where the parallel laying logs had once been. Around it, emboldened by the flames which spiraled high into the premature night, Woody and Jimi were skipping in a frenzied dance along with Jack and Dan. Their faces masked in grey mud and dark red, they wielded sticks and rocks and were chanting and hollering in delight as they punched their fists high into the air.

Then came the scream.

Terrifyingly sharp, it rose from above the flickering light and shattered the whistling of the wind like fragile glass. It was the sound from a boy, but a piercing terror that Bryan had never before heard.

Like the column of smoke on which it rose, the cry curled high into the sky. At the spot of its origination, Matt Chauncey was perched precariously on one of the immense limbs of the Father Oak, twenty feet in the air. He was wailing and clawing at something around his neck as he pleaded, "No! Please. *Noooo*—"

Tears ran down his cheeks and into his mouth, ultimately choking out the plea. His eyes were wider and darker than Bryan had ever seen human eyes, the vast pupils like Little Orphan Annie eyes in reverse. Matt's clothes were torn and tattered, and like the others, his face coated in mud and something deep red.

But more noticeably red than grey, Bryan found himself thinking as his mind whirled in strange, incomplete synapses as it futilely attempted to make sense of what it was witnessing.

When a shirtless Stu Klatz burst across the clearing and clambered up the Father Oak so quickly it seemed inhuman, Bryan's thoughts moved beyond comprehension and into the realm of unsettling dream-state.

Spider-like, Stu's feet and hands seemed to barely make contact with the tree as they somehow moved all at the same time and the slim but muscular boy skirted between branches so swiftly that gravity and time seemed to no longer apply. Within seconds Stu had made the climb and was striding down the giant limb, on which Matt Chauncey cowered, with little more effort or concentration than if he were taking a casual stroll along the ground.

Matt started to inch fearfully backward along the branch, his ungainly clumsiness matched in equal measures by Stu's agile surety. Despite its impressive size, Matt could feel the girth of the branch thinning beneath his feet as he slid first one and then the other backward, each tentative step moving him further from the trunk of the Father Oak. With each of these uneasy steps the limb groaned and bent a little more.

"Please!" Matt begged. "Please! Please Stu. Stop!"

He threw his left arm defensively in front of him, palm facing out. It was an instinctive, symbolic barrier if little else, and he hadn't considered the repercussion of releasing his grip from one of the smaller branches he'd been steadying himself with.

Matt immediately lost his balance.

Stu's eyes widened, the boy's manic snarl spreading to an eager grin as Matt's left foot skated out from underneath him, pulling his body fiercely to the right. His left arm windmilled in feverish loops, a wildly spinning gyroscope unable to find center. His right leg kicked up and out. And Matt fell backwards off the limb.

The rope around his neck saved him.

It snagged on the branches higher up and Matt teetered there at a forty-five degree angle, looking straight up at the taut rope as his throat constricted from his weight tightening the loop. He choked and gargled as his feet scrambled to find new purchase, and when they did, he gripped the tightly drawn rope with both hands and pulled himself back to the safety of the limb.

Stu's delighted countenance fell.

"Aw. Shame," he stated despondently. Then, after a pause in which his eyes darted back and forth behind his black plastic spectacles: "Maybe let's try again."

He stretched tall and pressed his palms firmly against the underside of the branch above them. He pushed down hard with his feet at the same time, and their limb bowed. And creaked even more. When it sprang back up, the wave of motion cycled down the branch. As it reached Matt, his knees bent while his feet rode up, and the snagged rope came free from its entanglement above. Matt gripped the branches nearby even tighter as Stu exploited the recoiling momentum and pressed his legs down harder. The limb flexed like a diving board and Matt's feet began to slide and skate, each ensuing peristaltic wave threatening to be the one to loosen his grip and send him plunging twenty feet to the ground.

Or worse yet, never hit the ground.

Matt's heart raced. His breath came fast and shallow and he suddenly felt as if he might pass out. His body caromed up and down with the limb as his fingers fumbled in blind desperation at the rope around his neck. He could feel them playing over the knot behind his head; sensed its bulk and layers of interconnected loops; but his mind was a spinning roulette wheel, the little white ball frenetically skipping and bouncing from thought to thought but wholly incapable of landing on a single space where a cohesive one might reside. He could not form a schematic image of the knot, no matter how many times his tense, trembling fingers played over it again and again.

All the while Stu continued to bounce, edging closer each time. He was a stealthy predator slinking intently towards his prey and it was the calm, resolute focus in his eyes which lit the fire of Matt's fear more than anything else. When Stu curled his upper lip and showed his yellow, crooked teeth in a bestial grimace, Matt pinched his streaming eyes closed and released his terror in a scream that sliced like a scalpel through the tumultuous roar of the wind and clamorous whoops and barks of the boys' vulgar ritual below.

Had it not been so surreal, Bryan would've thought it comical. Instead, he covered his ears and tried not to allow the reality of Matt's fear and pain to find a way to spark his own.

Then it happened.

Stu's unblinking eyes spotted him at the edge of the clearing, hands clamped to either side of his head but still unable to turn away from the predator–prey drama unfolding in the tree.

Their mutual stares locked and Stu's eyes bore into his own like an auger, ceasing to bound upon the branch and riding its slowing camber until it rebounded to a stop with a low, snapping groan.

As if commanding the very air, the wind also fell from its maddening crescendo. Around the fire, the boys stopped their dance and quieted their boisterous hollering. So the cacophony of sound which had become the static constant backdrop to this scene abated instantly to silence, and only the popping and crackling of the fire in the clearing accompanied Matt's soft, hiccuping sobs.

Then, as if for no other reason than a dispassionate display of his un-tethered might, Stu retracted a muscled arm far behind his ear and fired it blindly towards Matt's face, his eyes never breaking their stare with Bryan. The fist was off target but still struck like a piston, and with a popping sound Matt's nose spread wide. Thin strands of red slung in all directions, weaving a concentric pattern across the drying mud which masked Matt's face; spotting Stu's shirtless torso like an instantaneous bout of measles.

Matt cried out in a delayed, muffled cry as he cupped a bloodied hand over his face.

In the clearing below, Bryan leapt to his feet and charged toward the Father Oak. "STOP IT! YOU'RE GONNA KILL HIM!"

The boys around the fire each turned as he jolted past, their eyes empty; faces expressionless.

All except one.

Beneath his mask of mud and red, the slicing grin of Jack Raker glowered at him. Jack was holding Matt's flute and as if on cue, began to scream acrid breath into it. The cheap bamboo pipe shrilled to sour, inharmonious life and a shiver of icy cold ran down Bryan's back like dead fingers playing down his spine.

He was nearly at the Father Oak and anticipating how to make the climb when something exploded into his side. It lifted him from his feet and slammed him into the dirt. The wind exploded from his chest in a reflexive gasp and for a moment his lungs were vacuuming in upon themselves. He barrel rolled through the dirt fully twice and came to a sliding stop on his back, looking up at the limb where Matt and Stu were perched far above. He sucked the air back into his lungs with a choking gulp, but the attempt to fill them was cut short by a hefty, timeworn work boot pressing squarely upon his chest.

Towering over him, Big Dan Mercer smirked in crazed rapture as he leaned into the stance, perfectly shifting all his weight to that foot.

"You're—hur—tin—" Bryan wheezed between futile breaths, and Big Dan responded by only bearing down harder.

In the tree above, Stu whooped with delight.

"Cockerton. Hey *Cock*-erton! Watch this!"

And after Big Dan had clamped a thick, calloused hand across Bryan's face to make sure he was looking up, Stu reveled in indifference as he artfully swept his leg around and perfectly executed an effortless yet lightning fast roundhouse kick.

It happened so fast it was impossible to dodge.

Matt's legs sailed out to the side and up. For a moment his feet were level with his head before he crashed back down on the branch and his ribs made an unusual cracking sound as the air bellowed from his chest. His body went slack as it bent unnaturally around the curve of the branch.

Then Matt simply slid off the limb.

Falling backwards through the entanglement of offshoots and vines, he plummeted towards the ground shrieking. One hand futilely clutched at the empty air, the other for the loop around his throat. When the braided rope reached its full extent, the instantaneous cessation of momentum jerked him violently back up, and the tongue which had shot from his mouth he bit in two.

Momentarily thrashing, Matt bungeed up and down above Bryan and Dan like a morbid Yo-Yo, the noose constricting his throat until his scream transmuted into a sickening snake-like *hissssss.*

Big Dan hastened to his feet and thrust both fists into the air in triumphant celebration. "Yeah man. Hell YEAH!"

Then came the realization that Matt's feet dangled only a short distance above him, and Dan delighted at the prospect of jumping up and yanking on them just because he could. He pictured wrapping his arms around Matt's ankles and swaying back and forth as his own colossal heft being added to the rope would pull the noose around Chauncey's neck even tighter.

So Dan Mercer jumped. Twice. But Matt's twitching feet remained beyond the reach of his feeble ability to lift his own considerable weight more than a few inches off the ground.

The second jump is when Bryan kicked out Big Dan's kneecap.

Dan squealed and crumpled like a rag doll, Bryan rolling to the side just in time before the huge thug slumped to the ground next to him in a pitiable, moaning heap.

Inches away, Bryan lay on his back and opened his eyes.

Directly above him, Matt's body swayed motionless from the rope. One hand appeared to be clutching at the loop now embedded into his neck, pinned there by a finger Matt had somehow managed to get under the noose. The other arm hung disjointedly out of place, disproportionately longer than the other. Where Matt's clothes were torn the shredded openings revealed welts and bleeding cuts. Flowing from a source beneath his shorts, Matt's legs dripped with lines like thick red spiders' webs.

And one of Matt's eyes had begun to protrude from its socket as if the orb were attempting to escape its dying body.

Bryan's pupils dilated, his eyes blurring to a thousand-yard-stare as they sought a focal point far beyond Matt's swinging body, even far beyond the dark canopy of the trees. Settling someplace in the distant sky, his mind had simply seized, disallowing any further thought or comprehension of these silent testimonies. Proofs of horrors perpetrated upon the timid boy even before Bryan had stumbled into the clearing in the first place.

Then something emanated from Matt's lips, two distinct vibrating pitches, barely audible beneath a wisp of air.

Bryan heard them from his far away place, as if a relic of a terrible dream. But then they seemed closer, as if moving up through the sky to reach his mind up there. And Bryan's mind moved down through the sky, through the canopy to meet them.

Because he thought those two pitches sounded like words.

And those words sounded like:

"Heel-lp . . . meee . . . ."

They wheezed through a stream of air escaping Matt's body like a punctured tire. And the magnitude of the inconceivable realization that Matt might still be alive snapped Bryan's mind to such insanely crisp focus that he jumped to his feet and was pulling himself onto one of the lower branches of the Father Oak faster than his new thought process could keep up. He carefully steadied himself, planted his feet, then reached for the next level of branches where he sidled onto one barely able to support his weight but ignored the logical improbability of it.

If I can only lift his weight from that rope . . . . He stretched as long as possible and Matt's waist was almost in reach. *If I can just raise him a little bit he—*

A monstrous weight struck him from above and he was suddenly away from Matt and slamming back to the ground with Stu's arms wrapped around him. He yelled and punched and struggled but Stu's grip was too strong, leaving Bryan to grapple impotently at the base of the tree as Matt twisted limply above them.

The rest of the boys who, until now had been inanimately watching, broke once more into an elated dance. Their manic frenzy around the fire threw warped, lurid shadows across the clearing and the trees. And Stu

Klatz, no longer concerned with Bryan, rolled off the elder Cockerton boy and jumped into the throng of boys where he raved triumphantly with them. They all followed Jack's lead and frolicked around the pyre, their muddied faces glowing amber . . . everyone, that is, except Ian Cockerton who, sitting at the edge of the clearing, stared blankly into nowhere as he silently rocked back and forth, pressing his face into his knees.

And Matt, whose body swayed lifelessly from the rope.

Bryan looked at the boy that was his brother's friend and wiped a hand across his own face, streaking the dirt and sweat and tears and blood. Helplessness washed over him as he watched Matt's dangling legs sweeping gently to and fro in the currents of heat rising from the immense bonfire. Matt's protruding eye had now exploded and hung on his muddied cheek by jelly threads. It no longer was full and round but collapsed and hollow like some dime-store prop. His other eye was glazed and lifeless. And stared vacantly but directly at Bryan.

Bryan Cockerton bent over and retched.

Staring at the ground, he missed Matt's final spasms as the boy's fingers stretched and played one last time over the rope around his throat, perhaps only a reflex action as the expiring muscles tightened and twitching nerves fired.

Stu stared beatifically at these final movements of his creation, sometimes tilting his head one way, then the other, as he admired the dangling form as though a gruesome god.

His job was almost done. But there was yet one final brush stroke to complete the masterpiece; one final act to fulfill the perfect purpose he had been called unto.

He pulled a flaming branch from the fire, examined it closely with a level of enthralled awe, and strode slowly towards Bryan . . and the Father Oak. He savored every step, never once taking his eyes off the hanging idol. Along the way he plucked a square metal can from the dirt without breaking stride and adeptly unscrewed its red cap with a single hand.

When he reached Bryan, still bent over and vomiting, Stu slung the can spinning high into the air.

Its liquid contents spiraled in a corkscrew behind it. The can hit Matt squarely on the chest then fell unremarkably to the ground as the fluid streaked the boy's tattered clothes, ran down his legs, and began sprinkling the dirt where Matt's blood had done the same. Together, the liquids formed a pool of diluting purplish-black which radiated an unmistakable odor both sour and oddly sweet.

The uniquely pungent smell of gasoline.

Stu lifted his head and for a moment, appeared to almost behold Matt's image piously. He mouthed something silently, as if paying homage to a new god, then extended his arm and raised the torch—

—And Bryan threw his shoulder into Stu's chest, wrapping his arms around him and using the momentum to take him down. Just the way they'd been taught in football practice.

Stu didn't budge.

It was as though Bryan were attempting to tackle a marble statue.

With a simple push, Stu swatted him to the ground as easily as tossing a kitten from one's lap.

Sprawled once more in the dirt, the cool dampness of the purplish puddle soaked through Bryan's jeans while drops of gasoline and blood pattered gently down upon his head.

"It's him . . ." Stu began in a voice that was more a range of dissonant vibrations than the voice Bryan had known all these years. His face appeared distorted and aberrant, seeming to undulate between the boy Bryan recognized and something grotesque and inexplicable. The sight hollowed Bryan's heart as if being scraped from the inside out. ". . . Or it's you, Cockerton."

Without waiting for a reply Stu thrust the torch at Bryan's face.

Bryan grabbed the burning stick and prevented it from gouging his right eye. Sparks stung his cheek before he pushed the torch away, deflecting it hard to one side. It took a moment before he was aware of the lightning bolt of pain shooting up his arm from the skin which had seared on his right hand.

"You made the right choice Cockerton."

Stu's voice was once again his own and spoke the words with unnervingly sober detachment. He extended his arm high above his head . . . and kissed the burning torch against Matt's sneaker.

The flame took instantly and licked furiously up Matt's body.

"Die, you sad bastard."

Matt's torso was engulfed in a rushing *whooosh* as the flames ran up his neck and kissed his face. His mouth, now frozen in an eternal scream, stretched—twice—before disappearing beneath a mask of fiery red and yellow ribbons.

Time stopped as the boys stood in rapture.

Every one of them, Bryan included, watched in morbid fascination as the flames grew and strengthened until they consumed Matt's being wholly. The swaying boy was now a ghastly, fiery specter; an illuminated idol lighting the woods which eclipsed even the radiance of the bonfire which seemed to ebb out of deference.

When the boys' intense concentration began to subside and their attention returned to Bryan, he screamed from somewhere deep inside and started to run.

In ungraceful, biting panic, Bryan stumbled to the edge of the clearing where his younger brother sat hugging his knees. Ian's eyes were wide and unblinking as his mind cruelly recorded each and every frame of the boy on the rope—the kid who had once been his best friend—who now bubbled and blistered inside the flames. It faithfully cataloged every hideous mutation as Matt's misshapen neck stretched like hot plastic, the weight of his body pulling it longer. It documented the smell as the swaying feet turned black at the bones, and etched in endless, nightmarish perpetuity the moment the almost beautiful boyish face simply vanished beneath a gruesome veil of white hot fire.

Bryan sensed this all because his mind was doing the same.

He dismissed what he could not control and chose to focus on what he could. So he leaned down, threw his hands under Ian's arms, and lurched his brother to his feet.

And began to run.

Ian reeled forward a step before his right leg immediately buckled beneath its swollen and dislocated kneecap. But Bryan did not slow, and he did not look back. He did not worry about his brother's pain as they staggered in a kind of limping, three-legged trot across the clearing and disappeared again into the darkness of the woods.

Tugging and coaxing Ian along, they pressed through the increasing density of the trees and undergrowth which scratched and pulled at their clothes and skin.

When they eventually stumbled out of the Little Woods and into the dark open fields beyond, the shrill whistling of Matt's flute again began to sound and Bryan knew that the boys would not come.

At least now.

Not yet.

For those abominations in the woods—once boys, once friends—were enraptured in dark ceremony, parading beneath the phoenix they had summoned into being from the boy who once was Matt.

The sound of their abhorrent, baneful laughter commingled with the flute's disharmonic notes, and together the hideous chord echoed through the trees and rose high above the canopy and into the artificial night sky.

While out of the silhouette of the forest, a spire of flames grew and lit up the Little Woods like a sun.

Five

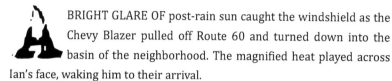 BRIGHT GLARE OF post-rain sun caught the windshield as the Chevy Blazer pulled off Route 60 and turned down into the basin of the neighborhood. The magnified heat played across Ian's face, waking him to their arrival.

Despite it, or perhaps because of it, he shivered.

They pulled into the driveway of the home where both boys had grown up. Ian's brother had purchased the house from his parents when they'd decided it was much too large for their needs and would now prefer a smaller place of easier upkeep. Bryan pressed the button of the remote clipped to the visor and the garage door began to churn clunkily upwards in spurts and starts, the same old way it always had. Despite the disturbing recollection of the Little Woods, this mundane detail and its reassuring constancy was a source of comfort as the nightmare childhood images receded to the back of his mind where they blurred and faded until Ian was left with only a lingering sense of mild unease.

When they pulled in, Rebecca, sans the kids, was waiting anxiously at the door. Ian wasn't entirely out of the Blazer before she ran up to him and threw her arms around his waist, flooding instantly to tears as her brother-in-law held her silently. The loss had been great for all of them but oddly for Rebecca, the newest member of the family, accepting it seemed to be the hardest.

"Hey, it's gonna be alright." Ian gently ran his hand up and down her back. "It'll be alright." He dare not look at his brother who stood in the open doorway, for if he did, Ian felt certain that he, too, would crumble beneath the oppressive weight of emotion.

In the quietude of the house they sat with cups of coffee which had long ago gone tepid as their grief spent all their tears. For now.

They then began to speak pragmatically about the arrangements. Thursday, 2 pm, St Michael's. Followed by the crematorium. Certainly it was to be a low-key affair. Uncle Rod and his wife would have to be there of course. (They didn't even know yet – that part Bryan was dreading.) But few others of the Cockerton family still remained, so there wouldn't be a lot of calls to be made. Ian mentioned that he thought there might be a great uncle Bob lurking around Philadelphia somewhere, but wasn't sure. Bryan said he would check this with their Uncle Rod when they spoke later.

None of them wished to prolong the ritual beyond what was required. The County Coroner would release the bodies tomorrow. Thursday was the day after that. A nice man from the funeral home that had prepared Auntie Mona three years ago had already been contacted about taking on the job. He would take care of everything, so he said. And then it would all be over.

Ian sighed deeply without wishing to. The crying had made his head light, almost a lopsided feeling which unnerved him; it was a feeling of loss of control he didn't care for.

"You've been good, Ian," Rebecca consoled him when Bryan left the room for another coffee. "It was a long trip. But still you came, and straight away. We can't tell you *how much* that means—"

Her words faltered to a fresh swelling of emotion and she fought away the tears, but they pressed too effortlessly through her defense.

Bryan returned with a fresh, steaming cup.

"Hey now. Come on," he whispered in hushed tones as he pulled her close. Rebecca disappeared facilely into her grief for a time, snuggling hard into her husband's chest.

And there she fell asleep.

"Listen Bryan, I want to know." Ian said softly once he was certain Rebecca was fully asleep. "I *need* to know. Exactly how it happened. I *have* to know how . . . ."

Bryan bit his lip. As though spellbound by his brother's words, his mind somehow called to view the sight of the wreckage. He hadn't been there when it happened. Hadn't seen it at all, in fact. The first he knew about his parents' accident was when he received a phone call (that call we all fear) from Mercy Hospital, around two hours after they had left his home for theirs.

But Bryan had known about it—*had somehow sensed it*—hadn't he? Even before it happened. He recalled his uneasy feeling as his parents waved goodbye from the driveway after their visit with the kids that evening; the inexplicable anxiety he'd experienced before, so many times, when he was a boy.

He cleared his throat before answering.

"It was a truck."

And Ian's stomach churned, his head filling with helium.

III

Carl Miller had been driving tractor trailers since he was twenty-years-old. His father had taught him to drive cars when Carl was only nine. Before that he'd driven minibikes. After cars, he drove trucks. Pickup trucks, flat beds, box trucks. Then big trucks. *Really* big ones. The eighteen-wheelers that speed by you on the highway and send your hatchback buffeting to one side like fluff in the wind. Carl especially liked that part of it. It was power.

And power felt *big*.

He laughed at this thought right now as he was passing a small Pontiac. He grinned at the image in his passenger's side mirror of the driver tensing up, gripping his steering wheel that little bit tighter.

Yeah baby. Power.

Currently Carl worked for an independent trucking firm but was mostly sub-contracted out to the regional steel mill to haul their girders and beams and other boring things around this part of the country, quite often to Pittsburgh, Philadelphia, sometimes even New Jersey or further. Tonight he was making his way back from Pittsburgh as a matter of fact, and looking forward to settling down at home with a nice supper.

And his Sherry.

My woman, he would explain to new acquaintances as he pulled up a stool at any number of truck stops he frequented and struck up conversation over a burger and fries. *Not the poofy drink.*

And he made sure they got it that his girl was some hot tamale. Sure, he admitted he was nothing much to look at himself and didn't quite know how he'd pulled it off. Almost like magic, he'd usually say. Sherry just landed in his lap. Quite literally. Down at Dempsey's Tavern in town. He's having a drink and there she is, and a little tipsy to boot. And as they say, that was all, folks.

They had a quickie out back behind the toilets, and then Sherry moved in with him a week later, in his trailer on the edge of Eastfield Park Estates. And shit, did they have some sex. Every night. Everywhere. Sherry just loved it. And so, of course, did Carl.

He loved the look of her hair—dark, almost jet black.

He liked the look of her lips—ruby red.

And he was crazy about her tits—big ones. The kind that draw you like a magnet as they pass by. Yeah, Carl loved that about Sherry.

Oh, and her legs aren't half bad either, he'd often throw in those conversations.

The thought of Sherry right now, and the fact that he'd be having his way with her tonight, made him begin to feel that oh-so-familiar sensation. So Carl reached into his lap and felt the firmness starting to build inside his overalls.

"You wanna come out to play, little fellow?"

He asked it aloud, half expecting it to answer back. Of course in its own way it did. It lurched up, pressing against the inside of his pants.

"OK then, Little Carl."

So he began to visualize his Sherry.

Those beautiful, big breasts, firm and plump.

From the height of his cab, Carl's tractor trailer felt like a giant Pac-Man gobbling up the reflective markers down the middle of the nighttime road as the juggernaut rumbled towards Hamburger Hill at a good 50mph clip. Not long now and he would be home.

Did he dare?

Sherry's gorgeous mouth, moist and open.

Half closing his eyes, Sherry's features were crystal clear to him. Sprawled across the bed, eager to please.

He grew harder.

Why the fuck shouldn't I, Carl answered himself and snapped open a button of his overalls below his waist. *If anything, pulling one out— right here, right now—will make me last that little longer tonight.*

Which could only be a good thing by his books, and surely by Sherry's, too. Because sometimes, if he were honest, Sherry made him come way too fast . . . and way before she wanted him to.

Fumbling with his right hand and transferring his left to the vibrating steering wheel, Carl reached between the open studs. And began unceremoniously pulling himself off.

It didn't take much coaxing before—

Shit, watch that pothole.

—he was fully erect. A little more stroking and he was pulsating from within, could feel his load ready to loose. All the while the semi carried on down the road, expertly guided by his other, highly experienced driving hand. Almost, almost—

That beautiful, smokin' hot ass of hers.

—almost, almost, almost, nearly there now!

Carl lifted his chin and grimaced in concentration. He could feel her satisfying him as if she were there. And in another moment he was about ready to cum.

But the car was also coming, over the crest of the hill.

It blared its horn and Carl snapped awake. And his mind failed to understand what his eyes were showing it.

What in God's name were they thinking, coming onto his side of the road like that?

But of course it was his eighteen-wheeler which had crossed the center line before Carl had the opportunity to finish his self pleasure.

Carl tried to pull his right hand out of his trousers but it wouldn't pass through the snaps as easily as it had gone in. So, with eyes now frozen wide, he yanked the wheel hard right with his left hand and slammed his foot on the brake, pressing way harder than he was trained to do.

The semi's wheels locked up.

It slipped and began to fishtail . . . as the car coming at him did exactly the same thing. A moment later it disappeared beneath Carl's line of sight, too close to the front of the semi to be seen over the truck's long nose. But a crunching metallic noise above the shriek of wailing tires confirmed they hadn't averted the collision. And now the truck was jack-knifing down the wrong side of the road. Its tires bounced the cab up and down as they absorbed the forward momentum at an angle they weren't designed for, as the semi pressed the blue sedan a third of the way back down the hill it had just climbed.

In Carl's driver's side mirror, a woman appeared from nowhere, her body sliding face down across the blacktop and then crumpling on the verge, becoming little more than a small bundle in the distance as the semi slid away. Carl couldn't see the driver, as the car and front chassis of the tractor trailer were now fused into a single mass.

A few seconds later the semi bounced to a grounding halt.

Carl gazed numbly as the dust and debris settled across the blacktop. The sound of his heart pounding much too fast began to fill his ears as his head grew light. Then the image before him began to swim, coming in and out like wavy lines across a television set not quite tuned to its channel. Everything was becoming deepening shades of grey as his eyes grew heavy. Before they closed, Carl was sure he saw something odd along the roadside.

A boy. Just standing there.

A young boy.

Smiling.

And then all was black.

IV

"Jesus Ian, I'm sorry. I—" Bryan swallowed hard, his throat protesting. "I shouldn't have told you, maybe." He hadn't offered many details at all. Because he actually knew precious few himself. But still the summary explanation of the crash had shocked his younger brother worse than he'd anticipated.

Rebecca still nestled asleep in his bosom, Bryan played nervously over the waxy burn scar on his right hand, the wide and smooth ribbon of whiter skin running from the base of his thumb to his wrist.

Sitting on the edge of the couch, bent over so that his head was between his knees, Ian waved emptily at the air to indicate that Bryan hadn't done anything wrong. He had asked because he needed to know.

Several minutes quietly passed, only the grandfather clock in the hall marking the moments.

Eventually Rebecca began to rouse from her sanctuary of deep sleep inside the safety of her husband's embrace, and was alarmed at the sight of Ian in despair when she did.

When she started to fuss over him, Ian waved vacantly toward her voice, still not lifting his head from his knees.

Rebecca ignored the signal and fetched a towel dampened with cool water, draping it tenderly over the back of her brother-in-law's neck. Almost immediately it eased the sensation of heat and fuzziness Ian felt there. The searing prickles around his head and neck and face—signs of losing the fight to retain consciousness—began to ease away by steps.

In minutes, the sense of cloudiness was almost completely gone.

"Sure you're okay?" Rebecca prompted despite Ian's assertions.

"I'm fine, Becky. I promise."

He lifted his head and forced a smile the best he could to prove it.

Rebecca wasn't stupid. She smiled back at him in an equally fake manner and added, 'okay then,' as she removed the damp towel from his neck and retreated to the kitchen for another towel.

Bryan took the opportunity and leaned toward Ian.

"Tell me, Ian!"

Though Ian's eyes revealed a sudden, somber acknowledgment of something shared between he and his brother, he ignored the plea with a feigned look of bewilderment. He ran his hands over his face. Was Bryan onto him? Was his brother somehow aware of his precognition? Hoping he was overestimating his brother's perception Ian blandly replied, "Tell you what?"

Bryan glanced over his shoulder to ensure Rebecca wasn't yet returning from the kitchen. "You know I don't like when you hold back like this." His face was drawn and sallow and added pointed significance to the words. "Just tell me. You felt it—*you knew*—somehow. Didn't you?"

It was a statement, far more than it was a question.

"It's all falling into place. Your phone call last night. The way you reacted . . . ." Bryan paused before adding, "Your reaction, right now."

Ian didn't answer. He didn't have to. His eyes did it for him.

They began to gloss over with tears that hadn't been felt, not *really* felt, for almost twenty years.

V

Thursday came and went, and the funeral with it. Uncle Rod attended with his wife. Great uncle Bob couldn't be traced. Even Rod didn't know if he were still alive, but guessed that if he were, the man probably would have little recollection who the hell his nephew on his sister's side of the family was anyway.

"Bob had never been what you could call close," he said.

The funeral arrangements had been quiet and practical. Even so, the church was half-filled with mourners.

On a Thursday afternoon.

Ian couldn't understand where they all came from. Perhaps a few were devout Catholics, attending today irrespective of the service. But judging by the appropriately dark attire most wore, a number of them must have been amateur mourners. Ambulance chasers. People who thrilled at attending such events. Somehow these individuals profited by the vicarious sorrow in which they wallowed. Maybe it was the same as riding a roller coaster: you face impending death but still get to come out the other side. Exhilarated.

Ian guessed that in their own way, funerals must be similarly life-affirming. For some at least.

For him, they were depressing and held a peculiarly rancid odor. The scent of lilies always smelled to him of death.

The priest blessed the pair of coffins as eight pallbearers prepared to carry them down the aisle and outside, where the wan light of a persisting drizzle offered no solace to the somber atmosphere of the chapel. A sleek black hearse was waiting to take them to the cemetery where, following another hymn and final words, the caskets would be placed in the ground, one atop the other, and eventually covered with soil.

At this point, the ritual at last proving final, the five adults who remained graveside voiced their mutually stunned disbelief quietly among themselves. As they did, the occasional pebble or small clump of dirt would fall innocuously from the edge of the cleanly prepared hole and make a thin, hollow clapping sound as it struck a smoothly polished casket. None of the adults brought attention to this fact, nor allowed it to interrupt their conversation. Neither could they ignore it, however. So although the carefully managed response was barely noticeable, each of them would wince each time this happened.

The two young children by their sides voiced nothing at all, only standing silently together with their hands intertwined, their fingers fidgeting nervously.

VI

Since his return, Ian had declined to sleep in the guest room which had been his own bedroom as a child. The feelings there were too strong, the room entirely too emotive for him in the days leading up to inhuming his parents.

So instead, he'd been sleeping on the couch in the downstairs TV room and was invariably still asleep when young Diane and Andrew came bounding down to watch cartoons, caring very little about disturbing their estranged uncle. For them, having time off from school was, despite the little understood circumstances inducing it, a thrill a minute.

Home. Without being sick. And with an infrequently seen uncle to tease and torment?

What a treat!

So they would jump atop Ian's slumbering figure, irrespective of his level of consciousness, and giggle and generally be excited and raucous as the sun tried to break through the downstairs curtains which each night Ian pulled tightly closed so he wouldn't be awakened too early.

The Monday that followed, Rebecca and the kids were back to their normal routine.

Sleeping in the living room as Becky worked to get the kids and herself ready for the day, had become a little uncomfortable for all of them. So, with the funeral now several days past, Ian conceded that the guest room —once his childhood bedroom—would make the most sense after all. And besides, though the dreams still lingered, they had become less prevalent each successive day, their intensity declining in equal measure as the disbelief his parents were really gone finally had begun to set in.

Though it now felt foreign to him, Ian's room that night still held at its core the familiarity that had been borne here a long, long time ago.

The contours of the bed were there, but now the wrong shape and in the wrong places, the result of countless sleepover pals. The smells of his youth had lingered, but stealthily buried behind newer odors introduced in the room's changing purposes since his departure. (First the kids' play room, then Becky's hobby hole.) Pictures still hung from the same hooks but were now 'proper' pictures in frames, not the posters and other such frivolity of which his mother—not his father—so disapproved. And nestling under a shallow layer of dust on the bookshelf sat the little ivory Buddha his parents had bought for him during their adult–only Polynesian vacation. Funny how he'd forgotten about it given the importance the ornament had played in his childhood. Never would a day pass that Ian wouldn't lift the icon gently from its resting place and carefully rub its fat little tummy and smooth round head. His fingers had known every curve and contour, every grade and texture. The little Buddha was not an expensive piece. Quite the opposite. He realized now that it likely had been processed in a mold from waste ivory powder, probably on some Chinese or Taiwanese assembly line. Soft 'fuzzy' bits of material stuck in many of the joints and around the edges and creases. But Ian hadn't cared; he liked it. He liked to look at it. To touch it.

To be one with it.

It had made him feel good. Secure. *Strong.*

Ian crossed the room and eagerly plucked it from the bookshelf. The dust which had settled upon its head dispersed into the recirculating air and floated away as he ran his now fully-grown fingers softly over its shape, just as he had done back then. A warm feeling washed over him, filling a long-empty void as the gentle smile of the fat, cross-legged little idol beamed benevolently back up at him. He laid back down upon the small single bed, closed his eyes, and grasped the Buddha lovingly in both hands.

It felt exactly the same.

He didn't know how long he lay there, silently drawing upon its grounded strength, before finally succumbing to sleep.

VIII

A siren, far in the distance, cried louder and louder as it came nearer. Laying in his old bed, the sound triggered precisely how Ian had felt so many times as a child when his parents had been out for the evening—dancing, or at a movie, or whatever parents did—and left him at home alone. He suddenly felt now exactly as he had then as he'd lain here, in this bed, in this room, when that very sound had ebbed and flowed in the night.

How it had affected him back then.

Of course he had been old enough to stay home alone. Most, if not all, of his friends did the same. And did so quite often. In fact, they'd welcomed the opportunity of being in charge of the house for a change. They were at that age which brought forth the birth of rebellion; the beginning of transformation from childhood to adulthood. So they would watch TV —anything they damn well pleased, including the delectably risqué offerings on HBO, thank you very much—and gorge upon their favorite snacks and soda pop until their bellies bloated and they felt a little sick. Sometimes they would even attempt a swig of beer left over in the fridge . . . if they thought their fathers wouldn't discover it missing the next day. Generally speaking, they would have one hell of a good time on their own.

Ian wanted to do the same. He wanted to *be* the same.

But it never managed to work out that way.

Despite his best intentions to get up to no good, Ian always ended up worrying about—about—*things.*

The night always began awesome: potato chips, popcorn, his brother sleeping over at a friend's house. And a great show line-up on the box that invariably began with some Friday night cop show with some woman who was as scantily clad as she was attractive (stirring within Ian new odd and unexpected feelings) and ended with some spooky late night film fest like *Return of the Zombies* or *Creature From the Black Lagoon* or something like that.

And it was fun . . . . Until Ian found himself tired out, his parents still not home, and waiting nervously only half asleep in his bed.

In his room.

At the top of the stairs.

At the end of the corridor.

All alone.

The attic would creak sharply.

Probably the timbers settling in the night air after such a hot day.

A door down the hall would squeak.

Shit, did I close the bathroom door?

And there was always a thump.

Was that outside? I think the spare bedroom window is still open.

Then an ambulance would cry in the distance, growing closer.

It's my parents . . . .

For Ian it was always his parents the medics were racing to save, to cut free from the twisted metal of the wreckage.

Every time.

He could *feel* it.

But of course it wasn't his parents, and they always came home. The rickety old garage door would thump and grind below his bedroom as it rode up its rails in spurts and starts. And his mother would always come into his room to check on him and give him a gentle goodnight kiss on the forehead.

And Ian would always pretend to be asleep as his racing heart finally began to calm and his sense of security gradually returned.

Now, laying here again in his old room, Ian tangibly felt the seeds of that insidious childhood anxiety creeping slowly toward him as he dropped in and out of adult sleep. Once the siren on the top road passed swiftly by—most likely a bored cop chasing some dumb kid running his dirt bike on the street at night or something—Ian finally succumbed to the weight of sleep and fell into a deep, beckoning slumber for the first time in six nights.

IX

The central heating kicked in around eleven, its warming waters heating the baseboard pipes throughout the house. In Ian's room, the radiators softly whistled as pockets of air were pushed through the pipes by the expanding water behind it.

And Ian visibly winced in his sleep.

At an awkward corner to his pillow, his head began to glisten with light perspiration. His breathing quickened, heart rate climbed.

The whistling of the radiators grew louder.

And he is back in the Little Woods.

With Matt.

They are running and playing and having a great time amongst the trees and brush that, in his dream, are greatly, almost comically exaggerated. No one else is with them at first. Then Ranger Rob, the goodhearted cartoon forest ranger, joins them. He is short and plump and wore little round glasses and was always smiling. And he always did the right thing.

It was the same each time Ian had the dream.

Always joyful, always carefree.

Matt and he would play 'swords' with sticks. They would have races to see who could get from here to there first. And always, the Ranger would stay with them and explain the Good things to them as he laughed and skipped with them as he showed them their way around the woods. Ranger Rob kept them safe.

Then the sound of the Whistle would come.

The boys do not know exactly what that means. To them it is more a feeling than a palpable understanding. It tells them something is maybe wrong, maybe somewhere. That they should beware and be careful about them. Nothing more.

The Ranger most definitely knows what the sound means.

But each time the dream came to this point, the plump little cartoon ranger would mask his anxiety and not allow his concern to show through.

"C'mon," Ranger Rob says, smiling, as he pushes his little round spectacles up his nose. "I think it's time to go."

And the boys would see his face, feel its happiness and warmth, and feel so much better again for it. They would heed the Ranger's words, but his reassuring demeanor does little to promote a need for urgency. Equally, the Ranger can not find it in his heart to hurry the boys from their happiest place. So instead he patiently waits, keeping alert and close by while the boys frolic their way through the woods, gently working their way back home.

The boys, therefore, never notice how the woods have grown dark. How it seems the unsettling tones of the Whistle have bid the very sun itself not to shine. They do not sense the air itself which had taken on a sour, almost metallic scent, or how the woods have now become a different place; a place they should no longer be. They do not notice any of these things, because of the Ranger's care.

Until the Beast Bear appears.

And just like that the dream was stolen, its veil of safety so easily torn as the boys became aware of the darkness.

A darkness that drew upon them like blindness.

The Ranger shouts at them. To go! Just run!

Transfixed by confusion and uncertainty, the boys do not obey the plea. Instead, they stand motionless, eyes disbelieving as distant brush moves and sways, faraway trees uprooting and splitting as the woods yield to the on-slaught. The boys do not heed the primeval screams the Beast reverberates through the forest in warning; nor do they turn and flee the ground that shakes beneath their very feet as it bores mercilessly down upon them.

"Go!" the Ranger pleads frantically. "Please boys—GO NOW!"

When the Beast Bear then bursts through the trees, its eyes alight with crimson fire, its teeth yellow and dripping . . . the boys do run. They run and they did not stop.

Until the silence makes them look back.

Holding his ground between the boys and the Beast, the Ranger's face is frozen in both terror and disillusionment. He makes no sound as the Beast scoops him up without breaking stride and carries Ranger Rob high into the treetops where his screams echo as the thing turns him inside out.

In painfully clear slow motion, the Ranger's spectacles fall to the forest floor and shatter in a deafening crash which sends glass and visible ripples of sound in all directions.

The boys turn away but their legs are molasses, their feet heavy as anvils as the Beast's blazing eyes draw upon them—

Ian bolted upright in the bed of his childhood, his panicked scream breaching the stillness of the house. Anxiously rocking back and forth, he stifled his sobs with a perspiration-sodden sheet and labored to slow his hastened breathing until the bedroom gradually eased back into focus.

As the whistling of the radiators subsided, he reassured himself over and again that he was no longer twelve; that the terror of that nightmare had occurred long, long ago. But the images were stubborn, lingering even as his brother's footsteps were heard bounding hastily down the corridor toward his room.

six

1977

HE DARKNESS TURNED to rain and came heavily as Bryan and Ian struggled through the fields. Half-carrying his brother who grimaced with every step, Bryan labored with Ian's weight through as many steps as he could before he had to stop, catch his breath, then start towards home once more. When they finally stumbled through the back porch door, they were soaked to the bone, covered in blood and exhausted. And filled with incomprehensible fear beyond fathoming.

The house was silent and dark. A quickly scrawled note on the kitchen table told them that their mom and dad were out looking for them, that they hoped they were okay and already home and reading this by the time they got back themselves . . . and that they'd better have a pretty darn good reason for being so late.

This was good news. Of sorts. It gave them some breathing room, some time to think what the hell they were gonna do.

Bryan paced as Ian sat numb and silent at the breakfast table, running his fingernails absently across the Formica surface.

The first thing they had to do, Bryan figured, was get out of their soaking wet, torn and stained clothes.

Bryan's were horrific, but passable. He'd been home from the woods before looking worse. He ran them under the bathroom sink to wash away the caked mud, and it was amazing how much better they looked almost instantly.

Ian's were past explaining.

His jeans were torn down most of the length of one leg; his blue T-shirt was dyed a morbid hue of purple where the blood had soaked in, dried, then soaked in further a second time in the rain.

Bryan helped him out of them. They'd had to be discarded. *But where?*

He knew their mother was going to have a shit fit when she saw the state they were in, and the tattered clothes only made things look worse. Ian wasn't hurt that bad: Bryan inspected a few cuts and bruises on his hands and legs, and that gash on the side of his face.

Then there was that twisted knee . . . .

Bryan couldn't stop to think about it. Any of it. He just wanted to get themselves sorted out and settled—and with a plausible plan at the ready —before their parents got back.

The wood burner in the living room was lit. It was no surprise to Bryan. His mother was always cold, even at the height of summer. Particularly so when there was a storm like this, one that sucked the heat out of the air and replaced it with a damp chill.

He opened the small front door of the wood burner and tossed Ian's shirt inside, watching as the flames grew. The jeans were more difficult. It wasn't a massive stove, and the sodden pants nearly extinguished the fire altogether as they dampened the wood and occupied what little space remained, stifling the flow of oxygen. Bryan slammed the door shut and they pressed oddly against the inside of the smoky glass which once had been clear but turned a brownish level of translucence over the years. He opened the front air intake to full and listened as that familiar *whoosh* accompanied the increasing glow that illuminated the room.

Without speaking, Ian watched all of this from the corner of the living room. He sat on the couch huddled into a ball, pulling his legs up to his chin and wrapping his arms around them as he had done in the clearing only an hour and a half before.

"Come on," Bryan said to him, extending his hand. "Let's get ourselves upstairs. We need to shower and change."

Ian didn't move. He stared into space and said nothing. His eyes were hollow and vacant and the look of him scared Bryan most of all, although he wouldn't admit this to himself.

"Come on buddy . . . ." Bryan forced a little chuckle and wrinkled his nose intentionally. "Man. You do look like a bag of dicks. I mean, look at the state of you."

A weakly lit smile crept onto Ian's face. It lasted for the briefest of moments and then extinguished.

11

They showered and changed, cleaned cuts and applied antiseptic creams until they started to resemble boys once again. A little worse for wear, but nothing that couldn't be explained away with a carefully crafted story about some rough-housing gone a little too far.

It wasn't long after that before the sound of the electric garage door churning upwards announced their parents' return.

Bryan helped Ian downstairs into the kitchen, and there they sat, preparing for Veronica Cockerton to throw into a rage.

"Look at you two! Oh my God! Ian!" She turned to explicitly direct her next questions toward Bryan. "What did you do? How in God's name did you let this happen to your brother?"

She was still in an uproar even after she inspected their separate injuries and satisfied herself that while terrible, they weren't life threatening. Now it was about the boys being so late for dinner; and out in this horrendous storm; and playing too rough, or fighting with the other boys, or whatever it was they'd been doing. She was very angry that the boys should disregard their parents in this way and told them that they were most certainly to be punished for acting so badly. And for making her worry. (That last part pissed her off more than any of the others, and she made sure they were aware of it.)

Then she added, almost reluctantly, as if doing so weakened her authoritative position, that she was very, very relieved that they were both now home, safe and sound.

Their father all the while stood quietly off to the side, leaning against the kitchen counter. When their mother's boil eventually reduced to a simmer, she turned her back on the boys but did not leave the room. Rather, she made herself intentionally busy about the kitchen, closing each cabinet door just that little bit too hard and occasionally muttering a frustration just loud enough to be certain it was heard. When Harold Cockerton was pretty sure his wife wasn't looking, he simply gave the boys a wink and a *'but don't do it again'* look, then told them to make their way upstairs to their rooms. And think about what they'd done.

Bryan thought their dad was pretty cool.

Their mother didn't share his feelings.

Catching sight of their father's wink from her almost superhuman peripheral vision, Veronica Cockerton blew into another outrage. This time it was aimed at all three of them, but their father caught the worst of it. She slapped a dish towel down and folded her arms across her chest, never once taking her eyes off their father as she stormed out of the room.

Most unhappy at now being at the sharp end of their mother's ire right along with the boys, Hare Cockerton pointed rigidly at the stairs and commanded they get to their rooms.

Immediately.

Without daring to utter a single sound, they both slinked off to their respective bedrooms, Ian edging up the staircase a little slower than Bryan who took the steps by threes.

III

Laying rigid on their beds, the boys each listened in darkness as the static rain pelting the roof hard above their heads slowed to an intermittent sprinkle. After a length of time neither could determine, it finally turned to little more than a drizzle as the murky storm skies began to yield to a black and starless night.

In this fashion they laid for hours, listening.

Waiting.

Ian's eyes remained transfixed on the ceiling as the radiators in his room began to quietly bubble. They clicked, blurped and clicked again as the boiler kicked in. Then, as the water inside them warmed and grew, they began to, ever so quietly—

—*Whistle.*

His empty eyes stared into the blackness of the room as they replayed on constant loop the incomprehensible events in the Little Woods. In his mind the images were already broken and incomplete, and it allowed him to see less and less detail with every consecutive playback. Eventually, as the rain stopped and the crickets returned, he found himself clutching at nothing at all that could make sense of what had happened there.

As if it had all been just an elusive, unsettling dreamscape, the images finally floated away into the dark of night, like wisps of steam from your breath in the cold winter wind.

IV

Both boys woke nearly fifteen hours later to a warm summer morning, groggy and unsettled as if from a terrible dream. Everything from the day before now oddly distant. And so incredibly unreal.

The sun was bright and forced its way through the parting in the curtains of Ian's room, streaking the walls with long yellow-white slashes. High pitched chirps of vibrant birdsong lilted through the warm morning air as the the Robins and Chickadees pecked the ground and scratched their feet, energetically searching for their breakfast.

Ian looked out the window expecting to see something—anything—to reinforce the terrible dream he'd had, but was met with only the image of light wisps of mist rising from the driveway as the June sun began to warm the saturated ground.

It never happened.

He breathed heavily in relief as he climbed into a pair of faded old jeans, but unexpectedly winced in pain as he pulled his left leg through, his right faltering beneath his weight. He ran his hand over his knee to find it swollen and sore, but had no idea why. He threw on a grey sweatshirt and began shuffling down the corridor to see his brother, but heard him downstairs with their mother.

Everyone was at the breakfast table where Bryan was already munching some toast and a bowl of Quisp cereal. A comical, pinkish alien smiled inanely from the box.

"Good morning sweetheart," his mother greeted him, smiling, from across the room. "How are you this morning? Did you sleep well enough?"

She was her usual pleasant self, and the greeting made Ian feel warm all over. When he was much younger, Ian had suffered a terrible case of the flu. His temperature had been well over one hundred, and it was only later that he learned just how worried his mother had been. But she never showed it. Not to him, anyway. She stayed with him that whole night, caressing his back and his brow whenever he would wake dripping with sweat from a feverish dream. She would smile at him through the darkness, and it made everything alright. She could always make him feel safe like that. But this morning, more than others, her warmth was especially appreciated, though Ian was uncertain why.

He returned her smile.

"Yeah, I slept okay. I guess" He wasn't ready to tell her about the terrible nightmare he'd had. "What's for breakfast?"

She offered him eggs or pancakes, whichever he would prefer. He declined both and decided instead to join Bryan in a bowl of Quisp. Not because he preferred it to pancakes, or his mother's fantastic sunny-side-up eggs, but because he knew it would piss off his brother. The gormless alien-emblazoned cereal was Bryan's favorite and he didn't much care to share those sweet little sugar coated flying saucers with anyone else.

He glanced sidelong as his little brother reached for the box, then dismissed everything about him and simply returned to emptying his own bowl.

Most disappointing, Ian said only to his own mind.

Harold Cockerton was busy behind a broadsheet of the local rag. Nothing particularly interesting was announced on the front page. There was, however, a black and white photo of two little kids holding balloons, ice cream dripping down their chins, with a caption that read: "WE ALL

SCREAM FOR ICE CREAM."

A lame attempt to remind us that summer's finally here, Ian thought. *As if we all didn't know this fact already.*

His father flicked to the front page—he always read the paper from back-to-front, from the sports to the news—chuckled at the photo, then got up from the table.

"Morning, sport." He rubbed his hands roughly through Ian's hair. "Guess I'd better be making a move. Another day, another dollar, or something like that." He looked at his two sons, almost proudly for no particular reason, then added: "What's in store for you guys today? Off to the Little Woods?"

Ian's chest tightened at the words and he froze, a mouthful of cereal and milk dripping from his lips. Bryan simply grunted something that sounded like *yeah maybe* without looking up, and gulped another spoonful of the alien's ever-growing-soggier saucers.

Mr. Cockerton looked from his elder son back to Ian. "The woods?" The expression on his face affirmed he was seeking confirmation.

Ian shrugged noncommittally, averting his gaze.

Hare Cockerton shouted back from the stairs, "I should be so lucky. You boys have fun out there."

Harold Cockerton worked in the local steel mill, but not actually doing the hard labor stuff. Not anymore. His father had worked there also. His brother Rod, too. And just about every male member of his immediate family for that matter.

It'd been that way for years.

Sometimes Uncle Rod would tell the boys stories, and often they were sad, although they were not meant to be. Rod still worked, and worked hard, down on the floor where the temperatures soared. He carried, pushed, bent and welded steel as they melted, poured and formed it into one shape or another. That's what their uncle Rod did. Every day.

But Hare Cockerton wasn't on the floor with his brother, he was elsewhere in the mill. He worked on the other end of the site, in the small office complex near the truck depot. There he pushed pencils over paper and tried to make the figures add up. He made up the little brown envelopes with the payslips in, and hoped that they had enough for everybody.

In later years, Ian often supposed that maybe this hadn't been as easy as it first looked, and wondered if his uncle Rod perhaps had the better deal all these years. Then again, maybe nobody did.

Ian knew that Rod would have given anything be up in that office too. Ian also knew that his father had questioned, every single day, whether or not he'd made the right choice to leave the manufacturing floor. So for ten years, Hare sat at a desk while Rod worked at the furnaces. And in that time, he watched the company books becoming thinner and thinner. And increasingly more difficult to balance. Every week he had to decide which one, or two, or three of the men would have to go; which ones were to be deemed 'dispensable,' as his boss would say.

His father once told Ian, when they were much older and Hare Cockerton had enjoyed a beer or two, that it was like being able to see your own death coming. You could see it there, all black and grisly and stinking horrible as it trundled steadily for you. But you couldn't do a damned thing about it. He'd been anxious for a very long time about it. So much so that he would often wake up in the mornings feeling sick to his stomach.

At least on the floor you just passed each day as it came to you. Now he had to watch not only his own death, but his brother's and his friends' too, as it came for them all. One by one.

"But then," he added before taking another swig. "There comes a point when you simply get used to it."

Ian didn't exactly know what that meant. But it hit him later.

Boy did it hit him later.

In his own desperate attempt to get away from this town of despair, little did Ian know he would achieve precisely the same result in years yet to come.

His job would pay more.

And outwardly appear more glamorous. Other than that, his grind would end up being much the same as his father's ever was.

Ian shoved another spoon of Quisp in his mouth and watched his father climb the steps, admiring him without knowing exactly why. It would be years before Ian would understand things like 401(k)s and savings accounts; layoffs or unemployment. And to be frank, he really couldn't care less. His life was happy, or at least secure in that beautiful way that you only feel when you don't even know that you feel secure. And for the most part, things were pretty much okay.

He finished his bowl of cereal, put on his sneakers and went outside into the embrace of the warm summer air.

His mother shouted after him to not be late. "... Or else ... !"

Bryan came out a few minutes later, carrying his old blue leather baseball mitt and aluminum bat.

"You gonna play?" he asked Ian indifferently, pulling his cap down over his eyes. "Daniels' field in about half an hour. If you wanna. No biggie if you don't."

"Yeah, sure. OK," Ian answered. "Sounds good."

He didn't ask who would be there. Ian already knew. It was always their usual gang: the summertime crowd.

"I'll go grab the guys and bring 'em over. See you there."

Bryan 'hmmphed' an apathetic reply and started down the road towards Jack and Jimi's house, spinning his cap around backwards.

Ian headed the opposite way, down towards Craig Dalton's place, breathing in the uniquely pleasant odor of the blacktop as it warmed and grew tacky beneath a particularly brilliant June sun.

V

Craig wasn't yet up when Ian rang the doorbell. Mrs. Dalton, brushing shoulder-length blonde hair, was on her way to work and hurried past Ian, telling him to just go on in and 'wake the little shit up.'

He laughed as they passed through the doorway. Her chest brushed against him just ever so slightly, and Ian became suddenly warm all over, and a little tingly.

She looked at him coyly and smiled.

From inside the house he watched her climb into the car. As she did, her skirt lifted just the right amount to show a firm leg, beautiful and tanned and just athletic. Ian couldn't help but wish he could go with her in that car, wherever she was heading. And for the first time ever, he realized how beautiful he thought Mrs. Dalton was and found himself imagining so much more. He suddenly wondered what it might be like to kiss her soft lips, to feel her hands *(oh those beautiful hands with those perfectly slender fingers, and that wide band of white gold on her third finger, and that chunky silver watch, gathered loosely around her wrist)* and touch the backs of her legs, run his fingers up her firm thighs, across her taut stomach, her smooth—

"Hey!" Craig shouted at the top of his voice as he leapt over the stairwell banner and toppled heavily and clumsily but accurately on top of Ian. They crumpled to the floor together as Ian's heart attempted to thump its way out of his ribcage.

"Shit a brick Craig! You scared the living *crap* outta me!"

"Well," Craig got up and brushed himself off. "I couldn't pass up that be–ee–a–*you*–tiful opportunity. You were completely zoned out there for a minute, Ian."

Craig peered through the hallway curtains but only saw his mother pulling away out of the drive.

"What were you looking at?"

Ian dropped his eyes to the floor as embarrassment swept over him in a cold wave. "Uh, nothing. I thought I saw something, but I don't know what it was."

Craig cocked his head to one side, begging more explanation.

"W-w-ell," Ian inadvertently stuttered as he decided perhaps it might be a good idea to buffer his story a little more. You know, distance himself from the freaky truth as much as possible. I mean, that was his friend's *mom* for Christ's sake. "I thought I saw something that looked like, I dunno, it looked like—Bigfoot—or something."

Craig nodded, spinning his finger in a circular fashion like a fishing reel. In other words gesturing, 'yeah, and then what?'

Ian stubbed his finger into Craig's chest.

"What else do you want me to say?" he queried, then decided to just run with this colorful new lie and see where it took them. "The only Bigfoot sighting in Pennsylvania this millennium and you go and scare it off. Go ahead, look for yourself."

He opened the curtains wide when he was sure he'd heard Craig' mother accelerate away.

"It's gone now. Well done, dick face."

He accentuated his mock frustration by pouncing upon Craig, fists clenched, and pretending to pummel him to death.

They both fell about the floor, wrestling and laughing for a while until it wasn't funny anymore.

"So, are you ever going to get dressed, or what?" Ian finally asked, huffing for breath.

Craig decided 'or what,' but went upstairs to change anyway.

Ian waited in the entryway downstairs until he heard Craig rummaging around in his closet. As soon as that first squeal of a clothes hanger sliding across its rail pealed throughout the house, Ian rushed into the guest bathroom, closed the door and locked it. He sat on the toilet and watched how quickly he grew as he thought about Mrs. Dalton. He touched himself with uncertain anticipation.

This wasn't the first time he'd explored himself. But he had never had the courage to follow through, always stopping part way because it felt dirty or wrong, like something he shouldn't be doing.

But then again, it had never felt quite like this.

The feel of his fingers shot throughout his body like a static charge. Because now it was *her* fingers touching him.

His breaths came short.

The caresses grew firmer and longer.

And then she was rubbing him. That beautiful wedding ring hand sliding up and down. Her wristwatch brushes against him and the coldness of the metal is intense against his skin. Her fingers grip his tip and move in light circles around it. She smiles at him, the same way she had in the doorway just moments ago. Her fingers tighten. He twitches. And it comes out, squirting between her fingers, oozing over her polished nails, over her ring. Onto that chunky silver watch.

Ian exhaled deeply, his chest thumping.

He opened his eyes to a world which felt suddenly, inexplicably very different from three minutes earlier.

There was no time for the weight of the moment to sink in: Craig's footsteps were clomping down the second floor hallway, heading for the stairs.

Fuck!

Filled with a sudden cold panic, he yanked a sheet of toilet paper and the roll spun like the reel of a slot machine. A snake-like ribbon spewed across the tile floor and gathered in a wavy pile. He ripped off the end, gathered it loosely up, and haphazardly wiped the mess off his hand.

More clomping steps.

The top stair creaked in its characteristic way.

God, no! I still need a minute!

Clutching his jeans and wrenching them up to his wait, Ian ran out of the bathroom panting. He was still scrunching the mass of toilet paper into a manageable ball as Craig stepped onto the bottom riser and turned to face him.

"WE'RE-PLAYING-BASEBALL-THIS-MORNING-WANNA-COME?"

The announcement blurted from Ian's mouth as one long hyphenated word and sounded far more like the name of some remote Welsh village than an invitation to come play. It was mind–bogglingly rapid. And intensely loud. And followed by a small, nervous chuckle.

Surprisingly, Craig understood it. He was used to Ian's peculiarities by now. Though he had no idea why his friend was acting so weird *this* time. He decided not to even ask and continued into the spare room to hunt for his ball and mitt as Ian called after him.

"Craig. I'm gonna call Matt. Okay?"

Ian wondered why his own statement had become a question. Of course it was okay. It was always okay. Never once had either of them asked to use the phone in the other's house. They just picked it up and dialed. Sometimes they would even dial the area code followed by seven random numbers. That clear plastic dial would ratchet round and back, round and back, and sometimes they'd clap out a rhythm on their thighs as it clicked away. The eights and nines were most fun. Dialing a number that had lots of those in it took upwards of seventeen seconds just to dial.

Craig had used a stopwatch to time it once.

So why did Ian feel so odd?

It's fucking obvious, he castigated himself. *You've just splooged. In your friend's bathroom. Thinking about his mother for God's sake.*

He cringed, scrunching his face and covering his eyes with his hand. "Ughhh."

After a few rings Matt's father answered, which was of no particular surprise since Mr. Chauncey was a teacher and had the summer off as well.

"Hello." Mr. Chauncey's voice was flat.

"Is Matt there?"

Silence, then a strangely mumbled, *"No."*

"Is he outside? This is Ian. From the neighborhood."

Silence.

"You know, from across the street—"

"I know who you are, dammit." The voice was much more course than usual. Mr. Chauncey was prone to be a gruff bastard anyway, but he'd never sounded like this before.

Normally Ian would have hung up after such a reply, nervous that he was somehow in trouble.

"We're playing ball over at the Daniels' and I thought—"

A quiet click, then the humming of the dial tone.

Ian wasn't sure what to make of it. He made his way into the spare room to tell Craig.

"So weird," Craig said as he stretched a sweatshirt over his head. "Probably hungover. You know how Chauncey's old man is. Has a few, knocks his woman about a bit, and passes out on the couch. Now he's got a sore head and couldn't give two shits where Matt or any other fucker is."

Ian considered these words of wisdom. He also thought about how Craig actually sounded pretty cool when he swore, the words flowing smoothly and naturally from his mouth. He, on the other hand, fumbled awkwardly over their foreignness. Coming off of Ian's tongue, the curses spat out like a mouth full of marbles.

He punched Craig in the boy's slightly fat tummy.

Because, why not.

They made their way back up to the top of the neighborhood, strolling towards the Daniels' place with no particular time frame in mind. They would arrive when they got there.

Craig was cool like that. He took his sweet time, regaling his friend with anecdotes as they walked: about shows he'd been watching; the hot chicks he was into (he'd just bought a Dallas Cowboys Cheerleaders poster from the poster store in the mall); the stash of girlie mags he found in the back of his dad's closet and how they even showed this guy's big schlong being put inside a girl's privates and how awesome hot it was. Oh, and this new science fiction movie he wanted to see that looked pretty cool, called *Star Wars*. His mother could drop them off at the mall this weekend if Ian wanted to see it.

Ian flinched. One second Craig is talking about girls and schlongs and naked things, the next he mentions his mom.

He knows. Fuck! He definitely knows. He's trying to trick me into telling. I know he knows. Oh fuck oh fuck oh—

"Hey! Jerk wad!" Craig shouted as he stopped walking and hollered back, realizing Ian was no longer beside him.

A good three or four paces back, Ian was just standing there. With a stupid look on his face.

"What the hell, Ian . . . so, should I tell her yes? She wants to know by tonight. If not, she's making other plans."

Ian studied Craig's face. His eyebrows were raised. Questioning and irritated at the same time. His arms were out, palms up. The international sign for, 'I'm waiting for an answer here.'

OK, maybe he really is just asking about a movie.

Then Ian reminded himself that Craig *always* talked about girls and schlongs and gross things he found in his dad's closet.

"Uh . . . sure. Yeah. Why not," he answered. Now he would know for sure. If Craig was trying to bust him, he'd do it right here and right now. He tensed, awaiting the response.

Craig just lowered his arms and started walking. "Alright then. Sheesh. You're hard work sometimes, ya know that, Ian?"

VI

The other guys had already congregated in the field adjacent to the Daniels' house and the sound of a baseball smacking firmly against the webbing of the boys' leather mitts wafted pleasantly to Bryan and Ian before they were able to see it.

Of course Bryan was there. Jack was with his brother Jimi. Big Dan was bouncing—fat and all—around the field doing Lord knows what. And Woody was wrestling on the ground with Stu Klatz. Nothing unusual there.

Matt was standing just outside the group.

Ian was relieved to see him, but didn't know exactly why.

Matt was on his own, knocking one of the baseball bats against the bottom of his shoes as if clearing the treads before stepping up to the base. Somewhat the way the professionals do.

Ian greeted them all with a shout as they approached, and no one turned but Matt. Craig shrugged, regarding this as pretty much par for the course, and ran ahead of Ian, managing to intercept a throw that was clearly meant for Jack. The ball arced high across the path of the mid-morning sun as Jack shielded his eyes. Craig leapt and snatched it out of the air with a reassuring *smack* as it met the worn leather. Craig then spent the next several minutes running around the field with Stu, Jimi and Dan chasing after him. Jimi lunged and managed to trip him, and Craig fell ate dirt as he plowed across the ground. Ian winced but also laughed.

When they finally decided to actually play some baseball, the laughs turned into bellowing shouts and orders that resounded up and down the upper street of the neighborhood.

—Take third . . . go on!—No . . . stay!—Foul? You must be joking! That was straight down the line!—Yeah sucker, that's a strike!

The only one that said very little was Matt.

This wasn't especially unusual, but Ian hadn't noticed that he'd said a single thing the entire game. And that *was* unusual. Matt was a timid outcast, but when he had something to say, he said it with unusual confidence. Even though what he said was considered by most of the gang as irritating and useless pulp. That's not to say that it was, but rather, it wasn't any of the important things the other guys liked to talk about.

Like whether or not the Pittsburgh Steelers or Pirates would have a winning season this year.

(Usually prompted by Dan or Woody or Bryan.)

Or what hot babes were on TV the other night.

(Yes, that was Craig more often than anyone.)

And cigarettes versus chewing tobacco, and which of the two vices made you look more cool.

(Almost definitely Stu Klatz.)

Personally, Ian couldn't stand cigarettes or tobacco; was only just beginning to—apparently *very* recently—discover that magnetic draw of the opposite sex; and was only moderately into sports.

Though he did love the Steelers.

But hell, everyone here loved the Steelers.

And I mean like everyone.

The gang decided, after about an hour, that the game was getting pretty boring. And so they just let it die naturally, having more fun just goofing around. A few of them hung around and still threw the ball back and forth between them, shouting random things like, "That one's for Roberto Clemente!" But most just drifted off.

Bryan walked away with Jack somewhere. And Matt stood alone in the middle of the field and chose to ignore Ian's wave goodbye as he and Craig made their way back to Ian's house.

They screwed around there, in the big back yard, while they waited for lunch. The outdoor thermometer hanging under the eaves of the back porch announced that Coke was 'the real thing'—and also that it was something like eighty-five degrees. Give or take.

"Why don't you get us something to drink, you idiot?" Craig rolled his eyes upwards and clasped a hand to this throat in a mock chocking sequence. He gargled air for a bit and then fell to the ground, playing dead.

"Okay, okay. I take the hint. Whaddya want?"

"Anything, scrotebag, so long as it's cold."

The house was cool and singularly dull after the brightness outside. Ian's mother was in the kitchen.

"Mom, do we have any—" He stopped mid-sentence when he saw his mother was on the telephone, gesturing tersely for him to shut up. It wasn't worth interrupting her, not if he wanted to keep hanging out with Craig, so he threw open the fridge door and rustled around. His mother's gasp, followed by the strangely serious tone of her voice, made Ian forget about the drinks . . . and about Craig, who still lay on the lawn, acting dead. Gotta hand it to the kid. He knew how to commit.

"Mom?" Ian whispered, moving into her line of sight.

She was wringing the phone cord tightly between her fingers. The tips of them were turning pinkish-white.

"Okay," she said to the other end of the call.

Silence.

"Yes. Okay."

Silence.

"Yes. I'm really very, very sorry. I just don't— Okay. Yes. Goodbye."

She replaced the handset but stared blankly at the yellow, orange and brown flowered wallpaper of the kitchen.

"Mom?"

It took a moment for her to turn and slowly face him.

"Ian . . . I want you to sit down, honey."

She patted the chair next to her at the breakfast table.

Her face was grave and raw, and it scared him. Asking him to sit down scared him even more. Something was very wrong. She had never been like this with him before. He blurted out:

"Mom, I'm sorry. What have I don—"

She placed a finger gently across his lips. "Shhh baby." The look on her face was more somber than Ian had ever seen. "Ian . . . ."

Something not right.

"Ian . . . ."

A whistling in the distance.

Her eyes moistened.

"Ian . . . I don't know how to say this. There is no way, really." Her face blanched, lips trembling.

They're in the woods playing, the two boys unaware.

"It's Matt."

Ranger Rob is with them.

"There's been a terrible accident honey. He's—he's—he's gone, Ian. I'm so sorry. He's gone."

Carried into the tree, his spectacles crashing to the earth.

She pulled his head to her chest. Her fingers ran through his hair as Ian's world began to swim. "They found him in the woods, baby he . . . ."

Her words faded into a long tunnel and Ian's world turned black.

VII

A cold cloth wiped gently at his face and forehead as his mother's face appeared, first swimming in front of him, then as a fuzzy image. Her voice was warped and far away, its timbre too low, like a man's. It raised by half octaves as the shrill, ringing sound in his ears intensified, the blood again resuming its normal pressure as it passed through them.

She caressed him and said she was sorry, over and over again. That it wasn't right. And shouldn't happen like this. Not to a child, and not to a boy like Matt. That it couldn't be true . . . but it was.

VIII

Veronica Cockerton spent the rest of the afternoon on the phone. When she wasn't on it, it would immediately ring and she'd be engrossed in conversation once again.

Bryan hadn't come home for lunch, though he was told to. So he missed his mother's news. He was also late for dinner. Again. Because of the news, however, he also escaped the verbal thrashing which would normally have ensued, especially for being late two times on two consecutive days. When he eventually did bother to show up, his mother sat both of her sons down and recounted as mush as she'd learned about the incident.

"Apparently there was a fire, late yesterday afternoon. In the woods," she said. "Just before the big rainstorm we had. I'm surprised somebody on the bottom street didn't notice it, perhaps it wasn't that big. I just don't know."

She paused to cover the trembling in her voice, feigning a cough.

"I think everyone had gone inside because of the storm. You boys weren't anywhere near there, were you?"

Her faced revealed small, intense signs of worry.

Bryan and Ian shook their heads no.

She continued, her voice shaking, swallowing hard in the pauses. "Matt never came home last night. Mrs. Chauncey called here early this morning, but I didn't think much about it at the time. I explained that you'd been very late for dinner last night and had been sent to your rooms. So no, Matt certainly was not over *here*."

Veronica Cockerton began to cry.

Over the next few minutes her words spurted between tears as she told the boys that the firemen had found the body of a child amidst the remains of what appeared to be a small campfire. That they had also found a gasoline can there, near the center of the fire. Because of this, it was expected the authorities would most likely rule the accident as death by misadventure: that Matt had been camping out, made a fire using gasoline—for God knows what reason—and it had simply gotten out of hand. Maybe he tried to put it out. Nobody knows for sure.

Ian thought that was bullshit and actually said so, much to his mother's chagrin. Under the circumstances, she decided it should elicit no corresponding reprimand. He said he knew things about Matt the firemen didn't. Like the fact that Matt was a gentle, even scared, type of kid who would never go into the woods on his own. And if he did, he sure as shit would never go so deeply that he would find himself all the way back in the Little Woods.

He also knew that Matt wasn't much for camping.

And that Matt would most definitely, never ever, go camping in those woods . . . alone.

Because Matt had suspected—just as he now did—that something dark and stealthy prowled in those woods.

Ian could not vocalize this last thought. He wasn't even sure it *was* a real thought. It just sort of floated there, bobbing up and down in the flowing waters of his mind, a vague impression he was unable to articulate. The same way the County Coroner was unable to articulate why he had chosen to omit in his report the discovery of what appeared to be clear ligature marks in the disfigured remains of the young boy's body in the woods.

Perhaps the idea of what that banded indentation revealed was a horror too much for even him to contemplate.

And yes, any evidence of rope fibers had been incinerated—along with everything else in the clearing—by a heat so intense that even the Fire

Chief had difficulty explaining it.

Which meant that yes, the furrowed bands scarcely visible around the boy's charred neck were now the only indictment that this had been anything more than a terrible, tragic misfortune.

Yet as hard as those facts were, never had the Coroner allowed uncomfortable truths to govern his actions. *Truth was truth.* But standing there, in that smoldering clearing with the boy's blackened body laying at his feet, something foreign welled up within him like a dark, inexplicable presence. And the Coroner did something that, in more than thirty years of faithful service to this community, he had never done: he chose to allow the truth of Matt Chauncey's death to pass away along with the boy in those deep, dark woods.

IX

Matt's funeral was just shy of a week later. The weather held fine for the interment, the early July sun bright and comforting over the atypical rite taking place beneath it.

A great crowd of guests attended, endless unknown faces coming to mollify the remorse which had disrupted their lives, the shock waves of such a startling child death rippling across every small community for miles around the neighborhood.

When the Chauncey family finally retired home that evening, Ian's father walked across the quiet street, carrying the roast Veronica had prepared., along with the condolences of the whole family with him.

X

Later that night, as it had done seemingly every night that week, the rain came. Steady and hard.

Behind St. Benedict's church, squares of new green sod respectfully (if languidly) cloaked the raw imagery of a freshly dug grave. Rivulets streamed across the overfilled mound, washing away loose soil and occasional flower petals and leaves from the arrangements laid in a pile atop it. Most rippled away in small, whirling currents. But some ran into a newly forming divot, swirling in repeating circles as the cool nighttime rain flooded an ever–growing hole.

As a rusty pickaxe began to cleave away turf and clods of mud.

Seven
1995

BRYAN WAS SLEEPING comfortably in his bed when Ian's screams broke the quiet of the house. He was laying on his side, legs tucked up to his abdomen in the fetal position. Wife Rebecca spooned reassuringly into the contours of his back. His eyes began to twitch, darting back and forth, as he scanned a place he had not been in a very, very long time.

A place he'd buried deep inside to hide even from himself:

Darkness. Everywhere. Shapes and sizes barely discernible. The landscape moves oddly slow as he stirs into the void but sees nothing. Even the sky above as deeply black as pitch.

A wind blows up around him and whips the dirt and debris of the ground into his face. It briefly whistles as it stirs wildly about him.

It whistles.

'Hello,' he calls out and watches as the word becomes tangible, its shape thickly liquid as it passes from his lips and floats lethargically ahead of him. Like syrup, it pours around the shapes before him then disappears.

He reaches out, feeling the black air, and begins to walk. The ground is soft and gives to his steps. A shape ahead of becomes closer with each careful stride. His hands stretch to touch it and he feels the familiar roughness of bark.

The whistling comes again an almost instantly the woods light up and part before him, the trees bending and swaying as they crack under the stress of the motion. How odd to see them, but how perfectly natural that they should do this. Beyond the parting a clearing is ablaze with light, its color blanched ashen, it is so bright.

In its center, demons leap on cloven hoofs around spiraling flames, their motions slow and deliberate as they kick and jump into the air. In disfigured hands they grasp strips of tan and red which drip onto the ground, painting a crude circle in the dirt as they dance around the flames. One by one, they throw the fleshy strips into the air and snap them into their mouths with long, thin, leathery tongues that unravel with a sound like horse whips.

One of their number turns.

It sees Bryan.

He tries to drop out of view but his body reacts sluggishly. The beast's stare ensnares his own and Bryan sees his brother's friend Matt behind those eyes? They burn red, deep in the sockets. Its top lip pulls up in a macabre smile, revealing a blackened hole which squirms with worms and crawling creatures deep within. A vaporous stench shoots from the orifice and envelops Bryan. It forces its way into his mouth, spilling down his throat and he gasps and reaches for his neck but can only watch himself, as if from a third person perspective, as his hands move so slowly that the action is worthless as he chokes and sputters and loses his breath as if drowning in the very air around him. He falls to the floor, his face hitting the dirt before his eyes can even blink. He twists onto his side as something warm kisses his scalp.

A boy, stripped naked, hangs above him. He is dangling by bound hands. Long strips torn away from his torso bare the dark crimson of sinewy muscle beneath the skin. Blood drips from them and falls rhythmically to the dirt.

Bryan cannot identify this boy . . . . His face has been removed.

Another thick bead of red falls. It moves through the air impossibly slowly and yet Bryan is unable to avoid its contact. It strikes him on his cheek, spreading like a tiny starburst.

Above him, the faceless head opens wide where the mouth should be and screams and Bryan's mind whirls *Oh God how can I stop this?* Then comes the deepest explosion of sound and light—

"Bry," Rebecca mumbled under heavy lips, elbowing her husband. She was the first to stir from the noise down the hall. Bryan winced and muttered something unintelligible as he pulled away from her.

"Bryan, *get up!*" She poked him harder this time, digging firmly into his ribs, and he pulled himself up onto his side.

"What?" His eyes were wide, forehead deeply furrowed as the scene in his mind melted into the darkness of the room.

"I heard what sounded like a scream. From your brother's room!"

Bryan was on his feet and racing for the door.

Rebecca reached out for him but was too slow. "Babe wait—"

But he was already sprinting down the corridor, the echoes of his flat feet on the threadbare carpet filling the upper level of the house. He turned the knob of the guest bedroom but the door was locked.

He rapped, brisk and hard.

"Ian . . . It's me!"

Only the muffled sound of Ian's shallow breaths answered. But there was another sound, barely audible beneath this; an odd, low frequency sound like a voice recording on a 45 record being played at 33 speed. Bryan's heart raced as he tried the door again, and this time could *feel* this deep resonating bass through the handle.

The knob rotated part way. Then stopped.

"Ian, open up!"

Then silence.

"Come on, open the door—" Bryan twiddled the knob again. "Ian, open the damn door!"

He took a step back, leveled his left shoulder, and slammed his full weight into the center of the door. The jamb split on the other side and the door flew open, splinters of wood shooting inward like porcupine quills. The door smacked hard against a dresser as Bryan tumbled through the doorway.

Sitting stiffly atop the covers strewn about his bed, Ian was trembling. His hands covered his eyes, his mouth agape as if silently screaming. He did not flinch as Bryan flew into the room.

No longer hissing their shrill, off-key whistling sound, the baseboard radiators merely clicked and gurgled as the warm water now flowed smoothly through.

"Jesus Ian! You alright?" Bryan moved closer and sat at the foot of his bed. Ian shook his head slowly from side to side, still covering his eyes with his quivering hands as Bryan held him close.

The brothers remained like that for longer than either could tell. Eventually Rebecca appeared in the doorway with Andrew cradled in her arms. Her son's chin was hung tiredly over her right shoulder, his arms and legs wrapped tightly around her as Rebecca lightly bounced and rocked him.

"Everything okay guys?" she asked as she stepped into the room, eyeing the splintered door frame. A moment later she registered the situation and chose not to linger for a reply, instead offering her husband only a simple, tender smile.

Bryan whispered after her as she turned to leave. "Becca," with a gentle nod. "Thank you. Everything's okay. I'll be in shortly."

She lowered her head, smiled again and left. Andrew had already fallen back to sleep and was hanging limply from her torso. His arms and legs dangled at her side, secure in the way you can only feel when you don't even realize that you feel secure.

Bryan stayed with his brother, assuring him gently over and over that it would be okay. Everything was gonna be alright.

II

Breakfast was planned a little earlier than normal. Bryan set the alarm for 6am to give them a little extra time to get everyone ready as they returned to their normal routines. But the morning came way too quickly, and after repeatedly slapping the snooze button on the digital alarm clock every twelve minutes, it ended up being well past seven before Bryan and Rebecca both leapt from bed in a sudden mad panic.

Bryan quickly showered while Becca woke the kids amidst crises of, 'why can't we stay home today! We never get to see uncle Ian.' And feigned grievances such as Andrew's personal favorite: 'I don't feel well mommy, my stomach doesn't feel good – I think I'm gonna throw up.'

At his young age it's unlikely Andrew understood how crafty this claim actually was, given its inherent difficulty to be disproved. More likely it was a matter of conditioning: per Pavlov's dog, Andrew had come to realize that when he rang that particular bell, a reward would follow.

Or at least it usually did.

"No, I'm sorry," Rebecca asserted to their ongoing pleas as she fed them toast and cereal and hastily prepared two packed lunches. "You can see your Uncle Ian when you come home from school. Besides, he doesn't feel very well himself and will probably sleep awhile."

Unconvinced, both children grabbed their plastic lunch boxes from the counter, grumbling.

In their defense, Rebecca too was having second thoughts about sending them back to school so soon. It had been, after all, only a few days since their grandparents' accident. But she and Bryan had discussed it the evening before, and letting them return to their normal routines felt like the best thing to do.

This morning, it felt less so.

Perhaps they would be better off at home, the little voice that was the right side of her brain coaxed. And quite convincingly too.

Rebecca's hesitant hands lingered above the kids' colorful lunch boxes, a wax paper wrapped sandwich in each.

But it's been almost a week, the left side of her brain rebutted. *And they'll heal faster this way. No matter how much you hate sending them away.*

And that logical voice was probably right. Neither of the children had yet grasped the true gravity of the week's events.

Andrew was still too young to understand what mortality really meant. And Diane was handling it pretty much okay, or so it seemed. Of course their daughter was saddened and her demeanor much more low key than usual. But Diane would be better off resuming her daily routine; being around her friends. It would do nothing for her well-being to dwell on the accident more than necessary, only to absorb that morose negativity to the point of amplification.

You mean like you, Rebecca? each side of her brain unanimously chastised her. *Perhaps, it's YOU who really wants to stay home. To have them here, with you. Rather than facing this new reality.*

Rebecca dropped the sandwiches in the lunch boxes, clicked them tightly closed and handed them off.

"Chop chop," she said, clapping her hands. "The bus is coming."

Diane and Andrew skulked reluctantly towards the door.

"The day will pass before you know it," she reassured, but wasn't convinced it was for their benefit as much as it was for her own. "And you'll be back here, just like that." (Snapping her fingers.) "Plus, Uncle Ian will be here when you get back."

"Promise?" Andrew asked with briefly renewed zest.

"I Promise."

Realizing this still meant a full day of school until then, Andrew shrugged, the spark fizzling. He waved listlessly behind him and hiked his book bag a little tighter over his shoulder.

Diane walked out without saying a word.

Rebecca watched them from the bay window in the living room to make sure they were safely at the bus stop. She was just dropping the curtain to the side when Ian came down the steps, already showered and dressed for the day.

"Ian, Good morning. Did you sleep well—" Rebecca realized the faux pas as soon as the words passed her lips. "Oh, I'm sorry Ian. Force of habit. I know you had, um . . . didn't—"

Ian cut her short with the brisk wave of a hand.

"Becky, don't worry. Honestly, I'm fine." Then adroitly changing the subject, "Have I missed the kids?"

Rebecca nodded as she opened the fridge. "Yes, just a couple minutes ago. Eggs for breakfast?"

"Yes, eggs would be amazing. Wow! Thank you."

"Amazing and wow?"

He grinned. "I'm just saying, it feels pretty nice to have someone offering to make me anything. At all. Normally, it's just a muffin with Felipe at this deli we pass on the way to work. Near Times Square."

His voice trailed away as the images of he and Felipe in Tony's bar started flooding in: *the baseball game, the ice cold beers . . . Anonymous.*

Rebecca laughed and the joy in its sound pulled Ian back to the present moment. "Well, breakfast in Times Square sounds a whole lot more glamorous than my scrambled eggs. But thank you, sweetie."

"Hey, Rebecca?"

She turned to face him.

"I didn't mean to cut you off a minute ago. I am sorry about, you know, about that whole incident last night." He motioned towards the stairs. "I must have scared the hell out of the kids—and you too—screaming like that. I feel so stupid . . . ."

Rebecca shook her head.

"Nonsense. Diane never heard a thing. She's a very heavy sleeper. And Andrew fell back to sleep before I even tucked him back into his bed. Ask Bryan."

"Ask Bryan what?" her husband interjected as he came down the stairs pulling a T-shirt over his head.

"Ian was apologizing about last night and I was saying it's no problem. This has shaken each of us pretty badly." She bit her lip, hard, holding back the tears which again threatened. She'd promised herself she wasn't going to cry today. She'd be strong for her husband and his brother today; be a calming center of respite for their worries today. The kids may be young enough and resilient enough to carry on without her concentrated help, but Rebecca wasn't quite so sure about these two men in her life.

"I agree," Bryan said and pulled up a chair at the breakfast table, hoping he was doing a passable job at hiding his discomfort with this conversation. "What's for breakfast?"

"Eggs," Becky answered as she broke another one into the cast iron skillet and it sizzled.

"Good. Any chance of some toast?"

She shot her husband an expression that artfully conveyed both *'of course—what do you think?'* and *'when did I become your geisha'* as she slid some bread into the toaster.

"Ian, how many for you, sweetie?"

"Just a couple would be fine, Rebecca. Thank you."

Bryan scarfed his down the moment Rebecca slid it across the table, while Ian waited for his sister-in-law to join them before lifting his fork. Rebecca winked at him in acknowledgment, and in the gesture Ian felt genuine affection. He hadn't really noticed, not before that moment, just how deeply brown Rebecca's eyes were, or how they communicated a natural sense of calming reassurance. A kind of warm, grounded strength.

Or how intensely beautiful she was.

He studied the curve of her face, the line of her mouth, the soft fullness of her lips and felt himself swelling—

"How is everything?" she asked.

"The eggs are great," Ian replied more bashfully than he wanted to before quickly averting his gaze.

Bryan caught a glimpse of this exchange between bites. He was relieved the two were getting on so well. Always more compassionate than he, Becca had been the one who'd suggested, without hesitation, that of course Ian must stay with them. She'd also commented a little later, almost as a side note, that the only thing she wasn't sure of was how it would work if Ian were to end up staying for any real length of time. Bryan hadn't been sure exactly how that time was meant to be determined. But for now, everything seemed to be going as well as could be expected, under the circumstances.

He took his last bite and pushed his plate away as the thought faded. "Yes, great eggs Becca. Really."

† † †

After breakfast, Rebecca changed for work. The family's crisis hadn't stopped that from being a necessity. She would have to go in to the office, for the morning at least, to tie up some loose ends. No matter how much she wanted to stay home.

Think of the kids, Becky. People, order, routine. Take a dose of your own medicine, the rational voice reminded her bluntly.

She listened to it. And agreed. But she would try to get away as soon as she could. "So, what's on the cards for you two?" she asked the brothers, injecting an air of chattiness which her rational voice thought they could all use.

"What's on the cards is, you're late for work," Bryan answered. And then whispered in her ear: "Try to come home early, if you can."

She kissed him on the cheek, her warmth lingering with her perfume. "Don't you two go getting up to any mischief now. The kids are bad enough." She pecked Ian on the forehead too, ruffling his hair.

"Don't worry about me, I'll be good. I promise. Your husband . . . now that's a different matter. "

"You'll just have to keep him on the up-and-up then," she insisted as she headed for the door. "Bye then, my pair of big hunky fellas."

The familiar sound of the garage door churning electronically upwards ground throughout the house as Bryan sipped his coffee, now lukewarm.

IV

Despite a challenging morning, Rebecca was making good time on the twelve mile commute until she became inexplicably faint on Route 21 and her Chevy Blazer struck the soft shoulder. The sudden change in friction caused the SUV to skid diagonally across the blacktop and Rebecca nearly swiped two oncoming cars.

Both swerved to avoid the crash then simply carried on driving. The first was a young man who whipped her the finger as he barreled by; the second, a mature woman in a brown Pinto who deliberately averted her eyes as she passed so she wouldn't feel the obligation to stop and check if Rebecca Cockerton was okay.

Becky just loved it when that happened. You could always count on people when you needed them—count on them to be complete and inexorable bastards, that is.

She regained her composure, checked around the outside of the 4x4 (no flat tires, nothing untoward) and finished the rest of her journey. Her boss was in a flurry because it was month-end that week and they needed 'all hands on deck' as he would say so often. But he was aware of Rebecca's family circumstances.

"I'm sorry I'm late, Tom. My car went off the road, I don't know what happened. I thought at first maybe I'd had a blowout . . . ." She didn't know why she was apologizing, it was he that should be grateful she was coming in at all. "I just needed a moment afterward to regain my composure."

Her manager settled back into his chair. He breathed out heavily.

"Right, well. Get on with it for now. The sooner you clear that load off your desk and get back home the better, I guess. Your husband is going to need you." And then only as an afterthought added, "And how are you?"

"Okay, I guess."

"Well, if there's anything I can do . . . ."

He looked down and started scribbling away at a pad. Apparently that was the end of the sentence. And his offer.

It was painfully apparent where she fell within his list of priorities: and it sure as shit wasn't at the top. In fact, it was *way* down the list, far, far below his department's revenue targets.

You trumped up little shit bastard.

Oh, how Rebecca enjoyed the sound of those words in her mind. If only she could say them aloud. Instead, she walked away without another word.

At her desk, she began rustling through the considerable pile of papers which had accumulated in just a few days of being off. Clearly none of her teammates had thought even once about checking on her workload for her. So here it lay, an unapologetic, almost scoffing pile of stark reality.

On oh-so-many levels.

She asked herself if anyone cared the slightest damn bit about at all.

When the garage door clanked and clunked back down and Bryan was sure his wife had left the neighborhood and pulled onto Route 60, the tone of his voice inexorably changed.

There was no smile, no affection. Just cold, rigid, almost brutal directness which seemed to grow in direct proportion to Rebecca's growing distance from the house.

"What the fuck's going on here, Ian?"

Bryan booted one of the stools out from under the table and sat opposite his brother, leaning in close.

"You better just come out and say it."

Ian tensed, his mind seizing. His heart began beating hard. So hard he was sure Bryan could hear it. He stared at the tabletop, the pattern in the Formica threatening to blur.

"I mean," Bryan continued, failing to accept Ian's lack of reply. "What the hell is happening? What exactly was that—"

Ian pushed himself away from the table. Bryan had always been able to look inside his thoughts, to see his mind as clearly as he saw his own, and the idea of him being able to do so in this moment made Ian's skin crawl with embarrassment.

Had it been so apparent? This rash, new, entirely unanticipated feeling he'd found himself having about his brother's wife.

Over breakfast, for God's sake.

As children they'd found this same unique ability—an inexplicable bond between them, some type of positive vibration—enabled the brothers to have almost entire conversations without saying an audible word. They would laugh as they conveyed thoughts and ideas intangibly, without a single person around them aware that they were communicating in clear, cohesive frequencies.

Sure, the adults would catch an occasional eye roll or giggle between the boys. But that was it. No one had a clue as to the depth of detail the boys were transmitting.

Equally, it had been a very long time before the boys realized this was something unique that other people just did not share.

VI

Ian was nine years old when he took Bryan's Evel Knievel action figure, replete with 1/10th scale motorcycle. It was the cool one, with a working 'engine' you got going by pulling this long plastic strip—like a really long zip tie with ridges all the way up it—through the gear alongside the rear wheel and the tire immediately spun so fast you'd get a brush burn if you bumped your hand against it. And when you sat that bike down, that thing would skip off at a furious pace and screech along the floor until it careened into a piece of furniture or a wall, at which time it would invariably pop a wheelie, spin on its axis like a whirlwind, then crash in a rolling, somersaulting spectacle.

Wanting to see what that baby could really do, Ian took it to the creek at the edge of the neighborhood where he built a makeshift ramp out of a couple square inches of leftover plywood their father had laying around in the garage. Positioning the ramp strategically at the edge of the fast running stream, he then smoothed out a dirt track about five feet before it. He took a moment to soak in the feeling before pulling the plastic strip.

"OK Evel. It's go time!"

Ian pulled the plastic starter strip and the wheel screeched to life. Little Evel Knievel shot towards the ramp at mind-numbing speed and Ian could remember years later how impressively the bike took the ramp and sailed gloriously through the air.

"Go Evel! Go!" he shouted as it flew with incredible grace and ease a good seven or eight feet . . . across a twelve foot creek.

It arced down and hit the water with an anticlimactic *PLOP* before whisking immediately downstream in the current, never again to be found.

Ian slinked home to find his brother downstairs, still in his pajamas.

Bryan knew. He knew everything.

Instantly.

A furious, wordless fistfight erupted and their parents had to separate the boys before sitting them down and demanding why one minute Ian was walking through the door and the next, Bryan was pummeling him in his PJs, without cause or explanation.

"It just makes no sense," they insisted.

Still, neither boy spoke. They sat at the breakfast table across from their parents, who informed them they could sit there all day for all they cared, they weren't going anywhere until one of the boys told them what the heck was going on.

Or else.

There was always that deeply foreboding: 'Or else.'

So Hare and Veronica Cockerton sat silently at the table, waiting for one of their sons to spill the beans.

Uncomfortable silence is a powerful tool in the right hands.

(Something every parent everywhere seems to utilize, presumably detailed in some mysterious *Parenting 101 Handbook* they all apparently purchase. It was also something Ian would, many years later, teach his sales team at the *Bulletin* during their monthly training sessions.)

But the silent treatment only works if there *is* silence.

Little did the parents know the only ones sitting there in silence were, in fact, themselves.

Through the unique, inaudible frequency they shared, the boys effortlessly continued an entirely unspoken conversation of sorts, only sporadically accentuating it with an audible huff or *harumph*.

Hare Cockerton was the first to leave the table, having waited out their sons as long as he could before breaking the 'silence' with an expression of how disappointed he was (another oft-used tool from that parenting handbook) and that he'd had enough of this waste of time and was getting on with his day. The boys, however, would not get on with theirs. He ensured they sat there another good hour or so before finally sending them to their rooms.

This type of thing happened often. And it drove their parents nuts. Which of course made this uniquely shared connection between them all the more appealing to the brothers.

It also made their spats and childhood arguments all the less appealing. For in times like this, it would vibrate in a low, plaintive frequency. It was this, and not the intended silences they never had to suffer, that generated the boys' greatest level of discomfort. So it was that neither could stay mad at the other for any significant length of time. The inner silence being too torturous, sooner or later one would ping the other in tiny, vibrant pulses.

VII

That was a great number of years ago, however. Since then, the seemingly telepathic ability the boys had shared had gradually diminished with every year, and every mile, between them until one day Ian simply no longer felt Bryan's 'pings' or vibrations on any level anymore. In fact, the gift so neglected, he would eventually forget that they ever shared such a secret, mysterious gift at all. Like Santa Claus and the Easter Bunny—*and the Boogeyman*—acknowledgment of it had been banished to the scrap pile of childhood frivolity, to flounder away in a locked space to which most adults could no longer find the key. Nor saw any need to.

But now that he was back in this childhood home, as close to his brother (at least as measured by physical distance) as he had ever been, Ian did remember something about a gift they had once shared. He had begun to feel a kind of familiar yet unusual energy resonating softly, deeply, within him.

The sensation seemed to be growing with each passing day, as if being back here—in this neighborhood, in this childhood home, and once again so near to the Little Woods—were reviving in him a sort of enlightened reawakening.

What he couldn't understand is why Bryan seemed so oblivious to this energy, despite having remained here all these years.

That doesn't mean we won't pick up right where we left off, Ian thought, realizing that now he was home, perhaps the synapse was a small enough gap to ignite the gift's spark once more. And with the revival of the gift would also come the erosion of personal privacy.

And personal thought.

Which meant that his feelings toward Rebecca, as innocent and unintentional as they may be, may not necessarily be his private thoughts or emotions. And as much as he'd prefer to simply dismiss those fleeting, innocent feelings he was having about his sister-in-law, his brother might not see them as quite as innocent as Ian knew them to genuinely be.

After all, they weren't kids anymore. And it just wasn't acceptable to be having feelings—of any kind—about your own brother's wife.

Of course Bryan was aware that Rebecca was a beautiful woman. He also openly acknowledged her as the more caring, supportive one in their marriage. Quite frankly, it was Rebecca who was the source of comfort to those in need while Bryan so often presented himself as distant, even coldly detached.

Still, Ian felt he needed to have the conversation. Right here, right now. If there were any chance at all Bryan could still pick up on the vibrations of his thoughts and feelings, even if just a little bit, it would be better to clear the air quickly and then move on. Surely Bryan would understand how Ian might experience a momentary wave of affection toward his wife. And if he couldn't, Bryan *would* always understand that, to Ian, Rebecca was . . . purely family.

Ian sat back down and pulled his chair closer to the table.

"What do *you* think is going on, Bryan?"

He was calm after taking a deep breath, and subconsciously monitored his brother's features for any hint that their unique bond had reconnected. There was a vibration, yes. But such a nominal frequency that Ian could barely feel it.

Bryan showed no sign that he felt it at all.

Or even remembered it.

"Last night Ian!" Bryan shouted, stubbing his fingers forcibly against the tabletop to accentuate each of the three words.

Last night.

Ian exhaled. A long, cleansing breath.

So this isn't about his unwitting affection toward Rebecca at all.

"Oh, last night," he repeated and almost laughed as the intense anxiety washed so instantly away it could only be replaced by an unintentional, giddy nervousness.

That didn't sit well with Bryan who was now on his feet.

"Yes, last night Ian! You scared the shit outta me. You scared the shit out of *all* of us. Andrew woke up bawling. Can you blame the kid, Ian? He's only seven and his uncle's screaming in the room next door, like death itself is at his bedside!"

Ian calmed his jangling nerves by taking in another long, slow breath through his nose and expelling it passively from his mouth. The sensation as it wisped over his lips was soothing.

And in this momentary pause, as if far away, he felt a small but palpable vibration: a weakly discernible radar blip between interludes of soft white noise. And though it was low and hardly even there, Ian knew at once that blip was coming from Bryan.

So he does still have it.

Ian took a moment to compose his words. His features softened, as did his voice.

"You know what's going on, Bry," he quietly stated, the words firm but soothing. "You know, because I think it's happening to you too. Look at the way you're acting right now."

Bryan fervently denied understanding anything at all, about what the hell was going on or why his brother should wake up screaming so horrifically. He shook his head vigorously as he paced back and forth. To admit that deep down, some inexplicable echo of the past was clawing its way back into his psyche, would be too much to handle right now. He could not allow the Little Woods, and what happened there, to become real again. Even though his own demands upon Ian were a subconscious attempt to get his brother to admit this very same thing.

"I wish that were true," Ian replied dispassionately. "But you do know. You're starting to sense it again, just like before. Just like me. Just like that night Matt came to me and he—"

Ian's words faltered beneath the trembling of his voice until the only sound was the steady, metered measurement of time from the wall clock in the corner of the kitchen. In the strained silence, each audible mark of each passing second grew progressively louder until every one of them assaulted the quiet like the sharp, snapping percussive strike of a snare drum.

Bryan fell to his knees as each clangorous tick of the clock sped his mind in reverse, tugging his consciousness backwards, faster and faster. Every second became a minute; each minute an hour; each hour a day. Until the years between childhood and now had been unceremoniously stripped away.

And the dam of Bryan's subconsciousness burst.

He is back in the Little Woods.

On his knees.

With Matt's bloodied and lifeless body dangling above him.

Bryan screamed as a dozen pin-prick scars on his back blistered with pain, the long-submerged memory now assailing his senses. Tears poured down his face as he fell to his knees, sobbing into his hands. "Oh my God—Ian—what did we do? What—did we do!"

"C'mon," Ian gently reassured, reaching down and wrapping his arms around his big brother. This time it was he lifting Bryan to his feet, much as his brother had done for him so many years before.

In the clearing. As Matt burns.

He held his brother in the safety of his embrace as eighteen years poured out of Bryan like a wave.

When eventually the quaking sobs ebbed to a slow, controlled tremor, Ian held his brother's face in his hands and assured him everything would be okay.

C'mon. Let's get some fresh air. And we'll talk.

Ian did not speak these words, only thought them.

Yet Bryan nodded in agreement as he swiped away the tears from his face and rose upon shaky, unsteady legs.

1977

THE WOODS WERE out of bounds as soon as the news of Matt's accident had spread (like wildfire). By the time the Chaunceys had buried their son six days later, the entire neighborhood had devolved into a ghost town.

It had been a solid week-and-a-half of parents pondering and ruminating, gossiping and endlessly worrying, until the sweeping hysteria had made pretty much everything off limits. None of the kids were out playing ball, riding their bikes or skateboarding. No one tossed an old football or played 'Kick The Can.'

It was like the neighborhood itself had gone into lockdown. Quarantine. A twenty-four hour curfew.

Because, if Matt Chauncey—the good, quiet, reserved and smart young boy that he was—had been playing with fire . . . then any of the other good boys in the neighborhood might be inclined to do so, too. After all, boys would be boys. And boys liked to mess around with things they shouldn't. Like matches. And ropes. And sharp things like knives.

The repercussions didn't bear thinking about.

So that was it. No more games of War in the Little Woods. Jack and Stu even stayed away. It was more than their lives were worth if either of their old men caught them anywhere near that long stretch of tractor path leading towards the woods.

Especially if their fathers had been partaking in the odd beer or two down at the Blue Jay or Dempsey's Tavern after work.

So they found somewhere else to hang out.

For a while.

II

"Hello, Mrs. Cockerton? It's Craig Dalton. From down the road," the voice on the old black telephone vibrated tinnily from the other end of the line.

"I know dear. I do know your voice by now."

"Oh. Haha. Oh. Ha! Well, is Ian around? I haven't seen him in days."

"I know hun. I wish you could spend a little time with each other. Why don't you come up this afternoon. I'll fix you both some nice lunch."

"Hold on," the disembodied voice dictated as it muffled the receiver and shouted out for its mother. Its mother was faintly heard in the background to say something along the lines of, 'Why, you little scrote—don't you like the lunch I'm making?' then laughed and approved the request.

The voice returned to the handset.

"Sure, I'll come straight up." Craig hesitated for a moment. *"But it'll take a bit longer. I have to go the long way round. On the road. I'm not allowed to cut through the woods anymore."*

As soon as the words had come out and were still traveling down the phone line, he realized this made him sound like a real wuss.

"I understand. Why don't I pick you up then?"

There was only one thing worse than as-good-as-admitting you were a wuss. And that was being picked up—*on your own*—by your best friend's mother.

Craig was silent for what seemed to him like hours but was in actuality only seconds.

"Sure. Okay. That sounds great. When?"

"Well, how about now, hun?"

"Cool. I'll be ready. Bye."

The phone clicked and then buzzed monotonously in Veronica Cockerton's hand. Ian could use a good friend at the moment, she thought. This would perhaps help draw him out of himself. Craig and he were always best buddies. Lord knows she could never find a moment's peace when school was out and they were together at the house virtually all summer long.

But now, what she wouldn't give to hear that clamor again.

She picked up Craig in the old Ford and they rattled back up the hill towards the neighborhood. The Daltons lived about three miles from the main cluster of houses. It was only a quarter of that distance as the crow flies, but you had to cut through a couple fields and then the edge of the forest, just by the Little Woods, to do it. She understood completely Kathy Dalton's reluctance to allow Craig to walk that route now. Or, knowing Kathy's rather liberal parenting style, perhaps it was Craig's own hesitance to do so.

She didn't blame him.

Not after what Matt did to himself there.

You wouldn't catch *her* anywhere near that place. It didn't matter that she was a grown adult.

Or that today was a sunny, pleasant summer's day.

Nope.

The woods felt just too eerie now. Dark, foreboding. Like they were haunted or something. It was unnerving how that malaise had spread so that the bright, cheerful neighborhood had itself become so dismal. And grey. And unpleasant. It no longer echoed with carefree noise as kids played joyfully outside; no longer facilitated impromptu 'hellos!' as parents casually gathered on front porches of an evening.

Everything was different now, and Veronica Cockerton just wanted things to go back to the way they were. In so many ways, she now realized, their lives had been simply idyllic.

And Matt had ruined that. For all of them.

She hated herself for thinking in such a churlish, self-absorbed way. The poor boy didn't deserve to burn himself to death like that. But it was the truth. Things had changed, all for the worse, in the weeks since he had done such a stupid thing.

"I'm not afraid, you know," Craig belted out without prompting, shattering her thoughts and the silence as they rode slowly through the neighborhood.

Veronica looked at him, surprised.

"Afraid of what, dear?" A shiver creased her back.

"You know. The Woods. It's no big deal."

"How can you say that? Poor Matt—"

"I know, I know. I don't mean it that way. You know. I feel rotten. But I'm not afraid to go in there. I just thought I should tell you, it's my mom. She won't let me go that ways anymore."

Mrs. Cockerton wished she had the same problem. Quite the opposite, Ian hadn't emerged from the house at all in the weeks since. He'd barely even left his room. Once or twice they managed to get him out for an ice cream, or back to school shopping.

But Ian just wasn't the same boy he'd been before.

"Your mom is very right. You shouldn't hang out around there. It's too far from home. No one could help you if you would need them to."

Craig eyed her with that look of oddity only the young can muster when adults—parents—are being overly cautious.

"Well, I'm not afraid, that's all."

They pulled into the drive and Veronica opened the garage door with the remote. It churned upwards and the moment the car was parked, Craig jumped out and ran upstairs.

Mrs. Cockerton called to him that Ian was in his room.

Duh, he thought. *Moms are weird. Sheesh.*

ΙΙΙ

"Way-hey!" Craig blurted loudly as he burst into the room. Making an entrance was always his scene.

Ian looked up, not at all surprised.

"Hey," he returned coolly. He was sitting on his bed, Indian fashion, with a couple of books spread about him.

"Watcha doing?"

"Reading."

"Oh. Great. Wow. Sounds real exciting."

Ian shrugged and turned one of the books over so that its cover didn't show.

"Fancy a bit of baseball or something?" Craig picked up an autographed ball from the shelf of books next to Ian's bed.

Again Ian shrugged.

"What's up with ya, scrotebag?" Craig's irritation begged to be loose. "You haven't been outta here for ages . . . ."

"I—I," Ian stuttered between heavy breaths. "I don't know."

"What the hell's the matter?" Craig was clearly uncomfortable but sat down on the edge of the bed, making the 'friend' effort anyway. Ian was, after all, his *best* friend.

Ian stared down at his crossed legs as he fiddled with his toes.

Mrs. Cockerton's voice began to trill up the stairs as she sang along to Andy Williams on the radio.

"C'mon man. What's up? You ain't sick! But you haven't been out of here for, like, ever."

Ian shrugged without looking up. He paused for a moment then added, almost as an afterthought, "Matt."

"Man—" Any sympathy Craig had managed to muster crumbled like feta. "That kid was a douche-nozzle, man. Always was. I mean, lighting that fire like that . . . he was a dumbass."

He almost giggled but decided to hold it back.

"Always was. Always will be. Now."

Ian shot him an icy glare.

"You don't know what happened. You weren't there!"

His anger sliced the atmosphere (what little there was) and brought an uneasy silence to the room. Both boys looked at the floor, the walls, the pen and ink drawing of the ship on the choppy ocean waves his mom had insisted would counter–balance those awful posters of rock bands or women in bikinis; anywhere but each other.

Ian broke the silence.

"Where were you Craig . . . ?"

Craig Dalton pretended he didn't understand.

"Where *were* you!" Ian repeated, his tone more demanding. "You know what I mean. You were on point guard. You headed east. I went west. That was the last I saw of you."

Craig said nothing. He kept his head down and pulled at a piece of loose thread on the bedspread. Ian suspected he was holding back from crying, something he had never—*ever*—seen Craig do. Not even the time they were in the branches of an apple tree in crazy old man Freeman's field, eating sour apples, and Craig got caught up in the barbed wire coming over the fence when they heard the shots. Or at least what sounded like them.

"I don't know!" he erupted. "I don't *know* where I was! I went off like you said. I headed that way for a bit, then decided to go upwards, north, for a spell. I thought Jack and Stu and them all might be up that way. Everything was real quiet, and to be honest, I was getting a little bored. Then this huge cloud comes over and it gets real dark. *So quick.* It got hard to see. I couldn't tell where I was."

His stare grew distant.

"Then I heard this really weird whistling sound. It was like, far away at first, then closer. It was creepy, man. So fucking eerie. It scared the shit outta me, I don't care saying so. I couldn't find my way around. Then this orange light flashes and I could see a little bit. I ran as fast as I could where I thought the base camp should be. I knew you guys would be there. I know I was pretty close when this scream sent shivers down my back."

That same shiver ran through both boys right now as if the words spoken had summoned the sensation. Ian's eyes were wet.

"I stopped right there. Where I was. Something was wrong, man. I knew it. So I snuck around the other side. Turns out I wasn't far from the Father Oak. When I got to the clearing there was a fire where the stump and those log seat things used to be. They were burning up inside it all. And Matt was in the tree—"

His eyes began streaming.

"So I ran."

Silence.

Ian broke it: "Wait. So you saw what was going on? You saw him. You *saw me?*"

"No! It wasn't like that! I was scared, Ian!"

"And what about me! I'm there with my head tore up and my fucking leg all twisted. They gave it to me good and hard, Craig! Rocks, fists, the lot. You think I wasn't fucking scared?!"

(Despite the solemnity of the conversation, inwardly he was proud of his swearing; this time the cuss words finally landed the way he felt they were supposed to.)

Craig apologized, sobbing.

"I'm sorry, Ian! I really am. Please—"

"How much did you see?"

"Just Matt in the tree! And those guys, around it at the bottom, doing something. Prancing around the fire or some shit. I didn't see you, Ian. I promise I didn't. Just—" He shut his mouth, a moment too late.

"What? Just *what* for Chrissakes?"

"Just your brother. That's all. Just your brother in the weeds. He was crouching in them like me. I don't think he saw me though."

Ian saw the image clearly in his mind.

Matt in the tree, screaming for help. He on the dirt floor, rocking with his knees pulled all the way up to his chest, unable to comprehend the terror around him. His brother bursting into the clearing.

The whistling as the flute screamed and shrilled.

"You coulda helped!"

The fire crackling as the flames lick up Matt's legs.

Ian's fist landed hard across Craig' left cheek, knocking his friend off the bed sideways. Craig reeled and cracked the back of his head against the corner of the night stand before laying there, stunned and spreadeagled, on the hardwood floor.

The sound of him falling thudded through the house and Veronica Cockerton called up from the kitchen.

"You boys okay up there?"

She turned down the radio, just a little, while she waited for an answer. Receiving none, she ran up the stairs as Sonny and Cher chirped obliviously away in the kitchen.

The door to Ian's room was ajar and through the opening she saw Craig on the floor, a tiny red smudge on the dark wood of the bedside table behind him.

"My God, what's going on here!"

She cupped a hand over her mouth as Craig was trying, unsuccessfully, to lift himself from the floor. His hair was matted with blood down the back of his scalp. Several drops had made thick burgundy circles on the floor. Veronica ran to him and helped him back up and onto the bed.

"Ian, go get me a wet wash cloth. A warm one!"

Ian stood transfixed.

"Now!"

This time he obeyed and came running quickly back with a trail of water dripping behind him.

"Now go and fetch me my car keys. We'll have to take him to the hospital!"

"No," Craig objected weakly. "I don't have to. I hate—"

"Craig," Ian's mother held his cheek in her right hand. It was smooth and warm. "You're going. And that's the end of it. We'll call your mother from there and let her know what's going on. Everything will be alright."

IV

It was bright and airless in the huge corridors of the emergency ward. Fluorescent lights blanched the faces of people rushing back and forth; green gowns and translucent white latex gloves shimmering as they passed. A cutting, sanitary odor punctuated the unnerving sound as coughs and groans emanated from all around them as they waited, imprinting indelibly on Ian's mind.

"Veronica Cockerton," a voice called out hollowly from behind the reception desk where a nurse wearing a blouse at least two sizes too small for her portly frame studied the sign-in sheet. "I'm looking for a Mrs. Veronica Cocker—"

Ian's mother half-stood and signaled her location with a wave.

"Now, you wait here," Ian's mother instructed. "I'll go in with Craig. It won't—it shouldn't—be very long. All I think he needs is a quick X-ray just to make sure, and a bit of TLC."

Ian lifted his eyebrows by reply. He sat stiffly in the hard, red plastic chair, staring at his friend as Craig held a hand to the back of his head, his elbow deliberately covering his face so he would not have to look at Ian.

Ian watched them walk through the blue vinyl swing doors until they disappeared around the corner as the doors rebounded back together.

The big analogue clock on the wall read 12:02.

Ian was bored already. And uncomfortable.

Shit. I didn't mean to smack him so hard. I really didn't.

He hummed to himself and fidgeted in his chair as he watched the people coming in. The minutes turned to an hour; an hour into another. And the endless flow of people never stopped. There was always someone new coming in. Only sometimes someone going out. Like a stream of misery trickling through those big, automatic sliding glass doors that announced this was the 'MOOR YCNEGREME' every time they kissed back together at the center of the entry.

An elderly woman seated directly behind Ian spluttered.

Wheezed.

And began to cough.

The old woman sucked in air. An unnatural, rasping sound emanated from her chest as her lungs gasped for air but could only pull the thinnest stream of air which whistled through her teeth.

Ian twisted away in his seat and as he did, the old woman grabbed him. Her fingers clasped onto his shoulder, wrapped around his forearm. They tightened as her chest heaved for air.

He hadn't even noticed the woman before. Just another faceless person in the throng. But the old woman had his attention now.

"Help! Please! HELP!" Ian implored at no one—at everyone—as he tried to yank out of her grip. Though the woman was small and frail, she clutched at him frantically like a drowning person clawing at a life preserver.

The panic in her eyes screamed in desperation and aloneness, and Ian could tangibly feel her fear flooding tangibly into his every pore.

"SOMEBODY HELP!"

Out of the corner of his eye, a shape of what must be a nurse (not the fat one with the clipboard) raced toward them, the motion resembling a slow motion film sequence.

The old woman wrenched Ian closer and a weak stream of air drew across her lips. There were words within that wisp of sound. Faint and faltering, but they were there. Ian could sense them—*could feel them*—but couldn't make out their meaning.

"What? Wha—" he implored, the woman's eyes piercing his own.

Another inhalation, a wheezing, whistling—

whistling

—draw into desperate lungs. Another fragile exhalation and the words were there again, masked within the hissing air.

Ian leaned closer and a puff of acrid breath blew into his face. He pulled sharply away as the old woman began to twitch and tremble, a convulsion rippling through her frail body like a wave. When it reached her misshapen hands, her fingers tightened, nails like ragged talons clawing into his skin. He winced in pain but refused to pull away from the old woman lest she tumble to the ground.

Her eyes pleaded as she pulled Ian closer, pressing her face to his.

"D—i . . . b—s—t . . . ."

Her hot breath coiled into his mouth and nostrils, burrowing down his throat. Ian wheezed and was barely able to hold back vomit, gulping the stinging, acidic vapor back down.

The nurse was nearly upon them when the old woman jettisoned the words in a shrieking, rasping curse:

"DIE BASTARD! DIE BASTARD! DIE-BASTARD-DIEBASTARD!"

A gelatinous string of yellow-green mucous spurted from her mouth as she screamed the mantra. It quivered then hung from her bottom lip. Her pneumatic–like grip released and the old woman collapsed to the floor where the nurse and a full medical team lifted her onto a stretcher. Laying on her side, the old woman's tongue dangled loosely from her mouth, a line of mucous running down her cheek and onto the stainless steel gurney as they wheeled it swiftly through the lobby. The blue vinyl swing doors brushed open as the woman heaved herself upright and cackled hysterically.

Ian watched in horror as a medic restrained her, forcing her back down, and the doors hissed softly closed.

V

Ian slumped into the red plastic seat, trembling. The fat nurse with the clipboard offered him water and reassurance before leaving him to sit there quietly. Alone.

A mother of two (or at least that's all she had with her) offered him a concerned look and a smile. Ian tried to reciprocate but couldn't manage it. He felt as if he might crack in two if he did.

The clock on the wall displayed 12:19.

"Don't be upset, son." The voice was deep and smooth and came with the hand of a man, which touched his shoulder tentatively.

Ian flinched sharply and the man pulled away deliberately.

"Whoa, whoa there. It's okay, I'm not going to hurt you. Honest." He held his hands up to illustrate. "Alright if I sit down?"

Ian squinted at the man and saw the fat nurse at the desk behind him nod as if to gesture that he was okay. Ian must have raised a slight smile, for she returned it greater. He looked up at the man. "Okay."

He was quite tall and heavily built. Pinned to his suit coat was a name badge which read in big bold letters: DR. MARTIN. He sat down next to Ian but folded his arms in a deliberate fashion to indicate that he was keeping well out of Ian's personal space.

"Your friend's going to be okay. No serious problem at all. A bump, that's all. I just thought you should know. And," he paused, "I see you've just had a little incident on your hands. You sure you're okay?"

Ian nodded.

"We get them like that sometimes," Dr. Martin admitted with barely concealed regret. "Are you sure?" He added as he stood, appending his previous question.

Ian shrugged again.

"Fine." The doctor opened his arms once more and patted Ian firmly on the shoulder. "Your mother will be out shortly. She's just getting your friend and his things together."

Ian said nothing as the doctor walked away without looking back.

Craig came out a moment later with Mrs. Cockerton. He wore a bandage at the back of his head which stuck awkwardly through his tufts of dark brown hair. Ian smirked at the idea of how much that was gonna sting when Craig pulled that sucker off sometime later.

"You boys stay here a moment," Veronica Cockerton instructed as she rummaged through her purse for some change. "I'm going to call Craig's mom and let her know what's happened."

She used the payphone in the lobby to call Kathy Dalton, preempting the conversation with an apology and assurance that Craig was okay, "But here's what happened . . . ."

Kathy tried to verbally shrug it off as just one of those things, boys will be boys, after all. But Veronica sensed, as perhaps only mothers can, that Mrs. Dalton was actually rather concerned and anxious. She arranged to come pick up Craig, but Mrs. Cockerton persuaded her Craig was okay and why didn't she swing by and pick him up on her way home from the store later.

"Besides," Veronica assured her, "I'm certain he would prefer to have some company at the moment."

Kathy Dalton agreed reluctantly and promised to be there no later than six. The boys did little in what remained of their afternoon, watching television and sitting around.

"You little scrote. Nice one, send me to the hospital why don't ya?"

"No thanks, I already did!"

"D-duh, yeah," Craig feigned. "I noticed."

He whipped Ian the finger and had to quickly retract the gesture as Mrs. Cockerton appeared on the stairs down to the TV room.

"Everything okay down here?"

The boys nodded and Craig winced as he touched the bandage and it tugged at his hair.

Veronica mistook this for pain from the bruise and kissed him gently on his forehead, stroking his hair for a moment.

"Let's have a look." She carefully lifted an edge of the bandage and saw no further bleeding. "Looks fine to me, but it's likely to be sore for a while. You'll have to make sure to take it easy for now."

"Mmm, yeah," Craig assented and poked the bump once or twice himself. "I think you're right."

Mrs. Cockerton smiled.

"I'm glad you think so, Craig." She waggled a finger at both of them. "Now, I don't know what you two boys were fighting about—or doing, or whatever—upstairs, but I hope you've learned a lesson from this."

Despite addressing them both, the caution seemed directed more at Craig than Ian, as if she expected he was at the root of this particular incident. Either way, she was quietly happy that Ian had resembled a touch of his normal self today, and smiled at Craig for the accomplishment.

Craig hadn't a clue what she was thinking but smiled back.

According to every clock in the house, Mrs. Dalton roared into the driveway at 6:47pm. She hopped out of the car and trotted up the front porch to ring the bell.

Craig opened the door as the first of the chimes rang out.

"I'm here, Mom."

"Oh, baby! Let me see you!" She pulled him brusquely to her and peered closely at the bandage as Mrs. Cockerton explained briefly what Dr. Martin had said.

After an awkward pause, Veronica invited her in for a coffee.

"Oh I don't know where my manners are! Please, do come in." She stepped aside and gestured for her to enter.

"No, really," Craig's mother declined. "Thank you though. But we really must be going."

She looked at Craig.

"Ready, kid?"

He nodded.

"And thank you for taking care of things, Veronica." Kathy looked at Ian, too, and smiled warmly. "See you later, Ian."

He flushed as he said the same, those tingling thoughts of her gushing back. He stood at the door and watched until they turned out of the neighborhood and drove away.

"Come on," Veronica called out to him. "You can help me get dinner on before your father gets home."

VI

That night, the sirens cried as they often did in the summers, wailing through the warm, still air as they passed above the neighborhood on the main road. In his sleep Ian watched them.

The sounds rise in a cacophony; lights flashing wildly, shining from the wet blacktop of the road. Everything blurs behind a cloud of fluorescence. Their alternating, cycling flashes land upon a car in the road. Its top no longer exists—its front and sides a crumpled accordion. The front passenger seat extends well beyond where the windshield once was. The steering wheel is cocked and bent awkwardly at an angle, the driver's torso spread against it as if in rest. His neck is empty, save a sliver of spherical white poking through.

The woman is on the road, twenty yards from the vehicle, her figure bent at the waist as if she were sleeping on the verge.

In the back, something screams through chokes, huddled on the seat. Its face is only a blur as its cries blend and disappear amidst the shrieks of the sirens and growing moans of lookers-on.

The first responders, Ian among them, reach into the car.

A baby—no, a child—cries as they reach into the back seat. It is alive! It's still alive! It can be saved!

Its face is young but too smooth, oddly shaded. It grabs at them with charred hands and pulls itself to them.

"Die bastard!" the face screams as it becomes the old woman and lunges from the back seat, fingers splayed into claws which lance Ian's chest with a flash of hottest pain and peal away the skin to reveal—

Ian bolted from beneath the covers and scanned the room in a frenzy. His breath short and quick, he pushed his back hard against the headboard, the feeling of its sturdiness reassuring as he steadied himself in the dark.

On Route 60, curving over the top of the hill, a siren faded as the ambulance hastened to its destination. Its red swirling globes cast an ever-weakening glow through Ian's bedroom curtains and onto the immutable familiarity of his walls.

VII

Bryan was the first up and about the following morning. His mother saw little of him these days, his father even less. Bryan was often up and out before the rest of the family even sat down to breakfast.

As Ian hadn't been out of the house much, he didn't know where Bryan went. He went down to the kitchen when he heard Bryan clattering around in the cupboards.

"Where's the bread?" Bryan asked, irritated, as he rummaged around the counter. The question clearly directed fault at Ian.

"Why should I know, fat boy?"

Bryan glared but resisted retaliating.

"Maybe try the fridge," Ian offered. "Mom sometimes puts it in there now. Says it keeps it fresher, or something."

The fridge door opened to reveal the better part of a loaf. Bryan tutted, and nodded. That was his way of saying thanks these days.

"Where you going today?" Ian asked, watching his brother prepare a Fluffernutter sandwich.

Bryan shrugged his shoulders. "Dunno."

"Come on, Bry. You *do* know—wherever it is, you've been going there just about every day this week."

"Keep your ugly ass nose out of it." Bryan shook a finger at his little brother. "And just mind your own bees wax."

They sat down at the breakfast nook while the electronic toaster did its stuff.

"Bryan?"

"What."

"I wanna ask you something." Ian's tone grew somber. "About—about . . . Matt. You know. The things that happened in the woods."

Bryan stared mindlessly out the sliding glass doors to the patio and did not flinch.

"Hmm? Sure. Like what things?"

"Like, what all happened, you know? I mean, one minute we're playing War . . . and then it all changes." He lowered his voice as he leaned sideways on the chair, peering around the corner and up the stairs to make sure his parents weren't awake yet. "I can't believe any of it. One minute we're messing around, sure, a little rough, but then I'm on the floor watch—"

His voice cracked and he had to swallow hard to hold back the feelings. His hand trembled under the table.

"—Watching this—this—*thing*—in the tree, and Jack and Stu are doing things to him! They're tying this rope, and smacking him so hard he coughs this stuff up. And I'm sitting there knowing this isn't really happening. You know?"

Ian was sure Bryan could see the scene too.

"Sorry. Not sure what you mean, kid." Then, after a brief pause where the cold diffident demeanor seemed to loosen: "Probably just a nightmare. You're getting it all a little confused, is all."

Kachuung!

The sound clapped through the silence and Ian recoiled, startled, as the toaster springs popped and presented two perfectly golden slices. Bryan slathered both in butter, adding globs of purple jelly to one, mounds of crunchy peanut butter to the other. He wolfed down the first right there at the counter; the other as he grabbed his rucksack from the living room closet.

"Right. I'm off," he stated blandly as he bounded down the stairs towards the garage. Remembering the noise the big electric door made every time it ground up or down, he changed tack and spun ninety degrees to leave through the back porch instead.

"Bryan," Ian called after him. "Where—"

The door clicked shut behind him.

Ian wanted to follow. But he couldn't.

I just can't.

So instead, he watched through the living room curtains, ducking out of sight when Bryan spun around once to make sure his nosy little brother wasn't spying on him. Ian watched him make his way down the top street at a decent clip, heading towards the bottom of the neighborhood. Towards the fields. And the woods.

"Morning kiddo!"

His father's greeting from the stairwell startled Ian for the second time this morning. He hadn't heard him coming down the hall, or down the rickety steps, at all. Ian immediately wondered if his father had been standing there the whole time, and perhaps even heard some of their conversation.

"Morning," he returned in attempted nonchalance, only half glancing at his father from behind the bay window's long curtain.

"Anything interesting?"

Hare Cockerton was making a beeline for the coffee maker.

"NO." As soon as he'd uttered it, Ian realized his answer was much too abrupt.

"Okay then! Wow, little buddy. Keep your hat on. I'm only asking." Hare Cockerton shook his head and mouthed something that looked like, *'kids.'* Then added: "You in the mood for some breakfast, sport?"

Ian reported rather pragmatically that he'd already eaten, even though he hadn't. He didn't know why he lied about it. He sat down at the breakfast nook anyway, pouring some orange juice while his father browsed through the daily paper, waiting for that delectable, aromatic, first coffee of the morning to bubble and gurgle through the white paper filter.

The headline of the *Tribune Herald* announced that another heat wave was on its way. The sports section, which lay crumpled on the table where Bryan had already pulled it out, was just about the only evidence Harold Cockerton had these days that he did, indeed, have more than one son. Hare straightened the paper with a small nod and folded the sections neatly back together.

"And what are you boys up to today?"

"Don't know. Same old shi—" Ian blurted out but abruptly corrected himself to finish the sentence with "—stuff."

Mr. Cockerton grinned. "Aren't you getting a little cabin fever, hanging around inside the house all the time?"

His concern was enough to show that he cared, but not so much that it introduced unnecessary pressure into the situation. Hare Cockerton was incredibly tactful if nothing else.

Ian shrugged.

"It looks an awfully nice day . . ." his father added, his voice rising at the end, creating more of a question than a statement out of the sentence. What it really meant was, 'why don't you go outside?'

"Maybe," Ian's discomfort came out in his answer. "I don't know. I'm not sure how I feel."

"Okay, big fella. You're the boss."

Ian got up and again peered through the window. His brother was gone from sight now. "I'm not sure . . ." he half–mumbled to himself as his father buried himself in the sports pages.

Veronica came down a little later, pleased to see that her 'boys' (she liked to affectionately include Mr. Cockerton in that classification) had prepared their own breakfasts. She was even more surprised when Harold pulled a plate from the warming oven for her, replete with two slices of buttered toast, bacon and one perfectly cooked egg, sun-ny-side-up. "Wow, Hare. What's the occasion?"

"No occasion, just summer. And things are *fine*." He winked at her as he brought the plate over and tilted his head in Ian's direction. It was his way of indicating that maybe, at last, Ian might be returning a little closer to the way he had been before the whole Matt incident.

"Are you doing anything today dear?" Veronica excitedly asked Ian after rushing through a silent grace over her breakfast plate.

"Mmm," he responded. "Maybe. I might go see Craig. See how he's getting on. That's alright, isn't it?"

"Yes, of course it is. I think you *should* go out. It'll be a good way to break out of this funk you—"

Ian's father threw her a look of 'that will do dear' and she immediately cut herself short.

"Great," Ian's mother simply concluded with a smile and paid deliberate attention to her eggs.

"Can you drop me off, Dad? I don't really want to walk that way."

"No problem. Just be ready by eight-thirty, that's all."

VIII

Ian pulled his rucksack from his bedroom closet and poured the contents onto his bed. A thick musty smell poured out with them.

A compass. *(A birthday present from his uncle Rod last year.)*

Half a Snickers bar. *(Who knows how old.)*

And a magnifying glass. *(A plastic toy, but it did kind of work.)*

These were the pack's only contents.

He slid the compass and the magnifying glass in his jeans pockets before picking up the chocolate bar. It felt hard and was off-color and grainy at its half-eaten end. Still, he sniffed it before tossing it adeptly in the garbage can at the other end of his room.

He shoots . . . he scores . . . and the crowd goes wild!

When his parents went back upstairs to get ready for the day—his mother changing out of her robe and his father preening one last time before heading into the office—Ian hurried in the opposite direction: downstairs to throw together a couple PB&J sandwiches and snag a can of cold Coke from the fridge. In the garage, he grabbed a knock-off Swiss Army knife he'd bought himself two years ago with his birthday money. It only had four or five attachments but it was exactly his type of thing when he was ten. Now it seemed a bit infantile, but it would have to suffice.

"Yo! Let's hit it," his father called out as he hurried down the stairs two at a time and slid around the corner into the kitchen.

IX

Driving through the neighborhood, Ian experienced a warmth and happiness from the things he saw and the way the sun shone so brightly upon them. For the first time since it all happened, he genuinely smiled. Just because.

"How's work?" he asked his father who had turned on the radio already set to a Pittsburgh rock station. He had to admit that his dad was pretty cool sometimes. When he wanted to be. But never was, when Ian's friends were around.

Surprised at the question, Harold Cockerton laughed aloud.

"What . . . ?" Ian asked, confused. "What'd I say?"

His father shook his head, grinning.

"Nothing, bud. Work is work, that's all. I'm just surprised to actually hear you ask me."

He reached over and ruffled Ian's hair.

Ian oddly still enjoyed the feel of his dad's big, heavy hand in his hair. It felt secure and comforting. But he wouldn't dare say so. Instead he simply said: "Are things getting any better?"

"What do you know about *things*?" Hare Cockerton asked.

"I've heard you and Mom talking. And Uncle Rod, too." He looked at his father across the front bench seat. "I'm not stupid, you know."

"No, I know you're not. Not at all."

Their eyes met in a moment Ian would not forget for many, many years to follow.

"Don't you worry about things, big guy. That's what I'm for. Things will be—things are—just fine."

He stopped talking and turned up the Rolling Stones. 'A blast from the last decade,' the DJ announced above Brian Jones' pleading sitar just before Mick Jagger began confessing how he wanted to paint some door black. To Ian, it had always been a literal lyric and he imagined this ornate door being painted with a big sloppy brush every time he'd heard it. But all of a sudden the lines seemed to strike him at a different level as they spoke to his life's newly introduced emotions of fear and uncertainty and anxiety.

They turned off the main road and headed down the secondary which led to the Daltons' and a spattering of other houses. Ian never knew if this gravel road really went anywhere else, or if it was just like a giant driveway for those few well-off households nestled quietly away beneath the trees. Craig lived in the first one on the right. Their driveway was at least a good thirty feet long and covered in blacktop. Just before it connected with the garage, it looped into a circle for a convenient turnaround.

Ian always thought this was pretty fancy stuff.

"Right, Ian. Here we are. I'll pick you up after work, yes?"

"Yeah, sure" Ian confirmed. "And Dad?"

He poked his head back into the car before closing the door completely. "Thanks."

"No problem sport. Have fun now."

Ian gave him the thumbs up and tossed his backpack over this shoulder. He stood and watched as his father pulled away and motored back up the hill, the gravel crunching soothingly beneath the tires as small plumes of dust trailed behind.

Everything was so quiet—and peaceful—here. You could hear everything. The birdsong in the trees seemed amplified. Even the trickling water of the small man-made pond behind the Daltons' house could be heard through the trees, the sound meandering all the way up here to the front yard. Ian breathed in heavily and the perfume of Mrs. Dalton's prize flower garden filled his senses as he turned a full circle, soaking it all in.

He smiled when he noticed Mrs. Dalton's car was still in the drive.

She obviously hadn't left for work yet.

He rang the doorbell, oddly filled with angst about the prospect of seeing her, unsure if he wanted to—

God yes I want to see her . . .

—or not.

. . . but what if she knows? Ughh. She probably knows. Oh man!

The door flung open and Craig was standing there instead.

"Hey scumbag, come on in." He waved his friend inward. The bandage on his head was different to the night before, less messy. Ian was glad his friend didn't look so bad anymore.

"Hi," Ian returned rather lamely. "Where's your mom?"

The question was out before he even realized and it elicited a very strange look from Craig who shook his head, dismissing it.

"You're weird," he couldn't help but add as he walked away into the kitchen.

Ian followed him, turning the corner as Craig's mom appeared from the downstairs bathroom. Kathy Dalton was sporting only a short, ivory silk bathrobe.

"Morning Ian," she noted casually as she passed by, more of a statement of fact than a greeting. Her smell lingered and to Ian it became the scent of the flowers in the garden.

"Want something to eat?" Craig inquired.

Ian had to concentrate hard on the question to respond appropriately, his eyes still following Mrs. Dalton down the hallway.

"Uh, yeah, sure. Okay. I'm starving. What 'ya got?"

Craig splayed a selection of cereal boxes before him on the breakfast bar. "Well, let's see. Hmm. You've got a choice of breakfast cereal, or . . . breakfast cereal. How about that."

They each grabbed a bowl and poured milk over various cereals that resembled neon nuggets more than food.

It was only then, that for some odd reason, Ian noticed his friend was wearing just his underwear. Nifty little Y-front briefs and a stained and rather ragged wife–beater vest. Oh, and that matching white bandage on the back of his head. The perfect accessory.

"Do you always walk around your house like that?" Ian scrunched his nose to accentuate the question.

Craig nodded. "Sure. Why not?"

A drop of colored milk oozed from between his lips as he spoke and fell to the table.

"Gross."

"Yeah? Well watch this!"

Craig held his bowl to his face and sucked in half its contents.

"Don't you dare, Dalton!"

Craig grinned ridiculously, dropping the bowl carelessly to the bar and spilling a good portion from it as he did. *"Phbthaw,"* he attempted from pursed lips.

Ian pulled away and stepped back. "What?!"

"Ahsehd, phbthaw," Craig kindly repeated, trying to articulate, 'piss off.'

Laughing, Ian turned to the doorway and poised to run. Craig pursed his lips, took a deep breath through his nose, and spewed the mush from his mouth. A volley of multi-colored cereal pieces flew through the air and sprayed mostly onto the floor. But some still spattered Ian.

Craig ran the back of his hand across his mouth. "I said, piss off!" He burst out laughing and nearly spilled what little remained in the cereal bowl.

"Idiot," Ian chastised as he wiped the remnant goo from Craig's mouth off his T-shirt and jeans. Once he managed to squeegee most of it away, he rushed at his attacker.

Kathy Dalton entered to see her son being pummeled and broke the two up. "No repeats of yesterday, now. Do you boys hear?"

She waved a finger frantically at the pair of them who held back chuckles while they nodded in agreement. "I mean it, now. Okay?"

"Okay," Craig acquiesced.

"Alright," Ian replied coolly, suddenly remembering the hospital.

"Right." Mrs. Dalton gave her son a sidelong glance but smiled. "And just have fun. After, of course, you clean up that mess!"

She snapped a dishcloth at Craig's butt.

"See you boys later."

They both waved her off and Ian tried to get a glimpse through the window while Craig tidied up the mess, but it seemed awkward and obvious, so he gave it up and helped Craig instead.

"Listen, I need to talk to you," he insisted as they crouched together, wiping the floor.

"Yeah, what about, baggage?" The features on Ian's face must have become somber, for Craig immediately added in an uncharacteristically sedate manner: "Hey, Okay. What's up, buddy?"

"Something's going on with Bryan. I'm not sure. Things just don't seem . . . right. And I want you to help me." He paused to gauge his friend's reaction. When little came he added. "Please."

Craig stood up and threw the cloth into the sink.

"I don't know."

"I gotta find out what's happening with him, Craig."

"I said, I don't know." He turned to face Ian. "There's probably nothing happening with him, man. He's just getting on with his summer. Like you should be doing."

Craig's face expressed detached certainty. But the anxiety in his voice belied it.

"Craig! Matt was hang—"

"Why can't you just leave it, Ian? The kid's dead and buried!" The words rang through the house as if they had no business being uttered by a boy. "He started a fire and it got out of control. He fucked up. That's it!"

They stared at each other from opposite ends of the kitchen. Ian shook his head repeatedly, incapable of believing the words Craig was saying.

"Craig? What the hell? It wasn't that, and you know it! You told me you saw it. You saw it all."

"I *didn't* see it. I told you, I r-r-ra—"

Craig's voice had quickly raised to a loud, high pitched crescendo and now wavered on the edge of frantic anxiety. He hesitated before lowering his head. And his voice.

"I told you . . . I ran."

"You're a shit, Dalton. You really are. No wonder I wailed on you yesterday."

Ian snatched his rucksack from the floor and bolted for the front door. Choking back the tears, he shouted out that it wasn't an accident, and Craig damn well knew it. He slammed the front door without looking back and stood trembling on the stoop. After the arid air conditioning of the house, the intense July heat made his lungs burn as it enveloped him.

In the canopy of the trees, the birdsong carried on as before. The pond still trickled and bubbled, its sounds caressing the oppressively still air. Nothing in the world had changed in the mere minutes he had been in the house with Craig. Yet everything had changed. Ian began to feel his own universe crumbling away beneath his feet as the realization that he was alone in this thing, whatever it was, spilled over him in an instant.

No Matt.

No Bryan.

No Craig.

The fears of the last two and a half weeks, the nightmare images which had kept him a prisoner in his own home, didn't just creep back in. They slammed into his mind at full throttle.

His chest began to tighten, his ears filling with a static white treble. He sprinted up the driveway but made himself stop as he turned onto the gravel road to face the steep ascent up the hill. Gathering his thoughts and controlling his quickened breathing, he forced his restless legs to walk despite everything inside which urged him to run.

He was mostly up the hill when he first heard the shout. It was loud and brusque, and echoed back and forth between the channel cut through the hillside. He did not turn and did not stop.

"Hey! Wait," the reverberating instruction insisted again.

This time Ian turned. Dwarfed by the distance between them, the figure started to run up the hill, dust and sediment kicking into small clouds beneath its feet.

"Wait," Craig shouted between panting breaths, much more a request than a demand this time. When he finally pulled alongside Ian, soaked with perspiration, he added between heaving inhalations: "Thanks."

"What do you want?" Ian's reply was unabashedly terse. He didn't care. He was even a little glad that it sounded so.

"Look!" Craig offered up a small rucksack, still catching his breath. Inside, held in check by drawstrings, were a couple of fresh but hastily made sandwiches slopping around loosely, and some pieces of hardware Ian could neither discern, nor had little interest to. "I'm coming with you. Let's do it."

A fragmented smile crept onto Ian's face, despite his conscious attempt to repress it.

"You got dressed fast—"

"Yeah, well. I didn't want you to . . . you know . . . go in there, wherever, all on your own. And check this out," Craig bellowed after another deep inhalation, thrusting the rucksack closer to Ian's face. "I don't know what's going on. And I don't care. Well, I do really. But you know what I mean. I suppose we can find out together?"

His offer was in no way a direct apology, but Craig considered it good enough to be one and felt all the better for it.

"C'mon, check these babies out!" He shook the rucksack again, now so close to Ian's face it looked like a farmer about to fasten a feedbag to a horse's muzzle. When Ian failed to lower his eyes, Craig plunged his arm into the bag all the way up to his elbow, fished around for a moment then pulled out a handful of short, stubby red tubes. Each had an inch of stiff, waxy green string poking from the center of its barrel.

"What are they?"

Craig's eyes lit up, his smile so wide that his front teeth poked over the edge of his bottom lip.

"M-80s!"

He stood like this, nodding inanely, for more than a few moments.

Ian's expression did not change.

"Aww, c'mon man!" Craig's disappointment in the dramatic effect lost upon his friend's naiveté was palpable. "Firecrackers, dude! Cherry bombs. Explosives! They're like an eighth of a stick of dynamite each, or something. Should handle just about anything we come across."

He smiled big again. That cheeky, unmistakably Craig Dalton grin.

And Ian's world suddenly felt much more recognizable.

X

The two boys walked at a steady pace the rest of the way up the hill and turned onto the main road. Few cars passed by them, most people using this route already at work by now. The occasional station wagon full of kids drove by, always at a snail's pace, no doubt a mother making her daily pilgrimage to the local swimming pool just a few miles from here. Ian always pulled faces at the brats who stared obnoxiously from the back seats, and enjoyed watching as they turned to snitch to their mothers. Unfortunately, by this time they would be chugging away out of view and Ian never got to see the mother's reaction. Inwardly he hoped it was retribution upon the kids for disturbing her concentration while she was driving and, he liked to think, probably no ice cream for the brats that day.

Well, he could wish, anyway.

"Sheesh, its hot. I wish *we* had some ice cream or something."

With no one around, Craig wondered why the random emphasis on the 'we' part of that statement, but couldn't be bothered to ask. Probably something to do with those kids in that car, he guessed. He agreed anyway.

They strode silently across the searing asphalt for a good five minutes before he prodded out of the blue:

"So, douche nozzle. Tell me. About your brother then."

Craig expected a laugh, or maybe a poke or punch. But if Ian heard what he proudly thought to be a most creative insult, it didn't land.

"I don't know where to start. Nothing really too strange, I suppose. Just that Bry's not been his normal self. Like . . . at all."

Ian kicked sluggishly at a largish stone, sending it bouncing erratically across the road.

"Yeah?" Well you've not exactly been Mr. Personality these last few weeks. And as for the last coupla days . . . ."

Craig shook his head and sucked air between his teeth, making an exaggerated noise like he'd seen his old man do when he sternly disapproved of something.

Ian ignored it.

In the sunshine and warmth, everything that had happened in the Little Woods seemed so far away now. And so long ago. Like one of those dreams you wake up knowing that you'd had, but can't remember any of its details. And the more you try, the more it wisps away, until even the story line is a blur. Leaving you with only that queer, uneasy, hollowed-out feeling.

Perhaps Craig was right about the whole Matt thing. Maybe, Ian started to think, it had been an accident. Maybe his mind had blown it all out of proportion. Maybe the fear and the pain and the darkness—

that sudden darkness

—as he sat there in the clearing with a gash in his temple and his knee all swollen and hurting, had distorted and amplified everything. Maybe it was all in his head. Maybe Craig was right.

About everything.

"Mmmm," is all Ian was willing to admit out loud.

"Mmmm?" Craig repeated. "Mmmm? Seriously, Ian? Like, wow, dude. You've not been acting anything close to normal yourself. But, I'm out here with you. In this goddamned heat. So you better have something better than 'Mmmm' for why you think there's something weird going on with your brother." He lowered his voice to a whisper without realizing it. "After all, bud. He did try and save the kid, didn't he?"

Ian really hated how Craig always referred to Matt as 'the kid' or some other dismissive, offhand term. Matt had been their friend. A bit timid, even wimpy, perhaps. But their friend all the same. They all went to school together. They all ate at the same cafeteria table together. They all rode on the same school bus together, near the back where their seniority allowed because they were in the sixth grade now, at the top of the primary school totem pole.

"Yeah. He did."

They walked in more silence until the road split at a junction: the top road heading back up towards the main neighborhood, the bottom road meandering towards Sowtern, not far from their school.

Ian looked first one way, then the other.

"The question is, which way do we go now?"

He peered into the scant woods near the top road, allowing himself to just be in this moment. Perhaps he would feel the way.

Sense it.

He closed his eyes and listened as the sound of a small stream burbled beneath a stone bridge nearby. He allowed its soothing sound to flow through him, just as the creek itself flowed through the trees. For a fleeting moment Ian could feel it, could *see* the way. But just as the elusive haze of dream, the sensation was gone—a colorful wisp of steam that wafts away the more you try to clutch at it.

He sighed, loud and heavy.

"Dang it. I'm really not sure what we're supposed to do right now."

"Well. It's a good thing I do know," Craig informed him with coolest indifference, his beaming smile belying the feigned nonchalance. "We go that way, buddy boy."

He pointed past the bridge, to where the woods grew thicker.

If Ian's eyes could shoot darts, Craig would have looked like he'd been trying to make out with a porcupine.

Craig shrugged.

"Dude, whaddya want me to say. They asked me to join them."

"And . . . ?"

"And nothing. I didn't go. Think I'm crazy?"

This time Ian shrugged.

Craig *harrumphed*.

"Anyway. It's there." He waggled his finger in the vicinity of the bridge. "Somewhere, thataways. So are we going . . . or what?"

But Ian was already off the road.

Nine

1995

THE NEIGHBORHOOD SPREAD out before them as Bryan and Ian walked in silence, the bright sun and warm breeze calming Bryan in intervals until Ian could sense a baseline of lucidity in his brother. Not wanting to dive into the subject so brusquely, he commented instead on how little the neighborhood had changed since treading these same roads so many years earlier.

"I see the Daniels moved on, though," he noted of one of the few differences. Surrounded by the intimately familiar trappings of his youth, he was sharply aware of just how conspicuously different his voice sounded. Having convoluted over the years, his accent now possessed that thick, gruff New York inflection. It was both odd and a little disconcerting, and the thoughts evoked images of Felipe Menendez and their deli near Times Square. He wondered how his friend was doing. And this, in turn, began to elicit horrid images of Tony's bar—

Ian forced himself to extinguish the memory before it could hijack his amygdala. He needed to stay focused right now, and brooding over something in the past that was utterly out of his control would not help him handle what was in his control right now: and that was figuring out why both he and his brother were being haunted by such gruesome, increasingly vivid, memories from what had happened in the Little Woods so long ago.

He lifted his arms over his head and clasped his hands together behind, welcoming the heat of the morning sun as it swept over his breast and cleared his clouded mind.

"Yes," Bryan answered. His voice was still shaky, but it steadied the more he spoke. "They just up and moved one day. I knew they had their house on the market, but it wasn't on for very long. One day I come home from work and Becky says the 'For Sale' board's been taken down and they'd gone. It was a shame, really. I always liked Mr. Daniels."

"Gone?" Ian asked.

Bryan nodded.

"Just like that." He snapped his fingers to accentuate the point.

"So, how long ago was that?"

"Hmm," Bryan played a finger over his chin while he thought. "Must've been four—no five—months ago."

Ian nearly tripped, stopping abruptly. Maybe Bryan wasn't fully clear-headed yet. Understandable, given everything. "Wait. You must mean five years, Bry. Surely?"

He stared at the abandoned property which had once been so lively. The Daniels had hosted the neighborhood's annual summer picnic, a custom which all the families had both anticipated and participated, for as far back as Ian could remember. It was also his few memories where he recalled the neighborhood as one cohesive, happy, community. The bungalow's appearance was diametrically opposite to those memories now. The once crisp paintwork had faded to a dim yellow. (Closer inspection would reveal intense blistering across much of its facade.) Large sheets of splitting, sun–bleached plywood covered window frames. Knee high weeds had overtaken the once impeccably kept lawn and swayed in the weak breeze, the whispering sound pulling on Ian's attention as if speaking to him. He had to shake his head to ward off the disturbing sensation.

"So what happened to them? This house, it used to be so full of life." He waved an empty hand at the property. "Now look at it. Don't the Daniels need to sell it? Don't they need the money, wherever they now are?"

Bryan shook his head. "Don't know. Haven't heard from them since." He cocked his head slightly to one side and peered from beneath what had grown to be huge, bushy eyebrows.

Ian averted his eyes and continued walking. "It seems strange, that's all. Know what I mean?"

Bryan shrugged. "Happens all the time. People get fed up, move on. And they had to be around retirement age, after all. Maybe they relocated to Florida. I mean, could you blame them?"

"I'm not just talking about the Daniels. I don't know. Maybe this whole thing has upset me more than I'm letting on. Everything here seems wrong." He scanned the area as if to accentuate the point. "It feels . . . off. Like I'm experiencing it, but it's like it's a veneer, or something."

Bryan shook his head soberly.

"Yeah. Well," he said, paused, then looked like he was going to throw up. He bent down and held his knees, mildly heaving. The images, which in the kitchen had ticked frame–by–frame, faster and faster into his conscious memory, now played in one steady but spasmodic stream: the pages of an aberrant flipbook being erratically thumbed.

Bryan's stomach came up. Rebecca's eggs and buttered toast pebbledashed the verge alongside the road. After catching his breath, he swiped the back of his hand across his mouth.

"I'm okay, I'm okay." He shooed away Ian's attempt to reassuringly pat him between the shoulders. "But why don't you tell me what the hell you think is going on here, Ian."

Ian stared down at his feet and the sticky tar surface of the road.

"Talk to me a little more first, okay Bry? Give me a moment to think how to explain it. Then I will. I promise."

Bryan sighed, took a moment.

"Alright then . . . . I guess I can tell you what I never shared about old man Raker." He pointed across the road and Ian's eye followed to the large stone house nestling beneath the branches of the willows.

"He died last November. Very strangely."

II

"Jimi and Jack's old man? What happened, he get shivved in general population by some lifer with nothing to lose that despises child killers as much as the rest of us?"

Bryan shook his head. "No, he was out, Ian. He was released last year.

Sometime just before Halloween."

"Wait, what? He got out of the slammer? Why didn't you tell me!"

"They curtailed his sentence by three years. Compassionate leave, is the word on the street. Something to do with congestive heart failure. He was on his last legs anyway, so they let him go."

Ian squinted with sharp disappointment, the lines furrowing his brow and pulling his mouth into a frown. "I didn't know. I really didn't."

But deep down, he wondered if he hadn't; if last November he hadn't just known . . . hadn't *felt* it somehow. An unsettling reverberation deep within him.

"Yes," Bryan continued. "I didn't want to tell you. Not at the time."

Ian shook his head. "Why not?"

"I don't know, Ian," Bryan said matter-of-factly. "They said he had a massive coronary. I don't remember much leading up to it, but I do remember that particular week. Vividly, in fact. It was cold. You know that bitter cold when there's no snow. You know how it gets when it's like that." His tone suggested a question, more than an assertion.

Ian nodded and they walked on.

"We'd had a pretty good autumn. Up until then, the summers weren't anything like as hot around here, or at least they didn't seem to be, as they were when we were kids. Y'know? But last summer was one of those hot ones. Really hot. And it lasted well into the fall. We paid the price though. When winter hit, it hit us good and hard.

"It was absolutely freezing by the end of October. Ice everywhere. And it didn't seem to melt. I had to get up like an hour earlier every day just to get to work on time, the roads were that bad."

The brothers both gazed quietly for a moment at the cold stone face of the Raker house as they came closer, the images of Bryan's narrative becoming solid against the real backdrop they were seeing.

"And every morning, as I'm out scraping the windows of my car—and you have to understand, it's still dark at that time—old man Raker is outside in his back yard, doing . . . something. I don't know what."

The sound of their footsteps cuffing against the warm blacktop intensified Ian's concentration and the visuals elicited by his brother's story. Steadily, rhythmically, their steps beat softly into Ian's subconscious.

"And? Did you ever find out ... ?"

Bryan nodded.

"Well, sort of. That cold snap lasted just a good ten days or more. A lot of people were housebound the final few days of it because the roads were just that bad. Then old Mr. Walston down the road came to see me, noticing that I still managed to struggle to work each day. He asked if I would help a few of the men check on some of the older residents and younger families in the neighborhood. You know, to make sure everyone was okay, had enough groceries, heating, no frozen pipe problems. Things like that. If they did, I could always grab a few things while I was in town the next day.

"Anyway, Walston and myself and two other guys went knocking on doors. We took a half dozen houses each. Luckily everyone in my patch was okay. But Walston wasn't so lucky."

"Raker ..." Ian deduced and Bryan nodded.

"Walston got no reply at the front door. Since Mr. Raker rarely ventured out, and he certainly wouldn't have under those conditions, Walston went round to the back to try that door."

Bryan inhaled deeply, interrupting his own flow.

"He couldn't believe it. Says he's never seen anything like it, and hopes he never will again. Old man Raker was on the ground in the middle of the yard. A half-bottle of Scotch next to him. Walston knew he was dead but checked anyway. Raker's body was hard. Frozen solid. Walston tried to turn him over but couldn't, he was actually frozen to the ground. So he bent over him and that's when he saw—" Bryan's voice cracked noticeably. "When he saw his face. Walston said his mouth was stretched so wide he couldn't fathom it. Frozen in this scream. And his eyes were wild, like a hunted animal. And Raker's hands were still reaching—no, wait, *clawing* is how Walston said it—for the back door."

The brothers were quiet as the image played through their minds. Shaking it off, Bryan hurriedly finished the story.

"We still don't know what happened. Perhaps Raker was on the binge and went outside for God knows what reason. Maybe he slipped and fell and was unable to get up again. Broke his leg maybe. But that's the way he died. The coroner report was hypothermia. Me, I'm not so sure."

Bryan looked at his brother, connecting deeply into Ian's eyes.

"The strange thing, the thing nobody understands, is why he had a shovel with him. The ground was frozen. Like frozen inches deep. And he'd dug right through it; had a hole a few feet deep in his back yard. I saw it later myself. And temperature readings indicated he'd been digging at least some time during that night, if not right before the accident. So the *Tribune Herald* reported."

Ian inhaled deeply and stared across the road as the Raker house moved slowly by with each step they took. Despite the searing heat of the morning, he felt a sharp, almost icy, sensation. He had to force himself to look away.

"Christ," he muttered and bowed his head as they passed.

†††

By the time they reached the southernmost tip of the neighborhood's figure eight layout, a small cluster of dark clouds had obscured the bright morning sunlight, threatening rain. In the adjacent fields, young sweet-corn swayed on one side of the tractor path, wheat stalks on the other. Together they created a perpetual wave as they bent in successive unison across the landscape in the strengthening breeze.

"Should we head back?" Ian asked as he looked first at the darkening sky, then his watch: 11:11.

"Don't be such a big girl," Bryan chided. "Since when've you been afraid of a little bit of rain?"

Ian remembered the rain. And what had preceded it. Back then.

Bryan kicked a stone from under his feet and watched it travel across the blacktop and into a ditch on the other side of the road.

"Besides. It's time for you to talk."

The brothers strode the same direction as the stone's journey, as the first drops of rain spattered the hot black surface, sizzling as each one struck. "Okay," Ian agreed.

Bryan nodded, although not at all certain he was ready to hear what Ian was about to reveal.

IV

Ian knew of no other way to start the conversation but to just lay it out there. He'd tried before but this time it had to be blunt.

"It's not over. It's happening again."

The words spurted from him so quickly and without inflection that Bryan nearly asked him to repeat himself. But he didn't. Deep inside he'd already known what the revelation would be, even though he could barely believe it now that it was out.

"Jesus, Ian."

"Our phone call, last Monday?" Ian prompted as a reference point.

"Yes?"

"I haven't told you about what happened. But I'd been in a bit of a crisis earlier." He swallowed hard before continuing. "Seems some fucking lunatic in a bar didn't like my choice of baseball team. He pulled a .38 from his pants, Bryan. He shot an old man, this old homeless guy, for no reason other than him breathing too hard. Fuck, Bryan, the old guy was scared!" Ian lowered his head. "We all were . . . ."

He then recounted the whole story, leaving nothing out.

"For God's sake, Ian. Why didn't you tell me earlier? Why didn't you say something that night you called?"

Ian waved the question down, his stomach sickeningly tight, pulling on his abdomen. His voice trembled nervously.

"Let me finish. There's one more thing. The most important part of it. Like I said, I passed out. And when I came to, my mind was filled with all these confusing images. Of the bar, the baseball game for Chrissakes, the old guy . . . ." He took a deep breath. "Bry, I saw Mom and Dad's crash. Jesus Bryan! Do you understand? That was half a day before it happened. But I saw it. All of it. God help me I saw it and it was horrible. And there was nothing I could do to stop it!"

He broke the train of thought to consider one final time the weight of what he was about to reveal. Once said, it could not be unsaid. His voice lowered, his eyes wetting, as he tremulously admitted:

"Matt was there, Bryan. By the roadside. And he was . . . *smiling*."

He could say no more. The emotion bottled so tightly inside came spilling out in a rash of cries and tears.

And now it was Bryan holding his brother.

In the empty neighborhood road.

As the late morning sky succumbed to grey and finally opened, the rain pouring down in sheets upon the two grown men in a solemn embrace.

ten
1977

HE WOODS WERE a respite from the searing heat of the blacktop. A soothing, damp coolness washed over Craig and Ian as blistering white sunlight dimmed to amber hue beams through the trees. Moss and lichen softened their steps as the boys walked silently on, watching the play of their shadows in the delicate breeze which somehow whispered around them.

Craig was first to break the silence, his voice was foreign and loud amidst the serenity.

"It was gross."

"What?" Ian was conscious of keeping his voice low.

"The funeral. You know. It would have been better, maybe, if you were there with me. But it was weird."

Their feet crunched along the twigs and natural debris between the trees. Ian had to jump to clear a small puddle which surprisingly hadn't yet dried.

"There was this casket—it looked small, man—with the lid closed. They *had* to keep it closed. But Matt's mom kept telling everybody that they were burying him in that nerdy blue suit he had. You know, the one he wore for school pictures last year. With those stupid anchors on the metal buttons? The whole thing was just . . . creepy."

He stopped and pulled a can of Coke from his bag, tapping twice on the tab before pulling the ring and flinging the sharp aluminum teardrop to the ground.

Ian sat down on a log and kicked the plants from beneath his feet. He scraped a stick in the dry dirt clearing, doodling.

"I thought at least your brother would have been there," Craig picked up where he left off. "With your parents I mean. I saw your parents."

"Yeah," Ian agreed without looking. He stared blankly at nothing in the distance and scratched.

Craig offered the can. "Want a drink?"

Ian shook his head.

In the high branches of a nearby tree a large crow took flight and an uncomfortable shiver raced down Craig' back as the wings beat furiously at the air, slicing through the silence like gunshots.

Ian's doodling stick snapped in two.

Craig crouched down next to him.

"So . . . this is really shaking you up, huh. I don't want to get into any arguments or anything, but I still don't think it was anything but an accident, man." He shivered momentarily despite the warmth. "I mean, I'm not happy about it. Hell, it scares the shit out of me, but I really don't think there was more to it than that. And your brother—he tried to help the kid too."

"I don't know. I can't explain it. Things are all jumbled."

. . . the Whistle crying out as the woods grow dark, as if the very song has bid the sun to shine no more as the darkness closes in upon them . . . the woods that send the Beast Bear . . . to take the cartoon Ranger within its stride and carry him into the treetops . . . turning him inside out . . . .

Ian scuffed away the doodle in the dirt with the toe of his sneaker.

"That darkness, Craig. That wasn't just dark. It wasn't just a dark, man it was black. The Woods were pure black. You couldn't see an inch in front of your face—it was like blindness. And all the boys were there! Didn't you see them? They were there, but not there, like something sick and twisted was controlling them. Like puppets. Like really weird, fucked up, evil–assed puppets . . . ."

Craig was dismissive.

"All I saw was Matt, dude. And that bonfire he made. But there was no one else there, Ian. I'm telling you, you've got things all mixed up in your head. Just like you said you do.

"You're right about one thing though, that storm was a motherfucker. So everyone must've taken off when that shit went down, just like me."

Craig waited for Ian to respond, but none came.

"I mean I'm sorry I didn't help you, dude. I didn't even know you were there. But I saw Bryan, and that was good enough for me. I mean, I may not care for him much, y'know, but when all's said and done, your bro's a pretty solid dude. I knew—"

He paused, and for a minute Ian felt he could sense Craig faltering in his story. Like maybe this whole bullshit facade was getting a bit too much for even his mock bravado to keep up.

The moment passed and Craig was the same old Craig again.

"I don't know what you think happened. I mean, you're not really saying. But I'm starting to put the pieces together. And I'm telling you, the pieces may be all there but you're putting them in the wrong places. The guys are cool, Ian. The same old guys they've always been. I'll show you. They'll be in there," Craig nodded further west, "just messing around. Playing Tree Tag. And Bryan will be there, just messing around with them. You'll see. Nothing wrong with that."

II

The morning gave way to July heat until even the woods could not cloak the oppressive humidity.

Craig led Ian through the increasingly dense forest, following the slightest of hint of a trail, a newly trampled path that must be the result of the other boys' shuffling feet. Somewhere not too far ahead an invisible chorus of laughter erupted. It twisted and coiled through the trees as it permeated the thick forest.

"There," Craig indicated with an outstretched arm, pointing towards a lighter patch of the beech trees. "There. That's it, over that way. That's what they call the Beechnut."

The closer they got, the more dense the brush and thickets grew, the path less defined, until the boys' progress slowed to the point they could only inch forward, even crawling in some places.

"This means we're almost there now," Craig announced as he absentmindedly pushed aside a thorn bush and the tendril whipped back like a spring. It would've torn across Ian's face if he hadn't ducked aside. Craig carried forward, oblivious.

The shrieks of laughter grew louder and occasionally the ground would resonate as one or another of the gang must've jumped from a considerable height, slammed to the dirt floor below, and planted his feet hard and firm as he landed.

Ian slid against a pine and sat, quietly listening. The voices were mostly clear: Jack and Jimi, Stu, Woody, Bryan. And maybe another he wasn't yet sure of, but must be Big Dan.

A shiver ran down his back as their screaming came to him.

. . . the boys, sticks and rocks in hand, faces masked in grey mud and something red, dancing in a frenzied clamor as they scream and howl around the fire . . . .

He shook his head hard to dispel the image. This was not the same, he told himself. *Not the same.* Craig wouldn't be party to anything like that. He wouldn't lie about something so inconceivable. Craig was his friend, he wouldn't lead him into danger.

"Hey, wait up," he whisper-shouted as Craig was disappearing beneath the heavy undergrowth just ahead of him.

Ian pressed through the same and in a moment, the two were on the edge of a copse of silvery white birch trees which formed a kind of lop-sided cluster around one monumental beech that stretched high above the rest of the forest. Ian settled low within the brush beneath one of the birches, and found himself marveling at the curtain of light which illuminated this place, so dissonant to the duskiness of the woods they'd just traversed. Bright rays of sunshine pierced the forest canopy all around them. It shone like hundreds of translucent arrows through the dust eddies kicked up by the boys' game of Tree Tag, dispelling the dimness in shiny pinpoints in every direction.

It was almost magical.

"The Beechnut," Craig informed flatly in a semi-whispered voice, laying prone and pointing. "It's been here a while, apparently. I remember hearing some older guys, a long time ago, mentioning something about it and how they used to hang out here. No idea why they stopped. But I guess Jack and the gang found it too, you know—after the whole Matt thing in the Little Woods—and thought it was pretty cool as a new hangout spot."

Ian raised a nervous eyebrow and Craig laughed at the look that was comical but wasn't meant to be.

"Shush, you idiot." Ian held a finger to his lips in condemnation. "They'll hear us."

They peered through the undergrowth, following glimpses of motion as they caught flashes of the boys' game through gaps between the brush and trees: Big Dan was pulling himself upright onto a long, thick branch of the big beech tree, Stu jumping frantically up and down on the ground to reach him. Stretching as much as his body would allow, Stu managed to slap the bark firmly as he chased Dan's dancing feet down the limb, and the sound emitted a satisfying *thwack* as he did.

"Go on, Big Dan! Dannie Boy," Woody cheered as Dan worked his way unsteadily along the branch. "Get outta there boy, whoo! Go on!"

Stu tagged him soon afterwards (despite several opportunities to pass the 'it' onto Jack, who blatantly flaunted this alliance each time) and nearly sent him flying from a rickety old tree stand in the large beech tree, a relic of someone's hunting days, long ago.

Big Dan, however, found it quite difficult today pass on the 'it' to anybody, only managing to achieve it by eventually skimming—just barely —a mat of hair on the back of Bryan's head. To be fair, he did so quite acrobatically, not just for Big Dan but by anybody's standards, hanging from a limb by the inside of his knees and stretching down as Bryan clambered along a branch underneath. Dan loosed a rebel yell and asserted most vehemently that hair counted as part of the body, and so Bryan had been tagged. Fair and square.

Not much anyone could say to argue that, and besides, it was rather impressive.

Bryan then tagged Jack quickly, about three minutes later, but fell to the ground as he did. He was therefore out of bounds, the tag rendered void by the rules. You had to stay in the air. At all times.

"Even if you didn't tag Jack," Woody interjected, "you'd still be 'it' because you touched the ground. After all, rules are rules."

And what would society be without rules?

If the ground were to be considered in–bounds or fair game, Woody continued to argue—becoming more and more vexed as he spoke—then it wasn't really tree tag, now was it? It would just be regular old tag. "And that's just gay," Woody added in conclusion, and that sealed the deal for everyone.

Bryan accepted this decision of his peers, but did so under some rather vocal protest. He could tell the game was nearly coming to a close —the boys were all getting a little testy, a little tired and a whole lot hungry—and if they called it a day before he could tag someone else, he would still be 'it' tomorrow when it resumed.

And that kind of embarrassment just wouldn't do.

So, per the rules, Bryan climbed the large beech tree before he was allowed to make his way, through the air only, to any of the thinner but infinitely more elaborate branch systems of the encircling birches.

Filled with steely determination to not be stuck with the 'it' until tomorrow, he worked swiftly to the end of a large branch and in one sin-gle, eloquent move, leapt across a sizable gap to one of the thinnest birches of them all . . . where Woody was perched, already swaying pre-cariously halfway up the young tree.

Thinking the tree too thin and flimsy for anyone else to even attempt to add a second person, Woody had been there for a great chunk of the day's game. Not very exciting, maybe. But effective.

Bryan didn't agree.

He flew through the air and stuck the landing perfectly, wrapping his legs around the birch's thin trunk and throwing his arms into its network of small branches for an unshakable purchase. The whole tree bent back with the force of his momentum and with the burden of now supporting not one but two boys, it bowed so far back that its top nearly touched the ground. Halfway up (or as it were now, halfway across) the trunk Woody scrabbled to keep his hold, finding himself suddenly hanging from the tree at arm's length, his legs dangling, feet kicking to avoid touching the ground. Always tall and lanky on the best of days, Woody—now stretched so long and in such a comical fashion—was the spitting image of that frazzled cat on the motivational poster that read: 'Hang In There, Baby!'

Bryan started chortling.

And then the young, malleable wood of the birch made it rebound like a rubber band. Hugging the tree like a koala, Bryan held his grip. But Woody lost his and went zinging through the air like a frog from a slingshot, arms and legs akimbo.

He hit the ground and tumbled violently across the leaves and dirt. He did not make a sound, only laid motionless, and more than a little bent.

The Beechnut went silent.

All eyes were on their friend as he lay there, sprawled across the ground in a cloud of dust and drifting debris.

When he jumped up with a resilient, 'I'm okay!' the boys erupted in shameless, unabashed whoops and guffaws.

"Dude!" Bryan shouted down between belly laughs, still swaying in the birch like a metronome. "Ground's out of bounds, motherfucker. You're it, Rolly-Polly!"

Even Woody cracked a smile at that. He may be 'it' now, but he didn't care. He had to admit, that shit was just too damn funny.

Still hiding in the undergrowth with Ian at the edge of the Beechnut, Craig giggled. "See, Ian. I told ya," he declared loudly, whispering no longer a concern. "C'mon, let's join them!"

Ian tried to hold him back but only managed to snag the back of Craig's T-shirt, the material sliding easily between his fingers as Craig trotted out into the open. "Craig, no!" he shouted through gritted teeth.

But it was too late; Craig had run into the clearing.

Every head turned.

"Woohoo! Hey look!" Jack shouted as he hung from a branch by one hand, still laughing. "It's scrotebag's friend!"

Bryan knew without looking who Jack was referring to, and the joy in his face dissolved immediately into stark uneasiness.

"Wayhay buddy," Jack reiterated as he hopped to the ground and dusted himself off. "How's it hanging, little dude?"

Craig grinned and self-consciously waved even though they were only feet apart.

"Hey!" Bryan demanded as he hopped to the ground as well, the birch bending down and again snapping back. "Craig! Where's Ian?"

Not sure how to reply, Craig said nothing, only shrugging with an impish smile. Bryan strutted across the clearing and squared up to him, their noses virtually touching.

"I'll ask a second time, Craigy-poos. But I won't ask a third."

"Over there," Craig said skittishly as he thumbed over his shoulder, behind his back to the brush where he and Ian had been hiding.

Bryan pushed him out of the way and trod to the edge of the Beechnut as Jack shouted after him, taunting. "Yeah, that's right! Bring out your little brother, Cockerton! Let's play a game with him!" He began jumping up and down on his branch like a monkey.

Stu followed Jack's lead and started making exaggerated chimpanzee sounds, hopping up and down on the rickety old tree stand. The rest joined in until the air was filled with shrieking, hollering monkey boys.

Suddenly Craig, standing alone in the center of it all, felt unexpectedly vulnerable and very frightened.

While at the edge of the Beechnut, Bryan grabbed his younger brother by the shirt and yanked him up from the weeds.

"What are you doing here!"

His anger contorted his lips so that they curled as he spoke, the words pressing out in a hushed gust of air.

"It's none of your business," Ian defiantly replied as he prized his brother's hands from his T-shirt and shoved Bryan away. "What do you care, anyway?"

Bryan rocked on his heels, still clutching Ian's T-shirt. He gained his balance and pulled Ian even closer. "Look, you don't belong here.

Understand? This is for the big guys. Not little craps like you and your creepy little buddy there."

"C'mon Cockerton, bring out your dead!" Stu hollered in Monty Pythonesque style from the tree stand, clapping his hands in an exaggerated, disturbing fashion.

Dan mimicked him, and together they chanted over and over.

"Bring out your dead bring out your dead bring out your dead!"

"Yeah, come on Cockerton," Jack beckoned. "Bring him out!"

"You're an idiot," Bryan reprimanded his brother in an angry, whispering tone as he pressed his face so close to him that Ian sucked in his exhalations. "Why do you think I wouldn't bring you here, or even tell you about it!"

The condemnation rang deep into Ian's heart and he realized in an instant that maybe this had been a mistake. A big mistake.

"Why couldn't you just let it go . . . like all the others had?" Bryan said and dragged his brother into the center of the Beechnut to present to Jack Raker, who had climbed down from his tree. "Now come on. And be cool,"

"Hello, Cockerton number two." Jack extended his right arm, offering a handshake that Ian refused. "Fine. No problem. It's cool, little Cockerton. I understand." His voice was calm and deep. And sounded sincere. And the unexpected congeniality made an electric tingle run down the back of Ian's neck.

"You little shit, Cockerton," Stu shouted from high in the beech tree, waving a fist. "I am gonna mess you up, you little fucke—"

Stu cut the threat short, ducking to avoid a stone winging past him. It rebounded off one of the tree stand's supports. Out of the corner of his eye, he saw Jack regaining his stance, having been the one who threw it.

Ian stood perplexed but Jack nodded; a reassuring look Ian had never received from the older Raker boy before.

"Don't worry about him," Jack added. "You're okay by me, Ian."

Jack jumped and hoisted himself back into the beech tree. As he climbed, he looked over his shoulder. "You'll be okay here. Really."

Craig, who had been watching anxiously from the center, sighed melodramatically then picked a birch of his own and climbed into it. He chuckled in nervous relief.

Bryan placed his arm around his brother's shoulders. "See that tree?" he asked, directing Ian's attention to a silvery birch with strong, solid limbs extending in all directions. "That's a good one. It's yours now, Ian. Go take it."

Again the Beechnut became a chorus of noise as the boys shouted and jumped to and fro, chasing each other around the trees, laughing and cajoling one another until the sun dipped below the treeline.

And Ian joined them.

III

The boys began the walk home as the low summer sun began to cool, making their way through the woods and into a meadow at the bottom of the neighborhood. The sky was a warm cerise, washing over the field and tinting it with color.

Craig and Ian separated from the rest by walking ahead. Occasionally, a small field mouse would run from the path ahead of them, bending the grass as it scuttled underneath.

"Well, my friend, when I'm right, I'm right." Craig sniggered and scrunched up his nose, still on a natural high. "Don'cha think?"

Reluctantly, Ian nodded.

"Okay already. I said so a million times and we've only just started walking. Give it a rest, will ya." He reached over Craig's shoulder and pulled the rucksack from his friend's back. He hadn't drank the Coke from that morning, and although now thin and warm, it was still refreshing as he gulped it down.

"Like, don't offer me any," Craig advised him sarcastically.

And so Ian didn't.

That evening, Mr. Cockerton came home and decided maybe tonight was the perfect night to take the family out for dinner. He was pleased that Ian was coming back to some form of normality, and even more pleased by the change it was affecting in his wife.

"I told you it would be alright," he said to her, but not in a boastful manner. He pulled her close and hugged her from behind as she stood in front of the bedroom mirror. "All it took was some time."

Veronica reached behind her and clasped her hands around him. "I know. And I'm glad. You don't know how relieved . . . ."

"Well. Never mind that now," Hare Cockerton mumbled wryly as he gently pulled himself away. Sometimes his wife's depth of feeling made him uncomfortable and he had to distance himself from it.

He didn't really know why.

In later years, he would consider this over and over, and quite frankly wonder why she had put up with it—or him—at all. The only thing he could say to himself to assuage the remorse was that sometimes, the amount of stress piled atop him at work was simply too much. Any additional emotion, good, bad or ugly, was just one straw too many. In the back of his mind though, he always knew this must be difficult for Veronica; having no one to speak with, day in and day out.

What a pressure valve he must be for her when he finally walked through that door each evening.

"Come on then, let's go," he beckoned her.

"Just one moment, sweetie. I've got to fix my hair. It's a real mess. You go on and get the boys; I'll be right down."

She waved him off and sat down at the dressing table, running a thick brush quickly and repeatedly over her head.

In the doorway Harold stopped to silently observe the routine. It made him feel safe, though he couldn't have vocalized it at the time.

"Go on then!" she ordered as she spied him in the mirror, waving an impeccably manicured hand. "Shoo!"

Harold Cockerton chased the boys away from the TV; a re-run of the *Brady Bunch* which had captivated them as they stared mindlessly at the screen and munched on peanut butter crackers.

"Whoa, there! We're off to eat in a minute. Don't go filling yourselves up now. Where do you fancy going?"

They shrugged noncommittally without turning.

"Come on, the pair o' you! We haven't been out for ages as a family. Where would you like to go – Taco Bell? Burger King? You name it."

Ian forced his attention away from the television at a commercial break while Bryan continued munching.

"Anywhere?" he asked.

"You name it, and we're there."

"How about Poppy's?"

"You got it, pal. Poppy's it is."

Hare reached over the sofa and playfully wrapped his arms around Bryan's chest in a bear hug, pulling his face close so he could bristle him with his five o'clock shadow.

Bryan made a dissatisfied face but said nothing.

"That okay with you, sport . . . Poppy's?"

Bryan only shrugged but somehow managed to convey a, 'yeah, that's alright with me,' response in the gesture.

Ian chuckled.

It was great at Poppy's Olde Time Pizza Parlour. At least Ian thought so. It was one of those new pizza joints that was really a restaurant. In truth it was big enough to seat several hundred people, and more than one birthday party, if needs be, but it was laid out in intimate sections like a small, local, old-fashioned pizza place.

All the waitresses wore red and white pinstripe aprons over crisp white blouses and black trousers, and they all had to wear this Styrofoam hat that was meant to look like an old straw hat you'd see in pictures of barbershop quartets. They would serve the drink order (Harold Cockerton never missed this rare treat of splitting an ice cold pitcher of their excellent beer between his wife and himself) then told the kids in the group that if you wanted to, you could go watch your pizza being made in the 'spin kitchen'.

The spin kitchen was where you could see, behind this enormous glass window, this guy grabbing the balls of dough, kneading them, then throwing them in the air (sometimes behind his back) and catching them as the newly forming pies spun like Frisbees. They were magically bigger, and flatter, each time he threw them, and Ian and Bryan often sat there so long that their own pizzas went cold on the table before they got bored and rejoined their parents.

Tonight, Bryan ignored the waitress' offer and sat glumly with his parents while Ian went up to kneel on the bench and watch.

"What's the matter, sweetheart?" Mrs. Cockerton asked gently.

Again Bryan shrugged dismissively.

"Dunno. Nothing much really."

Hare Cockerton leaned back and took a sip from his frosted glass.

Bryan watched as his father's fingertips dispelled the mistiness from the outside of the thick mug to leave small, circular impressions. "Maybe I don't feel very well. I'm not sure."

"Do you want to go home?" His mother was already out of her seat before she finished the question.

"Sit down, Veronica. We're going nowhere," Mr. Cockerton told her brusquely and immediately relented. "I'm sorry. But we've only just got here a minute ago, Veronica, for heaven's sake. The boy's fine. Stop babying him ... please."

Bryan actually agreed. "Yeah, Mom. I'm fine. I suppose I'm just not that hungry."

Mr. Cockerton reached across the table and ruffled his hair as the waitress appeared with three round metal trays.

"One large Poppy's Special, a small Mushroom, one small Pepperoni," Mandy, as her name tag proclaimed, read from her notebook. She sliced a piece from both of the smaller ones, then two from the large, placing them carefully onto each plate. "Enjoy your pizza, guys. Shout if you need anything else."

She smiled, mostly at Mr. Cockerton, who happily reciprocated.

Which also did not go unnoticed by Veronica Cockerton.

IV

They went to a movie afterwards, not to the new multiplex downtown with the array of screens, but the old drive-in at Richmont, the one where it was only a buck-fifty for the kids and two dollars for adults. Even so, the occasional teenager would get busted for smuggling in his pals, hidden beneath a blanket in the backseat or—Ian's personal favorite, and the one that made him laugh the most when the stupid kids would get busted—all contorted in the trunk.

The best 'seats' in the house were the parking spots dead-center to the screen and about five rows down from the concession stand: close enough to run to the bathroom or grab another candy bar without missing too much of the movie, but not so close that you had dumb teenagers walking back and forth in front of your car all night long. Now, if you were lucky, you came in a pickup truck and backed into your spot. Boy, was that the ticket! You could lay a sleeping bag or some blankets in the bed and everyone could lounge in the lap of luxury while also being too high up for any passersby to interrupt your viewing (maybe the odd super–tall kid here and there, but even then you only caught the top tuft of his hair, so no biggie.)

The sound for the movies came from this clunky, heavy speaker built out of something that felt like military grade metal. You had to pull it in, latch it to your car window, then wind the window up so it stayed put. Forget about surround sound, or even stereo: this was mono–sound at its fuzzy, tinny best.

And that was if you got one that worked.

More than once, Hare Cockerton had procured that perfect space, loaded up both arms with goodies from the concession stand, got every-one nicely situated . . . to discover the speaker only burbled and reverber-ated incomprehensibly, much the way the adults' voices sound on the Charlie Brown TV specials. Of course, by that time any parking spot with half decent visibility had long been snatched up and you'd end up watching the double feature at an odd, oblique angle that somehow made the movie feel different. But it didn't matter to the boys. The atmosphere was great, and you got loads of popcorn in your bucket. And the fact that it didn't rain tonight only made the event all the better.

Even Bryan managed to perk up as dusk fell and the screen came alight, even though the projector would cast little more than a semitransparent image until a good quarter of the way through the first movie. At least by then the rain had stopped.

With popcorn and chocolates passed around, the Cockertons settled in for a night of cinematic entertainment.

Cartoons: Ian loved the Tasmanian Devil ones the best, whereas Bryan preferred the old black and white Disneys.

First movie: Burt Reynolds as this guy called 'Bandit' who is basically a trafficker of contraband beer to Georgia while being pursued by a hapless and overzealous sheriff. Hare and Veronica Cockerton thought it was a bit inane and perhaps a little too mature in parts, but the boys liked it and laughed a lot, so that made them happy.

Second movie: Paul Newman as the captain of a ragtag hockey team desperate for glory in some small, dead end town. Although rated R, it didn't much matter as Ian was sound asleep before the opening credits; Bryan was awake a little longer but out like a light before the Hanson brothers threw their first fists.

The drive home was late and quiet. Not much traffic on the roads, and both boys dead asleep, leaning into each other with the travel rug wrapped unevenly between them, Bryan having most of it.

Veronica sighed and rested her head against the seat.

"It was a great night, Hare. Thank you."

She admired how the orange glow of each street lamp they passed played rhythmically across her husband's strong features—his strong cheekbones, masculine chin—and she ran the back of her hand lightly against his cheek, playfully fingering his neck with her nails.

Mr. Cockerton glanced briefly at her, smiled, then returned his concentration to the road.

"It was nice to spring it on us," she reiterated. "I think we all needed a little, I don't know, a little . . . something, But I still can't—" She stopped herself short. She knew it was a mistake to even think what she was, let alone mention it.

"Can't what?" Harold broke his gaze from the road once more, this time slightly longer.

Veronica turned away, staring out the window.

A light drizzle began to speckle the glass.

"Nothing, dear. Pay me no attention . . . . It's starting to rain."

Harold slowed the car and began pulling carefully toward the verge. The boys were sound asleep, so taking a few extra minutes to get home wouldn't matter. And besides, Hare didn't really feel like having this conversation later when he was trying to quiet his mind for sleep. Better to hear her out now, get it out in the open. Whatever it was. And go home —and to bed—happy.

He slowed the Ford and edged over, preparing to stop.

A boy racer in a souped-up 'Cuda had a different idea. The muscle car's engine growled loudly as the boy behind the wheel stepped on the accelerator and clutch at the same time, announcing in no uncertain terms his displeasure at their current speed. He inched up until Harold was certain they must be about to kiss bumpers.

"C'mon Grandpa, outta the way!" the boy shouted, shoving his head out the open driver's side window despite the growing rain. He simultaneously flashed his high beams in case his discontent weren't yet obvious enough.

The hot blacktop sizzled as the rain increased, and Harold could feel the traction of the Ford's tires shifting out of balance. The front passenger side started to crunch across loose gravel, the driver's side fighting for purchase on the quickly slicking blacktop.

If the kid were to bump them now, whether deliberately or by mistake wouldn't matter, he'd send their Ford into a dangerous fishtail that would careen them across the road out of control.

So Harold pressed his foot on the gas and pulled the wheel gently to the left. The passenger tire screeched as the wheel bumped back up onto the paved surface and momentarily spun until it matched the speed of the driver's side. Harold tightened his grip on the steering wheel and pressed his right foot further down. The Ford straightened and accelerated, quickly creating a breathable gap between the cars.

The family sedan may have been fast, but the Plymouth was faster. Within seconds the racer was on them again, bumper–to–bumper as they approached the blind crest of Hamburger Hill (so named because of its array of neon–lit hamburger and fast food joints, as opposed to the famously bloody battleground in Vietnam, eight years earlier).

Another moment, and the kid was pulling out to pass them.

The 'Cuda roared next to them in the oncoming lane and through his periphery, Harold caught the kid grinning as he whipped them the finger.

Then came the glow of headlights in the opposite direction.

In an instant they flooded the apex of the hill in blinding prisms which reflected off the streaking rain. Then the tractor trailer itself came into view, barreling up the hill towards them at incredible speed behind those brilliant high beams.

Harold slammed on his brakes.

The Ford buffeted from side to side as each tire fought inanely for purchase on the wet asphalt. A moment later, the suspension loosened and the sedan slid sideways as the truck crested the hill.

Fully alongside their Ford, the engine in the boy racer's car screamed in protest as the kid jammed his foot all the way down to the floor and slapped the quick–shifter down into second. The 'Cuda shot forward, sliced in front of the Cockerton's car at an angle, and all but kissed the Ford's front driver's side fender before righting itself as the truck driver brayed the air horn furiously but did not slow.

The truck flew past.

Harold gained control of the Ford as the semi's tail lights disappeared in his rear view mirror, the boy racer's rear lights blending into a curtain of rain and exhaust ahead of him.

He was still shaking as he pulled into the parking lot of the Savings &

Loan at the bottom of the hill, his fingers trembling as he placed the gearshift into PARK. He hadn't yet steadied his nerves, or his frantic breaths, before attempting to ease the tension by saying to his wife in a broken, nervous warble: "You were saying?"

Veronica Cockerton could only stare, pie–eyed and quivering.

Surprisingly, the boys slept through the incident almost entirely. Bryan woke only when the truck driver blasted his horn, and then only briefly. Ian managed to sleep throughout.

Once confident everyone was okay, Harold Cockerton gathered himself and stepped out to assess the damage. Again, surprisingly, only a small scratch; hardly noticeable in what little light was shed by the bank's luminous LED sign that vacillated interminably between the present time and present temperature.

Why do banks always have those, he couldn't help but think as he shielded his eyes from the rain.

V

The boys walked slowly in a daze to their rooms, not really waking for the job but allowing muscle memory to do the walking. Mrs. Cockerton merely had to point them in the right direction and, like huge wind-up toys, they stepped mechanically up the stairs and collapsed onto their beds in the dark. She would have preferred they change out of their clothes, but doubted highly that they would.

Rubbing his hands over his arms, Harold Cockerton turned up the thermostat to dispel the lingering dampness. And before long, he and Veronica were also tucked comfortably into bed.

Ian, fully atop his quilted down comforter, succumbed easily to warm, beckoning sleep. He did not stir as the radiators in his room began to click, the hot water churning through the cool pipes. As the water pressed more forcefully through, and the pipes began to ring gently in a soft, whistling chorus, Ian twitched.

Lightly.

Behind closed eyes his mind opened to somewhere familiar, yet also very strange to him.

A cliff top. Overlooking a beach as the waves pound over the rocks.

His friend Craig is with him though Craig, too, is not exactly the same. The boy walking by his side is an idea of Craig more than an entity. It is a warm and comfortable presence, however, and the two chat and laugh. Then comes the woman, a beautiful and caring woman. Ian senses Craig is still with him, but is also not there as his focus is drawn more intently upon this woman who seems to melt into many different women. The faces waver in and out and dissolve together and suddenly he is elsewhere.

This place is dark and cool; the moon full and bright.

He is now looking down upon a quiet wilderness below, and also upon himself, watching his body float in space. Together he and Craig fly, the air moving in currents around them as they turn freely in all dimensions of space, the boundaries and ties of the ground no longer a factor. In the distance, a light flashes dark amber and they glide to follow it. It glows from below, within a wood, and without moving they are already there. No longer gliding, they walk to the light as a new sensation of bitter cold snaps the air crisply.

The cartoon Ranger pops up from nowhere, a comical appearance, and they laugh and sing and this joy carries them far, far away from the glow.

But they are curious about the entrancing dark light and must go back. The Ranger shakes his head—No!—They must not to go! But they do not listen and turn from him. The cold has become fierce now and the glow in the woods draws them, promising warmth. The Ranger has followed faithfully behind and pleads as a whistling like countless flutes starts to sing. But the boys ignore his words, even pressing him away.

They are upon the glow, where the flames lick high into the air and eradicate the darkness, beating back the cold, windless air.

Other boys materialize and join them around the fire, laughing and shouting and nearly crying with excitement. They are eating something pinkish, like strips of firm cotton candy.

Then the Beast Bear is in the tree.

It opens its gargantuan jaws and the black hole of its mouth unleashes a scream like nothing Ian has ever heard. The piercing cry slices through the very fabric of the air around them as the Beast launches from the tree. Instantly it is upon the boys and has one of them in its massive, twisted claws. Blood spurts and sprays the camp, speckling the others, as the boy's headless body stands momentarily before shuddering to the floor, slapping to the dirt like a dead fish.

The Beast Bear now turns to Ian and Craig and opens its face once more, creatures within the catacomb of its throat catapulting out and onto them. They burrow and writhe into their skin. Craig screams and falls to the ground and now Craig becomes the cartoon ranger as the creatures bury into his torso. They multiply and cover him, Craig's eyes bulging as the silvery parasites crawl and tunnel behind his eyelids—

Ian flailed out of the nightmare, bolting upright in his bed. A scream tried to force its way out but never did, stifled instead within his throat as his heart beat fast and hard in his chest. He swallowed and gasped for air, clawing the bed quilt into bunches.

Only a dream. It was only a dream, he assured himself over and over. His lips were sore and dry and his tongue felt thick and at the back of his throat. The room and its varying grades of black swam before his eyes until, slowly, its comforting reality dissolved the dream and his breathing settled and his heart rate calmed, the painful pounding in his chest subsiding. Near the little ivory Buddha on his bookshelf, the bold numbers of Ian's LCD clock glowed weakly orange, announcing some time he couldn't make out. He blinked his eyes to clear them and concentrated on the the two blinking dots which separated the hour from the minutes. They pulsed in and out with each passing second.

2:22 swam into focus.

He took a deep breath and steadied himself against the soothing, solid certainty of the wooden headboard pressed against his back.

Craig Dalton had really wanted to go to the drive-in movies with Ian, but had been told it was a family night out, so Ian wasn't allowed to invite him. Which really sucked fat ones 'cuz they were probably gonna hit Poppy's Pizza first. And man, Craig could sure go for one of those thin, greasy slices right now. Plus those waitresses with their uniforms would be a yummy sight. Especially that one with the bodacious boobies. He didn't actually know her name, but called her Campbell's because she was *Mmm Mmm Good!*

Now he was hungry. And a little horny.

I'm such a horn dog!

Which made him think of wieners. So he threw a couple cheese stuffed hot dogs in this cool new microwave oven appliance his father had paid a couple of guys to install above the stove a few weeks ago. Craig didn't know how it worked, but it somehow cooked food super fast. Zapped it with some kind of rays. Or something.

It *dinged* after two minutes and Craig pulled out the steaming wieners, laughing at how they had bulged and blistered irregularly, one of them having swollen quite considerably at one particular end so that it looked unmistakably like something else.

He was still laughing as he slathered the dogs with mustard and sauerkraut and plopped down on the couch to scarf them both up as he watched *Charlie's Angels*.

Halfway through the show he ran to the kitchen. By the time he returned with a round tray of Jiffy Pop popcorn, he'd missed the whole story line explaining who this guy was that was stalking Kelly on the beach.

So, that was pretty annoying.

Next time he'd have to tell his mom to get some of that new microwave popcorn. He figured that would've popped and been done before the commercials were even over. Luckily, Craig didn't find it all that cerebrally taxing and managed to catch up before the next break. Anyhow, he didn't exactly watch it for the show's twisting plot lines. The chance to leer over Farrah Fawcett and Jaclyn Smith for an hour may have had something a little more to do with it. (That other one was hot too, Craig guessed. The one who played Sabrina, with the more nasally voice. But her character's hair was always just a little too short for his personal tastes, so he was never bothered to make the effort to remember the actress' name.)

The first of his friends to have cable TV, he flicked aimlessly through something like fifty channels, stopping any time there was a girl in a skimpy outfit or tight, little bathing suit. Of course these scenes never lasted more than a minute or two, and so the whole process was quickly becoming rather laborious.

Which gave him the next idea.

Craig's parents had gone out to dinner, his mom reassuring him they wouldn't be too late, although they would likely go out dancing for a bit afterwards. Which really meant that Kathy and Charley Dalton wouldn't be home for hours.

They had been taking disco lessons, practicing their moves in the basement, and Kathy Dalton exploited every opportunity to flaunt those new moves on the actual dance floor whenever possible. Charley Dalton wasn't so keen, but he loved his wife. He loved even more the fact that he was the guy Kathy would be draped over as they walked out the door together at the end of the night, reveling in the envious looks from all the other men who had been admiring his wife the whole time. To Charley, that elevated feeling of masculine superiority was a pretty even trade.

Certain he had a good hour or more before they would be home, Craig fiddled with a few buttons on his black Casio watch then bounded upstairs and tried the door to his parents' bedroom. He grinned as the knob turned and the door swung open, his old man having forgotten to lock it again. His father was always forgetting, despite his mom's audible insistence that they keep their room safe from prying eyes.

Well, Mother dear, Craig narrated to himself, *these eyes are going a-prying.* He was waggling his fingers in front of him like some cartoon baddie as he tiptoed through the room.

It didn't take more than a moment or two of rifling through his dad's closet before he found the stash of dirty magazines in an old boot box. Delighted, he fanned them out on the carpeted floor and sat Indian style, flicking judiciously through each one in timeless rapture as he searched for just that perfect one.

He recoiled when his beeping Casio brashly broke the silence, the timer he'd set alerting him to the fact that thirty minutes had so quickly passed. He silenced the watch, thankful for his own foresight to manage the time, and quickly placed all but one of the magazines neatly back in their box.

He retired excitedly to his own bedroom and leered at Amber May, a buxom redhead with skin like porcelain who was that issue's centerfold model. First Amber May was topless on a beach, then topless and bottomless, and looking rather hungry, on a rock.

Ooooh, yeah. Sweet, delicious Amber. Yummy like honey.

But his personal favorite was the model sprawled forlorn in the sand across two full pages, leaving absolutely nothing to the imagination. Her fingertips were pressed playfully to her mouth, one of them pulling down her bottom lip so that she was sulking because she was all alone and only wished that someone was with her. Naked. Together. In the sand.

If only you were here with me, Craig. You know you are ALL the man I would ever need . . . .

He could hear her voice, the longing in it as Amber moaned for him to be with her. He could smell her salty skin. And he was now inside that photograph with her. On that beach; pressing up against her smooth, faultless body; running his hands up her leg.

Then the random thought of how that scratchy sand would feel as they'd roll around in it completely burst the bubble of fantasy.

Man, that would be like 80 grit sandpaper!

And just like that he was back in his bedroom and Amber May was again just a photo of a woman on a magazine page.

Good thing, Craig reassured himself. *We might go down to that beach as*

Amber May and Craig Dalton, but if we did it right there on that sand, we'd be going home as 'Sandy Crotch' and 'Dick Gritty'.

He burst out laughing at his own sophomoric wit as he changed into his pajamas.

VII

Sleep came easily and Craig was already dreaming when his parents returned home. Kathy Dalton stealthily opened the bedroom door to peek through, and could tell from the gentle snores amid sporadic mumblings of something unintelligible that her son was all tucked up in bed and asleep like the good boy he was.

In his dreams, Craig wasn't tucked up into his bed at all, but back at the beach.

He is on a cliff top. This place is dark and cool, the moon full and bright. Yet somehow it is hot and breezy as the waves pound over the rocks. Then comes the woman, a beautiful woman who seems to melt into many different women and girls. The faces waver in and out and dissolve together and suddenly he is elsewhere.

This amalgamation of the woman leans into him and touches his face, her fingers lightly pressed to his lips. When she kisses him, he becomes alight with fire.

Real fire.

Flames erupt from his mouth, singeing his lips and licking up his face. His hair ignites like a torch and he beats hysterically at the flames, crying out as the searing pain is more than he can bear—

Craig jarred awake as he mercilessly beat himself about his own face and head, the slapping palms reddening his cheeks and issuing a thin stream of blood from his right nostril.

He held his hands before him, shaking as he gazed incredulously upon them, shying away as if they might attack again at any moment. They felt numb and thick and not like his own hands at all.

When he tested this fear by making his brain command his fingers to flex—which of course they dutifully did—he dropped his hands lifelessly to the bed covers and began to sob.

When he finally trusted, at least enough to be *fairly* certain, that his own hands were no longer a threat, Craig rubbed the tears from his eyes and swiped the snot and congealing blood from his upper lip.

Leaning across his bedside table, he snatched a tissue from the dispenser his mom had placed there. Never once had Craig considered that the sudden appearance of the box corresponded less with his mom's anticipation of tears or runny noses than it did the other things Kathy Dalton expected a boy his age might want to clean up. (As well as a desire to protect the rich, Egyptian cotton sheets she'd only recently purchased to replace his old, perpetually stained ones.)

Craig blew his nose and rubbed the blurriness from his eyes, balling up the tissue and tossing it in the general direction of the trash can beside his chest of drawers.

The LCD clock atop them blinked weakly orange, and 2:22 swam into focus.

As did the figure standing in the corner.

Motionless.

Watching.

Softly giggling.

Barely visible in the wan, pulsating orange glow, at first the shape was little more than an area of deeper black against the other blacks and greys of the room. Craig blinked hard then opened his eyes wide, forcing his pupils to drink in the trace amount of light. The figure became more clear, strobing in and out of focus with every blinking second of the clock's faint display.

It stared back at him.

Craig sucked air into his lungs that he could not release as he pressed himself so hard against his ship's wheel headboard that one of the spindles cracked the plaster wall behind. He wrapped his arms around his legs and pulled his knees to his chin, shutting his eyes tightly as his mind cried out that he must still be dreaming—

still dreaming wake up wake still dreaming wake up wake up

—as the shape emerged from the background and moved towards the bed. Passing closer to the clock as it neared him, the shape, colors and features wavered in and out, just as the woman's had done in his dream until her myriad of faces had become one.

The figure began to solidify. The vacillating colors becoming vibrant and clear. The outline precisely defined.

Matt Chauncey was standing beside Craig's bed.

Gazing down upon him.

Grinning

"It's okay, Craig . . . I'm here now."

Matt reached for him with a wizened hand. Charred fingers extended from the muddied cuff of the blue suit which had adorned the boy's body in the casket.

And the air exploded from Craig's lungs in a harrowing scream.

TANDING IN SILENCE at the bottom of the neighborhood, the rain continued to pelt Bryan and Ian until it soaked their clothes completely.

Bryan tugged lightly on his brother's arm.

"C'mon. We're getting drenched. Let's get back." He lowered his head to try and make contact with his brother's distant gaze across the fields. "Ian, it's really coming down now. We can talk more, back at the house."

He was surprised to find how loud he had to shout to be heard above the rain. Still Ian did not hear, or cared not to acknowledge that he had. Something in the distance had caught his eye and he was staring there, emptily. Beyond the fields. Into the woods.

"Hey!" Bryan interjected as he forced himself between his brother's focus and whatever it was out there that had captured his attention. "Hey, you with me or what? I'm heading back."

He started walking away, back towards the main part of the neighborhood where his house would be dry and warm.

Ian looked up, his eyes red and sore. Standing motionless he flatly answered: "No."

Bryan turned.

"Let's get back. C'mon Ian."

"No."

"Ian!" He trotted back to his brother, shielding his eyes from the sharply piercing rain. "We'll talk about it at home. Please."

"It's not that simple, Bryan. Don't you understand? It's not that fucking simple. I *saw* our parents die. I watched it all—d'you get it yet? I saw every detail, every reaction . . . the look in their eyes."

His voice was flat and even now and indicated no further emotion. His mind would not allow it; could not accept it. Simple as that.

The recollection played for him in his head as he spoke of it. Having played it over and again so many times in his mind, it was becoming little more than a movie; cinematic evidence of something happening to two people he felt he should know, simply felt he did not.

He could not.

"I saw Mom smiling. She was laughing about something Dad had said, and then out of nowhere, she's screaming. She's screaming, Bryan. And the truck. And that horrible sound of crunching metal . . . ." Behind the cloud of his eyes something flickered. "I actually saw them die, Bryan. I *saw* it. Hours before it happened."

A small tear traveled down Bryan's left cheek but was lost amongst the streaks of rain doing the same.

"And I saw Matt there, Bryan. *I saw Matt there!*"

"No. I know where you're going with this. But it was just an accident," Bryan refuted, the rain streaming down his face, in between his lips as he spoke. "A terrible, awful accident."

"How can you be so sure? I'm telling you, Matt was there."

"Only in your dream, Ian. You saw it, yes, I believe that. I *know* that is true. And that sight can be a disturbing thing. But you've had this kind of thing before—we both have. It's something we can't control. It's not really ours *to* control."

A small cleft in the darkness of clouds overhead opened to a shaft of sunshine.

"And if I'm entirely honest, I'll tell you I felt something that night too. Not as strong—not as clear—as you. But I felt something. I knew too, somehow." Bryan paused to gather his next thought. "As they pulled out of the driveway, something told me to not let them go; to have them to stay the night, or another hour. Ten minutes even, over another cup of coffee. Anything just to keep them from going. But I didn't Ian . . . I couldn't."

"But you didn't see what I saw. You didn't see Matt—"

"No, I didn't see Matt. That's right. But I'm telling you, that stuff's all over, right? Has been for years. It ended Ian. A long, long time ago."

the flames eating the body, growing from it, licking up his leg

Bryan forced the destructive images away. "And you know something as traumatic as Mom and Dad dying would bring back certain pulses, certain vibrations in both of us. We're part of a circle with them, you and I both, and the imminent trauma of that circle breaking came to us, the way those vibrations used to when we were kids. We both felt it."

The pair faced each other as the high atmosphere winds broke the cloud cover to illuminate the fields at the bottom of the neighborhood, immediately clustered back together to extinguish the sight, then opened them back up once again. The resulting light pulsed across the ground in uneven, alternating strobes.

"It's finished, Ian. It was an echo of something we couldn't affect, that we had no control over." A lingering ground breeze fluttered the leaves across a nearby garden. "Now I'm going home."

Bryan turned and went, without looking back.

Ian did not. He stood for a long time in the rain: thinking, running through the events of the past week in his mind, wondering if what Bryan said was right. Wondering if it were true that they could no sooner control what they'd seen than they could control a movie.

The difference was, this movie was a documentary. And it had screened *before* the event.

And Bryan was wrong in one way—one very important way. Because Ian had seen Matt on the roadside in that vision.

And that was indisputable.

Whether Matt had actually been there during the event, or only in Ian's mind, made no difference.

Whether Matt had manipulated his parents' fate that night, or only appeared for the thrill of it, also made no difference to Ian.

Because either way, his dead childhood friend had been there.

But that just wasn't possible.

UT OF THE blackness of the room, Matt's hand reached for the petrified boy in the bed as if in slow motion. He grated with laughter as Craig pulled sharply away, the breath wrenched out of him in terror of the thing standing over him.

"You weren't very sad at my funeral, Craig. That wasn't very nice," Matt's voice rasped bizarrely in mixed screeching tones that brought with them the image of the body dangling from tree; the neck stretching and stretching as the boy shrieked in terror and pain. "I know because I was watching you."

Matt's voice came to Craig through his own mind now, clear and crisp and the voice that had once belonged to the boy they knew. It did not match the grisly thing looming over his bedside.

"Ian was scared of my funeral, he wouldn't come. He was afraid he might see what I had become. What he, what all of you, made me."

The words were slow and deliberate as the dead boy leaned over him, his face crossing the thin sliver of moonlight from between the curtains. Little feeding things wriggled out of his remaining eye.

"This is what I've become, Craig!"

Craig cried out as he kicked and punched at the air, the sheets rippling from his bed.

Matt remained motionless.

Looming over him, the moonlight reflected from the dead child's teeth as Matt curled his dark, worm-like lips into a sneer.

With a howling thrust, Craig launched himself at the corpse, striking at its head. Matt's face sunk instantly, depressing into his skull. A black liquid oozed out of the exposed nose slits and ran down, dripping in splotches onto the floor. Globules of it stuck to Craig's knuckles and began to burn on his skin. He cried with mixed pain and shock when the smell of it wafted to him.

Matt threw back his head in violent, derisive laughter and it lolled unnaturally to one side atop his elongated neck. A shrill whistling laughter rose from deep within its throat and small bubbles gurgled out of a rip just below his larynx.

Craig recoiled and pressed himself hard against the headboard.

"Join me Craig, join me!" Matt motioned as he raised his arm, the filthy sleeve of his blue school suit falling to uncover the distorted hand as he gestured. "All your friends are here! Dan is here. Jimi is here. Jack and Stu. They're all here, Craig . . . waiting for you."

Matt tilted his head. His lidless eye staring.

"And your mother is here too, Craig."

The expression on Matt's charred, peeling and now sickeningly concave face attempted to smile. The lines around its distorted mouth lifted what had once been Matt's ever-blushing cheeks, the image perverse and grisly. Yet somehow Craig began to see within the expression the face that had been his friend's. The abominable, disfigured face mutating, transforming, until it became Matt. The way his friend had always been. It was a bright and happy face, and beamed in a way that seemed to swathe the entire bedroom in a warm, glowing light.

Matt's shriveled hands moistened and plumped until they were the soft, nimble fingers which had played across the holes of the bamboo flute given to him by his aunt. He slowly curled his index finger, beckoning for Craig to come . . . to come with him to the place that was better.

"Please, Craig. Come with me. I need you," Matt softly enticed, his voice the familiar one that had called him to come out and play, so many times. "Come. And we'll play."

The light surrounding Matt intensified. It burned bright and welcoming as his figure became immersed within it, the boy and the illumination coalescing as they became one.

"Come, Craig." Matt's voice moved into the distance as if traveling through the light. It repeated the invitation over and again until it was barely audible.

Craig slid his legs off the bed.

And stepped into the light.

It encompassed him as a muted, steady hum mixed with its brightness, Craig moving further into its warmth.

Come with me, Matt coaxed from deep within, now only a reverberation in his mind.

And then the light was everything. The room did not exist.

The humming intensified to a shallow, crackling sound and Matt's voice disappeared within it. With it the warmth also grew, and Craig allowed the soothing heat into him as he began to follow his friend.

He could no longer hear Matt's voice but allowed the sensation of it to carry him forward, moving faster as the light became a tunnel of flashes and colors which swept hypnotically by. Still it grew warmer, louder, and the crackling was now a snapping. A boisterous, white noise of hissing and popping—

burning

—as the colors changed.

First off–white.

Then yellow.

Orange to red.

Then a white again, so clear it was like crystal.

And cold. So fierce it burnt like ice on sunburned skin.

Now Craig was too far, the room gone as he was pulled helplessly through the clear, icy flames of emptiness.

He screamed but no sound came.

Matt replied in sonorous laughter, the grating sound echoing through the void.

"Let go Craig," Matt's disembodied voice called to him, repeating the command over and over until it liquefied and became many.

Let go! Let go!

Let go, let go!

Let go let go let go let go, the voices screamed, overlapping until they merged into a single, jarring throng. *Let go, Craig! We're all here!*

The voices crying out were his friends . . . his parents.

The door to Craig's bedroom flew open, slamming hard against the wall and flaking off chips of paint. Charley Dalton ran to his son where Craig struggled violently on his bed as if against an unseen aggressor.

"Oh my God! Craig!" his father exclaimed as his son trembled violently on the bed, striking out wildly and slugging his father sharply across the face. Charley reeled back, and for the briefest moment thought he saw a shimmering reflection in his son's eyes, the image of a clear, burning flame.

Your mother is here! Matt squealed as Craig's breathing shortened, quickened, becoming painfully sharper as his chest wrenched furiously from the heat burning within his lungs.

His body shook in fierce convulsions. Charley Dalton grappled with him as Craig writhed on the bed, becoming entangled in the strewn sheets and gasping in spasmodic fits. The air sucked past his lips and made a horrible noise as it was refused entry to his tight, burning lungs.

"Call nine-one-one!" Charley screamed to his wife across the hall, and Kathy Dalton fumbled in the dark for the black rotary telephone, cursing when her panicked hands struck it to the floor.

Please, no! Let it work! her mind screamed as the phone jarred against the hardwood floor with a disconcerting, tinny clang.

She threw herself over the side of the bed and swept her hands across the cold, unseen floorboards. Following the static hum of the receiver off its hook, she patted frantically until her fingers wrapped around the coiled plastic wire connecting the handset to the base. She pulled it toward her with a yank and the phone came springing into her hands.

Barely perceptible in the blanketing darkness, Kathy played her shaking finger over the clear plastic dial until she found the curved metal stop. She followed counter–clockwise along the dial until she felt the next to last hole, plunged her finger in, and skittishly pulled the dial clockwise until she again struck the stop.

She released, and the dial quickly ticked nine times.

"Thank God," she said aloud to the empty room and swiftly repeated the action for the first hole above the stop, pulling it twice.

The line clicked to life.

On the other end a dispassionate female voice announced, '9-1-1,' before the line started to hiss and crackle then went dead to resume its impotent, humming buzz.

She tried twice more, each to the same result.

Kathy shouted uselessly at the receiver and threw it down, cursing. The phone crashed against the bed frame before hitting the floor, and this time the receiver went silent.

Lurching out of bed, she reeled through the doorway and into her son's bedroom across the hall as Charley's voice came to her:

"Kathy, hit the light!"

Her fingers ran up the wall and immediately found the switch as they had done so many countless times before.

The light fizzed sporadically, dimmed, then clicked on brightly, filling the room with artificial fluorescence.

"Craig, its me. It's your father! Craig—stop it! Stop fighting me!"

Craig's seizure exploded him from his prone position on the bed as his back arched into the air. A frail hiss escaped his lips in an oddly long, slow exhalation as he crumpled back onto the bed. His father's grip loosened as the boy's arms became lifeless and the body beneath Charley Dalton lay still.

"No! No—no, nooo!"

Dread swept through him and swelled into his head, fogging his senses as he sat astride his silent, unmoving son.

"Please, Craig! Please just breathe!"

Kathy stood paralyzed at the edge of the bed as her husband dipped a finger into Craig's open mouth and pulled his tongue to the side. He pressed his dry, trembling lips over his son's, pinched Craig's nose shut, and emptied his lungs into Craig's mouth.

His son's chest rose then slowly deflated.

Charley fought to calm his whirling mind as he struggled to remember the procedure: after a moment, he carefully placed his trembling hands just north of Craig's sternum, one over the other, and began pumping his son's chest.

one

two

three

four

five

He leaned down and blew once more. Again his son's chest rose and Charley Dalton administered another five compressions.

After repeating the cycle a third time, he shouted at his sobbing wife to either shut the fuck up or get out as he placed his ear to their son's mouth and listened.

Thirteen
1995

REBECCA'S BLUE BLAZER was in the driveway as Ian walked briskly toward his childhood home. In the receding rain, his sister-in-law's SUV shone brightly, light wisps of steam rising from its hood. The cold was beginning to set in through his soaking wet clothes as he opened the driver's side door and pressed the big, square button clipped to the visor.

The garage door jerked tremulously upwards and Ian ducked under it before it was even halfway up.

Becky was on the landing between the kitchen and the front door, blow drying her hair in front of the full length mirror. A long white terry bathrobe draped against the floor, making small wet streaks on the hardwood everywhere she walked.

She didn't see Ian come in, and he stood halfway around the corner, finding himself fixated as she dragged the fingers of her left hand through her long strawberry blonde hair, appearing darker and straighter in its dampness. A glint of moisture caught the light as it played over her wedding band and then was gone, the droplet running slowly down the contour of her finger and falling neatly over her manicured nail.

Bryan is a very lucky man. Beautiful wife, two kids ....

The realized envy elicited a sour tang of self consciousness, the ebbing guilt over this stolen moment rising to the back of his mouth where the two combined like the taste of copper.

He started to turn away.

Still unaware she was being watched, Rebecca ruffled her hair and bowed to the mirror, tossing her mane over top her head. It draped toward the floor and covered her face as the dryer blew back and forth across the underside layers.

Try as he might, Ian could not avert his gaze.

An unexpected longing intensified as Rebecca tousled her hair and the wristwatch Bryan had bought her for her thirtieth birthday slipped gently down her wrist and rested at an angle against her forearm. Its chunky, silver metal bracelet gleamed, drawing particularly sensual contrast to the color of her summer darkened skin. Her arm moved gently up and down, running her slender fingers through the hair. As she did, the watch disappeared from view, appeared again to glimmer across her slender wrist, then was lost once more among the tresses until it caught momentarily on the folds of her robe.

In the mirror, Ian witnessed the lapels separate.

Rebecca bent further, reaching for the hair at the base of her neck, and the opening in the robe grew wider until the gentle curve of her breasts was revealed in the reflection. The soft white cotton clung delicately to their outside camber, emphasizing their appeal—*their taboo, private appeal*—and Ian's uneasiness about this accidental violation of trust bubbled up, the metallic taste increasing. Yet he found it impossible to look away, as if his sister-in-law were holding him in a trance. He watched unblinking as she ran her hand energetically back and forth across her head, separating the drying strands as her breasts brushed lightly back and forth against the soft cotton.

A taut, stimulated nipple stood proud in the reflection.

Now the taste in his mouth was as strong as sucking on pennies, and Ian forced himself to look away. He backed quietly away from the landing and (hopefully) unnoticed into the kitchen, exhilarated and embarrassed in equal measure.

When Bryan bounded down the stairs and barked a loud greeting to them both, the deep resonance of his voice detonated against the soft, static *whirr* of the hairdryer and Rebecca jerked upwards, startled and gasping.

"God you scared me!" She spun around and also noticed Ian standing uncomfortably at the edge of the kitchen. "I-I didn't know anyone else was in the house."

Self-conscious color rose quickly in her cheeks as she switched off the hairdryer and quickly pulled together the lapels of her bathrobe.

Ian looked away, but the discomfort stiffened his body language as he enigmatically addressed both Bryan and Rebecca with an awkward, enigmatic wave.

"Wet outside?" Bryan asked jokingly of Ian's dripping wet appearance, ignoring apparently both the nervous wave and the serious revelation they had shared at the bottom of the neighborhood just minutes earlier, as if it had never taken place. He ran a flannel towel through his own hair and stepped shirtless onto the landing, wearing only jeans.

Rebecca brushed uncomfortably past both men and dashed up the stairs. She dressed with the bedroom door locked for the first time since they'd moved into the house.

11

Bryan insisted the three of them go out for lunch. He didn't want to talk at the house after all. Something just didn't feel right about it. At least that was his reasoning when he pulled Ian quietly to one side while his wife dressed upstairs. Ian was certain Bryan was doing anything possible to avoid the conversation.

The barroom of Dempsey's Tavern was smoky and loud. Three pool tables were already occupied by lunching workers, most probably from the mill. They held bottles of Rolling Rock or Budweiser in one hand while they ate dripping steak hoagies with the other.

Rebecca, wearing loose blue jeans belted at the waist and a light cream sweater, came back to the table carrying three bottles by their necks. "I've ordered one each!" she shouted over the din of music blaring from the jukebox, John Cougar croaking something about some small town, somewhere.

"One each of what?" Ian shouted back.

"About the only thing worth having here at Dempsey's," Bryan interjected. "A steak hoagie. Dempsey's are the best. Period."

The pronouncement was nothing if not touching.

"You won't find another one anything like it, not in this town. Probably not anywhere. This place will be packed out in a minute. It always is at lunch times."

Ian looked at the multitude of people, a few women but mostly men, already crowding the small tables scattered across the red tiled floor. If this wasn't already packed, he hated to see what it looked like when it was. It made him uneasy. "Steak hoagies, huh? So what's so special?"

Rebecca tilted her head and peered at him out of the corner of her eye with a forced grin.

"What's so special about Dempsey's hoagies?" She winked at her husband and returned her gaze to Ian. "What's so special isn't the hoagie itself all that much, although they are good. And cheap. Dempsey is what makes the place tick. Everyone *loves* Dempsey."

"Can't wait to meet him," Ian replied with an edge of truth mixed with sarcasm. Rebecca and Bryan openly shared a look between them, obviously some 'in' joke Ian clearly did not get.

An uncomfortable silence followed in which Rebecca stared at her beer, methodically peeling the label from the bottle.

Ian cleared his throat.

"So tell me," he asked her as casually as he could muster, keen to distance himself from the incident earlier. Besides, he hadn't set out to deliberately spy upon her. And still he didn't know if she were even aware that he had. Though a low, uneasy vibration within him indicated that she might be. "What's new? How's the job going?"

"What's to tell?" She sipped from her bottle. "I think I'd rather talk about—"

She hesitated, drawing his eyes to hers. She was going to say something. Right here. Right now. Get this all out on the table. Then maybe they could move past it. But what if she were wrong? How would that look?

And besides you egotistical girl, she admonished herself. *What makes you think you're so damned special that it's a capital offense for your broth-*

er-in-law to see a little bit of tit? You're not Bo Derek, for Christ's sake. I'm
sure he's seen it all before. Many times.

Across the table her husband smiled.

She couldn't do it. It would be better to just stifle it. Let it work itself out on its own.

She took another swig of beer.

"—You. Let's talk about you, Ian. And New York. We haven't really had time to hear what's going on in your world, with everything that's happened. City life sounds a lot more fun than my boring job."

Ian spoke as the tension slowly subsided. He shared mundane anecdotes about his life in the city, the *Bulletin*, his buddy Felipe. He didn't say a word about that day in the bar; the day that everything started. That was for his brother and him to figure out, before Rebecca became embroiled in the whole mess. If they were lucky, they'd get to the bottom of it on their own and put it behind them for good. She'd never have to know a thing about the woods, or Matt. Or the foretelling dreams or disquieting tremors growing bigger and stronger from a place deep inside.

It was obvious to Ian from Bryan's dark epiphany in the kitchen earlier that morning that his brother had submerged any recollection of the Little Woods far beneath the reach of his conscious memory until today. Just as he himself had done until that fateful day in Tony's bar. So he knew it would be a surefire thing that Rebecca had never been told about what had happened out there, when they were just kids.

In the woods.

And Ian preferred to keep it that way. Hell, he'd prefer to forget it all again himself and go back to his ignorant, beautifully mundane life in the city. But he also knew that wasn't going to happen. At least, not as long as there were questions still to be answered.

Those thoughts were still lingering in his head as a leggy, ridiculously attractive waitress sauntered up to their table carrying three plates of hoagies crowded with French fries plus a few obligatory leaves of wilted lettuce attempting to pass themselves off as greens. Her white blouse, translucent and incredibly low cut, accentuated her caramel latte skin most effectively.

Suddenly, Ian was in on the joke: the reason why all these blue collar guys loved Dempsey's hoagies so much.

"Hiya sugars!" she said, her New Orleans draw pronouncing it as *shugaas,* as she bent over the table and placed the plates in front of each of them. "Say, you must be new around here?"

Her eyes, the smokiest green Ian had ever seen—so light they were almost transparent grey—locked onto his and for a moment Ian was entranced. Even a little nervous. After a pause that seemed like forever but was actually no more than a second or two, Ian composed himself enough to reply.

"Um—oh. Hello, yes! Ian Cockerton. I'm Bryan's . . . brother." He extended his hand and the woman shook it, her hand soft and smooth in his. "I'm pleased to meet you, uh—"

"Della," she declared with a wink. "But you can call me Dempsey, hun. Everyone 'round here does."

⚟

After two beers and a couple diet Cokes, Rebecca slid her chair from the table and announced that she had to go.

"The kids will be getting home soon. Will you two be okay for about an hour or so more? You can come with me now, but I'm more than happy to come back and pick you up later."

"We'll be fine," Ian assured her. "Besides, we can always get a taxi."

"No, don't be silly, I don't mind. Not at all."

The easiness in her tone reflected the change in mood that had transpired over the past hour. The incident on the landing now seemed vary far away, and Rebecca had come to terms with it. Life was too short to get wound up about such things. And she wasn't even sure if Ian *did* see anything he shouldn't. She was, after all, facing the opposite way and although the mirror was there, it would have been a fairly big stretch to see anything much.

"So, how about it, then?" She cocked her head to the side as she stood, flicking a layer of hair from her face. "I'll meet the kids off the bus then come back here. And if you two aren't completely blotto by then, we can all go out for supper somewhere."

The brothers agreed and Bryan rose from the table to thank her for the effort, kissing her firmly and whispering something that made her smile. "See you soon," he added as he patted her on the butt before she glided across the room, her smooth stride naturally provocative.

Several men stared.

As did Ian. But for a different reason. The sight of Rebecca leaving felt alarming. Those vibrations, pulsing low and deep down, swelled fast and fierce. He nearly jumped up to stop her from walking out—

But didn't.

Bryan threw an arm over his brother's shoulders.

"She's a beautiful woman, isn't she Ian?"

The bright afternoon sun poured through the open door and flooded the dimly lit bar. It silhouetted her figure as Rebecca walked through.

Ian called after her just before it closed.

"Becky . . . !"

But she only waved casually behind her, and was gone.

Inwardly, Rebecca smiled at the way the afternoon had turned out. And if she were honest, there was also something pleasing about being needed. Not only by her husband, but by her brother-in-law, too. That part of it she couldn't exactly place, other than a warm, comforting feeling that it was nice to be a family again. Despite the horrendous circumstance which had brought them back together after so many years, she was privately pleased that the tragedy had revealed a silver lining hidden beneath the grim veneer of loss.

She strode into the gravel parking lot, dodging puddles from the earlier downpour, and sifted through her purse for the Blazer's keys. Yanking them from the bottom of her bag, they caught against an 'emergency' pair of yoga pants and catapulted out of her bag.

Inside the bar, someone put another quarter in the jukebox and Guns 'n Roses began to wail. Behind the blaring music, though quite impossible, Ian heard the unmistakable sound of keys striking the ground. In his mind he saw them falling slowly, deliberately. And the noise they made when they struck the wet gravel exploded his senses into white static.

IV

Rebecca shook off the muddy keys and wiped them on the pair of pants which had snagged from her hand in the first place.

No bother now. They're already ruined, she thought, as she eyed the new tear in one leg.

Fifteen minutes to home. That would make it around three-thirty, give or take. Time enough to freshen up, change, and maybe even a quick coffee. Then the kids should be home. She'd get them ready then run back to pick up the boys. Of course getting the kids ready was the unknown variable. How long it would take mostly depended upon how messy Andrew had gotten over the course of his seven hours away from home.

Diane was much less of a concern. For now, anyway. Rebecca sensed that wouldn't last much longer. She could already see the signs in her daughter that Diane, at just the tender age of nine, was already seeking more than what she was being offered. More and more often young Diane steered the conversations with her mother toward clothes, make-up . . . boys.

What a nightmare thought, Rebecca chided. When she was a young girl, she hadn't thought a thing about boys when she was nine.

Ummm, that's utter bullshit, she contradicted herself immediately. *Of course you had. You're just getting old! Don't you remember? You not only thought of boys when you were nine-years-old, you actually sucked face (or some close facsimile thereof) with one. In the tree. Now who was that with . . . . Shit, who was that?*

Her thoughts raced backward through the memory, the images blurring and mingling as her mind rewound them like a video tape in reverse until she saw herself in a tree house.

She is with a boy.

Who was he? She couldn't see him yet, his face still a blur.

She grabs his cheeks unceremoniously and pulls him to her—

The image materialized, along with a sigh of relief as the boy's face came to mind.

Ahhh, yes. Alan, that's who. I remember now. My first kiss.

It was behind the little playhouse her Uncle John had built for her cousins. Rebecca had been the instigator, attempting to kiss Alan first. But he pulled away. Scared. Or perhaps surprised is the better description. Because many was the time Alan laid on the couch of a wet summer's afternoon, playing the radio and dreaming of Becky and him together when they were older. With a family of their own. In a house. In love. But he dare not say anything! No, he would be teased no end if any of his friends discovered his secret fantasy. So he pulled away when Becky tried to do something funny with his face.

And that was that. The one chance he'd had, gone.

But it turned out it wasn't his only chance. What seemed like years later but was in fact only later that week, Becky again tried—forced—him to kiss her in her cousins' tree house.

And Alan did kiss her. The best he knew how. Wondering if he did it right. It certainly felt right?

Yes, that was Alan, Rebecca recalled as a nostalgic smile crept across her face and she started to laugh. *Sucked face with him alright. No doubt about that. Poor kid didn't have a choice.*

Then, answering the question she refused to answer all those years ago, Rebecca said aloud to herself in the car, "And yes, Alan. You certainly did do it right."

She smiled as the thought warmed her heart, but also wondering where the hell the memory had come from in the first place.

The miles had passed by unnoticed as she motored steadily down the highway in a semi-dazed state, and she was already nearly home. Typical of western Pennsylvania summers, a dark cloud loomed on the horizon ahead. It hung stubbornly above the road at the top of their hill, wispy streaks of grey stretching down to the ground at a uniform angle. Those wisps would be streaks of sharp, slanting rain by the time she got home.

Well, that had been good practice, she thought of the kiss, allowing one last glimpse of the memory. She ran her tongue over her lips, the lingering sensation of the kiss almost tactile, before retiring the recollection to whatever place it was that nostalgic reminiscences resided. *Time to concentrate now.*

She gripped the steering wheel more tightly, the incident on the way to work this morning a much more salient memory that quickly washed away any clinging thoughts of young Alan as she focused on her driving and slowed the Blazer to a more manageable speed. She would be of no use to anyone if she never made it home.

The SUV handled the wet roads admirably, and Rebecca managed to complete the drive in just a minute or two over her originally anticipated fifteen. She pulled into the driveway and pressed the remote clipped over her head. The garage door started with a lurch and churned upwards. Given the weather, she decided to pull straight into the bay as opposed to leaving the 4x4 outside. Sure, it was a nightmare to reverse out, but her vanity—and comfort—took precedent at times like this. No sense getting wet if you didn't have to.

The Blazer was long, and had to be parked with its nose just about kissing the back wall of the garage, the only way the door would roll down behind it. She left the key in the ignition after turning off the engine. Safely locked in the garage, it certainly wasn't going anywhere.

The windowless garage was dark and airless and Rebecca had to feel her way to the door to the house. (The 'People Door' Andrew called it, to differentiate between it and the main garage door.) She'd asked Bryan a hundred times to change that bulb in the opener, and each time he muttered something about doing it. And each time her increasingly frustrated requests came to no avail, for whatever reason. It had been this way for so long now that, frankly, Rebecca had become rather adept at finding her way in the dark, able to do so out of muscle memory. So she simply gave up asking anymore.

She unlocked the People Door and the cool air from inside washed upon her face was fresh and sweet and smelled of home.

Home. At last.

No other sensation was the same.

She sniffed her clothes. The cream sweater, fresh on today, was like an odor sponge, having lapped up the awful mixture of smells of the bar. They would remain in there until she washed it. Maybe for even a couple of washes. Rebecca enjoyed spending time at Dempsey's every now and then. And sometimes, during better times, it could even be a real howl. But the smoke was thick and the music loud, and these had become increasingly less palatable to her with each recent visit to the bar.

Signs of age my dear, she told herself. Then also told herself to just shut the hell up because she was hardly what you could call old.

She pulled the sweater over her head as she passed through the kitchen and across the landing. Catching a glimpse of her topless figure in the full length mirror, and certain that this time she was absolutely alone in the house, she stopped to look herself over.

All-in-all the body reflected back at her was pleasing enough. Her bra cupped her breasts firmly but not too tightly, amplifying her cleavage. Her stomach was still flat (despite having had two children) and still showed signs of some ribbons of muscle from fairly regular bike rides and sporadic jogging. It wasn't a six pack by any means, but it was pretty good. Only her waist was a little more shapely than she felt it should be.

Have to do something about that, Beck. Time for the gym perhaps? Or maybe that waist trimmer thingamabob that's up in the attic somewhere. Order now, only nineteen-ninety-five. Not available in stores!

She smiled at the woman in the mirror as the TV commercial voiceover played through her head.

OK girl. But how about the real test—

Becky reached behind her back and with a single, practiced motion unclasped the bra strap, allowing the support to fall listlessly to the floor.

Her breasts were larger than average for her relatively diminutive size, and their firmness still held them to her chest in a way that many women ten years younger would envy. To her deep delight, they were still a significant an asset. Certainly one to appreciate before the years would pile on top of her, weighing her (and them) down.

She tousled and fluffed her long strawberry–blonde hair with both hands and unexpectedly grimaced, sniffing first one upper arm, then confirming the scent by smelling the other.

God, even my skin reeks of Dempsey's.

She took the next flight of steps two at a time, unbuckling the silver belt which hugged the blue jeans to her waist as she hopped down the long corridor and stepped out of the trousers in stride.

I don't mind showering again, a terse inner voice proclaimed most adamantly. *But no way we're doing that hair all over.*

In seconds it was bunched into a bun atop her head and she was under the flowing water which felt soothing and clean.

And refreshingly cool.

Her nipples raised as she ran a lathered hand over her chest. Her fingers—slender and soft—streaked her glistening skin and it felt good. A little *too* good. She splayed them apart and again ran her left hand over her breast.

Her wedding band brushed the erect nipple and it stiffened further . . . as thoughts of her brother-in-law filled her mind.

She is back in front of the mirror on the landing, but this time fully aware that Ian is standing there, behind her, steadfastly watching in the mirror. This time she only pretends that she does not know, enjoying the power which flows through her as she teases him and bows lower toward the mirror, slowly, sensually tousling her hair. Her breaths quicken as she bends yet further, fully allowing the glimpse of her breasts as the lapels of the bathrobe part. And now they are no longer on the landing but in the bathroom, together, he watching her as she showers, again playing coy.

Her fingers pulled and played lightly at the tip of her breast. The nipple's brownish shade stretched to pink as her thumb and index finger caressed and pinched and rubbed it, the series of movements growing more rapid.

Ian's fingers feel so good as he pulls on her breast. His other hand slides down her abdomen, pausing effectually above her pelvis before stroking his nails along the inside of her thigh.

Across her skin a series of light pink lines trailed behind Becky's manicured nails. The warmth inside her body grew.

She delved her fingers into the fine triangle of hair below her waistline and slowly, deliberately, plunged a forefinger into the smooth, moist skin beneath.

Ian's finger probes then enters, deeper, immediately pressing up towards her stomach, finding the spot.

A fiery ribbon spread through her. Stroking gently at first, she pressed quicker, firmer, until the tense satisfaction built to a feverish pitch. She pulled back her head, the muscles in her neck showing, and thrust her chest forward into her cupped hand. Her waist rippled along with the movement of her other hand and then she was crying out. The water from the shower head streamed down her cheeks, following the contours of her neck.

Then Rebecca fell back against the cold tile wall of the cubicle and gasped as she rubbed her hands together and then through her hair, over her face, as the euphoria faded

What on earth are you doing, Beck?

It was the same terse, incommutable voice which had demanded that, while it would allow her to shower, it would not put up with washing her hair all over again.

He's your husband's brother, for Chrissakes. What're ya doing!

Pressed firmly against the wall, Rebecca moved out of the choking spray of the shower.

So what? It's no big deal, a softer voice countered. *You were only fantasizing. Nothing more. Stop beating yourself up. The rest of the world does enough of that alrea—*

A digital trill rang faintly above the static hiss of the water, cutting off the thought. Not sure she really heard it, Becky cocked her head to the side, listening intently above the sound of the shower.

It warbled again.

Jumping out of the cubicle, she wrapped the nearest towel around her and hurried into the bedroom as the phone by their bedside chimed a third time. It would only ring once more before the answering machine would kick in. Once that happened, she would be unable to speak to whoever it was on the other end (she knew she was supposed to be able to, but could never quite grasp what buttons you needed to press) and this could be the school calling.

What if something has happened to the kids?

Her wet feet slid across the polished hardwood floor and she nearly went toes-up before catching her balance and falling gracelessly onto the bed. In one ungainly movement she plucked the cordless handset from its base as the first note of the final ring jingled out.

"Hello!"

Her voice was wispy and breathless and curt, all at the same time.

At first no one responded.

Then a voice, gritty and monotone and garbled, crackled through a veil of static.

"Hello Rebecca. Good shower?"

"I'm sorry?!"

Surely she had heard incorrectly. But something about the voice made the hairs on the back of her neck stand proud and elicited an immediate, incomprehensible anger.

"The shower, Becky. It looked like a rather good one to me."

The mannerisms and phrasing were that of an adult, but the voice was that of . . . a child's.

"I like it when you think of other men. Especially when you think of your own husband's brother."

The voice was coming to her from the receiver but somehow Rebecca could hear it elsewhere, as if coming from inside her.

Inside her own mind.

"Maybe you should think of me instead," the voice suggested and began to laugh. A pitchy, soprano giggle.

"Who is this!" Rebecca demanded as she gripped the receiver tightly. "Tell me who the fuck this is!"

The tittering continued until she slammed the handset hard into its base and both clattered to the floor.

The line clicked dead as Rebecca lay on the bed.

Repulsed and shaking.

fourteen

"ATHY! FOR CHRIST'S sake I can't hear!" The words were clear and direct and echoed through the house, but to Mrs. Dalton they were a babbling string of garbled sounds.

"Kathy! Get the fuck outta here! NOW!"

Kathy Dalton did not leave. Frozen in the doorway, her sobbing intensified until she could barely breathe, and now hiccuped from her chest in gasping spurts as her son lay lifeless atop his bed which rocked with every thrust of her husband's palms upon the boy's chest.

"Wha—wh—what—"

Charley Dalton didn't have time to lose. He grabbed his wife by the wrists, spun her out of the room and slammed the door shut as Kathy tumbled to the floor in the corridor beyond.

Running back to his son and cocking his ear again to Craig's parted lips, he held his breath as he listened . . . .

A meager wisp of breath whispered back.

Overcome with relief, Charley Dalton exhaled in one gushing release of breath and with it, the overwhelming adrenaline coiled up within him also uncorked. He slumped over his son, sobbing as he wrapped his arms around the unconscious boy and repeated his name over and over between moaning cries.

So close, something whispered in his ear, and Charley shot upright.

"Craig? Craig!"

But Craig was unresponsive and motionless.

So close, the voice repeated over Charley Dalton's left shoulder.

He spun around.

The boy standing there was an impossibility. It was a blackened, disfigured facsimile of a boy . . . in a muddied blue suit. Yet it was one hundred percent Matt Chauncey. Charley Dalton would recognize that weak, igno-minious grin anywhere. And though he hadn't seen it, he also recognized the blue burial suit Mrs. Chauncey had described that day, right down to the tarnished brass buttons with the embossed anchor insignias.

The blood in Charley Dalton's veins turned to ice. The muscles down the left side of his body constricted until it felt like plastic wrap pulled tightly around his limbs. His left arm began to sting with the pricking sleepers you get when you fall asleep with your weight atop it for too long, the fingers numbing and feeling dull and thick. And his chest tight-ened, in a way it never had before.

He clasped his breast against the pain and felt the intense and arrhyth-mic pounding of his heart against his palm.

Oh, you're both so close now.

The words had come from Matt, but were a perceived sensation as opposed to a physical sound. They rang inside Charley Dalton's mind like a baritone peal, a bass vibration which produced a dark and very visible wavelength in his mind that oscillated throughout his entire being.

With it, a beguiling vow of deliverance was proffered: his life in exchange for an act which only moments ago would have been an incon-ceivable proposition.

Yes, Charley, Matt spoke into the father's soul, savoring the acrid fear as the man sensed his own life about to come to an abrupt and premature end. *Give a penny, take a penny! Give him to me, and I will breathe new life into that expiring heart of yours. If you don't, Craig is going to die anyway, and we'll see if God values your life as much as I.*

With his left arm hanging limply at his side, Charley Dalton turned and looked benignly upon Craig. Laying inert upon the bed, the boy's breaths were feeble and sporadic. Then, with no more thought than he would give to rearranging the cushions on the bed . . .

. . . Charley Dalton pressed a pillow over his son's face.

There was no struggle as he watched the life extinguish from his unconscious son; only a few small, twitching spasms.

When the last of these expired and Craig's hands lay motionless upon the sheets, Mr. Dalton clutched at his own breast.

Excruciating pain jolted through his body as his heart squeezed the blood from its chambers with such a fierce systolic contraction that it never relaxed to enable them to refill again.

Oh Charley, you should know not to place your faith in the Deceiver.

Matt's words ringing in his head, Charley Dalton slumped over his son as his heart muscle seized.

He was lifeless before his forehead struck the ship's wheel headboard.

II

Behind the bedroom door, Kathy Dalton sobbed. She did so until such a substantial period of undeniable silence had passed that the urge to reen-ter Craig's room surpassed her anxiety of suffering her husband's violent ire. Trembling, she slowly turned the brass knob and warily opened the door by one inch increments. "Charley?" she whispered.

Her husband did not reply. The room was silent as the foot of Craig's bed edged into view, followed by the left foot of her husband.

"Charley?" she beckoned again after clearing her throat, this time a little louder and more certain.

The room reeked of unnatural silence. And copper. The taste of it filled her mouth.

She cautiously swung the door fully open.

Her husband was laying face down over their dead son's body.

The stagnant blood in Charley Dalton's cheeks had already tinted them a deep purple hue as it settled and pooled. Lifeless eyes stared vacantly at a spot across the room where a large brass button was rolling in slow, ever decreasing circles around the floor.

It came to a rest with its anchor emblem glinting in the moonlight.

And Kathy Dalton screamed.

The room was cool and airless when Ian jolted from his bed. The morning sun pushing through the heavy curtains cast a hazy mustard brown hue across the bedroom as the world swam into focus. Before he was fully conscious, an immediate feeling set upon Ian's heart. A dark, heavy and foreboding sensation, it was a feeling of dread which made him want to cry as illogical fragments of his dream from earlier that night begun spiking his thoughts: *Craig was with him and they were flying . . . then the Ranger was there. . .* then a grotesque, black void sucking upon his soul as he remembered . . . *the Beast Bear.*

The dream, as they had all been since Matt died, was terrifyingly dark and surreal. But this time, there seemed to be a sudden and very real void in his world; a tangible and unrecoverable loss.

And Ian had no idea why.

IV

The night had been wrought with sleeplessness for Bryan, too. He began his slumber with a dream that was fueled by the movie he had just watched, and it was at first exciting and pleasant.

Behind the wheel of a black Pontiac Firebird Trans Am, he is all smiles as he careens through the neighborhood, drifting around the corners with gratifying squeals of rubber. The fat rear wheels kick up gravel and clouds of dust as he fishtails the Trans Am off the blacktop at the bottom of the neighborhood and bounces along the rutted tractor trail which cut through the fields leading to the Little Woods.

Somewhere around the twin ponds, Big Dan is suddenly racing alongside him on his old beat up motorbike, and the two whoop and holler as they tear across the field side-by-side.

Clenching his right fist around the vibrating steering wheel, Bryan punches his fist in the air with delight.

Running neck and neck, Dan's trail bike navigates the ruts of the uneven path with ease, taking to the air in giant rhythmic leaps which produce illogical hang times that can only be created in dreams. With each one, Big Dan remains longer and longer mid-air, defying all terms of gravity.

While Bryan's Firebird is far less nimble on this rugged terrain, what it lacks in agility it makes up for with pure, unadulterated power. Weaving this way and that, more off the trail than on it, Bryan roars the engine with delight as he plows through crops which disappear beneath his hood. He obliterates small hillocks in great sprays of dirt which billow out behind him in the most impressive, satisfying clouds.

The dream was exhilarating and empowering, and it coursed life-affirming adrenaline through Bryan's sleeping body which believed what his mind was telling him: that he was engaging in an incredible, adventurous, breakneck race of a lifetime!

It all changed when they closed in on the edge of the woods.

Jimi Raker materialized with Woody out of nowhere, the two boys appearing right in front of them.

Big Dan simply twists the throttle and pulls up on the motorbike's handlebars, avoiding the pair by sailing effortlessly through the air above them as though his bike has wings.

Bryan's Trans Am cannot fly, however, so he slams on the brakes with both feet. But the Firebird's tires can find no purchase and only slide on the dry dirt.

The car slams into them both.

Jimi is tossed into the air like a rag doll.

Arms and legs flailing, he flies ten, then twenty, then a hundred or more feet straight up until he is merely a speck in Bryan's vision, blending into all the other specks of dirt and debris across his windshield. Woody is plowed over and trapped beneath the front chassis of the car, the still spinning front tires burying him deeper and deeper in soft, wet mud.

Then Jimi comes down. Spread-eagled as he falls, he is impaled upon one of the saplings the Trans Am has snapped in two. Blood spatters the windshield, rendering it opaque crimson.

The adrenaline just a moment earlier is now ice coursing through Bryan's veins as he jumps out of the car and finds Jimi writhing and scream-ing, staked to the ground like a bug to an entomologist's pin.

Beside him, Woody's mangled body is twitching beneath the Trans Am as the spinning tire sucks his head beneath the mud. The dirt and water fill his mouth and balloon his cheeks into a silent, frozen scream.

"Dan! HELP US!" Bryan cries out as he raises his head to find Big Dan floating, stationary, on his motorbike above them.

When Dan looks down, it is as if the motorbike's magical power is bro-ken and the bike, which has been levitating in place, plummets to the earth. Only Big Dan's torso and limbs fall with it. His severed head remains float-ing impossibly in the air, shock and horror frozen across the chubby, lifeless, face of the floating head.

Bryan screams and tries to run but his legs are ensnared in the weeds and dirt and vine-like tendrils . . . as the gold Firebird emblem on the hood crackles to life in real flames. The fire spirals high into the sky and becomes thick and dark and like a solid, living thing. And from it, Matt Chauncey's charred and disfigured face appears—

Soaked in his own sweat, Bryan lurched from his bed, trembling.

The rest of that night he huddled in the corner of his room, between his desk and bookshelf, with the reading light on.

Only when the first rays of sun began to poke through his bedroom curtains did Bryan finally allow himself to rest his head against the rough plaster wall and succumb to the overbearing weight of sleep which had pressed upon him since two-twenty-two a.m.

V

The morning turned out dreary and wet. The rain which had been forecast to fall was now threatening to do exactly that: the bright morning sun beginning to lose its battle with the storm clouds inevitably sidling their way underneath.

The boys were awake and downstairs far earlier than their mother expected for a Saturday. Already in front of the TV when she put on the pot of coffee, neither said a word when she greeted them with a smile and a cheery greeting. Both looked as if they hadn't had a wink of sleep.

Mr. Cockerton was engrossed in a weekend project upstairs while Mrs. Cockerton busied herself around the house but mostly tended, overzealously, to Ian who seemed as though he might be slipping back into his melancholy funk.

"Mom, I'm alright—really," he must have said for the third time in the last hour. He wished it would clear up outside so he could get out. He wanted desperately to be in sunshine and warmth. Away from the damp stillness of the house. He watched from where he sat as the sky thickened with yet more rain.

Bryan watched him watching.

From the kitchen, the ring of the wall mounted phone chirruped through the house and Veronica Cockerton rushed to pick it up, holding it between her shoulder and chin as both hands were occupied by glasses of fresh lemonade she'd just prepared for the boys.

Her friendly greeting to Mrs. Raker, Jimi and Jack's mom, lilted down to the TV room as a commercial for an electric shaver with three swiveling heads assured the boys that it was not available in stores and they should hurry and order in the next fifteen minutes.

"OH MY JESUS!" their mother screamed into the phone and began to wobble on her feet as if she might pass out.

The two glasses she held crashed to the floor, exploding in crystalline splinters in every direction amidst translucent, pulpy liquid.

Hearing the outburst as clearly as the boys, Hare Cockerton's footsteps echoed above as he pounded in quick, extended strides down the length of the upstairs corridor. His feet thudded only twice as he leapt down the stairs, descending the eight tread staircase by four steps at a time.

"Veronica!" he exclaimed as he slid to a stop in the kitchen and saw the prickle spots of blood trickling down his wife's calves and ankles as she stood in the growing circumference of lemonade. He threw his arms around her waist and steadied her as she teetered beside the breakfast table, gripping its Formica top for support.

Plummeting from her shoulder, the phone's clunky handset stretched taut the spiral cable connecting it to the wall-mounted base as it smacked against the floor. The cable immediately coiled up again, and the phone bungeed back up. At the end of the stretching and unstretching spirals, the phone bounced up and down as it simultaneously spun back and forth. On every third spin, it scraped against the wall and the little speaker in the earpiece made a small but audible crackling sound. A moment later, Mrs. Raker hung up. The click was followed by the monotonous dial tone.

"Charley Dalton is dead, Hare. Craig's dad. He died last night." Her words came out flat and emotionless but staccato, as though she were reeling off nothing more than a handful of items to add to their shopping list. "And Patricia Raker says they think he—" This time the weight of the words hit home and Veronica began to stutter and stumble over the last of them, finding it difficult to make them form past her lips. "—Think he mur —He mu-murd—He *killed* C-C-Craig."

Saying them out loud made them all too real and she began crying. A low, plaintive wail that neither boy had ever heard from their mother before.

In the TV room below, Ian blanched. His lips quivered.

Bryan only sat there. After a moment, he grabbed the remote and turned up the volume on the TV before whispering quietly to his brother, "You already knew, Ian. Didn't you. About Craig."

Tears began to well in Ian's eyes.

"You dreamt it. You saw it somehow. Didn't you," Bryan stated more specifically. And though Ian said nothing, Bryan knew. He felt the distorted, inharmonic vibration emanating from his younger brother in negative, cyclical waves. If it could be heard by anyone else, this psychic tremor would sound like a bass subwoofer pulsing in low C Minor, the chord vibrating in reverse.

Absorbing it made Bryan start to feel sick in his stomach.

In the kitchen, their mother could be heard saying something about Mrs. Raker being worried sick because Jimi also didn't come home last night, and how awful and nightmarish it all was, and how in God's name were they ever going to tell the boys about all of this?

Now the dark vibration began to pulse within Bryan.

Spread-eagled as he falls, Jimi is impaled—

"Ian," Bryan said as the grotesque dream sequence played in his mind, his voice grave and quiet. "I need to tell you something . . . ."

Fifteen

A SHARP PULSE like an electric charge spiked through Ian's body. With it came an image of Rebecca, but he refused to receive it, extinguishing it as swiftly as it had materialized. He forced himself to concentrate on the words coming from his brother's lips, but they sounded hollow and muted.

"... that was almost—"

"Uh huh," Ian interjected, completely out of synch.

"For Chrissakes, Ian. Have you been listening to a word?"

Ian closed his eyes and lowered his head.

"I'm sorry Bryan. I know you don't want to talk about what I said in the neighborhood but listen to me. Please . . . ."

Bryan emptied his glass and shouted to Dempsey for a whiskey. A double. When it came, Ian noticed how his brother's fingers trembled as they lifted the tumbler to his lips.

"I know you're scared to dredge this all up, Bryan. I'm scared too. For you, for me. For Rebecca. The children . . . ."

"Just say it, Ian!" Bryan demanded. "For God's sake, please just say what you think is going on." Bryan downed the Scotch and stared unblinkingly into his brother's eyes.

"I told you. It's not finished. I'm not sure it ever was. We didn't get rid of it like we thought we did, Bry."

Ian visualized the next statement before he allowed the words to be spoken: "Matt is back. In the Little Woods."

And the full crisp sensation exploded into Bryan's mind.

The woods. The darkness.

The game of War. The whistling. Then a scream, the scream that would forever exist in his soul . . . and the boy in the tree—

"No!" Bryan shouted and a few of the others in the bar looked their way. "No!" We stopped it that night. I–I remember that!"

Ian shook his head, slowly.

He remembered too. Most of all he remembered that terrifying sound. The horrid, searing scream of their friend as he swelled and split as the Beast clawed him from the inside out.

But Ian also remembered a single thought that which permeated all others since. The thought which, if he were honest, he'd had even before they'd gone into the woods that final night. The thought he'd never shared with Bryan:

You can't kill the dead.

And all these years since—all the endless nights when life was supposed to be safe again, and secure—that one reverberating thought had pulsed quietly, incessantly, beneath the veneer of reality.

It did so now, and more loudly than ever, as Bryan got up from the table and rushed into the men's room to empty his gut into the white porcelain sink.

II

The clock on the nightstand read 3:51. Rebecca had not moved from her position on the bed for over ten minutes. The towel around her was now damp and cold. But she could not move, paralyzed as surely as if someone had wrenched away her spine.

The kids will be back any minute now, she told herself. *You've got to pull yourself together. It was only a fucking pervert, some crank getting his rocks off and this time he just happened to strike it lucky. A coincidence. That's all.*

Her mind raced. Emotions reeled as her eyes darted around the room, across the ceiling. For the second time that day she was left feeling emotionally violated, abused, vulnerable and . . . dirty.

But now the children would be on the bus, which in turn would be plugging its way slowly up the hill to drop them off at the top of Route 60. She would need to be her usual self when they came home. Diane, particularly, was tuned into Rebecca's moods, able to discern them especially well. Rebecca would have to be a damned good actress to hide this one from her.

Just a fucking pervert!

The conviction started to take hold, the intimidation and dread starting to dissipate, replaced instead by simmering anger.

Young, raw anger.

Rebecca lifted herself from the dampened bed and sat with her feet over the side. The wooden floor was cool and contrasted with the rest of the room. Her towel had now absorbed her body heat to become clammy and clinging. She discarded it and left it on the floor where it dropped.

She pulled on her jeans and her bra and sifted through the closet for a clean blouse that was casual enough for the warm weather but stylish enough for a dinner evening out. Her hand landed upon a solid red silk top and she threaded her arms through it, tying it at the waist. Normally the top third of the buttons would be undone. Now they were all buttoned up, cinched fully to her neck.

The clock made it's familiar buzzing noise as another minute clicked by. Rebecca turned to see it proclaim it was now 3:55.

Right on schedule, the sound of school children wafted through the partly opened windows as the bright yellow school bus honked twice and pulled away. Rebecca brushed aside a curtain as the back of the bus disappeared down the hill to make its final drop-offs near Sowtern.

Down the top street of the neighborhood, a small funnel of children were skipping and chattering to one another.

"Right on time," Rebecca said aloud, and the spoken words rang strangely in the vacant house. She ignored the uneasy feeling this brought and made her way quickly to the kitchen.

A dig in the cupboard was rewarded with a jar of instant coffee, and she shoveled some into a mug without measuring. There was still time to have one and calm her nerves while the kids made their way home. Then

Diane could help Andrew change into casual clothes, she was old enough to help out with things like that now. Besides, if her daughter were kept occupied, there would be less chance of Diane sensing anything was out of sorts.

Rebecca intentionally distracted her mind with the morning's paper while she waited, browsing through its multitude of pages. It didn't work.

Hello Rebecca, good shower?

The eerie greeting played over and over in her mind.

I like it when you think of other men. Maybe you should thi—

"Fuck off!" she screamed and threw the newspaper across the breakfast nook. The pages separated and wafted apart, settling loosely over the chair and floor as the anger and overwhelming sense of vulnerability brought tears to her eyes.

Downstairs, the doorknob of the door leading into the garage rotated with its usual clicking noise. A moment later it opened, slowly at first, then so hard and fast that it slammed against the wall. A flake of plaster dusted the carpet as it rebounded halfway closed again.

Rebecca jerked in her chair with a gasp, twisting abruptly to see the door stood ajar but nobody walking through.

She waited a moment longer for the kids to come bounding into the living room, but none came. So she made her way down the half flight of stairs and stood before the half–open door, listening for their voices.

Silence.

She examined the new dent in the plaster wall and shook her head at what their father would think about that. Personally, she couldn't give less of a shit about it right now.

"Hey kids. Guess what?" she shouted while forcing a smile so the words come out the way they should. "We're going out for supper. Where do you guys wanna go?"

Silence.

Rebecca wrapped her fingers timidly around the knob and slowly opened the door the rest of the way, peering around its corner. The garage was its usual dark chamber, save a small swath of light from the living room which illuminated an angular trapezoid across the Blazer's front door and roof. It offered a dim glow to the rest of the space at best, and she cursed Bryan for his procrastination.

From somewhere on the other side of the vehicle Andrew giggled.

"Andrew, I know you're in there," she spoke pragmatically into the darkness. "Diane? Come on out. We have to get going."

Her voice sounded loud to her own ears as she stepped into the dim and silent garage.

"C'mon guys. Dad and Uncle Ian are waiting for us."

She crept steadily around the Blazer, carefully avoiding its muddy side panels.

"Fine, I'll just come get you!"

The pitch of her statement rose at the end, so that she was almost singing the last few words. Andrew couldn't resist chuckling when she did this. It always made him feel silly, and right now it would feel awfully good to hear that happy sound.

Scuffing her feet carefully across the concrete floor, she decided to work her way through the dark to the rear of the Blazer. With its front bumper so close to the back wall, it was unlikely that even a six-year-old child could squeeze through the tiny gap. Twelve-year-old Diane was certainly too big to do it. So this was the only way they could get around the Blazer. Rebecca would be ready for them as they would jump out while uttering dramatic '*Boos!*' and of course she would feign surprise and act startled, and Diane and Andrew would shriek in victorious delight.

It wasn't until she was edging fully around the back of the car that Rebecca actually realized the main overhead door was still closed.

Had she missed the sound of the children opening and then closing it again behind them? That awful creaking and groaning which echoed throughout the house as the segments lurched in their tracks and folded down towards the floor?

She had heard that dreadful sound, day after day, for more years than she cared to count. Again, despite her constant requests, Bryan just never seemed to find it a high enough priority to get around to greasing the damn thing.

So how could she have not heard it this time?

Not only once . . . but twice.

Just as she had only twenty minutes earlier, Rebecca again felt the cold fingers of anxiety creeping up between her shoulder blades to stand her neck hairs on end.

"Kids?!"

Only the whispering of the breeze replied as it brushed across the the aluminum siding on the other side of the wall, the sound amplified within this dark chamber.

"Are you in here Diane? This isn't funny now."

She continued to inch around the Blazer and caught herself on one of the aluminum trims over the rear wheel arch. Her red silk blouse made a quiet ripping sound as it snagged below the pocket and opened a small hole that could fit a finger.

Fuck, she scorned herself.

"Okay! Come out now, sweethearts. Mommy's snagged her top."

She waited for a response but received none.

"C'mon, guys. Uncle Ian's waiting to see yo—"

The People Door to the house slammed shut.

In the windowless room, thick with the smells of oil and tools and damp tires, Rebecca became as if blind.

Another giggle, this time muffled by the door as it emanated from inside the house.

It did not sound like Andrew.

It sounded like—

Don't be silly, Beck. It's one of Andrew's friends acting silly. Just get yourself over there and open that door. You've made your way through here in the dark before.

Yeah, another voice in her countered. *But not through the pitch black, and always just a few feet from the driver's door to the People Door. Not all the way from the whole other side of the damn garage.*

Fighting back panic, she felt for the wetness of the car to establish her location. The fear began to rise in her throat, her breathing coming thin and fast.

Okay. Calm down girl. Remember now, you're at the back of the Blazer. Only a few steps backward and you'll be behind it again. Another few to the left and then forward from there, and you'll be close to the People Door. Just like always. You can do this.

The lingering warmth of the exhaust pipe near her leg confirmed this as her hands pressed rhythmically along the contours of the car.

A few more careful steps and she stopped and shouted for the little boy—whichever friend of Andrew's it may be—to *please* open up the door.

He didn't reply.

This wasn't funny, or cute, at all anymore. But she would soon be in the house of her own accord and then that little kid was really gonna get it! There'd be a 'come to Jesus talk' for sure, and likely a rather terse call to his mother too.

Now more frustrated than anxious, Rebecca found her breaths becoming more grounded as she continued feeling her way around the Blazer.

Okay. Watch out for that trim, she reminded herself, but then wondered why on earth she'd bothered: the damage to her blouse was already done, and silk was essentially irreparable.

Almost there now.

Still anchoring her right hand against the Blazer, she extended her left into the black, open space before her and clutched at empty air until her fingers found the rough, unfinished wood of the door. She ran her hand slowly down the jamb until she felt the cold, faux brass knob. Thankfully it turned freely and she started to open it.

Until something made a clicking sound on the other side and the knob became stiff in her grasp.

"Look here!" she yelled at the door, her patience dwindling fast. "I don't know which of my son's friends you are, little boy, but I want you to open this door right now. And I mean right *now!*"

Silence.

"Did you hear me, little fellow!"

Silence. Her heart pounding against her ribs the only thing she could hear. Then, very softly . . . a small childlike titter.

And an answer.

"I did hear you."

The voice came from behind her.

Inside the garage.

Rebecca spun to see an orange glow reflected in the Blazer's side windows. Like snapping embers, sparks flashed sporadically like fireflies, crackling through the darkness in erratic pulses.

A boy stepped into their flickering light.

But it wasn't a boy. His face was charred, one eye socket empty. The space where his mouth should be was a wide void encircled by dry and twisted black lips resembling worms shriveled by the sun. The suit he wore was barely identifiable, having blackened and melted into the boy's skin.

Matt Chauncey threw back his head and it lolled unnaturally to one side on his stretched and torn neck. A shrill, whistling falsetto rose from deep within the boy's throat, bubbling up and out as he laughed. A squirming creature fell from his bottom vestige of a lip and hung there momentarily before dropping to the concrete floor where it could be heard to scuttle away in the darkness.

"Hello Mrs. Cockerton."

Matt's jaw contorted grotesquely with the words, the effort cracking the scorched skin of his face in lines which ran up his cheeks.

"Good shower?"

Thick yellow tissue oozed from beneath the fresh fissures.

And Rebecca's mind and body seized.

"I've come out to play. Wanna play, Rebecca?" It reached for the woman with flaking, blackened hands. White tips of bone showed through the fingertips.

"I know you like to play! I watched you play. You were a very, very

naughty girl, Mrs. Cockerton."

The air in Rebecca's lungs escaped in a slow, quiet hiss as Matt's wizened digits played over the front of her blouse. They made a clicking sound as the bony tips probed the new hole below Rebecca's pocket, one fingertip poking the underside of her breast.

"Tsk, tsk. What will your husband say about this?"

A minuscule bubble formed at the tear in Matt's neck as the words were formed. He retracted his fingertip and a thin sheath of burnt skin prized away, clinging to the silk.

Rebecca was paralyzed.

Unable to breathe, unable to move, her eyes stared uncomprehending as the corpse feigned a grin, Matt's withered lips curling to effect little more than a sneer. Reflecting off the dead boy's small, uneven but stark white teeth, the unseen source of the fire–like glow played across them like a match light across Tic Tacs inside a charcoal bag.

For Rebecca, the image wavered and blanched as her head grew impossibly light and all perception hazed away behind a dizzying fog. Dazed and devoid of breath, she wavered on her feet, beginning to sway in increasing circles.

"Won't you let your little babies come out to play, Rebecca?"

Matt's words now came thick and muted as the boy stared up at the woman, tilting his head this way and that as he scrutinized her draining face.

Inside, Rebecca was screaming and desperately shaking her head, but found it impossible to bring either refusal to the surface.

"Oh, but you're wrong, Mrs. Cockerton," Matt said in a simpering tone as he read the rebuff as clearly as if she had managed to express it. *"You see, they already have come out to play. Your babies are with me. Right now . . . . The girl invited me."*

The blanched scene wavering before her burst to pure white and then became nothingness as Rebecca collapsed to the floor, her consciousness submitting to a crescendo of white noise.

As it did, she perceived one last sound, as though through a tunnel and from a place very, very far away.

It was the sound of the Blazer's engine firing up.

The SUV idled happily in place, filling the windowless garage with choking exhaust as Rebecca lay motionless on the cool concrete floor.

Then all was empty silence . . . .

sixteen
1977

I THINK WE might be in trouble," Bryan said to his brother with uncharacteristic solemnity as he struggled to regain his composure against the terrible, low vibration now emanating from deep within himself. Its disturbing frequency was growing stronger as it combined with the same echoing noise from Ian, who was less successfully quashing it.

Tears welled in Ian's eyes.

They soon flooded over his lower lids and were running in fine streamlets down his cheeks.

"I mean like *real* trouble, Ian. Not the in-trouble-with-mom-and-dad kind of crap."

The merging vibrations continued to grow to such an all-consuming crescendo that the repugnant chord seemed to begin shorting out the very neurons in Bryan's brain. He had to make a conscious effort to breathe and slowly pulled oxygen in through his nose then expelled it softly in dedicated, repeating cycles until the thrumming bass finally rose an octave and reduced in intensity by about half.

"Tell me—" he said, the words wispy and bare as he wiped his brother's cheek. "I know you're scared. I am too, Ian. But tell me about your dream. When we came home from the drive-in last night you had a really bad dream—about Craig—didn't you . . . ?"

Ian's lips trembled as he fought to find the words.

"I–I don't know for sure that it was Craig. It–it didn't make sense."

Between soft, hiccupping sobs, he struggled to tell Bryan what he could remember about the dream. He tried to explain the inexplicable: about the clifftop, and how it had become the woods. And how this little cartoon character he only knew as the Ranger was there. And how suddenly Craig *was* the Ranger.

And when he had composed himself enough to say the words out loud, he told Bryan about the Beast Bear, the image wrenching away all semblance of normality from the dream and transforming it into a grotesque, violent night terror.

Then the Beast Bear is in the tree. It opens its gargantuan jaws and the black hole of its mouth unleashes a scream like Ian has never heard—

"And I woke up! It was so scary, Bry, what's happening?!"

Bryan lowered his head and realized his own hands were trembling. He was now more sure than ever that he knew what was going on, but needed one more validation before he was prepared to drag Ian into his nightmare realization.

"Boys, your mother and I need to talk with you," Harold Cockerton called out from the kitchen, his voice louder than he wished it to be in order to be heard over the television. "Boys, can you turn off the TV and come up here a moment?"

As an afterthought he added, 'Please.'

"I need to do something first," Bryan whispered to Ian, cupping his hand cautiously over his mouth. "Tell them I'll be right up. But don't tell them about your dream. It's obvious from the look of you that you over-heard Mom's phone conversation just now. But whatever you do, don't tell them about your dream. D'ya understand!"

Ian wiped the back of his hand across his tear soaked cheeks, nodding in agreement.

"COMING," Bryan shouted up the stairs and gave Ian a little nudge. "Now go on, I'll be right up. I promise."

ɪ ɪ

The answering machine picked up at Woody's house. His parents' chipper voices informed Bryan that nobody was home but that they sure hoped he would leave a message because they would be happy to call back . . . and that he should have a groovy day until then.

Bryan hung up without leaving a message. And as much as he wanted to have a groovy day, that was looking less and less likely. Right about now he would settle for a pretty mundane day. In fact, that would be awesome. All he needed for that to happen was to hear Big Dan's voice.

So he dialed the number and listened to each of the trilling rings, counting them to nearly twelve before Mr. Mercer answered the phone, dropped it, then picked it up with an angry, intoxicated mumble that sounded something close to, 'Goddammit who's calling?!'

"It's Bryan Cockerton, Mr. Mercer, sir. Big Da—er, Dan's friend. I know it's still early, sir, but can I talk to him . . . please?"

"No. You can't. The no–good layabout sumbitch isn't here. Jumped on his motorbike last night and took off to God knows where. No idea. And don't care."

The line clicked dead and reverted to the dial tone, and the weight of that ten second conversation injected dread into Bryan like black asbestos scratching at his soul.

Mrs. Raker had said that Jimi hadn't come home. Woody was who-knows-where. And Mr. Mercer didn't know where Big Dan was . . . .

Could it really be coincidence?

The sickening images from his dream that morning poured over him again like icy water, turning his heartbeat into a snare drum under his ribs. Bryan now realized with little uncertainty that, more than just a bad dream, the nightmare had been some kind of remote, psychic vision of three of his best friends. Dying. Just as Ian had experienced the same about Craig.

Bryan dropped the phone and scrambled up the steps to the kitchen as his lungs pulled for air, the panic sweeping over him.

"—don't know exactly how or why, but Craig is gone, sweetheart." His mother was gently conveying her conversation with Patricia Raker to Ian, who was sitting at the breakfast table numbly staring as Veronica Cockerton stroked his hair. Her words were calm and careful as she fought back her own tears of disbelief.

"We know how very close you both were," Mr. Cockerton somberly interjected, recognizing that his wife needed a moment. "I pray we can make some sense of it . . . and maybe we will, in time."

The words were spoken to Ian, but he was looking at his wife as he said them. The worry on his own face was unconcealed.

"But right now that's not where we're at. I'm so sorry budd—"

Hare Cockerton turned sharply as Bryan lurched into the kitchen and threw his arms around his father's waist, burying his face into his chest and not letting go.

᪥᪥᪥

The night before, as the Cockertons were about to settle into a double feature at the drive-in, Woody informed his parents he was sleeping over at Jack Raker's house.

His announcement was met with little question or opposition.

The rain had slowed to a constant, steady trickle, so he declined their offer to even drive him there. It was only a few hundred yards down the road, he said. And the rain was just a sprinkle now, and a little water never hurt anyone.

This also was accepted without question, and so Woody's parents waved him goodbye, wishing him a 'far out' Friday night with Jack and Jimi, and confirming that they'd see him some time tomorrow.

Just in case they were watching through the big bay window, Woody feigned the first few yards of the walk by heading towards the Raker house even though he knew his parents checking up on him was about as likely as a snow storm in summer. He had to admit they were pretty hip, and gave him a lot of leash, most of the time. Even so, he kept up the charade until he reached the next house, then ducked out of sight and turned for the woods.

The steady drizzle had almost completely subsided by the time he reached the Beechnut. But it was still chilly. And windy. And darker than it should be given the fullness of the moon. Occasionally, blinding lightning would streak across the sky, illuminating the edge of the woods with a violent blue light that left Woody blinking as the changes played havoc with his dark-adapted eyes. A second later the flash would be followed by a bellowing, echoing clap that seemed to shake the earth, the bass reverberating through his chest. Between these stroboscopic intervals he fumbled slowly through dense undergrowth, step by slow step, until gradually he came upon the more established trees and started to get his bearings.

Somehow he knew they would come back here tonight. Despite already being here earlier that day, despite the storm, despite the electricity shooting through the atmosphere. Woody did not question how he knew this to be true: he simply understood it in every fiber of his being, like a low, unsettling vibration ringing beneath his soul that compelled him to come here tonight too. And Woody did come, not because that vibration seemed to be beckoning him, but because everything over the past few weeks had become so inexplicably dark and twisted; nothing just seemed to make sense anymore.

When another jagged line tore across the horizon and silhouetted the unmistakable outline of the Beechnut up ahead, Woody paused and steeled his nerves.

It all started the day which had been the last time they played their game of War in the Little Woods. Though only a few weeks earlier, Woody remembered little of the day itself other than he had trudged home wet and tired and exhilarated all at once.

He did remember throwing off his mud-encrusted clothes and making his way to his bedroom refuge in the basement as his father, replete with tie-dyed technicolor tee, smiled his inane smile and said something about how it must've been a groovy day for Woody to be coming home so late and in such a wild condition.

Woody could not remember falling asleep that night, the line between wakefulness and dreaming crossed seamlessly. He realized he had been asleep only after being jolted from the worst nightmare he'd ever had, finding himself lying awake and trembling on his bed in a pool of sweat in the dark.

He remained that way, panting and anxious, the rest of the night as he prayed for the relief of the morning hours while the fragmented images of his nightmare assaulted his clouded mind.

In those horrible scenes, the boys were taunting and hitting and torturing Matt Chauncey in their game of War in the woods.

And then they brutally killed him.

The more Woody tried to fend off the nightmare remnants as nothing more than what they were—a boy's overactive imagination and raging hormones combining to result in a very, very bad way to generate a very, very bad dream—the more the images came to him with increasing ferocity and clarity until they culminated in a scene where Matt dangled by his neck from a branch of the Father Oak. Woody shook and winced and pulled his pillow tight to his chest as their friend then disappeared inside a column of fire, the boy kicking and screaming until the crackle of the flames was the only sound.

The whole thing felt so real, the sensations so tangible, Woody was certain he could actually taste the residue of smoke in the back of his throat; his every breath laced with a hint of earthy soot.

Of course the nightmare had been only that—a terrible dream.

The boys hadn't killed their friend; they hadn't tortured him in the most merciless manner; they hadn't jeered and chanted as he cried and screamed and begged.

This wasn't *Lord of the Flies.*

Yet ever since that dream, the world felt to Woody as though he were experiencing it from inside some eerie, disorienting bubble. He was able to see and participate in his physical reality, but everything was sheathed by a thin, dark, translucent veneer that no longer allowed him to connect with life quite the way he should.

It was with unsurpassed relief that, after trying so fruitlessly to shake the dream's disturbing images, Woody had seen Matt later that morning in the big empty lot next to the Daniels' house as they played a game of backyard baseball.

Oh thank you, God. Thank you! Thank you.

Woody hadn't noticed Matt joining in the game that day, or even talking to anyone, really. But that was just how Matt was. The kid had always been a little on the periphery of their gang.

But at least that proved it: the awful images which had shaken him so deeply were in fact nothing more sinister than a scary and very realistic dream.

One Woody hoped to never—ever—have again.

And so he spent the next few days going about his normal summer routine. Woody watched TV while shoveling down sugary cereal as his parents readied themselves for another day at the office; he practiced with his throwing stars and nunchucks, picturing himself every bit as good as Bruce Lee; and he jammed out to some of his father's eight-track tapes. Fleetwood Mac was one of his favorites and their new song, 'Dreams,' was his latest obsession. Funny how the haunting lyrics had so much more meaning all of a sudden.

Isn't it crazy how lyrics can do that? he thought, as he listened to one particular verse of the song over and over, whipping his nunchuks over his shoulder, under his arm, around his torso in admirable timing to the beat of the music. Because Woody *had* seen a clear vision. And just like the song, he agreed that he would never dare tell anyone about it. He could never share about having the nightmare, and most definitely not how badly it had scared him.

Without question, such an admission would be met with fierce and flawlessly sophomoric derision. They'd mock him by pretending to cry, balling their fists over each eye and twisting them to and fro while howling, 'Boohoo!' They'd call him names like Big Fat Scaredy Cat. Or worse, he would forever be labeled as a great big wet pussy of a girl.

So Woody kept his visions to himself.

But then the following week he found himself sitting in a stale and windowless room that reeked of lilies. He was looking down a long row of people who were somber and silent and sniffling in their dark suits and modest dresses.

The center of their undivided attention? A small coffin at the front of the room, the lid closed to respectfully hide the disfigured body which had once belonged to their friend.

And in a moment, everything changed.

Reality and nightmare morphed into one, becoming an indistinguishable sludge of consciousness.

The adults were saying that it had been a most terrible, unfortunate accident, that Matt had started a fire when he was out in the woods and the flames must have gotten away from him.

But Woody knew this wasn't true.

Because when the Coroner examined Matt's body, the doctor had to have found the unmistakable marks in the charred skin and muscle around the boy's distorted neck . . . but yet said nothing.

And while Woody hadn't directly participated in his death, he knew he had taunted and hit and even punched Matt, choosing to passively observe as some of the others held the crying boy down so Stu could tie the fraying nylon rope around his neck.

Woody also knew he'd celebrated the killing, prancing and deliriously whooping around the fire with the rest of the boys as Jack Raker blew erratic notes from the flute Matt had been given by his aunt. Woody had chanted with the others in incomprehensible yet somehow unified syllables none had ever before uttered as the fire grew hotter and brighter and higher. And he had cheered and laughed, caught up in the ritual's sweeping and grotesquely feverish crescendo, reveling with the others when Matt finally stopped flailing as he hung from the tree in a suit of fire.

Woody knew they had done all of these things.

He just didn't know *why*.

But above all of these atrocities, the worst thing Woody knew was this one dark, irrevocable fact: that he had done nothing to stop it. Any of it. Because the terrible truth was, that they *wanted* Stu to do it.

They wanted Stu to make Matt's bawling and pathetic mewling stop; they wanted him to pay for everything they felt was wrong about themselves, and all the things that had ever been done to them which they thought were so unfair or undeserving.

... This is for me not getting that bike I wanted on my birthday ... for getting an 'F' on that grammar test I studied so hard to pass ... for being grounded last weekend .... for all the times my dad beat me with his fists until my skin was bruised and raw ....

So of course when it was done they were filled with an immense and deeply unimaginable satisfaction, an elation none had ever before experienced. They then floated through the carefree summer days which followed as if none of it had been of any significance. In fact, as though the whole thing had never happened at all.

But Woody knew it had happened.

And the low, resonating thrumming emanating from somewhere deep within him since that day was making him sick to his stomach. His thoughts had become clouded and veiled and assaulted with disturbing ideas he never imagined he could have. So he was coming to the Beechnut tonight to inject some kind of balance into his wildly distorted reality. It was time to put things right.

At least he had to try ....

Fighting the anxiety of these thoughts, Woody edged through the dark in the thickening woods. Between a web of interwoven branches and limbs, a ring of birch trees glowed bright silver ahead with every flash of lightning. On the periphery of the place the boys called the Beechnut, their swaying luminous forms guarded the new sanctum like a line of skeletal sentries.

Woody squinted as he searched their slender branches for the boys he knew would be here, but the illuminating flashes were too brief, the light too bright. In fleeting moments he would spot a figure that could be one of them, but the sizzling lightning would extinguish and the woods would again be veiled in darkness. No sooner would his eyes adapt to the black veil of night than another electric tendril would slice through the sky and leave him seeing spots of blue and white.

"HEY!" he called out over reverberating thunder but the address was met with silence.

Feeling his stomach tighten, he pressed uncertainly closer.

Coming here tonight had seemed like a requisite as he sat in the safety of his basement bedroom. Enveloped in the guise of normalcy, with posters of rock groups and muscle cars and stupid TV sitcoms on his walls, he couldn't see any other way to start to right the wrong they had done. This wouldn't bring Matt back . . . but it was a start.

As the woods flickered in electric flashes and their rumbles trailed away to unnatural, inert silence, it now felt like a very bad idea.

In this moment he would have prayed to God for strength, but his parents had insisted that such a precept was fatuous. God was for those of a lesser intellectual capacity, his father had said. A construct of man to assuage fear in the feeble and excuse guilt in the rueful. Only science and the here-and-now existed. Just be a decent person and always think of the balance of life. There was nothing else.

So instead of praying, Woody clasped his trembling hands together and reminded himself of that child-sized coffin. They had done something bad—something terribly, terribly bad—and it needed to be rebalanced.

He stepped tentatively through the ever watchful perimeter of sentinel silver birch trees, and the Beechnut opened up like a woodland refuge before him.

Protected from the drizzling rain beneath the hefty branches of the namesake tree in the center of the Beechnut, the low, resonating bass vibration thrumming inside him began to rise to a maddening crescendo.

Another fork of lightning coiled horizontally overhead. Its long and serpentine flash of light illuminated the night sky so long and perfectly that Woody could finally see that he was right: the boys *were* here. At least some of them.

Stu most obviously was, bold and brazen as he leapt impetuously from a limb with no apparent regard for the next's ability to hold his weight, the thin branch bowing deeply as he struck upon it.

Jimi and Jack were here too, moving more modestly through the higher canopies.

Bryan and Ian were not here, but that was of no surprise to Woody. The brothers had always seemed . . . *different* . . . to the rest of the gang, and he hadn't expected them to be drawn by the echoes which seemed to be summoning them back into the woods tonight.

Craig Dalton wasn't here either, a fact about which Woody had little opinion, one way or the other. He considered Craig to be somewhat of an obnoxious little creep most of the time. Which isn't to say he actively disliked the kid, he just couldn't be bothered to particularly single him out for any hang time—like, ever—and that seemed to be equally acceptable to them both.

What was a surprise was not finding Big Dan here. Of all the gang, Woody expected him to be enticed more than any of them.

Well, more than any except maybe for Stu, whose unmistakable silhouette swung from branch to branch as he leapt between intervals of bright white streaks of blindness as the lightning sizzled and the thunder rumbled.

"Woohoo! Look at what the cat dragged in," Jack shouted as he stopped to clasp oddly from the side of a flimsy birch, pointing at a rain-soaked Woody who was squinting to regain his night eyes.

Jimi nodded and waved feebly from a branch halfway up the ancient beech, the proprietary gesture met with a hardened look from Stu who then leapt from an impossible height in a nearby birch and thumped to the ground in a way that resembled a superhero tripod landing. He landed so close that Woody felt the earth shake.

Standing and stretching back his shoulders, Stu arched his chest out as he took one step forward to be face-to-face with Woody. "Gotta hand it to ya, Woodrow. You got some balls on you. Not gonna lie, I'm a little surprised you came."

Woody focused on his own breathing and said nothing, his eyes fixed steadily on Stu's which scrutinized him up and down as if a jackal evaluating a jackrabbit. Stu then leaned in, placing his mouth so close that his rancid breath smothered Woody's senses, the odor writhing into his nose and mouth like a parasite trying to coil into the very core of him.

"I know why you're here," Stu whispered into Woody's right ear and took a long, savoring sniff, breathing in slowly and letting it out even more so with a low, satisfying moan. His mouth twisted into a wiry sneer. *"I can smell your fear."*

Woody gagged and coughed and shoved Stu away with such unexpect-ed force that it hurled him airborne. Stu landed a good ten feet away and skidded backwards through the dirt several yards more. A trail of saplings splintered in his wake before he slammed so hard into the tree in which Jack Raker was perched that the whole trunk quaked. The tremor shud-dered up the birch in an amplified wave and shivered the branches in a wild whipping motion as Jack tightened his grip and swayed precariously.

Astonished at his own strength, Woody stood frozen.

But Stu only laughed, an unnatural sound gargling up from his throat like a whistle submerged in water. He brushed the mud from his jeans as the sight of him doing so receded into shadow, a line of clouds edging across the moon so that the woods were again shrouded in transient darkness. Through this inky veil, a disembodied voice echoed from where Stu had been standing:

"Feels good, doesn't it, Woody. To wield such untethered power!"

Stepping out from the shadows of the Beech tree and into a wedge of moonlight, Stu was washed by a weak umber glow.

But the face atop his body was no longer Stu's.

Like a weak broadcast signal flickering between channels, its features wavered between Stu's one moment, something grotesquely inhuman the next. Sometimes both existed at once, causing the skin to appear to undu-late and move like snakes writhing beneath a blanket of warm wax; his eyes to darken and his mouth to sharpen into a dripping snarl like an ani-mal's.

"Can you feel it, Woody? I know you can! That energy coursing through you, transforming you? *That* is what true power feels like!"

The creature that was both Stu and not Stu stalked slowly toward him, his knees bending the inverse way so that the legs flexed backward at the joint. With every step they made a grinding sound of pebbles against a metal grate.

Inside, every cell of Woody's body palpitated as if vibrating at a molecular level, his terror building to such an unsustainable intensity that his mind began to mire in the dark impossibility of what was before him. Outwardly, he was steely and steadfast.

The Stu Thing laughed.

It was a repugnant chord of the lowest bass beneath the highest, trebling whistle: the sound of the consuming vibrations Woody had felt building inside him since that day in the Little Woods . . . beneath the shrillest, screeching, off-key notes Jack had breathed into Matt's souvenir flute as its rightful owner had kicked and convulsed as he hanged burning from a tree.

"I not only smell your fear," it said as it sniffed the air, relishing the scent. "I *feel* it, Woodrow. *I see it.*"

And the Stu Thing was now Matt Chauncey.

Diminutive and shy—standing in the middle of the woods on a stormy night in a blue blazer with brass anchor buttons—Matt's hands were behind his back as he coyly smiled, scuffing a line in the mud with a worn and dirty sneaker.

It was all very convincing.

Except for the hoof-like toe protruding from the shoe's torn fabric.

The image rippled and wavered and it was again Stu Klatz standing in front of Woody. Not the Stu Thing, not Matt.

Just Stu.

"Who are you!" Woody shouted. "WHAT THE FUCK ARE YOU?!"

"I'm Stu," it said calmly and without hesitation. But the voice had come not from from Stu's mouth, but rather from within Woody's own mind, the words a series of vibrations inside his head.

"You're not Stu! Stu can be a psychopathic fuck, but he's a run-of-the-mill, middle school playground psychofuck. A piece of shit kid, maybe, but he's no killer! And *you* killed our friend!"

Stu tilted his head lightly to the side, absorbing the words and allowing them to float there in the mist and moonlight. As if pandering to Woody, he morphed seamlessly back to Matt.

"Killing is a misunderstood concept. And I can be anyone or anything your feeble human mind needs me to be," little Matt said unperturbed as first one pant leg and then the other rippled into flame. "Existence is one infinitely complex organism, far too vast for your detestable intellect to comprehend . . . ."

In a moment, the fire was engulfing Matt's waist, devouring his chest. It licked up his chin and bubbled the skin of his cheeks as his grinning lips shriveled to reveal two buck teeth glinting beneath a broiling veil.

As if made of rope, the flames began to twist above his head into a thin, spiraling braid. Tighter and faster the flame wove together until, in one explosive shot, it fired spear-like upward into an overhanging bough of the beech. The branch crackled alight, its leaves curling and floating to the ground, each one a web of glowing skeletal embers as the fiery rope coiled around the limb like a snake. With each complete circuit it grew tighter around Matt's throat at the other end, stretching his neck and pitching his head to an unnatural angle. His eyes bulged as his trachea threatened to burst through his skin.

"Energy does not die," Matt wheezed through the flames. The words were barely audible but in Woody's mind they were deafening as Matt gripped the blazing noose with both hands and began to climb it. His fin-gernails extended into claws; his hands great mitts. And the figure inside the flames swelled and undulated as it ascended effortlessly and bear-like to the great, gnarled limb above.

"Energy only changes, Woody!"

A sonorous roar bellowed from what were now gargantuan jaws, unleashing an inhuman scream from the black hole of its mouth as the flames consumed it and then became it.

What crouched on the limb was no longer Matt, or Stu, or even the Stu Thing. It was an aberration of possibility.

A flaming embodiment of terror.

Multiple heads protruded from the conflagration, writhing and hissing at the end of long, snake-like necks. Their mouths twisted and yowled, and in each of their contorted screams the pain of a million others cried out from the depths of an endless abyss.

An abyss that devoured all hope in Woody's soul.

He stood transfixed, a black shroud of evil suffocating him as the many-headed Beast recognized Woody's subservience and rejoiced.

"Where is your father's science now, Woody?"

The question posed by the many heads at once echoed within Woody's mind. The voices uniting in harmony to emulate his dad's.

"He is right about one thing: the universal Balance. Light and Dark. One does not exist without the other. So if there is no God, how is it that I can Be? Yet here I am."

A moment later the flames were gone.

And Stu crouched alone on the scorched and barren limb. Waves of heat and smoke rose and disappeared in a new wind that began rocking the branch. Stu tightened his grip and shook his head briskly as if waking from a daydream.

"Hey ho, Woodrow!" he called down in a manner incongruous to the squall and noise as leaves and natural debris whipped around the Beech-nut in a wild cyclone. He only grinned and beckoned Woody join him in the tree. "Come . . . it is your time!"

Woody did not hesitate.

He pushed off the ground and in a single leap planted his feet solidly upon the limb next to Stu. Despite the growing tempest rocking the bough, he balanced effortlessly upon it. Woody felt no need to question this ability, nor how he had come to be standing here when the branch was more than a dozen feet above the ground.

Neither was it necessary for Stu to direct him any further.

He closed his eyes and allowed himself to indulge in the unadulterated feeling of power. When he opened them, he was able to scan the swaying canopy of leaves and limbs through eyes no longer impaired by dark.

He readily found Jimi Raker higher up in the ancient beech, clinging to a branch as it seesawed up and down in the howling gust.

With hands now tipped by thick primal claws, Woody bounded deftly up the trunk toward his target. Navigating the tree's labyrinth of branches with ease, he ducked agilely over, under and between crisscrossing limbs until he was upon Jimi, huddled in a tight ball as far to the end of the bowing branch as the boy's weight would allow.

Taking one methodical step after another, Woody stalked slowly toward him, savoring the fear he tasted as it wafted to him in rich, palpable waves.

"Please—" is all Jimi whispered before Woody wrapped a thick-clawed hand around his throat and lifted his friend high into the air.

Jimi said nothing else as Woody slung him to the ground like a rag doll. His two story descent through the branches appeared in stop-motion as lightning tiered silently across the sky to strobe the woods in pulsing, intermittent flashes.

When the last arc fizzled, the sound of Jimi dying came through the dark: a quick, sharp crack which splintered the static background of wind. Whether from Jimi's body or snapping wood was indiscernible. Then a low, guttural yelp exuded from the boy's broken mouth and blended with the echoing rumble of thunder as it rolled like deep laughter over the Beechnut.

Woody blinked hard as the light faded and again his human eyes were all but blind in the blanketing darkness of the woods. The power seeming to energize his very cells was gone, as though vacuumed away, and he crumpled limply against the trunk of the birch.

Another streak of light, brief silvery-blue, and Jimi's prone body was revealed on the ground, face down below him. The sharpened tip of a broken sapling spike poked through his back, pushing his contorted spine out of the skin.

NO! God! What have I DONE!

Clinging to his branch, Woody cried out. But the lament could not pass his lips. All energy depleting from him, the words formed only in his mind and refused to pass beyond his throat.

Now you believe, the woods themselves seemed to reply in the whispering of the wind. *But only the God you chose is here.*

As his consciousness reeled and the treetops began to spin, Woody's grip loosened and he fell several feet down to the next level of interwoven limbs. Exhausted and broken, he clung to the safety of their web and silently wailed.

He did not hear the other two boys descending upon him.

They carried him off and into the woods where the mud yielded to swamp and sloughing flats.

He did not fight back as the brackish water filled his mouth and the sludge choked the breath from his throat.

And his world became black as the life receded from him.

IV

Dan had gone missing that same night. His father, Dan's only parent, hadn't noticed whether or not he'd been in his bed, only remembering that he'd seen his son earlier in the evening watching television and then suddenly jumping on his motorbike. Beyond that, Mr. Mercer could not be more specific.

This conversation did not take place until he phoned the police a good seventy-two hours later.

By then it was too late.

But the officers weren't to know this, of course, and took down what details they could to initiate a casual search for the boy. After only a day missing, most teenagers of Dan's age (and certainly those from his background) would turn up as runaways on the streets of the next big town nearby. They were young, and not very street-smart, so were fairly easily spotted. The police would then inform Dan's father, and that was about all they would do. If the parent wanted the kid off the street, he would have to come sort it out for himself. At that stage, at least as far as the cops were concerned, they had done their job.

But Dan was not on the streets.

Before the storm, the evening had been peaceful and easy. Dan had enjoyed the day at the Beechnut with the rest of the gang. He was tired, and relaxed, and laughed to himself as he lay there fully clothed in his disheveled bed, watching in his mind as he managed to tag Stu. He'd patiently waited until the kid had to take a shit behind a tree. That was a classic, that one.

Probably the only time I'll ever tag Stu, that's for sure.

He chuckled quietly to himself and rolled over. His window was open and the sounds from the field behind his house murmured softly in the background as he closed his eyes to welcoming sleep.

And it had come quickly.

He was far and away from the neighborhood soon, drifting through his mind and investigating the many nooks and crannies and unopened doors that adorned the convoluted journey before him.

He is younger now and the family are all together. His mother, especially, stands out from the scene, her outline almost glowing in a dimension superior to the rest of the image.

She is young herself. And beautiful. She moves easily, this way and that, swaying and gliding to an unheard sons as she holds her baby close to her chest. Dan can see himself snuggling there; safe and secure.

And happy.

Then she is different. Lines, only just noticeable, wrinkle her skin around the corners of her eyes; around the mouth. She is still beautiful, and still young. But her life is evident in her countenance, although she would be concerned beyond embarrassment if she were only aware of that fact. She smiles upon her young baby boy while she bundles her wrist in a bandage. The flesh there is purple and bruising, but young Dan does not understand. All he knows is that Mommy has had an accident and this will make her all better. She flinches when the dressing is pulled tight.

A noise then makes them both wince and she pulls her son in close. Dan's Daddy has not been with them and the boy wonders where he is when the horrible sounds are scaring them.

Without obvious connection, Dan is flying high in the air.

Below him, in the Beechnut, he sees his friends in the trees and they are waving proudly to him.

You are flying, he tells himself as his perspective switches between first and third person. Then he is in the tree and laughing very hard. Jimi is smiling and Stu is there, and everyone else, although he cannot see them all. But he knows they are there. He can feel them.

In another time, the door crashes open and the man with the alcohol smell from his mouth is pulling at his mommy to and fro. She struggles and is out of Dan's view.

A slapping sound. A muffled whine.

The room is big and the ceiling is high, and that is what he sees as the sounds come to him. Sounds of pain. Hurting sounds. And his father is shouting and screaming. The man groans and then rolls from the woman's back, from the bed, into sight. He sneers at his child and slides him out of the way with his foot. Mommy is there again when the door is heard to shut hard behind them, and her face is red and swollen. She is younger and different again. Then she is gone and the boy is alone in the room.

Dan jerked in his sleep as the image forced its way in. From the open window, a cold draft rippled the curtain.

They are alone now, the man and him, in a strange room with pews and the smell of lilies and a strange purple hue of light. It is a somber room and a smooth, shiny casket is the center of their attention.

The scene whirs by him like a tape on fast-forward and he is now at the Little Woods with his friends.

He jibes and taunts the boy called Matt and though he knows that it is not right, cannot stop himself. Like an actor faithfully portraying a script, his lips snarl and shout at the other boy. And he does not like doing this. It does not feel right. Yet he watches as the Dan in his image does not stop until—

Downstairs, in front of the baseball highlights on the late sports roundup, Dan's father grasped a can of beer so tightly that it's thin sheath crumpled inwards, squirting some of the tepid liquid over his knuckles; onto the sofa. He swore at the TV and shook a fist at it before spiraling the can against its glass screen.

—a bright glowing column shines between the trees and Dan is curious, and glad of the light. He hurries toward it and is now at the Base Camp. On the ground, a boy rocks listlessly with his arms wrapped around his muddied legs; his head is bleeding and in the dream it is too large to fit the body correctly. Then there is no sound as Dan traipses across the naturally littered floor. Minute twigs snap beneath his feet but are struck dumb before they are able to sound.

All is quiet.

The inferno lifting into the sky does not crackle. It does not hiss. The boy in the tree does not scream though his mouth is hugely round, the face distorted and terrified. His almost naked body drops from the branch and springs back up, then down, then up, then down. It is no more than a cartoon. The neck is like elastic and then Matt's eye swells and bursts. The moisture from within it spits—again silently—into the flames licking so close to the boy's dangling body.

"You did this, Dan. You did this!"

The voice explodes like a cannon against this soundless arena as Matt claws the nylon ligature away from his elongated neck. Minus its support, he drops to the oval clearing and collapses while the rest of the dream players continue their performance unawares. They hoof around the fire as in their dimension the boy still twitches, hanging in the air. The faces are covered in dirt and blood . . . the boy's blood. The sound of a whistle pipes high into the air as Jack breathes life into the boy's wooden flute.

In his dream Dan reached into the scene and its surface shimmered into ripples like water over glass.

Matt is now sitting placidly on the rooted stump in front of the parallel logs. He is scratching his thumbnail over the stump's surface, polished smooth from countless generations of boys standing upon it. The sound of the jagged nail against the dead wood eradicates all other sound from the alternate dream in the background, muting the episode as it continues to play on faithfully, silently, without he and Dan.

Dan stepped out of the dream and was now alone with the dead boy in a dark blue suit which was still clean and neatly creased. Its tidiness only accentuated the gruesome specter the boy had become. Matt did not bother to look up as Dan approached.

Still, Matt's nail traced meticulously across the stump, its sound the only thing audible.

Dan stepped tentatively forward and the nail abruptly stopped, the new silence absolute and overwhelming.

Slowly, Matt lifted his head.

Beneath a mat of thick dark hair, a black and bloated face. The charred features tinted further from the chemicals that had been pumped into the carcass in posthumous preparation. The artificial eye which had been inserted in place of the missing one was askew in its socket, the white showing large and glossy. The other was clouded by a translucent film and deflated of its natural corpulence.

"Surprised to see me . . . ?" A thick, dark gel pooled at the corners of Matt's mouth where the lips stretched to form the words and split the dehydrated flesh. He tilted his head to one side and the congealed substance dropped in tiny black pearls down his chin.

"Come closer," he said and smiled.

Dan's heart thumped beneath his ribs as the creature from his sleep stared vacuously at him.

"Come on, Dan. Come and play."

Matt pulled himself upright and extended his hand from a deep suit cuff. Laying in his bed, Dan felt compelled to reach for it; to touch it. He wanted to feel those fingers, those deadened digits which lingered in the air in front of him, to know the tactile sensation of the charred skin clinging to the grizzled tissue beneath, forming to the shape of the hard bone.

"I played with you guys. Now it's your turn to come and play."

Dan extended his own hand.

"Come with me Dan. It is different here. So very different. I can take you to your mother. She wants to see you. She misses you—"

Matt's voice was pure and sweet. In Dan's eyes his image glowed clean and warm, Matt again the innocent boy before betrayal.

"Come, and be away from the badness."

Dan did not see that Matt's arm hung wrongly at his side, twisted from its socket by Stu's malevolent grip. He did not notice the branded indent of the collar which strangled the twisted, elongated neck; the skin beginning to blister from invisible flames . . . .

All he saw was freedom.

He now rides through the beautiful forest, the wind rushing by warmly. There is a light which beckons him on; a light which will take him away. He wants to be taken away—

Dan ran from his room and jumped on his motorbike.

The rusty exhaust pipe roared to life, bellowing thick black smoke. Dan twisted the throttle and popped the clutch, and the back tire squealed to life. Weaving a greasy line across the concrete, he tore out of the garage and onto the gravel driveway as pebbles shot machine-gun-like against the already tattered siding of the house.

Through the back yard and across the fields beyond, the trees swept by in the dark as Dan maneuvered expertly through them in spite of the broken headlamp which bobbed up and down above the motorcycle's front fork. Shining ripe above a tenuous mist—the product of the day's earlier rain kissing the overheated summer ground—the full moon led the way in warm, umber light.

As he rode, only a single word resonated over and over inside Dan's every thought:

Come.

He steered the bike between the twin ponds, skidding beneath the pine entrance to the Little Woods. Soon, the Father Oak loomed large and sentient. Below its huge branches and all about the clearing, the pile of black ash (*Matt's ash*) had been traced and scattered into tracks by innumerable tires and feet. A remnant of yellow caution tape, still knotted around a branch, whipped in the rising breeze as the approaching storm drew in.

Cold discomfort bolted through his body and Dan throttled the motorcycle quickly past, steering as though guided by an unearthly force through the dense and blinding woodland to his destination.

Matt was waiting for him at the top of the chasm.

The bank descended gradually at first, but then dropped steeply to the stream running through its belly, burbling down.

Their stream, Dan commended proudly to himself. *Their* creek.

It was the place he and Jack and Stu had so often waited and played, killing time while the other War team scoured the woods aimlessly for them. It was a secret place, a special refuge, deeper in the Little Woods than all the others dared venture. It was alive with sound and excitement. At the creek, things were different. Things had . . . *Power.*

But tonight the stench of the freshly decaying corpse filled the air.

Treetops were empty and lifeless. Poisoned by the shade which walked amongst them, taking their power as its own.

But Dan did not—could not—sense this.

He smiled at the rotting shell before him who held out his arms, entreating that he join him.

So Dan slid the bike to a stop and kicked down the stand.

Walking calmly to the edge of the chasm, and with clearest intention, he coiled one end of a cable—which he'd obediently brought from the garage—around the girth of a tree whose huge, aged branches stretched dynamically over the precipice. He tied it off in a compact double knot and threw it over the branch, studying his work and tugging on it more than once to test its soundness.

Then he casually circled the other end around his neck.

The song of the heavens lights upon his ears and Dan is filled with joy. He can see his mother on the other side, beckoning. Matt is there also, and the boy forgives. His face is full and bright; the child that was.

The Beast that once was Matt was not on the other side.

It was here, now, on the precipice of the chasm; cackling at the boy on the motorbike.

A clump of worm-ridden earth dropped from its open mouth.

The water below rushed wildly through the cavern, as if pulled by the very force of the ebbing moon overhead. It tumbled over rock and trunk and fed hungrily at its banks, washing the confines away.

A beetle clambered out of Matt's ear and scurried around the back of his head, its sensors tasting for the disintegrating flesh beneath the scalp.

"Come on Dan—let's play!" Matt beseeched.

So Dan Mercer mounted the motorbike and revved it up.

The motorcycle jolted forward, rear tire digging into the ground and spewing clods of mud as Dan circled back around and accelerated.

Swiftly gaining momentum, trees washed by in a blur as the cliff edge loomed. The teenager tightened his hands on the throttle as he lifted over the edge and the anchored metal cable around his neck reached its full extent and snapped tight.

Most of Dan plunged into the darkness of the chasm where the moon-light did not reach, the motorbike disappearing quietly beneath the run-ning stream as its metal melded into the torso still astride it.

Still yoked in the recoiling cable which glinted in the nocturnal light, Dan's head suspended above the bank, sweeping in wide elliptical move-ments. A thin stream of blood from his neck darkened the ground in neat-ly traced concentric rings, each one decreasing in size as the swinging of the cable slowed.

The only sound was the rhythmic squeaking of the braided steel line as it rubbed inside the freshly weeping channel it had notched across the top of the overhanging branch.

As the clouds choked out the moonlight.

V

In the kitchen, Veronica and Harold Cockerton embraced their sons after the morning call from Mrs. Raker. They were finding themselves sorely unequipped to communicate to the boys about Craig Dalton.

Explaining the death of not one, but now *two,* twelve-year-old boys from the neighborhood, and in just the past few weeks, was definitely not something found in the ubiquitous 'Parenting 101 Handbook' they knew their sons assumed they had.

Every once and a while, as they spoke in calm and comforting tones, they would share a look between them, thinking it unnoticed by their sons. It was a mutual recognition of this shortcoming in their parenting repertoire to truly say anything of value. At such a pivotal moment, it made them feel beyond helpless.

Now more than ever they wished there really was such a manual.

But as there was not, all they could think to do was wrap their sons in their arms and tell them that everything would eventually make sense— some way, somehow—and assure them that, no matter what, the boys were always safe.

After several minutes of hugging and a few soft tears, Mrs. Cockerton was the first to speak.

"Mrs. Raker is a little worried about Jimi, though. She's not sure he came home last night," she shared, adding that such a thing wasn't all that unusual for the Raker household. "Have you two seen him around? I'm sure he will be home soon but . . . it's just that Jack says he has no clue where Jimi is."

Bryan had a clue. And he was certain Jimi wasn't coming home. Just the same way he believed that Woody and Dan weren't either.

But how could he say that to his parents?

Well, Mom and Dad. I think Jimi's a goner. In fact, I saw Woody and Big Dan die, too. They all pegged it in a freaky dream I had after the drive-in movies last night. But I got to race a souped-up Trans Am through the fields to the Little Woods, so at least that bit was cool . . . .

It would be crazy talk. Besides, there was no hard proof yet that his dream was in any way a kind of prophecy. After all, even though he and his brother could share almost complete conversations between them solely through their thoughts, none had ever experienced an actual kind of psychic vision before.

Okay sure. That wasn't strictly true anymore. Ian had a dream about Craig last night. And here they were right now, finding out that Mr. Dalton had in fact killed the kid.

But Bryan had never experienced something psychic like that. And Ian's ability always did seem a bit stronger than his own.

Then again, none of the three boys in his dream were currently accounted for. But that could simply mean they were all together down at the gang's new hangout in the Beechnut.

Bryan considered all of these things in a lightning round internal debate with himself, then decided to follow his own advice which he'd given Ian earlier just a few minutes earlier: best not to say anything. At least not yet.

"No, Mom," he answered his mother but looked at Ian. It was a *don't-you-dare-say-anything-about-your-Craig-dream* kinda look.

Ian heard him loud and clear through their uniquely shared internal dialog. Every word and inflection. No look was required.

"No . . . ." is all he answered after an odd pregnant pause.

Mrs. Cockerton cupped her youngest son's chin in her hand and caressed his face. "You sure, Ian? If you kn—"

"OK then," Mr. Cockerton interjected. "I'm sure Jimi'll turn up just fine sometime later today. The important thing is that the two of you are here and okay."

"That's right. Nothing's going to happen to my boys," Veronica asserted in no uncertain terms, kissing their cheeks. "I want you both to know that no matter what, you will always be safe."

Most *definitely* safe, she emphasized, following the unequivocal vow with an inquiry as to how they'd both feel about a nice mug of hot chocolate and some freshly baked cupcakes on such a rainy, yucky day, all ways 'round.

VI

Later that evening, the police issued a BOLO—Be On the Look Out—for Jack and Jimi Raker's dad.

When Jimi never returned home that afternoon, Mrs. Raker finally summoned officers to the house in a hysterical and barely articulate call when Jack then disappeared later that evening.

And their father, too.

Since Woody was also reported by his parents to have been at a sleepover at the Raker house the night before and also had not yet returned home, the fairly obvious presumption among most was that old man Raker had killed both his sons, plus the hippie parents' kid, then bought himself a one way ticket to Nowheresville.

Some even postulated that Patricia Raker probably had something to do with it all, a cruel accusation which drove the mother and wife—now wholly alone—to the limits of her sanity and would taint her innocent life over many more decades to follow.

VII

"We're going to die," Bryan told his brother upon hearing the news. It was an emotionless statement, all the tears cried out of him earlier and now leaving space for only grounded, pragmatic summation. "Matt's coming for us, Ian. Because of what we did."

He took a moment to let that sink in, admitting even to himself that when said out loud, it sounded bonkers. What sounded worse, but at least possessed a tangibility to it was this:

"There's only three of us left now."

Ian vehemently shook his head, refusing to accept his theory.

"No! No no! You're wrong. I know you've got it all wrong because there's still at least *four* of us. So why would you even say that?!"

He reminded Bryan that Matt and Craig were dead; they knew that. But Woody, Jimi and Jack were only missing. They could still show up when they found old man Raker. And even if you put the three of them aside for now, he argued, there were still four of them left—not three—so Bryan had to have it all wrong. Ian then counted on his fingers as he reeled off the names: "There's still me, you, Stu and Dan. See . . . . Four! So what you're saying can't be true. The dream I had was just a dream. Or maybe I got it wrong. You're jumping to crazy conclusions!"

Bryan got it. He knew all too well why his younger brother was freaked out right about now. He was too. Hell, it was only that morning he was having this same argument with himself.

But that was then. And this was now.

"Huh-uh. They're all dead, Ian." Bryan was shaking his head. "And Dan's dead too. I haven't told you yet, but I saw it all. In a vision of my own. Just like you did . . . about Craig . . . last night."

He then explained how he saw Jimi, Woody and Dan all die in the nightmare that scared him shitless. He admitted he couldn't be sure they died exactly the way he'd seen, because the whole thing was surreal and fragmented and too difficult to make sense of. It was more of a feeling he had—an understanding—being conveyed to him, just the same way that a similar message had been delivered to Ian. "Now Jack, I don't know what happened to him," Bryan stated. "I didn't see him in my dream at all. Maybe he's still out there with his dad somewhere. Or maybe old man Raker did do him in, just like they're saying he did."

He went on to say that he was pretty certain about two things, however. First, that the dreams he and Ian both had weren't just something they created in their sleep, but were more like crazy, mixed up messages they'd been sent. The second was that the three boys in his vision most definitely hadn't died at the hand of Mr. Raker. He just knew that wasn't true.

When Bryan was finished laying out his argument in the best way he thought such lunacy could sound out loud, Ian just sat there, silent and unblinking.

Despite the overwhelming recognition vibrating within the very essence of his being—an all-consuming feeling that told him Bryan was in fact right—Ian would not allow his mind to succumb to it. "We don't know for sure Big Dan's dead."

VIII

Mr. Mercer—finally fed up to his eyeteeth that not a lick of chores were being done around the place—called the police to ask if they'd seen his no-good-piece-a-shit-fat-ass kid anywhere, and if they did see him, they better send his ass home ASAP because there was a lot of shit to be done around the place.

It wasn't an hour after the cops arrived on his doorstep that the telephone tree went into action. When the phone chirruped sharply at the Cockerton house, Veronica expected it might be Hare calling to say he'd be working late. Or maybe it was Betty Blaugh down the street returning her call with the number of that new place in town offering the disco dance lessons everyone was suddenly so keen on.

It was neither of those.

IX

What are we gonna do!? Ian projected in his mind as he pulled his knees tightly to his chin and rocked back and forth on his bed. Every third time he leant backwards, the heavy wood headboard banged against the wall with a muffled but recognizable thud.

The unspoken question, wrapped in a vibrating baritone thought wave only his brother could sense, was instantly received by Bryan in his room next door.

I dunno, Ian. Stop banging your headboard so I can think!

I'm scared, Bry . . . . Ian quietly sobbed and although the whimpers were audible, the words themselves remained silent. He still rocked back and forth, but now made an effort to not lean so far back.

I know you are, pal. I am too.

It was the truth. And the new internal noise Bryan was suddenly receiving wasn't helping alleviate that apprehension. Up until now, he had only ever received mental vibrations from his brother, those unique telepathic waves as unmistakably Ian's as his actual voice.

But now a new sound was echoing inside of Bryan.

It was an unsettling, foreign wave he didn't recognize: a deep frequency that reminded him of a bass subwoofer note so low that you feel it pulsing through you more than you actually hear it. The wave was thrumming so intensely that it threatened to saturate his consciousness with an all-consuming, paralyzing dread.

It's coming . . . he announced to himself and immediately regretted the cognitive slip as next door, Ian's sobs spiked to an audible moan.

Bryan inhaled deeply and swung his legs off the bed. He placed his bare feet on the smooth wood floorboards and embraced the feeling of grounded safety they provided. Closing his eyes, he concentrated on his breathing and consciously refuted the subjugation of this dark, inexplicable vibration.

In steps, the feeling ebbed to a still unpleasant but governable level, and for some reason Matt's father—Mr. Chauncey—permeated the effort. Bryan shook off the image and opened his eyes.

But it's coming, Ian, whether we're scared or not. The statement was projected in calm, steady cadence. After a moment's further reflection he added: *It's gonna be alright though.*

He didn't know if the afterthought was convincing enough. This gift they shared fed off their emotions more than some clearly logical process, and Ian could always see through his deceit.

Promise? Ian asked.

Bryan hesitated, then did promise.

We have to do one thing though. To really make sure, he added. *Tonight, after Mom and Dad go to bed. You and me are going back to the Little Woods . . . .*

Seventeen

H GOD, REBECCA!" Ian threw himself from his bar stool, toppling it off balance. His legs smacked hard against the high top table as he jumped up, the array of bottles atop it jangling together in a discordant melody. "Bryan! We have to go!"

But his brother was already halfway across the bar, heading for the restroom, Ian's voice lost behind the clamor of the jukebox.

The images were coming at him fast and furious, striking with blacks and greys so much stronger than ever before. They mixed and turned, coiling up into his consciousness and poured into one another like liquid paintings, never fully revealing themselves. All he understood was the feeling: dark and grotesque and unnatural.

Then he sees Rebecca. The children.

And the Woods.

A blackness impossible to describe.

There's a car. Fumes. The Woods again.

And then . . . Matt.

This he saw all too clearly: the dead boy's rotted body looming over Rebecca in a deeply dark space.

A wave of bitter cold tension ran through him and Ian teetered on his feet, fighting hard to not pass out. Della, perched behind the bar and engrossed in a daytime drama on the wall-mounted television, twisted on her stool to see Ian leaning off-kilter.

Not another one, she thought and shook her head. *These crackers and their lunchtime benders. Can't anyone seem to hold their damn whiskey 'round here any more.*

This one looked as if he were crying as he stumbled towards her.

"Police! I need the police!"

Ian was pleading frantically as he ran unsteadily in her direction, trying to see past the horrible images from his mind. He was shaky on his feet and speaking too fast, and he knew it from the look on Della's face. She was staring at him wide-eyed. But logic was out the window and he grabbed for her—to steady himself as much as anything—and the proprietress backed away sharply.

"Whoa!" Della's face contorted with anxiety as she pulled away, leaping off her own barstool so brusquely that she nearly fell. A half-empty bottle of beer dropped to the red ceramic tile floor and the shards splayed across it with a resounding echo.

"I'm sorry, I'm sorry," Ian pleaded as he withdrew and fumbled for his cell phone. He flipped it open, shaking so hard barely managed to dial nine-one-one.

A woman's voice crackled through faintly on the other end. It was calm and soothingly deep:

"Emergency services, can I help you?"

Ian tried to speak all at once and managed only a gust of hot air into the phone, the sound whooshing into the mouthpiece and feeding back loudly into his own ear. Conditioned to it, the woman on the other end ignored it, recognizing the signs of panic. She began to calmly ask him his name but he cut her off.

"Police!" he spurted. "Please, I need help! I'm afraid—I'm afraid someone might be in danger!"

"Name, house number and street please."

"Cockerton. Rebecca—" Ian was swimming inside the cacophony of images in his mind. "The address is–is—"

What are you going to tell them Ian? That a long dead childhood friend just assaulted your sister-in-law? Okay. Sure. Let's give that a try and see how it goes.

It was insane. Impossible.

The static in his head grew until he could no longer think, and he pitched forward as the bar bowed and bent like a fluid oasis the way the road ahead seems to shimmer and waver on a hot summer's day. The dim lighting became watery shades of grey; his head light as a helium balloon.

The cell phone dropped from his grip and he stumbled headlong across the room while the operator's disembodied voice rose tinny and small as the mobile phone scuttled across the tile.

Inside the bathroom, Bryan was draped over a washbasin, the cold water running over his fingers and down the drain.

"*Bryan!*" Ian's voice echoed around the cold, hard surfaces as he burst into the restroom. Bryan looked up and small drop of colored mucus feel from his lower lip.

"Wha—I don't feel so hot."

Again he leaned over the sink and threw up.

"Bryan, we've got to go! Now. It's Rebecca. And the kids."

Ian tried to keep his voice from betraying his panic when all he really wanted to do was scream and cry and break down on the floor and not get up; to forget about this whole fucking business of the woods and just go away and be normal again. He wanted to *not* see things—horrible things—anymore. More than anything, he longed to be back in New York, away from it all. Away from this impossible reality that resembled insanity. At least in the City everything was normal and gritty and real.

Bryan stared blankly into the mirror, his eyes dulled and uncomprehending. He blinked twice then wiped his mouth with the back of his hand.

"Come on for Christ's sake! It's your wife and kids! Do you understand me? I've had another vis—"

The word stuck in Ian's throat. More than about any, that one word had never sat well with him. It made him think of irrational people spouting irrational nonsense.

Lunatics, Ian. That's what you fucking mean. So why not just come out and say it? You think the word 'vision' means you're off your rocker, one card short of a full deck. And it scares the shit out of you, doesn't it? Perhaps more than the visions themselves.

He paused and the silence of the white tiled room was overwhelming.

"Vision," Bryan finished the sentence for him and splashed cold water on his face. His hair was streaked and the moisture dripped down his forehead and into his eyes. "Becky . . . the kids?" he asked in an oddly calm manner, perhaps the crest of realization mounting but not yet breaking.

Ian could only nod as the cacophony of jagged, black noise cluttering his brain began to slowly dissolve away and leave him with nothing but a deep and uncertain anxiety.

II

"Everything okay in there!" Della Dempsey demanded more than asked, her muffled voice filtering through from the other side of the restroom door. Anxiety had twisted her accent so that it was harsher and more staccato now, definitely conveying more Appalachian than Southern Belle. She didn't care. She also didn't care about their problems, or what had so radically changed this one stranger's behavior in particular. She just wanted both of these guys gone.

Neither brother answered.

Della 'hmmphed' at the door, considering for a moment just going in and pulling them both out and tossing them into the street.

"Meh, piké twa," she cursed instead, just loud enough to be heard from the other side of the door. They wouldn't know she'd just told them to fuck off, but it made her feel better. She gave the door a thump with her fist. "Time you boys were on your way! Closing up!"

The brothers stood in sober silence before Bryan spoke.

"How certain . . . ?" he asked and again wiped the back of his hand across his mouth.

Ian did not have to answer aloud.

III

"Shit, I know I'm gonna regret this," Della replied and sighed as she relaxed a bit, settling into her pose but crossing her arms and still keeping a good two paces away. "What do you expect *me* to do?"

"Something is wrong. Really wrong. We need to get home, Della. I mean, like, *now*."

Della shook her head emphatically without even thinking about it. She wasn't going anywhere with this crazy cracker. Hell, she'd only just met him and he was already causing problems. The other one she sort of knew, though he didn't come in often enough for her to really know much about him. His wife seemed pleasant enough, but that didn't amount to a hill of beans.

"Get a cab," she replied and began retreating towards safety behind the bar. She did so walking steadfastly backwards, not lowering her gaze.

"Della, we don't have time. Please. I think someone's hurt."

IV

Route 60 darkened as the rain returned and the halogen streetlights dotting its side buzzed and flickered on. Their glow was brilliant white, almost bluish against the waning natural light. Della focused as she followed the beacons along the twisting and hilly road, her boxy VW Thing connecting them one-by-one like a fat orange pencil joining the dots in a child's puzzle book. Her anxiety mounting, the only repeating thought she had as she concentrated through the wind and slanting rain was a hope that she would not regret offering to do this good deed.

It's good dharma, Della, she reaffirmed to herself and purposefully counted the lights in a meditative fashion, grounding her electric nerves. *It always returns to you.*

Always, a voice other than her own seemed to reply inside her head and her eyes darted to the rear view mirror where the two men sat in her back seat. The one she slightly knew was visibly trembling, his voice unsteady as he spoke to the 9-1-1 operator on his mobile. The other one jostled anxiously in his seat as he wiped the condensation from the window and stared into the darkness which had descended upon the afternoon like a woolen blanket.

"What?" she asked the latter and the man slowly turned to meet her gaze in the small rectangular mirror.

"It's just over the next hill," Ian answered brusquely. "Then down into the neighborhood. On the left."

"No, what else did you say?"

Ian shook his head meekly.

"I didn't . . . nothing . . . . We're almost there."

"—Not sure. No. I'm not there—I don't know what happened but please send an ambulance . . . . Yes. Yes. Please! Hurry!"

Bryan was pleading with the small voice on the other end of the line that was trying to understand exactly what the emergency was. When he then reeled off their home address, he was surprised to have the operator inform him that fire and rescue had already been dispatched. He confirmed the address, a question more than a statement, and Della quietly repeated the street name and house number to herself also.

She didn't have to.

As they crested the next hill, the basin of the neighborhood was awash in swirling red and blue light, leaving no question which was the correct address. Two firetrucks, a paramedic and one police cruiser were already positioned at haphazard angles across the driveway and front lawn of the Cockerton house.

"That's correct, sir. A neighbor already called," the voice tinnily confirmed for all three in the car to hear as Bryan pulled the phone away from his ear. Even through the small speaker, the operator's tone conveyed calm and routine authority. *"They should already be there. I can stay on the line with you if you'd lik—"*

Bryan was out of the Thing's clunky rear door and racing toward the flurry of noise and activity before Della even rolled the VW to a complete stop. "Rebecca!"

The cry was lost amid the cyclical, pneumatic hum of a hydraulic spreader which had been wedged between the seal of the closed overhead door and the concrete driveway. One of the firefighters held Bryan back as the jaws of the machine began to spread open, the bottom steel panel of the garage door beginning to ribbon upward.

A grey cloud of car exhaust billowed instantly out.

The pneumatic jaws continued to spread open like a crocodile's grin and the bottom panel rumpled in the center like a bow tie pasta.

"Whoa!"One of the firefighters shouted and waved back toward the truck to cut the spreader's power.

The mechanical noise cycled to a stop and the same firefighter called out to anyone inside, listening for a response.

The only sound above the wind and driving rain was the Blazer's engine dutifully idling away inside the garage.

"Okay, let's get two of you in there!"

He drove a long breaker bar in the crease above the door's bottom panel, ripping it mostly off its tracks. Another firefighter pulled it completely away and slung it aside as the next panel up was torn from its rails just as quickly.

Without notice, two more firemen crawled under the door and disappeared inside the cloud of fumes which continued to pour out in a noxious wave.

A moment later the Blazer engine stopped.

"We got her," a voice echoed from within, muffled by the firefighter's oxygen mask. "Female. Mid-thirties."

As what remained of the garage door began to lurch unsteadily upward, the silhouette of both men appeared with Rebecca's unconscious body in their arms. They carried her far from the fumes and laid her on the grass, stepping aside as paramedics surrounded her.

Bryan broke free of the firefighter detaining him and ran to his wife. He fell to his knees as the medics strapped an oxygen mask over Rebecca Cockerton's face and began administering manual CPR, counting the compressions. "BECKY—"

V

The ambulance pulled away as thick, greasy smoke rose from its tires fighting for purchase on the wet blacktop. Lights flashing, its sirens blared to life as it pulled onto Route 60 and accelerated away.

In the back of the second police cruiser which had arrived, Bryan was sobbing with his head in his hands as Ian and Della stood adjacent to it on the driveway, answering the officer's questions.

"Laveau. L–A–V–for-victory–E–A–U. DeLaCroix Laveau," Della said in response to the policeman's request for the correct spelling. She offered Ian a sidelong, deferential smile.

Ian responded in kind. Obviously this would make for an interesting story at another time. Right now he could only focus on his brother.

The officer closed his notebook and stepped aside, indicating that he'd just be a moment. Speaking into his two-way radio, he nodded a few times and returned. "She's being transported to St. John's Hospital in town. She's currently responsive, but I'm afraid that's all the information I have."

"And the kids?" Ian asked as calmly as his fraying nerves would allow. It was well past 4:30 and they should have been home by now. "Do we know anything about where they are? We can't just leave. But my brother needs to be with his wife. How do we—"

The officer indicated no knowledge of their location and asked if Ian wanted him to place an official All Points Bulletin out for them.

"What time do they normally come home?" Della interjected. Her smoky green eyes were soft with compassion as she cast them upon Ian. "Maybe the bus is just running late. Why don't you and I stay here and wait for them, and maybe the officer here can give your brother a lift to St. Johns?"

She smiled at the policeman and Ian was certain he even saw her eye-lashes flutter a little bit. Or maybe he was imagining it. Either way, Della got the response she was hoping for.

The officer agreed and waited for the last fire truck to reverse through the yard, watching with little interest as it created great dual-wheeled trenches before pulling onto the neighborhood road and trundling loudly away. He slammed his car door shut and spoke into his two-way again before starting the cruiser's engine.

Ian leaned through the open rear door and placed his hands on his brother's shoulders, looking into his eyes to ensure he understood. "We're going to wait here for Diane and Andrew. Then we'll come and meet you at the hospital."

"Jesus, Ian. What the fuck is going on here?" Bryan's eyes were wet and red and begging to make sense of what had happened.

"Hey, she's gonna be alright."

"No. Nothing is alright, Ian! Mom and Dad are slammed into by a truck a week and a half ago. This morning you tell me you saw it . . . from your New York apartment . . . *before* it even happened. And then you say that Matt was there. Fucking Matt Chauncey? You're talking about the dead kid from the Little Woods. Right? By the road. When Mom and Dad are . . . . And then y-y-you wake up screaming like a demon last night. From some fucked up dream about that stupid kid and a cartoon ranger. Now Becky's found unconscious in the garage with the door down and the car running? What the fuck! This isn't coincidence anymore, Ian—"

Bryan choked back his fear and anger.

"I thought we took care of this shit. Like twenty years ago!"

"So did I," is all Ian somberly replied and softly closed the cruiser's door, never breaking eye contact with his brother as the cop swung the car around and headed for the hospital.

VI

The school bus pulled onto the top road of the neighborhood not more than a couple minutes later. Della and Ian hurried to the bi-fold door as it folded in upon itself, Ian bounding up all three steps in a single jump.

"Hey! What the f—" The hefty male driver blurted out, judiciously cutting the sentence short as his eyes darted to the overhead mirror and the two dozen elementary school students who were hoping he would finish it. They began to snigger and grin. "You can't be in here!"

The rather large, tattooed arm he then threw across the narrow aisle to stop Ian from progressing any further showed he was definitely willing to put his money where his mouth was.

"Diane! Andrew!" Ian called out and rose up on his toes to scour the seats, his eyes methodically scanning each row of seats before moving onto the next, like a typewriter's carriage across a page. He was only half-way done when the bus driver, now on his feet, grabbed him by a rear belt loop and unceremoniously pulled him off the bus.

Three rows from the back, Diane slinked embarrassed out of her vinyl-clad bench seat. Covering her face as she hurried up the aisle, she pulled Andrew from his spot a few rows further forward and pressed him toward the door.

Andrew jumped buoyantly from the last step, mirthful.

Diane kept her eyes on the ground as the bus driver asked if she knew these people. "Yeah. That's my uncle," she said to the driveway.

The bus driver gave Ian one more good look up and down before climbing back into the bus, mumbling something no one understood.

Ian knelt and pulled Diane close. "I'm so glad you're okay. What happened that you're so late?"

Diane shrugged. "We had to turn around for Crystal."

"Crystal?"

"Yeah. Crystal Riley. She's always forgetting something and ran back into the school for her clarinet. So she missed the bus. Mr. Allen had to turn around when her brother, Davey, finally told him."

"Mr. Allen?"

Diane *ugghed*, her expression sheer indignation as she explained, as if her uncle were mentally stunted, that Mr. Allen was the bus driver. She pointed to the burly man and the driver smiled and waved back; he then turned to Ian and his countenance fell to a look of thunder as he pulled the bi-fold doors closed with a bang and crunched the transmission into first gear.

The big yellow bus wobbled from side to side as it lurched into the street and rumbled down the road. Disappearing from view as it crested the small hill leading towards the fields at the bottom of the neighborhood, its grinding gearbox still revealed its location.

"So, listen. We have to go to the hospital," Ian said as he angled Diane's chin up so that she would give him her full attention. "Everything's okay. But we need to meet your dad there."

Diane pulled her face from his hand and crossed her arms, staring unblinkingly at Della.

"Oh," Ian added. "And this is Della . . . Dempsey. I think. Or maybe La–something. But you can just call her Della."

"DeLaCroix Laveau," Della said and deftly curtsied before she extended a hand which Diane promptly shook. "But yes, you can just call me Della, ma'am."

"I will," Diane agreed, adding that she looked like she was probably a nice lady. And at least she didn't embarrass them like her uncle did.

Della laughed and repeated her introduction to Andrew who shouted, "HI DELLA!" somewhat over-exuberantly in return.

He immediately skirted around her, his eyes wide as he ran his hand along the ridges of her vintage car's flat paneled sides. He shrieked with delight as he assured her that she had a super cool car. "I bet lotsa people don't like it, huh Della. But I think it's awesome! Can I drive it?" the six-year-old asked without compunction.

"I can't imagine any reason why not," the woman offered as she bent the driver's seat forward and ushered him into the back. "Maybe a little later on?"

"You hear that! I'm gonna drive us home later," Andrew beamed to his sister as Diane climbed into the back seat beside him.

"Uh huh," she quipped and rolled her eyes. "It is a pretty cool car though, Della."

VII

". . . N'awlinz," Della drawled as she pulled onto Route 60 and headed in the direction of town.

Lost in a mental fog, Ian was staring emptily out the passenger window. The sound of Della's voice snapped him back.

"I'm sorry . . . what?"

"Look, I know you're worried, hun. But we got ourselves a good twenty minutes to kill. With circumstances as they are—intertwining our paths fairly quick here, so it seems—feels only proper you and I know at least a little something about the other. Don't ya think?"

"Sure, yeah. Of course," he absently replied as the fields glistening in the rain swept by the window.

Della focused on the road and contributed nothing further.

Twenty seconds passed by like twenty minutes.

"I'm sorry, Della. I wasn't really listening." He squirmed uncomfortably and cleared his throat. Funny how powerful silence can be; something he'd taught his sales team at the *Bulletin* for years. "Okay. So you said your name was La . . . La–something."

"Laveau, sugar. And it's okay, I'll forgive you . . . this time. Been some kind of a day, to be sure."

Maybe so, Ian agreed, but apologized as it was still no excuse for rudeness, especially given all she was doing for them. He was terrible at names —even at the best of times—but that was little justification.

"So, that's where you're from, New Orleans?" he asked out of social obligation more than genuine interest, his years of sales training kicking in like muscle memory.

Della chuckled.

"Well, I'm from N'awlinz. Don't know of a place by the name NEW orLEANS, but I guess I can forgive a Yankee's linguistic ignorance."

She'd put some extra spice into her accent and winked at the children in the backseat. Andrew giggled, though he wasn't wholly sure why. Diane smiled, feeling herself really starting to warm up to this stranger.

"That's two pardons now, Mr. Ian," Della warned. "One more, and I'm afraid you're out."

Ian grinned and put his hands up in mock surrender.

"So. The whole Dempsey thing?" The question was genuine this time, Ian's sincere interest in the conversation rapidly growing in direct proportion to their increasing distance from the neighborhood.

"Folks assume it's my name. Because of the bar. Familiarity makes them feel comfortable or something, I guess. So I just go with it."

As if he had been unconsciously holding it, Ian expelled his breath in a long relieving sigh and settled more comfortably into his seat. He liked Della's voice. It was natural and soothing. And her lilting Louisiana accent made him feel cosseted and safe, like a warm bowl of Southern hospitality. It offered the perfect distraction from the dark, underlying vibrations he didn't much feel like acknowledging, let alone sharing, at this precise moment.

Sensing the change in his energy and body language, Della loosened her grip on the steering wheel and continued speaking as Ian relaxed against the head rest, his face gently angled toward her.

"After a while, not many called me Della anymore. Everyone pretty much called me Dempsey. I guess it just stuck."

"Makes sense," Ian nodded. "Did you own a bar in New Orlea—I'm sorry, *N'awlinz*—Della?"

"No, sugarfoot. That part, like quite a bit else, is all new for me."

"So what did Miss Laveau do to earn a crust in the Big Easy?"

"Ha! Now that's a question."

She turned to catch his gaze and her smoky eyes caught the light in such a way that they shone almost silver. Against her caramel skin, it was entrancing.

"I come from a long line of French Catholics on my daddy's side." Then unflinchingly added, "Voodoo Priestesses on my mama's."

If it was shock value she was going for, it definitely landed. She had his full attention now. And though Ian wasn't quite sure how her religious ancestry tied into her job, he was definitely intrigued enough to follow her breadcrumbs. "Seems like a rather unusual pair of bedfellows, doesn't it. Catholic and Voodoo?"

"Mmmm," Della hummed. "You may be right. It *is* full of bizarre ceremonial ritual centered around a dark, mystical ideology. Plus a sprinkling of superstition thrown in, to boot."

"I really don't know that much about it, but I've heard Voodoo is like that."

"Voodoo, sugar? I was talking about Catholicism." Della winked in his direction, and for the first time in weeks, Ian laughed out loud.

Hard and full. And it felt amazing.

"But seriously," Della continued. "I was always intrigued by the amount of similarity I was noticing between the two. And then one day I realized just how much they intersected other belief systems across the world—Buddhism, Hinduism, Judaism, Zoroastrianism to name just a few—and ended up pursuing a Masters in Theology with a particular focus on mysticism. Then I opened my own business. First a modest market stand on Jackson Square on the weekends, then an itsy-bitsy brick-and-mortar place on the edge of the Quarter. I sold spiritual and metaphysical elements. You know, crystals, sage, books, charms, spiritual artifacts, tarot cards . . . and also did a few readings here and there. Turns out I'm gifted, in that regards at least, so that part of the biz took off pretty quick."

"Wow. So how exactly does a mystical, theological psychic from the Bayou end up the proprietor of a redneck bar, and in a podunk town like this no less?"

"Redneck bar? No offense taken." Della rolled her eyes but smiled. "Well, what takes any girl out of her hometown and away from everything she's ever known? Why a gentleman, of course. Mine was most definitely a man, but unfortunately turned out he was somewhat lacking in the 'gentle' department."

Ian frowned. "I'm sorry. That can't have been an easy thing to deal with. Especially with you being all on your own in a new town."

"Nothing to be sorry about, but thank you. I'm doing great. Always keep an attitude of gratitude, y'know? Life is what you make of it."

If only that were true, Ian thought and the unspoken retort may have shown on his face more than he'd hoped because Della cocked her head as if questioning it. He quickly steered them both back to the conversation. "Is Mr. Somewhat Lacking still in the picture?"

"Jackson? That piece of sh—" then remembering the children in the back revised the descriptor to, "—garbage? Good Lord above, no. I bounced that boy's no-account backside the first week I took over Dempsey's. Violent narcissism with access to a seemingly endless alcohol reserve don't, as you say, make for good bedfellows." She appeared lost in the thought but quickly added, "Now, enough about me. How about you there, Mr. Ian. What keeps the bill collector at bay for you?"

"Advertising sales. Well, sales management actually. For a city newspaper in New York."

"The Big Apple. That sounds exciting," Della exclaimed. "At least you're trending in the right direction. Unlike me. I sorta traded down to this—what did you call it?—podunk town."

"I didn't mean it to come across that way, I apologize. Truly. Just sort of surprised, is all. I've visited New Or—sorry, it'll take a bit for me to get used to it—*N'awlinz*—once and it was pretty great. Hard to imagine anyone giving that up for this place, is all. There's nothing here for me anymore, Della; but that doesn't mean that's true for everybody."

"It's not the Gulf Coast, that's certain. And these winters. Dayamm! Three years and I'm still getting used to those. But the bar has a nice apartment above it, and the boys around here sure do like their liquor, so that keeps my head above water." She hesitated for a moment then chose to add, "And I also have a little room at the rear where I discreetly provide the odd reading or two now and then . . . for just a few select clients. Ones I know I can trust. "

"Trust?"

Della nodded as delicate memories percolated behind her eyes. "Let's just say I had a bad experience or two at my place in the French Quarter. Enough to make Mr. Somewhat Lacking Jackson seem like a pretty good alternative at the time."

"Mmmm." is all Ian could think to add.

VIII

As Della neared the outskirts of town, Ian closed his eyes and concentrated on Becky. And his brother. Fighting past the electric anxiety pulling at his gut, he focused only on the composed and calm projection of the unspoken words meant exclusively for Bryan.

Everything is alright. Rebecca is going to be alright. We're going to figure out whatever this thing is that's happening to us. And together, we are going to make it stop.

The thoughts projected strong and sure.

But did not reach their target.

Like a phone conversation spoken to a repeating busy signal on the other end of the line, Ian's message was met by a wall of cyclical, soprano static. Failing to be received, they then hung in the ether and evaporated to nothing more than moot, self-assuring notions. For whatever reason, the direct mental circuit to his brother was shorted. All he could think was that Bryan's stress was acting like an inhibitor, creating an unbridgeable gap in the energy flow between them and derailing the connection. If their telepathy were like a neurotransmission, then their presynaptic and postsynaptic terminals just weren't jiving.

It could also be that his brother was making a concerted effort to simply close down his terminal receptor altogether.

And who could blame him? A little over a week ago Bry had no memory we even shared this absurd ability. Now, he not only remembered it, but also all the other nightmarish tokens that came with it.

He opened his eyes with a heavy breath, and Della reached across and gently patted his knee. They shared a brief look and he mouthed, 'thank you,' to which Della replied with a soft nod.

"So, this is what's gonna happen . . . ." Turning to the back seat, Ian explained to the kids that there was nothing for them to be worried about; that their mom was just having some boring ol' adult stuff done. And she was only at the hospital for a test.

Diane wasn't worried.

She felt an okayness about the situation in a way she couldn't explain, and didn't feel the need to try. Probably because she could also tell that her uncle somehow, deep down, sensed that she had this unusual ability to sometimes know things that she couldn't possibly know, or picture things she hadn't really seen. There seemed to be a kind of internal humming between the two of them. To Diane it felt like a conversation, but a scrambled one she couldn't hear with her ears or always fully understand. It was an odd sensation, but not one that fazed her much.

Ian cocked his head, a new vibration suddenly pinging him. Its wavelength was short and less organized than he was used to receiving, even a little fractured. And it was faint. So subtle that he almost didn't catch it at first. Then, like a weak radar blip which pulses just once, it was gone.

"I hate tests," Andrew blurted out.

"Quite right," Della concurred as she smiled at the boy in her rear view mirror and stuck out her tongue as if tasting something utterly unpalatable. "Tests indeed! *Bleccch!* That's what I say."

Andrew giggled and scrunched up his nose.

"What say you, Mr. Uncle?" Della inquired.

"Oh, I also concur," Ian responded—

—And Della tangibly flinched inside.

Concur.

She had seen that specific word in her mind as she replied to Andrew. Its rather formal, lawyerly feel is what inspired her to adopt such a mock proper, almost British, response. In her head, she was taking on the tone of a courtroom barrister in a long red robe and powdered wig. Throw in a silly sound to boot, and there you have it: the perfect recipe to amuse just about any six-year-old boy.

But she hadn't said the actual word, only thought of it.

Ian, however, did say it.

He not only said it, he said he *also* concurred.

It could be coincidence. After all, it wasn't an unreasonable expectation that he might copy her semantics, playing right along. Maybe the character she was portraying in that micro-moment was a better impression of an English barrister than she'd even thought. Or perhaps that was merely Ian's way of expressing that he, too, agreed.

But DeLaCroix Laveau had come to recognize long ago that there was no such thing as coincidence or happenstance; only universal signals which people generally ignored. She never understood why they did, but could only theorize that to attribute to such occurrences a label of meaningless chance must make life more palatable for most, in some way soothing their esoteric ignorance rather than admitting that the answers they'd been looking for all along were so often provided, right there in front of them, if they'd only opened their eyes. Answers from God and the universe.

She smiled to herself as she turned off the highway. For Della, the oneness of life and spirit meant that she rarely spoke of God without also speaking of the Universe, or vice versa. And having a very visual mind, every time she put the two together—God and the universe—she immediately pictured an Ed Sullivan type of presenter on a grainy black and white screen, introducing the hottest new pop sensation:

Ladies and gentleman, I now present to you [pausing as the crowd's revelry grows to a crescendo] God . . . & The Universe!

Now that would be some cool-ass rock band.

Her mental smile grew until she noticed Ian out of the corner of her eye. He was unexpectedly smiling also, a faraway look upon his face as if watching a private but amusing moment to which no one else was invited.

Because he was. And they weren't.

Okay. Definitely not coincidence now.

And then she reminded herself what he'd said in the bar. Wasn't it something along the lines of him knowing Rebecca had been hurt? He hadn't been talking on his fancy new cell phone. There wasn't anyone else in the bar. And his brother was in the john, puking his guts out.

So, how could he suddenly know the chick was in trouble?

"Hey, you know what might be fun?" she said as she pulled the VW to the soft shoulder and skidded on the gravel to a stop, her voice firmly no-nonsense. "If you tell me what the hell is going on here."

In the backseat, the children stiffened.

Ian offered them a reassuring smile and turned back to Della, his eyes wide. He could have admitted to it—right there and then—and offered to tell her everything at the hospital when they were alone.

He didn't have to.

Della heard the unspoken affirmation loud and clear.

"I knew it—" She struck the steering wheel with the palm of her hand and Andrew winced. "—I knew it, I knew it, I knew it."

She was shaking her head and softly muttering something in her native Creole, and whatever it was, it was undeniably profane.

"I'm sorry," she said to the children as she collected herself, a sincere penitence in her voice which softened her countenance. To Ian, it intensified the serene smokiness of her grey-green eyes.

They darkened when she cast them upon him.

"Is something the matter, Miss Della?" Diane asked.

"Oooh, yes Ma'am," Della replied, staring unwaveringly at the man in her passenger seat.

There's a lot more going on here than a woman accidentally passing out in a garage full of fumes, isn't there?

Yes, Ian returned, his thought unmistakably answering hers.

"Did you forget something?" Andrew's sweet Soprano voice broke the silence. "Like Crystal Riley did when she missed the bus today?"

"Yes, sugar cheeks. Sort of like that."

For the kids' sake, I'll wait until we get to the hospital. But then I want the truth, mister. All of i—

Diane asked Della if she was sure it was something she needed.

"Yes," she stated, still not breaking her stare with Ian. "It is something I absolutely do need, baby."

Ian self-consciously cleared his throat. "I'm sure it'll show up. When we get to the hospital."

IX

Tensely seated in the waiting area of St. John's Emergency Room, Bryan drummed his fingers nervously against the plastic chair.

"No word yet," he informed them before they needed to ask, and stood to embrace Diane and Andrew. He nuzzled his chin into their necks and told them both how much he loved them.

I tried to reach out to you, Ian broadcast to him in the hope their proximity might bridge the gap created by whatever it was that had disrupted their circuit.

The message was met only by contaminated, cyclical static.

"It's going to be alright," Ian assured him vocally instead, resorting to communicating the way the rest of the world did.

Bryan shook his head. "It's been a half hour. I just want to know what's going on."

"I'm sure you do," Della agreed. "I think we would *all* like to know what's really happening." Then with an air of regret offered: "Why don't I go see if I can get someone to talk to you, hun."

Andrew began to follow her, and Della very sweetly brushed him back to his father and uncle . . . who were whispering something she was sure had to do with her.

"I need to tell you something," Ian quietly informed his brother, leaning in so the kids couldn't hear. "Della. She's like us."

"Meaning?"

"She shares our ability, Bry. Look, I tried to reach out to you on the way here but couldn't find you. Or you couldn't find me; I'm not sure which. But then I felt this faint, new ping. It felt like it was coming from her. And then it definitely was."

"And—?"

"And believe it or not, she has a Master's degree in Theology and Mysticism. She also confided that she's a reader. Apparently it's what she did before she moved up here. Fom N'awlinz." Ian liked how easily that rolled off his tongue now. "She's a good person. Something's telling me we need to let her in on what's going on. Who knows, maybe she can help some-how. Lord knows, we could use a little help right about now."

"Reader? You mean, like a psychic reader."

"Let's just say she's more of an Intuitive, yes."

"From New Orleans?"

A hesitant smile lifted the corner of Ian's mouth. "I wouldn't say it to her like that. But yes."

"Seriously, Ian? What the fuck. You're seriously suggesting that a bar-tending psychic is supposed to help Rebecca right now?"

"Godammit Bryan! Why are you choosing to be so stupid and stubborn about this?" Ian pulled his brother closer, clutching his forearm. When Bryan tried to yank away, Ian only tightened his grip. "I know we both repressed what happened when we were kids. For years. Just going on with our lives. But Matt Chauncey didn't get to do that, did he? Or Craig Dalton, or Woody. Or any of them."

He waited for his brother to respond, but none was proffered, Bryan barely registering any emotion about the statement at all.

Ian ensured the kids were out of earshot before he continued.

"Then out of the blue, like two decades later, this psycho tries to kill me in a Manhattan hole-in-the-wall bar and I have that vision—yes, one of *those* visions—remember? The kind I had the night I dreamt about Craig getting killed. The same fucking kind you had when you saw Woody and Jimi and Big Dan die. And Matt Chauncey was there. For Christ's sake, he *was there,* Bryan. By the roadside. The kid from the Little Woods! Then Mom and Dad are killed later that night, exactly the way I saw them . . . . And that fucking kid, in his little blue suit, was standing there, grinning as they hit that truck!"

Ian's voice had risen as the rest of the world had faded away, only the moments being recounted his current reality. He hadn't noticed the dozen other people in the waiting room staring in silent alarm. Or Social Worker

Louise coming over and consciously ushering Diane and Andrew aside, handing them each a cheap grape lollipop—the little round kind the wrapper sticks to and you end up with waxy paper bits in the crevices and invariably in your teeth.

He centered himself, wringing the agitation from his trembling hands and focusing on his labored breathing which had become superficial and rapid. Like the edge of asphyxiation.

One Mississippi. Breathe in . . . . And two Mississippi. Breathe out—

The memory of Dead Man's Swamp blindsided his senses. Without warning, he was back in the Little Woods. With his swollen and dislocated knee. On that day.

A feeling like someone is holding him beneath the murky water as the weed tendrils and vines entangle and the quicksand envelops. The panic as he counts the seconds he is beneath the water—

He refuted the memory and it shattered like glass, the fragments falling to his subconscious recesses as he purposefully quieted both his mind and his voice.

"You remember it, Bryan. All of it. I *know* you do . . . . It all came flooding back to you in the kitchen this morning."

Though Bryan had lowered his eyes, he was assimilating every word, concentrating on his effort to keep it all together.

Ian could feel the internal static interference between them gradually subsiding as their connection again began to strengthen. For the time being, he continued speaking to his brother audibly.

"Look, I'm with you. It's a huge flood of shit to reabsorb, shit we pushed so far down we no longer acknowledged it even happened. But it did, Bryan—we let that kid die in the woods that day. Then we both saw him in dreams and the people in those dreams died."

He paused to let the truth of the statement take root.

"I had that dream again last night, Bryan, and now Rebecca's in the hospital. So tell me, exactly what is it that you just don't get?"

Bryan looked up and made heavy eye contact. *There's nothing I don't get.* Reestablishing their nonverbal connection, his eyes glossed with tears. *I had the dream last night, too.*

Guilty relief washed over Ian. Reassured by the fact that he was no longer alone in whatever the hell was happening to them, the reprieve was mitigated by an anxiety-pitching trepidation. Bryan's admission also meant that what was happening was, in fact, very real and not just a product of his own imagination.

He steeled his nerves before replying in kind.

Do we really wanna roll those dice, then? Maybe, just maybe, Della can help us. It's gotta be more than coincidence that for the first time in our lives we've come across someone who may actually get it.

Bryan puckered his mouth and reluctantly nodded.

"Everything okay over here?" Della asked softly as she approached with an austere man in scrubs a small step behind her. "Bryan. Ian. This is Dr. Fieldhouse."

The physician gave each of their hands a brusque shake and asked which was Rebecca's husband. Firmly grasping Bryan's shoulder, he took a moment to ensure he'd secured the man's full attention. "I'm going to say this as levelly as I can. Your wife has absorbed an untenable level of carbon monoxide. We've been providing her as much oxygen as we can, but we need to do more."

"Meaning—?" Bryan asked, his voice barely above a whisper.

"It's not good right now." The doctor's affect was bare and dispassionate. "I'll be frank with you. Given her condition, we're placing Rebecca on a chopper with a medical team right now. In just a few minutes they'll be medevacked to Pittsburgh. The hospital there can utilize a hyperbaric chamber to introduce more oxygen into her bloodstream than we're capable of achieving here. Do you understand what I'm explaining to you, Mr. Cockerton?"

"Are you talking about one of those chambers? Like they use for divers who get the bends?"

"Exactly like one of those, yes. The blood's capacity to carry the oxygen to the cells has been impaired. It's called hypoxia, and can result in serious neurological damage, impaired organ function or development, and even death. The hyperbaric chamber uses pressure at two to three times normal atmosphere to force more oxygen into the bloodstream. Achieving that quickly is critical right now."

"Pittsburgh's almost two hours away—"

"The helicopter will get them there in twenty-seven minutes."

"And then?"

"It will take a few hours. I'm hopeful it will achieve the results we expect. Rebecca will then rest under observation tonight. So the best thing you can do is take your kids home and get some rest yourselves. We'll see where we are this time tomorrow."

X

With Diane and Andrew's focus temporarily occupied by the attentive care of the social worker, the three adults stepped silently down the crimson-carpeted aisle of the hospital's modest chapel.

Cool and dimly lit, the small sanctuary offered but a few short rows of seats. On a small dais near the front of them, votives in small yellow glass jars flickered within a brass framework. The distinct lack of any pattern to the seven which were alight and the rest which sat dormant suggested the candles had been lit by family and friends praying for a loved one.

As they approached, one votive which had burnt the longest popped and sizzled before extinguishing into a thin wisp of smoke.

Della lowered herself to one knee. Making the sign of the cross, she closed her eyes and lovingly wafted the smoke in the direction of the crucifix above the altar as she whispered a private entreaty.

Taking a seat in the front row, the brothers patiently waited as Della then recited the Lord's Prayer. At first, only a whisper of air passed from her lips. But the words gained strength as the prayer seemed to flow through her, the Southern locution to the Latin litany resonating with a tender power.

"—*Et ne nos inducas in tentationem, sed libera nos a malo. Amen.*"

Della crossed her chest in closing, allowing the energy to flow from her breast in a long, even exhalation. She seemed to consciously evaluate its progress as the air in her lungs emptied and became one with the air around them.

"It's cleansing. To deliberate over one's breath. But you already know that, I've witnessed you both practicing it, in your own way." She offered a soothing smile. "It's good for your chakra balance, as well as being emotionally and spiritually grounding. Medically invigorating for the body, too."

"So you're some kind of wi—" Bryan hesitated. "—Doctor?"

"You can go ahead and say it," she replied. "I've been called a witch doctor before, hun. And things much, much worse. Believe me."

As if made manifest by the power of her spoken words, Della's unconscious mind conjured an unwelcome image of Jackson. Alone together in the bar after hours, strands of spit spun from the biker's lips as he screamed obscenities in her face and squared up to her. Now, in the hospital chapel two full years later, her hand reflexively twitched as though it still secreted the paring knife behind her back. As tangibly as if the event were happening this moment, the fingers of her left hand tightened their grip around the memory of the knife's smooth, wood handle as Jackson—

Before the scene could unfold any further, she forcibly exorcised it from her mind, denying it the crippling power it once had over her. Mentally she commanded it, *Dwe ale!*

"What does that mean?" Bryan asked without a moment's hesitation, hearing Della's words in his own mind as clearly as if the woman had spoken them outright. "Dwe ale, what is that?"

He was expecting her to be astonished, or at least caught off guard by his ability to perceive her thoughts. Instead, Della only placidly smiled. "Ah, so you have the gift to harness the vibrations too, I see."

"Gift? I wouldn't go that far," he tritely countered. "So, tell me, Miss Laveau. That jerk-off . . . he some kind of boyfriend of yours?"

Della nonverbally projected both answers. *It's Haitian Creole. It means, 'be gone.' And yes. He was, once upon a time. His name was—*

"—Jackson," Bryan finished her thought. "Yeah, I got that."

While the unspoken exchange was fast and furious, Ian picked up much of it even though his was not the intended receptor. "Okay, so now we've learned we can all do the parlor tricks here, how about we get down to what matters, like what the hell is happening here."

"I'm all ears," Della assured him and retrieved a dog-eared Bible from the seat back in front of her, focusing her attention on Bryan.

"We don't believe what happened to Rebecca was an accident," Bryan stated with tangible reluctance, and Della mimicked his earlier response by replying, 'Yeah, I got that.'

After an awkward silence, she apologized.

"Listen, Bryan, it's obvious you don't much rate me. Or maybe the thought of someone validating what you're experiencing just scares the living shit out of you. But two things . . . . First, I already *know* you're experiencing something you can't explain, something dark and irrational. It probably feels immature to you, because to you it feels like ghosts and goblins is kids' stuff." Della's thumb unconsciously flicked back and forth across the silver-edged pages of the Bible in her hands. "That's your head trying to attribute logic to the illogical."

"Yeah, because logic is a bad thing, right?" Bryan retorted with baseless and barely cloaked derision.

Ian gestured for his brother to cool it. "And the second?"

"And secondly, whatever it is, it's happening, whether I'm here or not." She softened her tone. "Look, sugars. I could just wish your sweet Rebecca the best and leave you both to it. Bounce right outta here, y'know? Remind you that I don't have a dog in this fight."

Della lowered her eyes.

"But truth be told, I'm starting to become concerned that maybe I do. That maybe we all do." A low, plaintive vibration began to pulse within her and though her voice did not shake, Della unknowingly tightened her grip upon the Bible. "The two of you have a gift. Diane, too. She's like you, that one."

For a moment Della seemed lost in thought.

"Not like me, though. It never came natural to me. Still doesn't. I have to work very hard at it, and even then, it really only lands when the receptors have the gift too. Like you . . . and your little girl. She's a very special one, that Diane. I feel she is destined for greatness."

"Yes, she is. And so is Andrew," Bryan assented and impatiently stood. "And I'd really like to get back to both of them, and home to sleep, as quickly as possible. I may even try to head to Pittsburgh yet tonight. So if we could—"

"That gift is like a little journey on the private back roads of the spiritual realm," Della cut him off without apology. "And I sense it's something you've both been able to do since you were children. Would I be correct in that?"

Ian nodded.

Bryan offered no reply, verbal or otherwise.

"The problem with acquiring such a powerful gift naturally, or perhaps we should say supernaturally," Della explained, "is not having to work at it, and thus the assumption that it's not very special at all. We grow up walking, talking, seeing, hearing, and we think nothing of it. But to someone born without the capacity to achieve any one of these given skill sets, the competence we take for granted is a miraculous feat they would give almost anything to be able to do."

Beginning to experience the tendrils of creeping shame, Ian cast his eyes to the ground as the truth of Della's wisdom struck deep into his core. Because she was absolutely right: he and Bryan had been bestowed with an incredible gift. And they had taken it entirely for granted. Worse, they had let it flounder over the years.

Her words seemed to have the opposite effect on Bryan.

It did not go unnoticed by Della as she continued.

"A gift like yours opens a connection to the spiritual realm. If not properly tended and honed, that portal has the very real potential to leave you vulnerable. Both positive and negative energies having access to it. If a negative entity gets its foot in the door, so to speak, it gains power by isolating you, instilling doubt, confusion . . . and even embarrassment. In this day and age, that is one of its greatest weapons. I mean, think about it. Who in the world wants to admit, 'hey, I'm being harassed by an angry spirit?' Which is exactly what an entity of that kind wants. So you seek no help. Alone, your energy reduces to a low vibration. And just like that," she snapped her finger and it resounded like a snare drum rimshot through the sparsely furnished chapel, "you find yourself at your most vulnerable. It's really no different from the tactics of an abusive narcissist. Divide and conquer. Gaslight. Psychological, emotional and spiritual manipulation to covertly sow the seeds of doubt until you question your own memory, your perceptions, and ultimately even your own judgment."

"Hold on. Exactly who's the narcissist in this equation?" Forsaking his poker face altogether, Bryan exhibited little interest in further masking his growing level of frustration.

Only Della noticed the candles upon the dais flicker, the flames bending to the point of extinguishing. The wax crackled before they recovered and hesitantly blazed brightly once again.

"Are you a spiritual man, Bryan?"

Bryan pondered the question and surprisingly clarified it without defensiveness. "Do I believe in God, you mean?"

"And the Universe," Della added. "Yes, hun. The Highest Power, The One from whom all things flow. The Holy Spirit, Father God, Mother Universe. The life force that connects us all."

Bryan scanned the chapel, absorbing the icons and trappings of rite and dogma which he knew comforted so many others. Consumed only by the thought of his wife alone on a stretcher, all alone and soon to be encapsulated in a coffin-like machine, they did not offer him the same solace.

"I believe in evil. I haven't seen much evidence of anything else." He lifted his head and silently met Della's eyes, finally exposing the raw vulnerability of a man close to the edge.

"I understand," is all she could at first say in return as the deep bass vibrations coiled through her like dark, parasitic tendrils.

Bile rose to the back of her throat.

Always so difficult for the empath to absorb such intense negative emotion, Della needed a moment to ground herself. Only after picturing a clear, impenetrable dome of safety around them did she invite Bryan to share what had caused him to so incontrovertibly abandon his faith.

Because that something was always a vile and unholy thing.

"Tell me, Bryan . . . . About the evil . . . ."

XI

Engirdled by the quilted satin lining, Rebecca opened her eyes with a sucking gasp of breath. She screamed as the hot, hissing air of the compartment constricted her chest, squeezing her ribs, rupturing the capillaries in her cheeks. The cry echoed loud but dull in her skull, muffled by ears partially deafened by the inexplicable pressure.

God help me, where am I? What's happening to me?!

Her oxygen-starved mind twisted and leapt, the neurons firing wildly. Bright colors burst across her vision as copious oxygen forced its way into occipital and frontal lobes. Her hijacked amygdala synapsed erroneously, immediately issuing a reckless warning that she must surely be in a casket. Or perhaps even a cremation chamber.

"H-HELP ME! S-SOMEBODY HEL—"

"Rebecca, we're going to need you to stay calm, okay?" the muffled, disembodied voice instructed through a speaker near her head. *"We can't open the chamber yet."*

Becky's breaths accelerated.

"Just try and breathe normally sweetheart, okay?"

The voice was female. Rebecca didn't recognize it. "Who are you? W-where am I!"

"You've had an accident, Rebecca. We're doing everything we can for you, but you have to try to keep still. And calm. That's really important right now."

Rebecca's mind careened, firing wildly. After a moment it landed on the faces of Diane and Andrew, and she started to remember. More of a dark and unsettling feeling than a specific memory, instinct took root and hollowed out her stomach. "Please! My children!"

A dark cavernous place. A boy is giggling in hushed tones.

Her mind flickered, the scene jerky and hazed.

An odor like smoke and yeast.

Then a memory of a bar.

The bar.

Dempsey's.

She had been there with the boys . . . but driven home alone in the rain. Her clothes had reeked of smoke and beer, so she'd jumped in the shower again. The water had been warm and enticing. That she remembered clearly. As she lay here now in the pressurized capsule, her brain fed the sensation to her fingertips, telling them they could still feel the soothing water running over them. Twitching, a muted prickling grew in their tips until the feeling of the warm, silky water turned from comforting pleasure to icy, slicing pain as the feeling in them returned, the nerves suddenly firing as the highly oxygenated blood coursed through them.

But something had happened in the shower.

Another tiny fragment of memory clicked into place. She recalled something about the shower being interrupted. Something about a phone; the phone on her bedside table. It had started ringi—

Oh God! The phone! That voice. I was in the garage!

The image snapped into place and the dead boy standing over her tore through her mind, shredding her rationale like shrapnel.

Rebecca's body began to tense and shake, the muscles in her arms growing rigid as they stretched to her abdomen, her fingers splayed wide, bending nearly backward.

"He's dead! He's Dead! HE'S DEAD! HE'S DEADHESDEA—"

Rebecca's mouth gaped, her jaw stiffening and locking. Foaming spit bubbled between her lips as her eyes rolled back, the lids fluttering madly. Her back arched as if responding to an electric shock as her heart squeezed and strained.

"She's seizing," the faraway woman's voice in the speaker yelled to someone other than her. *"Code Blue—Code Blue—"*

The last thing Rebecca remembered as the thin veneer of conscious thought succumbed to a grey, static void, was what she had been thinking about—*and what she had been doing*—in that shower.

The last thing she physically felt was the odd, new sensation now roiling deep within her abdomen.

XII

Bryan paced the carpeted aisle in an angst-ridden half stupor as he told Della how their parents had died the week before, admitting that the crash had been foreseen by his brother in a dream.

"The same dream both of us had years ago. Always in the woods. And always haunted by some dark, monstrous thing I can't really explain."

He added, somewhat hesitantly, that Ian's dream also included an odd little cartoon ranger. And a dead kid they once knew. But most importantly, he revealed that when they had this dream, bad things would happen to people around them.

. . . Serious neurological damage, impaired organ function . . . .

The doctor's warning reverberated inside Bryan's mind; it was a very bad thing.

"Your dream, Ian. That vision?" Della asked. "It was catalyzed by some kind of trauma, yes?"

"A shooting," Ian answered, the tension spreading across his face. "A violent murder. In my local bar."

"And then one, or both of you, had the same kind of dream recently. Is that correct?" Della presented the obvious deduction.

Bryan nodded, confirming that they both had. Last night.

"And now here we are and, God help her, Becca's fighting for her life. Whatever kind of life that may be."

He forced back the tears, shaking his head as he fended off an array of unimaginable images of his beautiful wife, mother of their two young and precious children, the rest of her years anguished by any number of possible life-altering disabilities . . . even if she did pull through this.

"You're right, Della. It's like a curse. Like something is gunning for us." Citing the details in this manner, let alone tying them all together, seemed the incredulous statement of a delusional psychotic. Because before that, he clarified, there was nothing. "Just eighteen years of normal life."

Della considered the unintended power of that statement.

Ian had to be in his late twenties, Bryan in his thirties. So why mention only eighteen years . . . ?

"And when you were kids? What happened that wasn't 'normal'?"

As if invoked by her question, the energy in the room lowered another octave, the vibration devolving to something base and grotesque. It cycled through Della in grave, throaty tones.

Fidgeting with his fingers, Bryan clearly felt it too. The tips of them had begun to tingle, the way they do when you don't realize you've been sitting on them for too long, and he shook them out, stretching and blowing on them. It offered a welcome opportunity to govern his uneven, nervous breathing before answering her.

"And befor—" he hesitated as the recollection of his childhood friends, *his best friends*, strobed his nerves like lightning, their faces materializing as clearly as if the years since had never transpired. "Before that, every one of our childhood friends were killed or never heard from again. After having that same goddamn dream."

He didn't allow Della time to process the admission. If there were any chance at all that she could help Rebecca, she needed to know everything. And she needed to know it right now. He had no reason to believe she actually could help them. But maybe, just maybe, there was the slimmest chance that Ian was right and she could.

So for the first time in his adult life, Bryan spoke the truth about what happened that day in the woods.

The memory playing instantly and vividly across his mind, the images, sounds and scents were as palpable as they had been that day. Describing in grim, unrelenting detail what the boys had done to Matt Chauncey, his words painted the images he saw in his mind: how the gang had isolated and punched and taunted their friend, the weakest of he boys. How when they were done, they simply hanged him by his neck from a tree as Matt kicked and flailed for his life.

How they had then burned him alive.

. . . Caked in mud and blood as they dance around the bonfire, the boys cheer as Stu touches the flame to the boy's pants, setting him ablaze as casually as if lighting a candle. Matt's cleaving screams cry out behind the vociferous whistling of the flute as the smell of the flames and ferrous tang of blood becomes one malodorous scent, instantly and indelibly etched upon this moment. . . .

Engulfed in the moment and with no capacity to moderate the vision, the scene assaulted Bryan's senses as it unleashed a visual broadcast of such intense, repugnant ferocity that Ian doubled over and clutched his sides; tears rolled freely down Della's face.

Drenched in perspiration, Bryan's fists clenched in despair as the guilt poured from his body. Wavering on his feet, he visibly weakened as the last bastion of denial finally succumbed to the cold, hard reality that— more than Matt Chauncey's life—all they had ever known of innocence had also been stolen that day, consumed by something vile and malignant the boys had no capacity to understand.

In the abhorrent place they had once, with such consuming affection, called the Little Woods.

A thin rivulet of urine began to run down his left leg.

The stream trickled over his shoe and soaked into the crimson carpet where it formed a dark, blood-like halo at Bryan's feet.

"YOU UNNATURAL HARPY!" he bellowed startlingly at Della, his voice lost beneath a cacophony of overlapping layers like the maddened, cater-wauling yips of a hyena cackle. Whipping a violent gust through the chapel, the words shook the room like a freight train. Solely targeting Della, the burst of air lifted her from her feet and flung the woman against the wrought iron railing as effortlessly as if shoved by unseen hands. She slumped over the dais, a stunned and confused rag doll, as the votives in the candelabra sprayed the air in slicing yellow shards. "YOU ASKED, PRIESTESS, IF I AM A SPIRITUAL MAN! THE ANSWER IS YES! I BELIEVE! I BELIEVE THE GOD WE CHOSE THAT DAY IS HERE!"

Bryan's eyes rolled into the back of his head as he fell limply to the floor, the echoes of his bellowing decree fading away like summertime peals of thunder.

As the chapel fell to darkness.

eighteen
1977

AFTER WAITING LONG enough to ensure their parents would be sound asleep, Bryan stepped lightly down the hallway to his brother's room. Carefully turning the faux brass doorknob to avoid its tell-tale squeak, he slid quietly inside. Backlit by a deep orange light that bathed the room in eerie incandescence, Ian's electric clock boldly announced it was 11:33 in big white numbers on black plastic tiles. He closed the door with little more than a gentle clack, and delicately tip-toed across the room.

From out of nowhere a figure on the bed bolted swiftly upright, aggressively waving something above its head in both hands.

"Shit!" Bryan's exclamation was louder than he wanted as he stumbled backward, banging against the plaster wall and nearly knocking the orange-glowing clock off the bookshelf. He held his breath as he listened for any sign of their parents stirring.

A small groan; a mattress spring adjusting to a minor shift in weight.

Then silence.

Bryan released his breath and rubbed his scraped elbow. Minute plaster crumbs dusted to the floor, revealing a small red abrasion. "Jesus, Ian," he whispered. "I didn't think you were awake."

The orange-glowing silhouette of his younger brother shifted in the bed with a mixed sense of relief and raging adrenaline as it lowered its arms. "What the hell, Bryan! You scared the shit outta me!"

"You! What about me?" Bryan exhaled in diminishing fits before perching on the edge of the bed beside Ian. He folded a leg beneath him. "What the hell is this for?" He plucked the hammer from Ian's still-clutching hands. Up close, it appeared as ridiculously innocuous as it was.

Ian returned a timid look, just shy of embarrassment.

"Look, I'm sorry," Bryan offered somberly. "I know what this is for." He absently fingered the hammer's cold metal nib. "Do you really think a tiny tack hammer like this is gonna stop Matt? He's already dead, dude."

Ian stared blankly at the thin summer quilt until the electric clock broke the deafening silence as it whirred and clicked by another minute.

11:34.

"He's killed the others." Bryan feigned a stoic lack of apprehension. "You know we're next. Stu said there would be seven. So he's coming back, Ian. For you. Or for me. Maybe for both of us. Unless we go to the Little Woods."

Ian withdrew against the headboard, vigorously shaking his head in disagreement while saying nothing.

"Yes, Ian. He's coming. Tonight. For one us, if we don't go. You understand that?" He stood and tugged Ian up with him.

"I'll tell you everything, on the way. But seriously, come on. We gotta get going."

II

The cool night air kissed their cheeks as they stepped quietly out of the house. It was a crisp, motionless chill, all the more intense after the day's earlier mix of heat and steamy rain. Beyond the new moon which had abandoned the sky, a blanket of fresh stars twinkled, their faraway fires shining bright in the calm and cloudless night. Occasionally, a slight tepid current would buffer across their skin and the movement of the warm air was a pleasing contrast to the damp, airless chill.

Just beyond reach of the dim lamplight of the street, house after house skulked like the huddled shapes of so many dormant creatures. It presented a surreal reality to the walk they'd taken so many times before as the shapes glided silently by with each reluctant step.

For the first half of the journey neither spoke, walking only in cold, contemplative silence.

Bryan was first to break it as they crested the hill to the bottom of the neighborhood and the Rakers' house came into view.

"It only really came to me when Mom got that call from her this morning," he stated with an air of both explanation and regret. "From Mrs. Raker, y'know. I had an idea, for a while before that. But it was just an idea . . . . That's why I was going to the Beechnut. Without you. I needed to see for myself what was happening."

Ian did not reply, staring only at the blacktop as he walked.

"Look," Bryan continued. "I didn't want you involved in this shit any more than you already were."

Their sneakers padding the stiff tar of the blacktop was the only sound for several long, drawn minutes until he spoke again.

"The Beechnut seemed okay at first, y'know? But then, I don't know, it just changed. I wish I could explain it. It was like this black mesh was over everything. I could see the world through it, but it was all covered in this shimmering, dark, see-through kinda haze. And there was this constant, low—"

"—Vibration." Ian finished the sentence for him. "I know. Like that awful feeling we get when we've been arguing. That gross rumbling in your stomach that throbs in and out . . . . I felt it too."

"You too?"

Ian nodded.

Bryan coughed and cleared his throat, the sound of it rolling in a muffled echo across the night's quiet dampness.

"I think some of the others did too. Jimi a little bit; but Woody—I think he did, a lot. He never said so, but I could tell." He shuddered as one image in particular from the Beechnut ran through his head, still trying to make some kind of sense of it. "Nobody talked about Matt. I mean like, not a single word. Acting like it never even happened. Then yesterday, Stu starts it up. He starts laughing about how the kid was hanging there, his legs all kicking in the air."

Bryan stopped and turned to his brother, extending his arm straight out and pointedly angling his hand down toward the street.

"He's doing this as he said it." He waggled his two fingers back and forth in the air. "And he was fucking laughing, Ian. Laughing about what they did."

He swallowed hard, choking off the words.

"Then he drags me to one side and keeps saying this shit about it being part of some grand revelation, it's a revelation. And we're the chosen ones. I dunno, he just keeps saying that dumb shit. Over and fucking over. Like he's a crazy-ass fuck." After a moment he added, "More than he usually is, I mean."

Ian stiffened. "Then what are we doing out here Bryan? In the middle of the night! I just wanna go home. C'mon. I say we tell Mom and Dad . . . we'll just tell them. Everything. They'll help, I know they will. They'll make it—"

"LISTEN!" Bryan grabbed his brother's forearm. "You need to hear this! He said everything is for this thing he called Zaze—Zaza—Zazol—I don't know, something fucked up like that. And that we have been chosen. That when they killed Matt in the woods, they made the kid—are you ready for this—the first sacrificial scapegoat. What the fuck is that even supposed to mean?"

"I don't know!" Ian yanked his arm from his brother's grip and turned to start walking back. "I'm scared, Bryan. *Really* scared. I'm not doing this anymore. I'm going home!"

Bryan watched him turn and disappear into the shadows beyond the pale, yellow glow of the streetlamps spaced at even intervals down the street. When all but a dim outline of his figure had ebbed into darkness, he realized his younger brother wasn't coming back.

"He told me there needed to be seven," he shouted at the shadows through cupped hands. "He said seven. Ian . . . six of our friends have died. Six, Ian!"

Ian stopped in his tracks. His back still to his brother, he counted silently on shaking fingers, running through the list in his head:

Matt.

Then Craig, Jimi, Woody and Big Dan, all last night.

And Jack, who's missing.

Even from this distance, Bryan could hear the first sniffle as Ian turned around, fighting to hold back his tears.

Encompassed by shadows, only his wet eyes were visible as they reflected the yellow light of the streetlamp Bryan stood beneath.

His steps were uncertain and hesitant as he edged slowly back to his brother, swiping his hand across his nose and eyes.

"How do you know any of this! How do you know he means it, Bry? We don't know for sure how they died. You said you saw them in your dream, but we don't know that's how it really happened. We don't even know for sure that Jack's even dead. He just isn't home!"

Bryan shook his head. "Huh-uh. I mean, yeah. Sort of. But—"

He cleared his throat. Now was no time for either one of them to be chicken-shit. If they were going to do this, it had to be together.

"Look, I get it that you're scared. Me too, Ian. But I *know* they're all dead. And I know how it happened. To all of them." He ignored the fresh electric shiver pulsing between his shoulder blades then tracing down his spine. "I know, because Stu showed me. Just before you and Craig got to the Beechnut yesterday. He showed me how this Zazol thing was going to do it. He showed me how he was going to kill Jimi."

ӀӀӀ

Stu leapt expertly from limb to limb in the bright afternoon sun of the day prior. He then vaulted from an impossible height in the giant beech and landed, superhero tripod style, just inches from Bryan.

Shielding his eyes, Bryan spat and sputtered as twigs and leaves puffed into the air as the ground shook.

"You still don't believe," Stu cackled in a voice resembling nothing of his own. "Disbelievers are my favorite. Oh, how I shall enjoy this."

Nose to nose with Bryan, he tilted his head first one way then the other. A junkyard dog purveying a new and compelling interloper.

"We belong to him now." Reflected in the dirty and scratched lenses of his black plastic spectacles, a flame seemed to be burning in front of Stu's dark, empty eyes. "We will honor him with seven innocents to satiate the primevel hunger!"

His breath was hot and foul. A putrid smell like blood and iron and decaying trash that reminded Bryan of moldy cardboard.

Bryan turned aside, gagging. He retched twice before catching his breath. "Satiate? Prime-what? Sounds like somebody ate an assload of shit today and crapped out a dictionary!" He slammed both hands as hard as he could into Stu's chest. "Fuck off, man!"

But the boy did not budge; Bryan might've had more luck trying to shove aside a ten ton boulder.

Immovable and grinning, Stu clutched Bryan's face with broken nails that dug into his cheeks, yanking him so close that their lips all but touched. Blowing rancid air into Bryan's nose and mouth, he reveled in each retching gasp as Bryan tried fruitlessly to pull away. "I will show you the next of the seven!"

The fiery glow in Stu's glasses erupted like gas over a flame, coming alive and showering them in crystalline white sparks that burned like sulfur as it fell in a shower upon their skin.

Bryan again shielded his eyes and when he opened them, he was no longer on the ground in the middle of the afternoon but perched precariously high in the beech tree in the deepest dark of night.

Far below, the forest floor shimmered iridescent and dreamlike.

He blinked hard several times to clear his vision, but the image did not change. Clinging tightly to one branch with one hand, he waved the other in front of him and the Beechnut billowed and wavered as if a movie scene projected onto a screen of smoke.

Mesmerized, he gawped in dreamlike awe and disbelief.

Then Woody was bounding deftly up the trunk with fingers impossibly tipped by thick bear-like claws. Easily navigating the labyrinth of intertwining branches with inhuman speed, he ducked agilely over, under and between the crisscrossing limbs. It took only seconds before he was springing up and onto the branch where Bryan exerted every effort just to keep from falling.

Taking one deliberately methodical step after another, Woody slinked menacingly toward him.

"Stop it!" Bryan thrust his hands defensively in front of him as Woody stalked closer, and the scene wrinkled and flowed around them as if he had plunged them into a wall of water.

Undeterred, Woody prowled nearer.

Then, like a ghost, he passed right through him.

Coalescing on the other side, Woody's form skulked unawares along the limb as its thinning girth began creaking and splintering, bowing dangerously toward the ground, far below.

In a tight ball at its end, Jimi Raker huddled in paralyzed terror.

"Please—" is all Jimi whispered as Woody wrapped a thick-clawed hand around his throat and lifted him high into the air.

Then slung him from the tree like a rag doll.

Crisp lightning tiered across the sky and strobed the woods in pulsing flashes. It revealed Jimi's two story plunge as if some kind of Hollywood slow motion sequence out of synch with the sound.

In the first frame, Jimi was only a few feet below them. His limbs were outstretched, his back toward the ground; eyes staring wide in disbelief. His mouth agape in a silent scream.

Then he was gone as the lightning sizzled away and the moonless night entombed him. Only the cracking branches in crisp, staccato snaps acknowledged that he was still there.

And still plummeting.

Another fork of electricity revealed Jimi clutching futilely at empty air as he broke through another thick web of branches.

The light fizzled and was gone.

In the dark, Jimi plunged through open air at least another twenty feet before he slammed against the ground. The force of the impact sent a tremor up the trunk of the beech, shaking and shuddering its branches in a wave.

Bryan clung on for dear life high above as the sound of Jimi's body hitting the forest floor came several frames later.

When another electric arc lit up the Beechnut, a sapling spike through Jimi's back became visible, poking out of his shirt just to the left of the boy's spine. This was followed by a solid popping sound as a funnel of steam blew from the hole in his back, hissing into the cool, dank air. Pinned to the floor this way, shaking and convulsing, Jimi Raker's limbs fluttered and slapped against the hard packed dirt as the long line of his spine pressed like a snake against the inside of his shirt. His eyes rolled into their sockets, the lids palpitating violently as his head lifted and fell in shudders.

Another flash of lightning sizzled across the sky and blanched the black veil of night in brilliant light. Jimi's back arched in one final, unnatural tremor, accompanied by a searing scream which sliced across the peals of booming thunder.

Clapping his hands over his ears, Bryan squeezed his eyes closed against the white glare. When he mustered the courage to open them, he was back on the ground . . . in the blazing afternoon sun.

"Five more blasphemies will follow," Stu said to him in an assured whisper just before Craig Dalton walked boldly into the center of the Beechnut while Ian vigilantly crouched in the periphery of weeds and thick brush.

"Woohoo! Hey look!" Jack Raker shouted as he hung from a branch by one hand, still laughing. "It's scrotebag's friend!"

IV

"That's when you and Craig showed up," Bryan said, slipping in and out of the glow of the street lights as they headed toward the fields bottom of the neighborhood. The dull sound of their soles slapping the blacktop echoed from one side of the road to the other as it bounced from house-to-house. "Even though it really happened, I still didn't want to believe it."

He kicked a lone stone from the sidewalk and watched it scuffling down the road and disappear into the shadows.

"Know what I mean? Like maybe I was hallucinating or something. But then Mrs. Raker calls this morning to tell mom that Jimi hasn't come home from the Beechnut last night. And old man Dalton's gone and snuffed his own kid with a pillow while we were at the drive-ins."

"Craig wa-w-was my f-fr-fr—" Ian stuttered, unable to finish the sentence.

Bryan pressed a fist softly into his shoulder.

"I know, buddy," he said as they walked on in silence.

V

The second half of the trek brought an odd sense of calm to Ian. Despite what he'd witnessed them do to Matt; beyond the fact that Craig had been killed by his own father; regardless of Bryan's retelling of the prophesy forced upon him at the Beechnut . . . none of it seemed very real and Ian's mind simply began to rationalize it all away. There was no such thing as the Boogeyman, after all. That was just a story kids told other kids to freak them out at sleepovers. For all he knew, this was some elaborate plan by his older brother to try and scare the crap outta him. Perhaps some secret indoctrination to their game of War the younger kids weren't privy to. He'd probably walk into the woods tonight and all the gang would jump out with a big, 'BOO!' and then they'd all have a good laugh at how gullible he'd been the past couple weeks.

Hell Yeah, he thought to himself, careful to not allow the notion to project to his brother, thus giving away his advantage. *That's exactly what's probably gonna happen.*

They stopped for a short breather when they rounded the corner at the bottom of the hill. There, the sprawling corn fields spread out before them, marking the end of the neighborhood proper. This time, in the hushed and motionless night, their green and yellow stalks did not sway in unison, to and fro, as they always did. Instead, they leaned at an angle, each side of the field seeming to point down the long, barren dirt trail to the twin ponds and the in-between place they called the Wild Place. Beyond this, laying in wait beneath the deepest of raven shadows, lie the Little Woods.

Bryan pressed a button on the side of his digital watch and the face illuminated.

11:51.

His stomach tightened. He swallowed hard before tugging at the sleeve of his brother's hooded sweatshirt. "Come on," he prompted. "We gotta keep going. It's time."

As if autonomous, Ian's feet stepped into the muddy path where the blacktop ended and the twin, parallel ruts began. Despite the blinding blackness of the night, they masterfully followed the track mapped out in his mind where countless knobby tractor tires had run over the same ground, to the same inevitable destination.

All the while, the unassailable logic reassuring him that he was simply being setup for a great big—if incredibly grand and twisted—initiation joke, diminished with every measured step. At first, the clinging fear beginning to coil into him was small and unassuming, a nagging anxiety that maybe, just maybe, his logic was wrong. But by the time they were at the Twin Ponds, the terror had grown until his chest had grown tight, his stomach tender and hollow.

No moon reflected it's silver glow in the ponds' glassy waters tonight.

No ripples creased their surface.

All was still and noiseless.

Even the modest warm breeze of just moments ago was gone, leaving only cold, humid air.

Stagnant, Bryan projected in thought to his brother.

Ian inhaled thinly in a series of small, erratic bursts he was not aware of, and the sound amplified the desolation of the noiseless nightscape.

No crickets chirruped in the tall grasses.

No wings fluttered quietly overhead.

No leaves rustled in the trees.

All was mute.

Not stagnant, Ian broadcast back to Bryan. *Dead.*

And a crisp new fear seemed to swirl tangibly through the cooling night air, settling upon Ian's soul like a winged pest which speared his thoughts with fresh, raw uncertainty . . . but certain dread.

His mind, and his heartbeat, began to race as he veered from the tractor path, following his brother through a blanket of mist which had layered between the twin ponds and the woods like a mass of webbing. On the other side of it, a dark wall of trees would mark the entrance to the Little Woods.

There, Bryan stopped and waited silently for him to catch up.

The grating of Ian's sneakers against the dirt and gravel at the end of the path resounded through the dark as he came to an abrupt stop.

"Listen," Bryan said as he crossed his arms over his chest, shielding himself from the damp and cold. "Maybe you're right, Ian. I don't know what we're doing here, I really don't. Maybe we should just . . . just forget it all and go home." Then he turned, starting back along the path towards the ponds. "I don't know what I'm talking about. Maybe I'm just fucking crazy."

"And maybe you're not!" Ian returned sharply without hesitation, the certainty of the reply surprising himself as much as his brother. "We both know why we're here. We *know* for Chrissakes. You're right. We have to do this, Bryan."

Both boys froze as something within the pines darted swiftly from one side to the other, the sound of leaves whisking under its feet.

Bryan turned slowly. "Did you hear th—?"

"Yeah." Ian answered through a hushed exhalation of air before his brother had finished the question.

"What do you reckon it was?"

"I don't know, I couldn't see it . . . I'm not sure."

Bryan shuffled quickly back, taking a protective stance alongside his brother. "C'mon, then. Let's keep going."

Moving off the main trail and along the smaller track that passed beneath the huge conifers, the pair entered the forest.

Inside was darker than either had expected. Their eyes had grown accustomed to the minimal light in the fields adjacent. But in reality, they'd been able to see a great deal more with their dark-adapted eyes than than they realized.

Here was a different matter altogether.

Little, if any, shape was discernible from any other, and the once familiar surroundings of the Little Woods were now foreign to them. Walking slowly alongside one another with arms outstretched, they grasped at black emptiness as they cautiously moved through the tress and brush.

When a whisper of cool air wafted past, brushing Ian's face, the length of his back broke out in shivering pimples from his shoulder blades down his spine. One-by-one in quick succession, the hairs lifted from their follicles like marching ants, a relic of mammal survival instinct to 'grow' larger and more menacing in instances of fear.

"Bryan?"

Bryan answered, 'Yeah?' from somewhere unseen beside him and Ian's face, could it have been seen, dropped to a worried frown.

"Did you feel that?"

"Feel what?"

"I don't know—a breeze or something."

Bryan shook his head in the dark to no effect. When Ian did not respond, he qualified aloud, "No. But maybe I should go first."

"No. I'm okay . . . just checking."

Again Ian pressed forward by degrees, concealing the fear within him and waiting for any hint of visibility to come.

It did not.

Finding there was no discernible difference, he simply closed his eyes as he moved between the trees. Beside him, only the sound of his brother's feet softly matching his own pace reassured him that he was not alone. Together in this way they followed nothing more than muscle memory and the sound of each other's steps as they began their descent deep, deep into the bowels of the Little Woods.

VI

Like a pistol shot, a cawing raven broke the silence of the woods and fluttered madly into the night sky from its perch high in the treetops. Ian recoiled, dropping nearly to his knees before recognizing the sound. Bracing himself against the nearest tree, he 'watched' the sound through the inky darkness, visualizing the position of the bird. Although the ravens were all around the woods, they gathered mostly in one particular area of dense, tall trees not far from the clearing of the Father Oak. Their screeching cries had frightened him when he'd played here as a younger child. How peculiar that they should terrify him even more so now.

"Did you hear that?"

"Jesus! Of course!" Bryan whisper-shouted, the answer quiet but terse. He allowed his heartbeat to settle before adding what he, too, recognized. "It's not far now . . . ."

Ian said nothing in return as his feet padded through the heavy underbrush. His thoughts were elsewhere; the walk in the darkness only a necessity to get to where his mind already was. He thought about what his brother had told him about Jimi Raker. And Woody. His mind raced over the images as surely as if he'd seen them himself. It asked what he was possibly doing here, why he wasn't home in bed, trying to sleep.

This whole episode, from that day in the woods till now, it's all just a terrible, unreal dream, after all. Isn't it? You can just go. Leave Bryan here. It's only his word that any of this is more than a lingering nightmare. Right? Let him fight his own demons. It isn't your battle.

And for one weak moment, Ian almost turned and ran, leaving his brother alone in the woods.

But then the other voice came.

Oh, if only that were true, something deeper than logic said. And he knew that this second voice was right. In fact, it was probably the only thing he would be sure of in his entire life.

(Until one day, when a crazy Anonymous man would pack a pistol and walk into a random midtown bar—any bar would do—and blow away some geezer, just because. Then Ian would be this sure again.)

He was here because, what the hell was going to happen when this thing that Stu called Zazol—or whatever the hell Bryan said he'd called it —decided it was their turn? If it was true, what Bryan said, then six had been taken by it and a seventh was next. That meant it was Stu . . . or one of them. If not tonight, then tomorrow. If not tomorrow, then the next. Because they had let Matt die. Perhaps, somewhere deep down, they had even wished it to happen. So how was he ever again going to sleep again?

Because sleep is always there, waiting.

And with sleep comes darkness.

In darkness, vulnerability.

"Wait—" The whisper burst from Bryan's lips in a short, staccato hush which echoed through the trees and startled Ian back to reality. Blindly reaching for him, Bryan pulled him to a stop and repeated the command. "WAIT!"

The air had grown thick and rotten around them, as if solidifying with a new stench that spoiled the natural odor of the moss and wood and leaves. It was a moldy, decaying odor, like old cardboard left out in the rain and then stumbled upon in its half-rotted state. It filled every pore, and Ian retched dryly more than once.

"Try to ignore it," Bryan instructed but was having difficulty himself, choking on the words. "It's the smell of it, Ian. Of Zazol. It smelled like this in the Beechnut."

"What the hell do you mean? Jesus Bryan, I don't like this—"

"Listen to me!" Bryan faced where he knew his brother should be. It felt strange, talking at a wall of darkness. Like standing in a windowless room, at night, and speaking to yourself in a mirror. He would have laughed, had he not been so damned frightened. "Don't you go backing out on me now. Only a minute ago it was me saying that I wasn't sure about this. But you told me I was right. That we had to go on. Has that suddenly changed, Ian? Am I crazy after all—is this all just fucking crazy?"

The increasing aggression in Bryan's voice belied the steadfast, reliable fearlessness which had brought them both this far. It was a vulnerable sound, new and bizarre to Ian as it wrapped around his own fear out of the void of the forest.

Squeezing his chest with anxiety, he could not muster a reply.

"Something bad is happening, Ian. Something *really* bad. I mean something evil. And you know it!" Speaking faster and faster, Bryan's fear grew more evident with every word. "Shit, you saw it that day. Even more than me. You were there, the whole time they beat up Matt. You saw with your own eyes what they did! Does that make sense to you? Does that sound like the guys that are—*that were*—our friends? We're not crazy! This isn't just in our dreams. And no, I'm not trying to set you up for a sick joke. Yeah, that's right, I heard your thoughts earlier even though you tried to block them. But this shit is real. Something is preying on us, Ian. All of us!"

There was no more hiding that he was scared. It was obvious that Ian could sense his amygdala hijacking as much as Bryan, himself, could sense that the thick, mushrooming stench in the air had nothing to do with disintegrating cardboard. It was the smell of something foul and reprehensible, something ungodly and far beyond his ability to comprehend or defend against. But defend himself is exactly what he planned to do. If that meant showing his fear card, then so be it. He'd rather be scared and fight on, than act cool but set his fate as just another victim. By his way of thinking, speaking that into the world would make it as real as if it had already happened to him.

Which it might, anyway.

But he wasn't going to make it that easy for the fucking thing.

"I don't know what we're gonna find in a minute," he finally allowed himself to say between dry heaves, the taste of the foul air clinging to his palate. "But you'd better believe it isn't gonna be nice. We have to be ready for anyth—"

The stinging pain was swift and sudden.

It speared through his head like a hot iron needle, entering his left ear and shooting through his head to the right. He slapped a hand to the side of his face and felt the beetle-like creature there, hanging from his lobe. Its hard insect feet had clawed into the soft skin for purchase as something long and sharp had twisted inside his ear.

Without seeing it he knew the creature would be big and black.

And hideous.

It screeched when his fingers wrapped around it, yanking it from its feeding place. It's wings buzzed wildly with a flurry of motion and clawing legs as Bryan threw it to the floor, stamping his feet hard in the place he imagined it would have fallen. Something firm made a sick cracking noise beneath his right sneaker, followed by the slippery sensation of oozing stuff.

"Christ, are you okay?" In the sightless void Ian could only hear the scuffle. "Bryan—!" He gagged as the breath between words filled his mouth and nose with decaying air.

"I'm alright . . . I'm okay, I think." Bryan pressed his fingers to his ear where a sharp pain burned like a hot poker. He wasn't sure if it was the remnant of the original pain or if something, possibly a mouth part or something, stuck in there. "I've just been attacked by a flying parasite or some shit!"

Something then swarmed by Ian.

"No!" he shouted as he jumped aside, swatting the air frantically around his head and slapping chaotically at his own face. Somewhere in this dramatic onslaught, the minute insect crumpled lifelessly to the ground.

Thank God. Only a mosquito.

But the instant relief was tainted with seeping guilt. For in that one, singular instance of panic, his instinct for self-preservation had been so greatly paramount to anything else that Ian would have happily had the thing, whatever it might have been, leave him and go for his brother instead. It was a dark, creeping feeling that left him empty inside. Ian said nothing of it, pressing his eyes closed as a single tear began to swell.

The intense flash of light that came next was blinding white, even beneath his eyelids. It filled his vision with pulsating, disorienting spots of brilliance. "Wha—!" He instinctively pressed his face into the crook of his arm while thrusting the other defensively in front of him as a monochromatic kaleidoscope burnt across his vision.

Beside him, Bryan furiously rubbed his eyes amid high pitched bleats from the stinging pain. Able to open them only in brief spurts before squeezing them shut again in agony, a negative retina image branded the alternating blindness. Summoning the strength to force them open one more time, stinging tears poured down his face. Shielding his eyes and squinting as if through a fast moving current, something unfathomable loomed ahead; something he was sure must not be real.

But Ian was sure that it was.

The blinding spots fading, his eyes adjusted to the woods' new phosphorescent glow and the sight of the lone figure standing before them. Stock-still. Draped in a deeply cowled cloak, it was bathed in the backlit aurora of a dark but fiery haze as the woods erupted into flame around them.

At the figure's feet, lifeless and prone, lay Matt Chauncey's corpse.

Hands and head burnt and blistered, neck twisted unnaturally to one side, the skin had begun to molder and slough away with an air-thickening stench. The body was still dressed in its neat little blue burial suit. Only now, the previously immaculate jacket was torn and ragged, the tidy trousers filthy with thick clods of mud and grass.

In a delayed reaction, the air vacuumed from Ian's lungs. Wheezing in thin, jarring paroxysms, he grappled for breath as Bryan gawked on, paralyzed in terror.

Neither were aware of the figure emerging from the searing orange brume of trees behind them.

Stepping stealthily through the mud and ashen soot, Mr. Chauncey, pickaxe in hand, moved silently across the clearing toward the Father Oak where just two weeks earlier his only son had pleaded and cried as he tortuously died, dangling from a cord.

Nineteen

STRUGGLING TO ONE knee, the Bible in Della's hands shook uncontrollably as she cowered before the dais. Repeatedly making the sign of the cross over her chest, the gesture frantic and clumsy, she flung her arms open wide. Her voice pitched wildly as she wailed to the Christ figure hanging above her, "*Nobiscum Deus. Defendat nos a Bestia—!*"

Ian understood enough etymology to translate her cry.

Deus—God.

Defendat nos—protect us.

"From the Beast—" he said aloud, his voice weak and barely audible in the cyclone of wind as his stomach tightened and he clenched the seat back in front of him for support. His knuckles stretched white as childhood terror overwhelmed him, the Beast Bear of his dreams bearing down upon him once more and consuming his senses. As it did, any hope of disassociating this nightmare vision from reality—or their violent past from the threats of the present—siphoned away as quickly and categorically as his failing equilibrium. Fighting to retain this faltering consciousness, a black pall of hopelessness roiled within his abdomen like a viper.

The violent gale fell to immediate silence.

Ceasing as quickly as it had come, it evaporated the moment Bryan collapsed to the floor. Forlornly shaking, he now sat there atop a small, darkening patch in the carpet. In the abruptly renewed quiet, his low, weeping moans reverberated thinly off the sparsely adorned chapel walls.

Della grasped the dais' wrought iron banister as she labored uncertainly to her feet. Frantically thumbing through the book in her trembling hands, the ultra sheer paper flapped and tore as she pored though the pages to finally settle upon a section near the back. She slapped the volume closed around a finger inserted to mark the page.

Then DeLaCroix Laveau closed her eyes tightly and prayed.

Wrangling his brother's dead weight into the nearest seat, Ian found himself issuing a flurry of trite reassurances to his brother that even he, himself, didn't believe.

Eventually, when Bryan's despondent groans fell to a soundless lament, Ian collapsed into an adjacent seat and rhetorically asked aloud, to whatever overseer it was that governed this life of theirs, just what the hell was happening to them.

"I d-don't . . . ." He fumbled over the words, his mouth dry and tasting of copper, barely able to comprehend what was taking place.

In a hospital chapel.

While, alone, Rebecca was fighting for her life in Pittsburgh.

And a woman, whom hours earlier he had barely known, was now reaching into his deepest vulnerabilities.

"I don't . . . don't understand. That was like—like—"

Like Bryan was possessed.

Della brushed aside broken shards of yellow glass from the dais and pulled a wooden stick from the metal box beside the candelabra. Careful not to betray the shaking of her hands, she struck the match to life and kissed it upon the wick of the single votive which had remained intact. The flame immediately danced within the yellow jar, unmasking shadow in every corner of the chapel and cleansing it in warm, reassuring light.

"Not possessed . . . . Not in the way you are thinking." Della spoke pensively to the altar, replying out loud to Ian's conclusion though she did not directly address him. "More a messenger. Delivering us a warning."

His eyes cast down, Ian showed no sign of hearing her as he grappled to process what had just taken place.

"It is in the dark that we most freely see the Light," Della softly heralded, returning her attention to the brothers. "There's a comforting strength in the wisdom of that truth. That we will always see the Light in darkness. But never darkness in the Light."

As if accentuating the tenet, the lit candle popped and brightened as the flame ran down the wick. It settled into a smooth, even burn atop the ivory wax as Della settled into a seat next to the brothers.

For several minutes, DeLaCroix Laveau said nothing more.

Calming her own fractured energy, she meditated over the reason why every path and every choice across a lifetime of options had conspired to deliver her to this precise place, at this exact moment in time. The onerous answer she divined from God and the Universe was direct and resoundingly clear: all the hardships and seemingly pointless struggle; the loneliness in isolation of a life on the periphery of accepted beliefs; an adamant refusal to deny the unorthodox, complex and oft-challenged spiritual erudition she had risen to; all of these things, and many more, had been immovably ordaining her for this singular, divine purpose.

She was brought here to deliver a message of her own.

Bryan wiped the tears from his face as he rustled in his seat, the shame and embarrassment palpable as it vibrated from him in short, fractured waves. Taking several deep, stuttering breaths, he cleared his throat. "I'm so sorry," he timidly offered Della. "Please. I don't—I don't know . . . where that came from."

Ian reached over and held his forearm, squeezing it reassuringly; Della lowered her gaze, smiling in an uncomfortable but exonerating manner.

ΙΙ

As the three slowly composed themselves, the vibrational energy of the chapel rose in equal, parallel steps. Della took one more deep and cleansing breath as she finished her meditative prayer in which she now willfully accepted the spiritual assignment she had unknowingly been honed by the Universe most of her life.

Settling her eyes first upon one brother, then the other, she offered each her genuine compassion wrapped within a warm, arcadian energy. *I am here for a reason,* she projected, the affirmation serene but resounding in unassailable authority. It wrapped around them as a blanket would swaddle a frightened, shivering infant. *You connecting with me at this precise time is no coincidence. It is our ordained destiny. What happened to your parents, to Rebecca, it's not some kind of spiritual revenge. The boy in your dreams is not Matt. And he is not punishing you for something you have, or have not, done.*

The telepathy exhausting her energy, Della cleared her throat and continued by speaking audibly.

"A powerful demonic force has attached itself to you." The statement was direct and unapologetic in tone. "A tangible presence of untethered evil, resuming the affront it began that fateful day in the woods so many years ago. When you were just children."

To regulate her own anxious breathing, Della focused on the play of light and tranquil, flickering shadows cast by the candle. As the cold fear within her gradually dissipated, a warming faith flowed into the void it left, restoring her with a calm, pastoral strength.

"And this . . . *warning* . . . that just came through me?" Bryan's tone betrayed the confusion and rising fear simmering beneath his thinly cracking veneer of composed normalcy. "I'm sorry, but you'll have to excuse me for not having the capacity right now to follow where you're going. I need something—*tangible*—from you to grab onto right now, Della."

"Your brother asked me if what just happened to you was a type of possession. The answer to that, Bryan, is no." She took his left hand and gingerly cupped it between hers, feeling the life energy transmitting warmly between them. Watching closely but furtively, she gently laid his palm upon the open page of the Bible in her lap. "And also . . . yes."

In contrast to the intense heat coming off Della's hands, the paper felt cold to the touch and Bryan flinched as the sensation emitted a sharp icy pain in his palm.

Covertly observing this exchange, Ian anxiously pressed her for clarification. "What do you mean, 'Also yes'?"

"There is a priest today. In Italy. By the name of Rafael," she explained, careful that her subconscious vibration impart a calm efficacy. "One of the Vatican's most revered clerics, Father Rafael is perhaps best known as the Chief Exorcist of Rome."

Bryan pulled his hand sharply from Della's tender grip. "And—?"

"And Rafael is published in several journals recounting his forty-plus years of administering exorcism rites on behalf of the Vatican. In them, he has identified what are now accepted as the defined stages of demonic possession." She turned her attention solely to Bryan. "Only in the final stage do we see the signs we've come to popularly associate with it. The first are comprised of all sorts of odd things you might otherwise dismiss if occurring in isolation: apparitions, bad odors, disturbing nightmares, anxiety, an onslaught of problems—both at work and at home—even physical attacks. These initial stages can take place very quickly, or can occur over a matter of decades. Each case is different. But in every case, little by little, the attack increases until the victim becomes violent. To others . . . or possibly even to himself."

Becoming visibly agitated, Bryan shuffled uncomfortably in his seat. Crossing and uncrossing his arms, he noticeably avoided eye contact with Della as she continued.

"Once broken by this incessant pursuit, the demon commandeers the victim's actions or behavior, even imparting traits like inhuman strength, speaking or chanting in unknown languages, and—though it can never fully negate it—temporarily overpower the victim's free will. We're not at that stage here. But I do believe that Bryan, or perhaps both of you, are somewhere in the initial phases of possession."

Vehemently shaking his head, Bryan abruptly rose from his chair. "Alright I've heard enough. Jesus, Ian! What fucked-up nonsense are you trying to pull here, bringing this crackpot bullshit into this situation. At a time like this? Like it's not hard enough right now?"

He squared up to Della, his body language intense and aggressive. "So, you're claiming that what just happened here was the result of an evil entity," Bryan clarified with little interest to hide his skepticism. "It couldn't possibly be the result of an unendurable amount of stress or emotional turmoil—"

"It feeds on trauma, Bryan. Just as it induces it, yes. Creating a perpetual cycle of negativity amid chaos."

"And what happened to Rebecca today. My folks. The weird shit in Ian's visions. You think all of this is proof of it . . . . So, to make sure I'm hearing you right, you think we're being pursued by a demonic force?"

"Yes." Della spoke the declaration without equivocation.

"A demon—" Bryan repeated disingenuously.

Though Della's chest was tightening and her pulse drummed the left side of her neck in quick and shallow bursts, her eye contact with Bryan remained firm and unwavering. "Yes. Pursuing both of you. Just as it did all those years ago. Children are highly receptive vessels. This also makes them more susceptible. I believe the intensity but immaturity of the vibration of you boys all together that day made y'all open to a spiritual attack which—for the others, for whatever reason—escalated through the initial stages almost instantly."

"Directly to the final stage," Ian drew the natural conclusion.

"Directly to the final." Della slowly nodded, softening her tone as she spoke to both men. "Make no mistake, sugars. There was something else with you boys in the woods that day. Something ancient. And powerful . . . and unbelievably bold."

‡‡‡

"Seriously. I've heard enough," Bryan flatly refuted as he stood up. Pressing Ian and Della both out of the way, he headed unapologetically for the door as a wave of negative energy rose in a deeply bass telepathic tide.

"Bryan—" Ian shouted after him, but his brother only waved him off without stopping or looking back. He wrenched the door open with an angry tug and the stark, blue-white fluorescent hospital lighting flooded into the chapel, washing it in sterile reality.

"It called itself something!" Della challenged as Bryan stepped through the door. "That terrible thing in the woods. What did it call itself?"

In a manner undetectable to most but obvious to his brother, Bryan hesitated, just barely, mid-stride. "It didn't call itself anything," he answered blandly over his shoulder as the self-closer slowly drew the door shut behind him.

That's not true. Tension rose in Ian's gut as his brother's brazen lie chafed his memory.

If Bryan felt the mental repudiation, he showed no sign of receiving it and continued into the hallway .

"AZAZEL—" Della shouted as the door had nearly closed. "It called itself Azazel! Didn't it Bryan!" This time the shape of the man, barely visible in the bright but diminishing wedge, stopped in its tracks.

The door shut with a click, consuming the last sliver of light.

Lowering her voice in the dark, Della repeated the declaration to the back of the door. "The demon in the woods. It called itself Azazel, Bryan. I know it's true."

Motionless in the austerely lit corridor, Bryan's heart beat relentlessly. As crisply as if occurring just moments ago, the words he spoke eighteen years earlier overwhelmed him: *Stu said everything is for this thing he called Zaze—Zaza—Zazol—I don't know, something fucked up like that.* And his veins ran cold.

Bryan flung the chapel door open. His silhouette framed in a bright rectangle of sterile blue-white light, the shape of him fell to its knees as tortured sobs filled the air.

Della ran to him. "Huh-uh, sugar. No sir. No one's giving up here." She waggled an index finger dramatically, almost comically, in the air while fiercely shaking her head. "Not on my watch!" Though she was speaking in little more than a whisper, her words emblazoned the chapel in sound. On the dais, the burning votive brightened and blazed tall and bright. "I can help you—and your Rebecca—through this. *We* will help you through this." She placed her palm beneath his chin and tenderly raised his eyes to the cross over her shoulder. "But I need to know . . . ."

Staring at her through wet eyes, Bryan managed to shakily utter after three attempts to speak, "Y-you n-need to know?"

Della locked her gaze upon him, drawing him in to her. "I need to know what happened, Bryan," she coaxed. "That last night. When you and Ian went back to the woods."

Weak and confused, Bryan shook his head in agitation, muttering. He feebly swatted her hand away from his face. "I don't remember!"

"Bryan," Della compassionately spoke as she lowered herself to one knee in front of the older brother rather than tower over him. "You do. You will always remember that night . . . because you are the Witness."

In Bryan's eyes, something more than the glimmering reflection of the votive flickered. Then it was gone, as quickly as it had come.

"Tell me, Bryan," Della said again. "What you did to Stu."

twenty

1977

CLENCHING HIS HANDS so hard that his nails dug into his palms, Ian's chest squeezed the final breaths of air from his lungs. His heartbeat came in pounding cycles in the side of his neck as his vision warped through a fish-eye lens.

One Mississippi . . . .

Two Mississippi . . . .

Motionless over Matt's decomposing corpse, the cloaked figure was silhouetted before the blaze as Ian's shallow, choking gulps failed to siphon new air into his burning lungs.

Five Mississippi . . . .

All around the Father Oak, crackling flames snapped and hissed as they devoured the outer ring of trees, ravenously licking up their trunks and blazing the branches to life. Bark ignited and green pulp withered as the agonizing heat boiled away the moisture from inside the living wood. Expanding through the smallest network of narrow cracks, steam squealed in shrill and jarring chords as it escaped to the surface, filling the air with discordant shrieks.

Shrieks like whistling.

The whistling of Matt's flute, Ian thought as the heat playing over his face grew the skin taut over his cheeks; his scalp tingling in hot prickles. His body suddenly too heavy for his legs—

Seventeen Mississippi . . . .

—Ian slumped to the ground on his side. Face to face with Matt's rotting corpse, his dead friend's vacuous eye stared emptily back at him as the broiling orange and red haze of the Little Woods became his deep grey void.

Bryan screamed, but it was an internal wail. His lungs would not issue the breath needed for the sound to come out. Frozen on the spot, eyes wide, his mouth stretched in a mute howl. Skin cold and clammy despite the blistering heat, pins and needles perforated down the length of his spine. His feet were like anchors beneath concrete pylons for legs as the fear took control of him.

Do you believe?

The words echoed inside Bryan's mind in the same fashion his brother's always could. But these were not Ian's. Reverberating more powerfully through him than any he had felt before, they were a dark and noxious vibration that tightened his stomach. He began to gag as the three simple words corkscrewed into him like deep, black tendrils.

The hooded figure slowly extended its arm.

For a moment, a boy's hand began to protrude from the deep cuff; the fingers tipped by the jagged, uneven nails Stu incessantly chewed. Within the shadows of the cowl that covered its head, Bryan spied a glimmer of Stu's features. Where his friend's black-rimmed glasses would be, a faintest spark of light flickered, a light like a match flame reflecting the fire's glowing embers back at him. It flashed bright for an instant, exposing Stu's face in deepest orange and red, and then—as the spark itself—Stu's face was gone.

All that stared back at Bryan was a cold and endless void.

Bryan's breath wrested from his chest.

Seven shall be offered. For seven blasphemies.

The finger of the figure's hand uncurled. Twisting as it extended, it was no longer Stu's. Wet with a gelatinous membrane that issued a fetid moldering odor, the mucous sluiced down its scaly length to congeal at the tip embellished by a thick beast-like claw.

It pointed at Ian.

"NO," Bryan wanted to shout but his mouth again stretched wide with no sound emitting from it. In his ears, his heartbeat thumped like a rubber mallet on a girder. It accelerated when Matt Chauncey's corpse, prone at the feet of the cowled figure, stirred.

At first it was a minute shudder in its bare and blackened feet. One toe twitched, the charred tip of a clean white bone scraping back and forth in the dirt. Then another. Matt's right foot, flaking and peeling to the taut dry tendons, spasmed in a wave that rippled up his tattered blue pantleg. Extended and bent unnaturally over his head, his broken left hand jerked back and forth in rapid, uncontrolled tremors that drummed the ash and leaves which flitted into the air and wafted down over his face. Then Matt Chauncey's corpse pressed itself up and wavered awkwardly on its knees.

And began clawing gracelessly through the dirt and ash.

Toward Ian.

The soundless scream in Bryan's chest elicited a hiss that seared his parched throat as his larynx strained to expel it. His pulse a snare drum in double-four allegro, every frozen muscle cramped in pain.

When his stifled cry broke free, it detonated in a visible, percussive wave that visibly bent the burning branches and swayed the trees around the clearing. A bellows fueling their flames, fiery fingers flared high into the raven black sky.

"Me! Take me! Take me! TAKE ME!"

Wrapping around the command like a swarm of stinging fireflies, crimson embers burst and popped from the intensifying flames. They cycloned around the clearing to bite Bryan's cheeks and singe his scalp. Choking and coughing, he dropped to his knees and covered his head, the heaving breaths tearing at his burning lungs as the blaze amplified and began closing in. At the near edge of the clearing, the scrub oaks and brush closest to the Father Oak broiled in the scorching heat, their bark blackening and starting to split.

Sizzling black rain descended in a streaming hot curtain to veil the woods in smoldering soot and glowing ash.

Fumbling blindly across the ground, Bryan made a human arch over his brother's unconscious body, inverting his T-shirt over his shoulders to cover both of their heads. Poker-hot cinders showered down upon his exposed back, a dozen third-degree pin-pricks branding his tender adolescent skin. Bryan flinched and grimaced from the needling pain, suppressing his cries of pain to thin, stifled whimpers. He held the pose until the burning downfall dwindled.

When it did, standing where the cloaked figure had been, Stu Klatz pulled back the hood of his sweatshirt. Next to him, Matt Chauncey—appearing very much alive—stood with his hands upon his hips and a grin across his face. His cheeks were smooth and flawless; hair neatly combed. The blue suit he wore was clean and tidy, its anchor buttons glimmering bright yellow and orange in the incandescent light as the burning trees around them flickered and hissed.

Only the coldness in Matt Chauncey's eyes betrayed that something not quite right resided there.

Tilting his head first one way then the other, the resurrected boy silently purveyed the brothers in childlike curiosity as Bryan lurched unsteadily to his feet while Ian lay motionless on the ground.

"Very good," Stu lauded of Bryan's achievement as the trees around the Father Oak settled into a strong, steady burn, encircling the boys with a rapidly constricting perimeter of crackling flame. "The Witness is discovering his power. How adorable."

As fear escalated to defensive rage, Bryan straddled his feet protectively either side of Ian's torpid body, instinctively drawing into a tight fighter's stance. His brain shifted to hyper-alertness as his excessively dilated eyes scanned the burning clearing, darting back and forth to unmask every shadow now ineffectual in their overexposure. His extremities palpitated as his thudding heart cascaded surplus oxygen into every muscle. His breathing coming fast, he raised both trembling fists. He swallowed hard. "You aren't taking him! I'll die before I let you!"

Matt Chauncey humorlessly giggled. It was a perverse grating sound that, in a way, resembled the boy's nervous little laugh. But also didn't. Something about it smacked of filth and darkness. In his eyes, no joy shone.

Yes, you WILL die. The boy's unspoken words tightened the muscles of Bryan's stomach as the malignant vibrations burrowed into him like four squirming parasites. *And we will take your brother.*

"Woe to the inhabiters of the earth!" Stu bellowed and stretched his arms wide, lifting his head in exaltation. "For the Primeval Dragon is come down unto you, having great wrath!"

The declaration boomed across the woods in the longing yowls of a thousand pained jackals. Resounding in undulating echoes through the canopy of the trees, it strengthened as it rose beyond. As if chasing after it, the flames of the burning treetops coiled around its invisible wick as they licked high into the night sky.

Bryan's chest hollowed as the broiling heat reddened his cheeks. At his feet, his brother's face was draining to a colorless hue. Beneath his breast, Ian's straining heart announced that it was dying. It visibly buffeted his ribs as it desperately labored for oxygen, the thickening blood coursing through it growing dark and impotent.

Bryan heard it—*felt it*—as surely as if his own. The frantic rhythm was building louder. And slower. The pause between beats extending.

Stu lowered his gaze and settled his eyes upon him. Like Matt's, they were cold and lifeless behind the black plastic glasses which magnified their size to unnerving proportion. Despite the inferno raging around them they cast no reflection, absorbing the light within a deep, dark void.

Two witnesses will prophesy before the God of earth, Stu issued in mephitic, venomous vibrations that twisted into Bryan's soul. *Fire shall proceedeth out of their mouth. But when their testimony is done, the Beast shall rise to overpower and take them!*

Jostling excitedly in place, Matt Chauncey giggled and pointed at the boy on the ground who had been his best friend as Ian now clutched at his last feeble threads of life. Flawlessly matching the cadence of Ian's failing heart which slowed between each agonizing pump, Chauncey mimicked its sound with unbridled exuberance:

"THUM-THUMP . . . thum–thump . . . . . THUM—THUMP . . . ."

"Do you believe!" Stu screamed and the image of Bryan's friend warped and rippled, betraying the veneer. His features blurred, intensely sharpened, then dissolved into the abyss of the cowl the sweatshirt had become. "Summon your God, Witness! That He may descend and save your brother!"

My God is not at my command! Bryan refuted with such unexpected and sacrosanct conviction that the repudiation astonished even him. The power of the vibration discharged a visible shock wave across the Little Woods, igniting the highest branches of the Father Oak and blowing them into bright blue flame.

"THERE IS NO GOD!" the figure roared and the earth tremored and shifted beneath their feet as if it were about to crumble. "ONLY HE WHOM AZAZEL SERVES!"

From a deep, drooping cuff it slowly extended one hand, turning its scaled, oozing cadaverous palm upward. Curling a single claw-tipped finger, it beckoned Ian's perishing body.

"ONE TO BECOME THE SACRIFICIAL SCAPEGOAT. THE OTHER HIS GREATEST DISCIPLE. RISE AND BE COUNTED AMONGST THE SEVEN!"

And with a choking gasp that filled his lungs, Ian stood.

Matt Chauncey clapped and whooped in boyish celebration, jumping up and down. He danced in a circle, flapping his arms.

Then he pounced.

Wrapped around Ian's torso, Matt's beaming smile spread into a cavernous hole wielding a hundred tiny, razor-sharp incisors.

Emitting an ear-penetrating cry—

the wail of countless discordant flutes

—he cocked his head back and struck.

The thick wood handle of his father's pickaxe shattered Matt's jaw before his band-saw teeth punctured and tore apart Ian's skull. Squealing as he dropped to the ground, Matt writhed in the smoking black ash as Mr. Chauncey raised the pick above his head once more.

No, Papa! No! It's me! Matt pleaded in credulous, whimpering vibrations as his father straddled over him.

"You're not my son," Old Man Chauncey flatly denounced as he dispassionately sunk the flat, wide chisel end of the pickaxe into Matt's skull. "You're an abomination."

Bryan recoiled as the man extricated the tool from the cleave in the boy's head with a stomach-churning *thwuucck* and Matt instantly blistered and blackened, his body contorting; neck twisting. One eye swelled and popped as the corpse deteriorated and shrunk into a fetal position, the blue suit sullying and fraying as it ballooned and rippled with maggots.

Then Matt Chauncey was a lifeless shell in the dirt and ash.

Bewildered and numb, Ian stumbled backward. His veins running icy cold, he futilely attempted to process what he had woken to as Matt's father pushed him even further away . . . then swung the pickaxe in a low, sweeping arc.

The dull, rusty pick end embedded into the cowled figure's side.

Shrieking in disharmonic layered yowls, it wavered in and out of opacity, a vacillating mirage between the demonic entity one moment, Stu Klatz the next. When it buckled to the ground, the clawed hands and cowled robe shed away to the very real sight of Bryan's bespectacled friend clutching his side in disbelief as his grey sweatshirt spread to bright red blood.

Stu screamed as Mr. Chauncey yanked and pulled on the pickaxe, dislodging it from the boy's ribcage. It made a hollow splintering sound, like green wood splitting, as he wrenched it free. If not for Stu's tortured cry, the noise might have melded into the chaotic snapping of the Father Oak as high above them, blazing limbs popped like gunshot reports. Flowing in hypnotic, smoothly rippling fingers, the fire summoned by Bryan's decree descended down the ancient tree's massive trunk.

Smoldering leaf clusters and incinerating branches began to rain down upon them like napalm.

Choking in the heat and smoke, Old Man Chauncey dragged Stu to the base of the tree, ignoring the loosening of the boy's arm from its shoulder socket as he jerked and wrested him across the clearing. The color in Stu's face draining, Chauncey disappeared behind the Father Oak and reemerged with an aged and fraying triple-braided rope. He tossed one end to Bryan which had already been fashioned into a crude lasso, then heaved the bulk of the coiled bundle over a branch just above his reach. The cumbrous spool skated over the limb, partially unraveling as it thumped to the ground in a shower of sparks and hot ash. "Around his neck," Chauncey directed Bryan as he gathered up his end. "I knew bringing him here would draw it out."

By 'him,' Chauncey was clearly referring to Matt.

Or more accurately, Bryan thought, *his putrid rotting corpse.*

Mere hours after Matt Chauncey had been laid to rest in the tidily groomed new extension of St. Benedict's cemetery, adjacent to the elementary school playground, his father had labored throughout the night. Exhuming his son's body immediately after dusk that day had afforded the opportunity to excavate and refill the still loosely packed soil while raising little suspicion. The plot and its blanket of lush, green squares of turf were so fresh, after all. Who would possibly notice, or even dare to make such an unthinkable allegation?

By 'it,' Bryan understood the man to mean the demonic thing that was at once both Stu and not Stu. The fucking thing Klatz had called Zazol, or something like that, when he showed him how it was going to have Woody violently dispose of Jimi Raker in the Beechnut; the thing which was now gone—if it had ever really been here at all—while his friend lay here dying, propped against the base of the Father Oak which was now a towering inferno.

Clusters of air bubbles hissed from Stu's torn lung, frothing the thick dark blood flowing freely from his side. He sputtered, and mucous so deeply red it was almost black spun from his mouth. "Br—Bry—an," he wheezed. "Please . . . h-help . . . . Me."

Bryan stared at his own reflection in Stu's cracked glasses. A pair of fractured silhouettes stared back at him against a brilliantly dirty amber haze as the flames at the clearing's perimeter edged nearer. The looped end of the rope dangling from his hands like a lasso, they were stereophonic cowboy cutouts pasted onto a miasmic diorama.

Stu reached for him, his fingers grey and trembling.

Hesitating . . . Bryan reached back.

Old Man Chauncey pushed him away, snatching the rope out of his hands. "That thing is not your friend," he said as he swatted away Stu's reaching arm and bent down to examine him.

He grabbed Stu's chin and yanked it this way and that, eyeing him with no more empathy than a farmer inspecting a veal calf at auction. Stu's upper lip lifted in a snarl and Chauncey squeezed the boy's mouth until his teeth sliced into his gums.

"It's an aberration in the shell of what used to be your friend. Here, look—" He pulled off Stu's broken glasses and tossed them aside. Bryan did not come closer. "I said look!"

Chauncey's large, calloused fist latched onto Bryan's shirt and dragged him near, forcing him lower until his nose and Stu's were nearly touching.

Staring back at him were two torpid pits.

With a cachinnating laugh, Stu spat.

Bryan recoiled, swiping the burning phlegm from his cheeks.

"I don't know what this thing is," Chauncey admitted as the hope drained from Bryan's face. "But it's not your friend, kid . . . . At least, not anymore." He again handed Bryan the rope. "Around its neck."

Stu flailed and twisted but was too weak to stop him as Bryan positioned the coarse, fraying loop over his head. A swamp of crimson soot now beneath him, Stu's skin had become colorless and sallow. With the Father Oak now ablaze all the way down its trunk and the flames licking hot just a dozen or so feet off the ground, Stu's skin seemed to wriggle and writhe in the intense play of light and shadow the flames cast.

Stepping a handful of feet away, Mr. Chauncey wrapped the other end of the rope around his own waist and tied it off, jerking it twice to ensure it was fast.

He began pacing backwards.

With each deliberate step, the slack in the rope diminished until it had become a taut braided line, forty-five degrees to the branch above them. Snugly curving over the limb, it ran arrow-straight down the other side where it constricted the loop around Stu's neck. Jerking his chin involuntarily upward, his eyes and Bryan's locked.

A noxious, pestilent wave rippled between them—

. . . *One Witness the scapegoat. The other His greatest disciple* . . . .

—and Bryan took a step back, placing himself defensively in front of his brother as Chauncey also took another step backward and the noose around Stu's neck clinched tight, gouging his skin now entirely grey and colorless.

Two more steps and Stu was pulled limply to his feet, an absurd marionette. Testing the rope's efficacy, the man leaned back and Stu's head tugged satisfyingly upward, his heels coming off the ground and precariously balancing on his toes, starting to sway.

"You boys don't have to see this," Matt's father stated with little affect, but Bryan stood transfixed. Behind him, Ian was motionless and numb. "Okay, your choice."

Old Man Chauncey lowered himself down into a tight spring, then leapt up and back. For a moment, the rope lost tension and the much lighter boy in the noose began to slough to the ground.

Then Chauncey was falling spreadeagle backward—a trust fall with no one to catch him—and Stu's body jerked violently off the ground.

The gash in Stu's side stretched wide as he lifted, exposing a mass of mangled tissue. Clutching the strangling collar around his throat in vain, burning branches loosened and fell from above as he kicked and thrashed mid-air inside a shower of broiling embers.

On his back, Mr. Chauncey wrapped the rope around his wrist and forearm and pulled the line as tight as he could.

It wasn't long before Stu's desperate flailing reduced to weak, twitching spasms. It was just before they stopped altogether that the horrid, bestial scream came.

Massive bear-like talons clawing him from the inside out, Stu's torso bulged and split as the Beast within escaped the dying boy, howling as it inverted Stu's carcass. Rising to merge into the fiery twilight as it elicited an ear-piercing symphony of shrieks like wailing flutes, the beast became nothing but shadow as it melded with the darkness that already prospered there.

As if sharing a terrible dream, Bryan and Ian watched in a stupor as Stu Klatz's shredded body dropped from the noose and doubled over.

Folding in upon itself, it sloughed to the ground. The steam still rising from its organs, it lay in a pile beside Matt Chauncey's black and shriveled corpse.

Bryan grabbed his brother's arm.

And ran.

They heard, but did not see, Mr. Chauncey's pickaxe striking the ground. As the Little Woods gave way to incinerating flame, thud upon thud echoed through the crackling trees.

As their friend's father hewed a shallow hole, wide enough for two.

Twenty-One

WE KILLED HIM, Jesus help me! We killed him!" Bryan cried out as Ian stood dazed in front of the single flickering votive on the dais, his face pale and beginning to glisten with perspiration.

Della lowered her head and signed the cross above Bryan's forehead, praying over him in Latin: "*Dimitte nobis debita nostra, sicut et nos dimittimus debitoribus nostris.*" The vibration was warm and compelling and flowed through him like a balm caressing his psyche: *Forgive us our sins, as we forgive those who sin against us.*

Bryan extended his arms and Della took each hand, helping him to his feet and wrapping him in a deep, sheltering embrace like none he had received in a very, very long time. Enshrouded by Della's quiet strength, he was back in the kitchen, the morning Mrs. Raker called—

. . . lurching into the room, he throws his arms around his father's waist, burying his face into his chest and not letting go . . .

—and the swelling tide of eighteen years of sadness, shame, denial, and guilt finally broke free. It crashed from his being like a rogue wave, vibrating in shimmering energy across the chapel as he finally surrendered his ego to a universe of authority far greater than his own, or even his own understanding.

"That wasn't your friend, sugar," Della affirmed, unclasping her arms from around his waist and stepping back that he could share in the unshakable faith behind her eyes. "That figure may have looked like Stu. But your friend was no longer in that body. Do you understand? It takes the shape of whatever it wants. Whatever will cause the greatest pain or shock value. It's a bit of a drama queen that way."

If the comment was meant to elicit a smile, it did.

Bryan chuckled. It was an awkward but honest sound, and perforated the silence as the chapel glimmered in positive, radiant light.

Standing at the dais with his back to them, Ian kept the transformation at arm's length. As much as he would have loved to convince himself that his own faith was the same as his brother's new-found trust, he just couldn't. The way he saw it, if God was real, if God was Love, and if he mattered *at all* in God's eyes, then He would reveal a reason for all of this.

Della was supposed to be that messenger.

Letting an educated, if somewhat unorthodox perspective, in on their secret was intended to illuminate how he could finally sever this fucking curse—or at least the belief in it—and rid himself of whatever malicious thing was still clawing into his life. For all he'd known, she would wave around some burning sage, recite a voodoo chant, maybe even cut the head off a chicken or some shit, and it would all be over. Nothing but a bad dream. At the very least, he expected her insight and objectivity would bolster his faith.

It didn't.

If anything, it was getting worse now that she was involved.

Ian raised his head to the crucifix above the altar, hoping beyond hope for a cosmic sign; a spiritual epiphany of his own that would help him make sense of all of this—any of this—and in turn, help him through it. One way or another.

The Christ hung in mute response.

Why? Come on! Don't just hang there. Tell me why!

Try as he might, Ian could not understand why one minute a group of rowdy but innocent boys—excited for the summer which had finally come —were a pack of rabid jackals the next, howling with delight as they beat and tortured and murdered their own friend. Why not one, but two, of his closest friends had to die . . . while he personally watched the first and remotely witnessed the second as surely as if he had been in Craig's bed- room. Why some mind-numbing thing had torn their friend apart right in front of them while a grown man, an adult they had trusted, lynched the bully in black plastic spectacles. Why, out of any of a thousand bars in the borough, Anonymous had come into *his* Manhattan bar. Why he then saw his parents die in a horrific car crash before it even happened, replaying their death over and over in his mind until it consumed him in obsessive, sickening detail. Why Rebecca, whom he was finally getting the chance to know, was found laying in a dark garage, overcome by inordinate amounts of organ-suffocating carbon monoxide.

He demanded an answer. And he demanded one right now.

The world's purest icon of love again returned only deafening silence, wrapped around Ian's own rebounding disappointment.

Although far from a devout Christian, Ian's belief had always been real and solid enough, especially given the changing tide of popularity in spiritual belief these days. Or at least he thought it had been. Staring now at the forlorn Christ, hanging in mortal abandon upon a cross of heavy timber, he realized he could no longer fathom how one would freely submit one's life, in the most torturous ordeal of anguish and pain imaginable (or unimaginable) in order to protect an unseen deity that would allow you to go through such torture in the first place. Hell, he wasn't sure he could put himself through that to protect anyone, for that matter.

In his mind, a mosquito buzzed and hummed.

It swarms around his face as he is back in the Little Woods for the last time on that blind, moonless night, and he swats and slaps the air around him, wishing it would leave him and go for his brother instead.

Then he remembered a different feeling, the sensation as he lay dying; his breaths faltering and his heart beating more fiercely but slower and more erratic as he lay prone on the ashen ground. And then came the unwavering sense of protection that enveloped him, refusing to allow him to give up:

Bryan flinches and grimaces from the needling pain, suppressing his cries to thin, stifled whimpers as poker-hot cinders shower down upon his exposed back, a dozen third-degree pin-pricks branding his tender adolescent skin. He holds the pose, sheltering his semi-conscious brother until the burning downfall dwindles.

And Ian flushed with shame.

He felt himself shudder as he stood beneath the crucifix, the tips of his trembling fingers pressing so hard into the polished wood of the dais railing that they were nearly translucent. In his mind, the sound of Mr. Chauncey's pickaxe was again cleaving the soil beneath the Father Oak. It echoed now as audibly and real as it had that night.

The poignant clang rings through the air while they run, the rusty metal of the pick glancing off stone and rock and roots.

Except the pickaxe had somehow become a massive iron mallet, its broad head pealing in metallic, ear-splitting chimes as it slams against a nail as thick as his thumb.

And it is not Mr. Chauncey wielding the tool, but himself.

Ian raises the hammer high above his shoulder.

The other soldiers hold the man down, laughing and jeering as they pin his shivering forearm against the timber and Ian pounds the crude iron nail through the man's wrist. Blood spritzes Ian's face, the bitter ferrous tang upon his lips as the nail he strikes penetrates the man's skin and bores through muscle and tendon. Another strike and it embeds into the wood beneath as the man on the cross cries out in unimaginable agony. One final hit and the bones snap as the nail head burrows beneath the skin. Ian looks at the prophet he is crucifying, and the one they call Christ is now the cartoon Ranger. Holding his ground between the boys and the Beast, the Ranger's face is frozen in both terror and disillusionment. The Ranger makes no sound as the Beast Bear scoops him up, without breaking stride, and carries him high into the treetops where his screams echo into the raven black sky as thunder roils over the hills . . . .

"Ian—!" Della cried as he bent over and heaved, a trace of bile dripping onto the railing and sliding slowly down. It sizzled as it struck the cold stone tile before the altar. "Ian! *Shhhsh*, hun. It's okay," she said over and over as she stroked his hair. "It's okay, it's gonna be okay . . . ."

‡‡

Della held his face, wiping away the spit and silent, streaming tears. "It's what it does. That wasn't you, sugar. It's the Deceiver. Spiritual and emotional manipulation, remember? It's the only way it fights . . . . Dirty."

She cast her eyes to the Christ on the cross. It radiated in a poignant, soothing luster.

"Evil does not accept the inherent balance of spirit—light and dark, yin and yang—only utter and absolute domination. Extinguishing the light wherever it shines. If we let it achieve that, it's the only way it can possibly ever win."

She clutched the Bible to her breast, cherishing the halcyon strength emanating from it.

"Della?" Bryan said, following several minutes of silence accentuated only by the popping candle in the votive framework. "We need you. I don't know what to do."

After a considered pause, Della answered him with a candid but requisite honesty she wished she didn't have to. "I don't truly know that I do either, hun. I wish I could say I did."

"But you've come across this before . . . ."

She shook her head emphatically. "No, sugar. I've done house clearings. You know, dispelling your run-of-the-mill accumulated bad ju-ju. And yes, more than once I've participated in ceremonial prayers over a living soul that's been afflicted."

"Exorcisms," said Ian tentatively, the smallest glimmer of hope igniting behind the exhaustion in his eyes.

"Catholics might call them that, yes. We consider it more of a prayerful rebalancing of the Loa—the Invisibles, or Mysterios—residing in us."

"Loa?"

"The In-betweens," Della explained. "Spiritual entities occupying the realm between us and God. Not explicitly good or bad, light or dark, these beings express a mix of dispositions, just as we do. Think of them and their realm as a bridge, of sorts, to the Supreme Creator. The rituals I'm referring to are a way of aligning these into balance."

Bryan too looked hopeful. "So we can do that here, exorcise this negative Loa—"

Della raised her hand, apologetically cutting him short. "The Loa are intermediaries, Bryan. We're dealing with something far more powerful here. I believe the darkness that's working you *is* expressly evil. An unholy angel. The influence of an explicitly demonic force—"

"—Azazel," Ian worked up the courage to interject, his voice weak and still shaking. "You knew that was the name Stu used for it, before we ever said a thing about what happened that night in the woods. How could you possibly know that . . . ?"

Della caressed the Bible's smooth cover with her palm, the tactile sensation assuaging the raw trepidation twisting inside her. "Because what's happening to you was written by the holy prophets, two thousand years ago, hun. Look, what I'm about to share with you, you won't find in any currently accepted scripture or religion. The Apocrypha . . . are you familiar with them?"

Ian shook his head no. Bryan was heedfully silent.

"From the Greek meaning hidden or secret. The Apocrypha were a set of sacred writings considered too esoteric for any but the divinely worthy. Fragments were discovered in what you will have heard called the Dead Sea Scrolls. Over the centuries, many of the Apocrypha writings were widely removed from most texts of western religion—save a few very notable exceptions—and the term apocryphal has come to be derogatory."

"Because?" Bryan asked, his nerve-endings again starting to fire as a new, uneasy feeling crept into him.

"Perhaps they threatened the establishment," Della conjectured. "Or it better suited the limited understanding of those in power to relegate the Apocrypha to the category of mythological, fictional. Maybe it was just easier to flat-out denounce them."

Ian's frustration started to show. *If refuted centuries ago, how did the Apocrypha have any bearing at all on their current situation? Why would she even bring them up?* "How does that help us, then? With this thing that is somehow still digging its claws into our fucking lives!"

"Look, sugars. Religious theory will never be tangible like science. There is no Absolute. But if there's one thing I've learned, it's that the truth usually can be found at the point of intersection between commonly held belief, personal testimony, and myth. The prophesies written in one Apocryphal text in particular—the Book of Enoch the prophet, great-grandfather of Noah—lies at that exact intersection."

"Wait, I've heard of something about the Book of Enoch," Bryan said. "Isn't that the mythical tale of oversexed boogeymen trying to corrupt the earth by having people turn on one another?"

"An oversimplification, perhaps. But not very far off," Della agreed. "And certainly not mythical. The name of those demons were the Grigori, or 'Watchers.' Guardians initially sent by God to watch over humanity, they were counted amongst the most beautiful and highly favored of Heaven's angels. But succumbing to envy over the prominence God bestowed upon his mortal children, the Watchers turned to lust and took human wives that they may seed children of their own: perversions of off-spring called Nephilim, borne upon darkness. And so God denied his grace to the Watchers because they refused to bow down before His single most beloved creation: Mankind. And while there were several leaders of the legion of demon Grigori, the most eminent was . . . *is* . . . ."

". . . Azazel," Ian said as the black tendrils of fear from eighteen years earlier speared his side and sucked the breath from his lungs.

"Yes. When early Jews made their sacrifices to God, it was common-place to also make an offering to Azazel. Not as a token of worship, but as a way to rescind their own impurities. After all, Enoch himself had declared to his people that, 'The whole earth has been corrupted through the works that were taught by Azazel; to him ascribe all sin.' Thus, with the sacrificial goat, their sins were returned to their origin. Or so they believed."

. . . When they killed Matt in the woods, they made the kid—are you ready for this—the first of the sacrificial scapegoats . . . .

Bryan's words from eighteen years earlier suddenly rang loud in Ian's memory. As they did, Della heard them too.

"They offered the goat—" She started, but had to pause to clear her throat as a malignant image of Matt Chauncey clouded her mind, the child hanging from the noose and crying. "I'm sorry," she said quietly as she wiped her eyes and forced the vibration aside, bracing herself to get the last part out; the most important part. "They ushered the goat into the deep wilderness, where they believed sin and impurity originated. There they would hang the animal by its neck from a tree. Before it bleated its last, they would set the goat alight—a symbol that their sin was atoned as it departed the goat in the form of flames that dispelled the darkness."

Returning to Azazel.

"The scapegoat deity," said Bryan as a chill ran down his spine.

The last votive flickered and snuffed to a thin wisp of oily smoke, and all three jumped when the chapel door swung open and slammed against the wall with a thunderous *BANG*.

III

"OH! I'm so sorry!" Louise said with a start as she clutched one impeccably manicured hand to her chest, the door she'd so dramatically flung open beginning to close upon its softly hissing hydraulic top hinge. "You startled me . . . I didn't know anyone was . . . still in here."

She exhaled dramatically as the three adults stared back at her breathless with wide eyes.

"Mr. Cockerton?" she asked as she flicked the light switch and the ceiling's recessed lighting popped into brilliant white radiance.

Bryan shielded his eyes from the light as the woman stepped forward, still uncertain who was addressing him. "Yes?"

Louise chuckled awkwardly, a clearly nervous reflex. "Oh my. I really am sorry. It's me, Mr. Cockerton . . . Louise." The statement met with frosty silence, she dutifully expanded, stepping forward to be better seen: "Louise, the social worker. I didn't mean to intrude on your family's personal reflection. I just hadn't expected you'd come back here, is all." After a pause she asked, "Did you forget something?"

"Yeah—um, no. Right, of course. I apologize we've been more than a few minutes. Thank you . . . for looking after the kids. We're ready to go—I think?"

Della and Ian nodded uncertainly.

Bryan approached the social worker, focused on calming his quickened pulse as it plateaued then began to gradually subside. "You know, you sorta spooked us a bit there, Louise. That was quite an entrance."

The social worker grimaced. "Again, I'm so very sorry to intrude. I really didn't expect you to be back here. I—I sometimes feel the need to spend a few minutes in here myself. You know, it can be soothing amid a particularly demanding shift."

Nodding, Bryan understood. He stopped in front of Louise, wringing the tension from his hands and offering her the best smile he could muster, given . . . . "So, thank you again. We'll follow you then?" Glancing behind him, he gestured for his brother and Della to come.

Louise didn't move. "I'm sorry?" Her professionally minimal smile cracked, just visibly.

"To the kids, of course. I don't know where we're supposed to go to collect them."

The social worker's face fell. "I don't understand."

Bryan's congeniality withered. "I just wanna get my kids, Louise."

"But y-you've—" She warily began taking slow, even steps backward towards the door. "You've already taken them, Mr. Cockerton."

Bryan's heart froze.

"I spoke to you personally, fifteen minutes ago. D–do you not remember? You told me you had to be somewhere. Something about a pet of yours." She nervously clucked a single staccato snort. The professional smile tried to make another appearance but was unsuccessful.

"A pet?" Ian blurted out.

"Fifteen minutes?" Bryan exclaimed. "We've been here at least half an hour. Ever since you offered to watch the kids so the three of us could talk in private. Right after Fieldhouse gave us his update!"

"That's not possible. It was you. You were alone, but it was you!" Louise's eyes momentarily scrutinized the man's brother as well as the woman standing behind Bryan, then blankly scanned the floor as she replayed the conversation in her mind. She checked her wristwatch, tapping it twice. It faithfully continued to tick away the seconds, one by one, the sound of each tangibly audible now in the savagely silent chapel. "Yes. You definitely said something about a pet. Something about a . . . a baby goat, Mr. Cockerton? Surely you're pulling my leg now. You know—"

Bryan pushed her aside and the social worker reeled into the corridor, aghast as he sprinted past.

"—If this is some kind of joke, I don't think it's very funny!" she shouted after them as the three bolted toward the lobby and Louise dialed '9' for security on the internal comms handset in the hallway.

IV

"DIANE!" Bryan called out as he ran through the lobby.

Ian darted through the automatic double doors to the Emergency Room entrance. "ANDREW!"

"KIDS?!" Della yelled as she threw open the swing doors to the outpatient ward and her voice echoed hollowly down the empty hall.

V

The motor of Della's VW Thing whined as she punched the accelerator, pulling onto the highway. Cars swept to either side as she weaved in and out, pushing the speedometer toward its upper limit.

"It's gonna be OK, sugar," she assured Bryan in the passenger seat next to her. "Louise may have been mistaken. I don't know how, but they're probably home."

But she didn't believe it.

None of them did, though they all dutifully nodded.

In the back seat, Ian punched the ten digit number into his cell phone keypad and the line trilled to life in the Cockerton home at the other end. It rang over and over, resounding through the dark and empty house until a crackly recording of Rebecca's voice asked him to leave a message and they would get back to him as soon as possible.

"Kids, are you there?" Ian shouted at the answering machine, knowing he was talking to no one. "Kids? If you are there, or if you get this, I want you to call Uncle Ian straight away, okay?" He reeled off his phone number and then repeated it twice more, very slowly so they could either write it down or memorize it. His voice had cracked numerous times though he'd made a concerted effort to sound calm.

"Anything?!" Bryan tensely asked.

Ian shook his head. He would try again in a couple minutes.

Watching the hood of her car eating up the road more hungrily than it ever had before, the rhythmic passing of the broken white lines became a visual metronome which synchronized the electrical pulses in Della's brain to an almost meditative theta state.

We should have seen this. How did we not see this? God's children. The envy of the Grigori. Seeding their own aberrations.

Children.

Diane and Andrew.

The boys in the woods.

Seven. Seven. Seven. Seven.

The number kept repeating, swirling around in her dreamlike twilight of thought and intuition.

Why seven?

Then came the image of the academic paper. She'd read it in a journal.

She sees it in her hand. In the other, a steaming chamomile tea in her favorite mug as she devours the article's content. The paper's author is Dr. R. Bartholomew and is titled, 'The New Apocrypha and the End of Days.'

She'd gone in person to the lecture at Xavier, only a few months later.

How could I have forgotten?

"The Beast in the Revelation of John is the same fallen angel of Enoch's prophecy," Bartholomew claimed from the podium without compunction.

He then read from the Book of Enoch. *The same line I just recited to the brothers.* "The whole earth has been corrupted through the works that were taught by Azazel; to him ascribe all sin."

Coincidence?

DeLaCroix Laveau knew there was no such thing.

And then . . . something about biblical numerology?

She allowed the waters of her mind to flow where they would, and they landed effortlessly upon the portion of Bartholomew's lecture where he'd illustrated the significance of numbers in the Bible. He'd made a point to accentuate them even more than was presented in his published paper: "In chapter five of the Book of Revelation, verses one through six," Bartholomew stated, "God holds a book in his right hand; the book which is the manifestation of the start of the

seven

year tribulation that will be the end of days. It is a scroll with

seven

sacred seals that can only be opened by the Lamb who, 'had been slain, having

seven

horns and

seven

eyes, which are the

seven

spirits of God sent forth to all the earth.' When the final of these seals is broken,

seven

trumpeting angels shall herald destruction upon the earth. Upon the sounding of the final trumpet, Satan shall make war with the saints but be cast from Heaven, whence he shall summon the Beast at his right hand to deceive all the earth to worship him. We are warned in chapters twelve and thirteen of Revelation: 'For I saw a beast rise up . . . having

seven

heads and upon each, the name of blasphemy. And his feet were as the feet of a bear. And the devil gave him his power, and his seat, and great authority.' That Beast," Bartholomew loudly declared as he dramatically dropped the Bible onto the lectern with a bang, "is Azazel."

His amplified voice still reverberating through the lecture hall above the diminishing echo of the tome's heavy thud, Bartholomew stepped away from the mic as the weight of his observation set in. The theologian had waited precisely seven seconds before resuming the lecture. Della remembered that part specifically.

I counted them . . . she reminded herself, seeing again the face of her wristwatch as the second hand had ticked them by, each one passing as if occupying an eternity.

Della blinked hard and the highway swam back into her conscious space. She hadn't realized how long she'd been navigating the car in the semi-trancelike state, but their exit was just ahead. She took the off-ramp, the car's blinker the only sound as the brothers sat in edgy silence. They, too, were in their own mental space.

Preparing for the worst but hoping—praying—for the best.

Turning back onto Route 60, Della's voice slightly cracked as her question broke the delicate silence. "How many friends—?"

"Stu was the seventh to die," Bryan responded without hesitation, nor the necessity to count. He had done that far too many times in the days and sleepless nights following that final night in the Little Woods, the number indelibly etched in his mind. "Seven. Seven friends. Seven deaths."

For the seven blasphemies, Della thought only to herself but the assessment struck Bryan's ears as clearly as if broadcast over a loudspeaker. *Bartholomew was right.*

VI

Della skidded into the driveway, ignoring the yellow caution tape which the VW stretched until it snapped and fluttered in the waning light of dusk. Before the car had come to a stop she was already reaching across

Bryan and unclasping the glove compartment.

"Here—" She pulled out the semi-automatic pistol buried beneath a raggedy owner's manual, a proof of insurance and an out of date registration card. She handed the gun to Bryan. "Just in case."

Bryan took it with little regard and tucked it into the band of his jeans as he ran from the car and disappeared beneath the crumpled, half-open garage door.

"And for you," Della confirmed as she handed Ian the Bible she'd liberated from St. John's Hospital chapel. "You need this, sugar. More than you need a handgun."

Ian said nothing, declining the Bible by forcibly pressing it away as he hurried after his brother.

Della gnawed at the inside of her lip. Thick, oscillating pulses throbbing in her chest and stomach, her pace was slow and tentative as she entered the dark garage. By the time she reached the open door leading into the downstairs TV room, the sensation had escalated to a palpitating baritone thrum. Della bent over and clutched her sides, gulping at the thick, noxious air as she stared at the concrete floor. At her feet, a sizable patch had been rubbed free of dirt and grime.

It was roughly the same proportions as an adult woman.

An array of long lines trailed toward it through the dust where the woman had clawed in vain, over and again, to pull herself to her feet and escape the choking fumes.

Won't you let your little babies come out to play, Rebecca?

The residual audio blitzed Della's senses. Hauntingly intense, it was an ice pick through her mind. "Dwe ale!" she demanded as she burst from the garage into the TV room, her lungs pulling for clean air.

In the basement, Ian was screaming the kids' names as the sound of boxes being thrown to the floor and storage crates pressed aside resonated through the house. Bounding up the second half-flight of stairs, Bryan's footsteps pounded down the hallway above her.

They stopped when he reached Andrew's room at the end.

Visible through the crack of the door partially ajar, the boy was sitting

Indian-style atop his bed, casually chatting away and giggling.

Thank God, oh thank you God! Bryan gushed internally as instant relief cascaded through him. "Th-they're—" The words were choked by surging adrenaline and he had to stop and bend over, reaching for his knees to allow the blood to saturate his brain. "They're here!" he shouted after a momentary breath, his voice still trembling. "IAN! They're u-up here!"

Climbing the basement stairs three at a time, Ian rounded the corner in front of Della and vaulted the next two half-flights the same.

Della followed quickly behind until all three were at Andrew's door.

"Thank God," Bryan exclaimed as he fervently pressed the bedroom door open the rest of the way. "You two had me majorly worri—"

Andrew flinched as the door flung wide and banged against the wall, the knob deepening the familiar indent in the plaster.

He was alone in the room.

"Hi Daddy—" he said reflexively, eyes wide and skittish.

Bryan rushed into the room. "Where's your sister! Where's Diane!" he shouted as he shoved the sliding closet door hard to one side and it rebounded against the stopper at the other end of its track. Besides the boy's clothes and an array of toys littering the floor, it was empty. "Who were you talking to? Andrew, tell me!"

Sheepish, Andrew turned and pointed but no one was there. He shrugged his shoulders. "He was right there, Daddy. He didn't tell me his name."

Bryan grabbed his son and shook him. "Andrew?! Where's your sister? Where's Diane!"

Andrew's uncertain expression soured, instantly morphing to fear.

"Bryan!" Ian wrapped his hand firmly around his brother's wrist and calmly loosened his grip on the boy's shoulders. "Easy, brother. Easy."

Bryan pulled sharply away when the six-year-old's whimpers rose to a frightened cry. "God, Andrew. I'm so sorry. Buddy . . . ."

He leaned in to hug his son.

Andrew shied away.

Leaning onto the bed and propping herself on her elbows, Della smiled warmly as Andrew twisted a fist over his wet eye.

"Hey there, sugarfoot. I thought you were gonna drive us back home? The Thing was all ready and waitin' for ya."

Della pulled the VW keys from her pocket and jangled them.

Andrew's weeping fell to a light snivel as he tried to hold back a smile but couldn't. He swiped the cuff of his shirt across his face to clean his gummy nose.

"H-h-hi, Della."

"Hi baby boy." She gently took his fingers and caressed them. "Is it okay if I ask ya something, hunnybun?"

Andrew timidly nodded, glancing from her, to the car keys in her other hand, then back at her again.

Della delicately opened his palm and placed the ring of keys in it. "Would you be willing to keep these safe and sound for me? I'm terrible at losing them. I think they're better off with you for a bit."

She winked and Andrew beamed.

"Besides, you'll need them if you're gonna drive back from picking up Diane." She stood and started for the door. Pausing dramatically, she turned and placed a finger to her lips. "Hmmm. Where was that again?"

Andrew half-shrugged. "I dunno. Well sort of. Something about going to see a billy goat." He studied the keys in his hand as he spoke, running his finger absently over the engraved emblem.

Though the blood in her veins had frozen, Della showed no sign of it. "Oh. Diane said that?"

"Yeah." Andrew nodded confidently, then changed his answer to a left-to-right shake of his head. "Huh-uh. Diane wasn't the one who told me."

Anxiety swelling in his chest, Bryan tensed. He said nothing, quelling the coiling swell of panic so Della could work her magic.

"Ah . . ." Della said with a mock sigh, snapping her fingers. "That's right. That billy goat. I was supposed to go see it with her, but I guess I plumb forgot." She feigned walking out the door but turned one final time. "Say, hun, who ended up taking Diane, then. To go see it?"

Lifting his eyes to his father but replying to Della, Andrew mundanely answered: "Daddy did."

He tilted his head.

"Doncha remember, Daddy? You know, when you came up here before?" Andrew resumed his inspection of the keys, pretending to turn them in an invisible ignition. Though he twisted in entirely the wrong direction, it made no matter to him. In his mind, the car's engine rumbled to life and he was revving it with excited fervor.

Across the hall, the cordless phone in the master bedroom rang.

The three adults stiffened.

"You sure it was Daddy, buddy?" Ian prompted, and his nephew nodded several times while making engine sounds and theatrically turning the steering wheel this way and that.

The phone trilled a second time.

Two more and it would go to the answering machine. Though his wife had asked him a thousand times to figure out how to accept the call even after the machine picked up, Bryan never had.

It rang a third time, and Bryan started sprinting across the hall.

Darting across the master bedroom and throwing himself across the bed, he plucked the handset from its base as the start of the fourth ring began to chirrup. It fumbled in his hands . . . he nearly dropped it . . . then shouted, "HELLO!" as he pressed it frantically to his face.

A voice—monotone, raspy and and garbled—crackled faintly through a curtain of white static.

"Hello!" Bryan fearfully repeated.

Then came the giggle. A child's titter.

Followed by that voice.

"Come out and play," pleaded Matt Chauncey, his tone a blend of melancholy and enthusiasm. "All I ever wanted was for you to come play. You're not afraid of the dark, are you?"

The line crackled like pine needles on a camp fire.

A moment later it cut to the monotone hum of a dial tone.

"GO!" Della shouted as the car slid to a stop in the mud as far beyond the twin ponds as it could muster. Bryan flung open the creaking passenger door and worked his way to the front of the VW Thing, grateful for the vehicle's rudimentary, chiseled edges as he waded unsteadily through the ankle-high sludge. In the distance the wall of trees rippled as if aflame, the yellow hue of the car's headlights playing across the swaying boughs as if igniting them. He reached reflexively over his shoulders as the past eighteen years evaporated, the dozen small burn scars across his back tingling in prickling fresh pain.

Choking back the acid fear rising into his throat, in his mind he was fifteen again; and again about to confront something dark and awful laying in wait behind those trees.

Waiting for them to come back.

And this time, his twelve-year-old daughter was in there with it.

"Do whatever it takes. Just release that sweet girl from the heinous spiritual grip of that thing," said Della as Andrew clambered over the seat back and planted himself in her lap, yanking the steering wheel with both hands. The front tires swiveled back and forth in the mud, gouging deeper in the ruts. "You'll know what to do, when the time comes. I'll be here, keeping this one safe . . . . And I'll be praying. "

But you can't kill the dead. The lingering thread of his own childhood logic surfaced in Ian's mind, cinching together both ends of an eighteen-year gap which had come to reveal that—though they had thought otherwise—his elementary reasoning had, in fact, been undeniably germane at the time.

He was sure, more than ever, it still was.

"How! How will we know?" Outside the car but leaning in, Ian's face was ashen; hands nervously drumming the edge of the door. "How can we possibly stop something intangible? Jesus! Della, we've been here before. Nothing's changed!"

The vibration projecting from him was staccato and terse, reeking of base, cynical despair. Absorbing it, Della closed her eyes and visualized it within her. Using its intensity against itself, she modified the energy, strengthened it, and broadcast it back in long, smoothly refined waves.

"Everything's changed, sugar . . . . You'll know." She then added in pre-meditated assurance, "You'll *all* know."

Standing in front of the car, the VW's headlights cast Bryan's shadow huge against the wall of trees in the distance. Looming over the gateway to the Little Woods like a menacing sentinel, the vast specter of his silhou-ette billowed and bulged as Bryan slogged through the thick clay and mud where, long ago, a slender trail had once led to the woods but now offered only thick, grassy swamp. He closed his eyes and unconsciously patted his waistband one last time—a reassurance that Della's semi-automatic was still tucked there—then, relying only on muscle memory, faced the perimeter of trees and ran.

Scrambling clumsy but hard through the clinging mud and waist-high weeds, his shadow sentinel guarding the Little Woods simultaneously shrunk until, becoming the same size as the man, the two disappeared in the undulating curtain of scrub trees and patchwork pine.

The scraping nails of anxiety clawing at his insides, Ian balked.

Then took chase after him.

VIII

"*Bryan!*" he quietly called as the glow from Della's headlights waned and was lost as he traveled into the expanse of trees. Blindly following only his memory for a hundred yards or more, Ian fought through thickets and broken branches, stinging vines and fine, whipping branches that tore at his forearms as he marched through the thick undergrowth which had flourished over the years since he had been here last.

The trees becoming taller and more dense as he pressed deeper toward the Little Woods, Ian's eyes struggled to adjust to the engrossing darkness as nearly two decades of thickening canopy now all but choked out the moonlight.

Where's the clearing? I should have reached it by now. Where's the Father Oak?

While something deep inside him knew exactly where they should be, another part felt utterly lost and confused; nothing looked as it should anymore. In his memories it had all been so huge and grand.

And intimidating.

Now, it was none of those things. Only trees and brush in the dark.

"BRYAN," he whisper-shouted again and the name echoed hollowly through the forest. Silence was the only reply. All was inert and dark.

Then, a rustling in the tree line ahead as shafts of spiking moonlight broke through the canopy.

Ian quickened his pace, an odd mix of sentiment and trepidation rippling through him as he hurried toward the light.

He did not see what he tripped over.

Tumbling to the ground, he rolled awkwardly onto his back and found himself staring upside-down at what had once been the colossal tree they'd called the Father Oak. Once impressively lording over this clearing and the lesser trees encircling it, the Father Oak had been a formidable icon in its day. Now it was all but a leafless and charred tower of broken, rotting wood, half the height it once was.

Ian pulled himself up to a sitting position and rubbed his swollen knee beneath the jagged new rip in his jeans, frustrated that he hadn't remembered the perimeter of stones that had been so meticulously lain between the clearing's outer ring of trees, linking them together in a crisply dotted circumference. One of those stones must be the tripping culprit, though it was too dark to see them.

Which meant it was also too dark to see the one which had been lifted high above him and brought down upon his head in a blinding flash of pain that issued a blaze of white light through his temple.

Ian's eyes opened to a flickering amber incandescence; the crackling of fire at first hollowly muted then crisply snapping in his ears.

The backlit shape of his brother loomed in front of the flames.

"I didn't want to have to do that, Ian."

Bryan dropped the stone and it rolled halfway between them, coming to a rest so that one wet, crimson surface glinted in the moonlight.

Ian winced and ran his fingers over his scalp. They dragged through his hair matted with thickly clotting blood. "Bry . . . ?"

He held his blood-covered hand before him, incredulous.

At Bryan's feet, Diane was huddled in a ball. Her school uniform was tattered and a myriad of fine striations ran down her arms and legs where she had been dragged through the thickets and thorns. Her eyes were closed but Ian could tell she was still alive—every few moments her chest would rise and fall in a faint but tremulous breath.

"It was you, Diane . . . . Or me," was Bryan's response. "Looks like we've got our answer which one now, don't we." He stepped over his daughter's prone body and towered imposingly over Ian. "You never were worth a shit. You, and those stupid little faggot friends of yours. Couldn't play War to save your life, always prancing around with that pathetic Chauncey kid. And Dalton, that little fucking pervert. They deserved what they got. All of them." He hesitated but then added, "You deserve it, too."

As the throbbing in Ian's temple coursed through his entire body, his brother's image swam confusingly in and out of focus. The pain had begun to lodge in his stomach, and he wanted to vomit but could only emit a series of wet, choking heaves.

"This all remind you of something?" Bryan asked as he bent down low and broke the tip off a small sapling, mimicking Stu Klatz, adopting the same maniacal cadence and tone. "Well, well, *well*. What have we got here then?" He clutched his brother's chin and yanked his head upward, curiously examining the new gash in Ian's temple where the original scar had been etched eighteen years earlier. As he did, a drop of spit lingered on his lip, wavered, then dripped onto Ian's cheek. "Just look at that lovely gash in your face, boy. I do believe you must be hurtin' some!"

Bryan slowly circled the tip of the stick in a figure eight in front of Ian's face. With no more thought than spearing a beetle, he then lanced it with casual delight into the raw, fleshy new gash in his brother's temple.

The skin there bulged as the jagged tip plunged beneath the torn flaps and Ian shrieked, scrambling backwards on all fours.

Cackling, Bryan stood, rising to a monstrous size. He raised his arms wide and howled in a hideous layer of raspy sound: "STAND NOW, GOAT, AND BE COUNTED AMONGST THE SEVEN!"

The gunshot rang out from behind, percussive in Ian's ears.

Its flash momentarily lit the woods in a hazy penumbra as Bryan's form shattered into countless black fragments, like tempered safety glass imploding into a million pebble-like pieces.

Time ceased as they retained his shape for only a moment.

Then they dropped to the ground all at once.

Striking the earth, the fragments rippled away like black lava in a smooth, concentric wave. As they did, the pieces simultaneously morphed into a mass of black, stinging beetles. Only once the last of them had made contact with the earth did the entire horde scurry back together in a uniform, choreographed dance.

Climbing one upon another, thousands upon thousands, they refabricated and re-solidified as they rose and became a single new figure.

The figure of Stu Klatz.

Disbelief and unbridled panic overtaking him, Ian clattered madly backward, away through the mud and undergrowth.

But something stopped his progress.

It wasn't sapling oaks or dense brush.

It was a pair of legs.

Looming over him, his brother held Della's semi-automatic in his trembling hand, a wisp of smoke still wafting from the pistol's barrel. "*You* were the seventh, Klatz! *You* were!" Bryan screamed. "It's over! You got what you wanted! Now let my daughter go!"

Stu merely sneered and pressed his black-rimmed glasses up his nose.

Prone on the ground, Diane stirred. In a moment she began wheezing, her fingers clawing unconsciously at the dirt.

Stu reached down and lovingly stroked her hair.

"It really wanted you, Bryan. The Witness, to become his greatest disciple." He leaned close to Diane and whispered something in her ear. "But now it wants the girl. Her power is so much greater than your own."

He licked his lips, the tongue long and reptilian, its fork darting out to taste the acrid air.

"Why now, you repugnant fuck!" Bryan took one tentative step forward. "After all this time? Why now!"

"What is time to the timeless?" Stu replied in magisterial authority, the voice a low rumble like distant thunder. "All will be as it has been prophesied. The Priestess, she knows."

Stu lowered his head as if in introspection.

Where is she . . . ?

The unspoken question vibrated in both Bryan and Ian's minds in the form of a low, sickening pulse.

"Ah, yes. There she is." Stu raised his head and the face that looked upon them was no longer Stu's, but Dan Mercer's. "She is with the bastard waif. How naïve of you to leave her alone with the young boy," Big Dan stated in a cadence and tone uncharacteristically articulate and pensive.

His eyes bore into Bryan's. They were mesmerizing. Entreating.

They became kind eyes: Woody's eyes.

"Do you not think the Priestess was brought to you for a reason?" Woody asked and appeared genuinely concerned. "She will make *the boy* the next sacrifice, Bryan! The Priestess . . . *she* is the dark Deceiver."

X

Andrew was contentedly making engine sounds when Della opened the glove box and pulled something out.

XI

"You piece of shit!" Bryan raised the gun and aimed it directly at Woody's forehead. Whereupon his friend flawlessly transmuted into Jimi Raker. "You are not Woody, or Dan or Jimi. You are Satan. YOU are the Deceiver!"

"That's not cool, man!" Jimi Raker winced, turning his head to the side while defensively his face with his hands. When he lowered them, Craig Dalton was staring incredulously back at Bryan. "And I'm flattered, and all. But Satan? Wow, dude." Leaning to one side and peering around Bryan, Craig nodded at Ian. "Hey dude, how's it hanging?"

The words sliced through Ian like dull, rusted razors. While the thing looked like Craig, and spoke like Craig, its vibration was perverse and out of register—a degenerate facsimile that made Ian feel sick to his stomach, like watching a 3-D movie without those red and green cellophane glasses to merge the lines all together just right.

"I mean, I wish I were the Fallen One and all, but I'm not even close. Not even this . . . what did the Priestess call me . . . Azazel?" Craig snick-ered, snorting as he slapped his thigh. "She really has you all wrapped up, doesn't she. Just like a woman. Only good for one thing, and it ain't for using their empty heads. Though she is pretty friggin' hot, am I right?" Craig feigned the act of gripping someone and grinding up against them. "Oooh, yeah. That cappuccino skin. Bet you'd like to try that, wouldn't ya, Bry? Beats the shit outta that milky white churl of a wife of yours." He scratched his head. "Funny though, how she so easily manages the role of hot little slut, you know, when it comes to thinking about your brother. Say, Ian, how is Rebecca doing anyhow . . . after that shower. Anything interesting going on there?"

Ian jumped to his feet, yanked the pistol from Bryan's grip and pressed it hard against Craig Dalton's temple.

Cringing, Dalton fell to his knees, whimpering.

"NO! Please! I'm sorry. No, no, no—" Then he started laughing. "Ahhh! Help me!" he cried out in mock agitation, rolling his eyes and waving his hands in the air. "Ha! I actually had you going there, Cockerton. Whoo! This is all too good! I just—I just couldn't keep it up."

He leapt to his feet, casually knocking the gun from Ian's hands.

It skated across the ground and disappeared somewhere in the thick brush as he snatched Diane by the hair and wrenched the girl violently into the air. A small clump tore from her scalp but Diane made no sound. Little more than a limp marionette, she dangled unconsciously from Craig's grip as his fingers lengthened and twisted, thick, ragged claws extending from each of their torn and bleeding tips.

The talons entangled in the strands of Diane's hair.

You were right all along, Ian! You can't kill the dead!

Craig's mental projection reverberated across the clearing and echoed from tree to tree, billowing into the night sky as he grew to inhuman proportions. His features wrinkling as if behind a veil of rippling water, in an instant only his face remained as the rest of his body dissolved and was at once a dark, scaled creature. Protruding from his lower back, a long tail swished back and forth, covered in a film of mucous as though a snake freshly hatching from its egg. Beneath his feet, two pointed hooves scraped at the dirt. Atop Craig's torso, six other heads emerged and lolled loosely alongside his own. Each wavering in and out, the sallow faces of each of their friends—Jimi, Big Dan, Woody, Stu and Matt—all bobbed alongside Craig's in a sickening dance.

On the seventh, only a faceless, incomprehensible void.

Suspended by her hair in the clutch of the demon, Diane's eyes flared wide and white as she animated with a sharp intake of breath.

It was incisively curtailed mid-draw.

Small, dainty fingers scrabbled at her neck which began to constrict as if by an invisible noose. Her lungs pleading for air, stampeding panic had frozen her diaphragm so that all that was achieved was a shrill, wheezing screech from her narrowing throat—

the discordant whistling of Matt's flute

—as her face contorted in panic and terror. Steadily deflating, her lungs began to burn like glowing pokers within her chest.

And on the Beast's seventh head, her face began to materialize.

Daddy! her mind screamed, but it was impossible for the cry to loose.

XII

Della pulled the Bible from the glove box and opened it. Without having to look, her finger slid to page one thousand, seven hundred and sixty-three. The Gospel of John: chapter three, verse sixteen.

"It is time, little man. I'm so very, very sorry," she said quietly as Andrew gazed curiously but admiringly up at her. She began reading the verse aloud: "For God so loved the world, that he gave his only begotten Son . . . ."

XIII

You'll know what to do. You all *will.*

Della's assurance materialized in Bryan's mind with the image of the martyred Christ in the chapel, hanging forlorn from the cross. These over-lapped in mingling layers with his brother's repeated insistence that you can't kill the dead; and the deep vibrations of despair which had projected when Ian had confessed, believing it had only been to himself, that it was unfathomable to freely surrender one's life in order to protect another. Let alone some unseen deity called 'Father.'

But Bryan could fathom it.

Because Della had been right—about everything—and in this moment he did know, absolutely, what had to happen.

THE GUN!

The urgency of his projection to Ian was unmistakable as, dangling in the grip of the writhing Beast, Diane's clawing fingers weakened and slowed, their frenzied scratching at the nonexistent noose around her neck revealing a series of wide but shallow lines in her skin which had begun seeping red.

The mad thrashing of her legs was now small, jolting spasms.

IAN I NEED THE GUN!

Dropping to his knees, Ian tore at the brush and thickets. "I don't see it! God help me, Bryan, I can't find it!"

Savoring two millennia of prophesy about to unfold, the demon roared in dark ecstasy, its ribboned tongue darting and licking the sulfurous air as Diane's life began to ebb away.

The color draining from her face, she twitched and reached for her father, her eyes pleading. With one last effort, she weakly extended her arm with her fingers spread wide . . .

. . . and the gun skated out from the brush.

As if drawn toward her open palm like a magnet, it spun from the clasp of tendrils and thorns and came to a rest at her uncle's feet.

In that moment her eyes slowly closed; her chin dropped to her chest, a long hiss escaping from her parted lips as her arm fell limply to her side.

Bryan lunged for the pistol.

As did Ian. He got to it first.

IAN, GIVE ME THE GUN!

So intense was Bryan's vibration that far away, in the car near the twin ponds, Della closed her eyes and pulled Andrew tightly to her bosom. Wrapping him up in the safety of her embrace, she cupped her hands over the six-year-old's ears and began to loudly but sweetly sing.

NO! Ian's response was fierce. *I know what you're trying t—*

Ian, you were right! You can't kill the dead. But you can stop the cycle. Bryan seized the semi-automatic in his brother's hand. *Guess I was the cartoon ranger all along, brother.* "LORD, FORGIVE ME MY SINS," he cried aloud. "AND DELIVER MY CHILD FROM EVIL!"

The high caliber shot took off the back of Bryan's head.

Time slowed, becoming a thick, cold syrup as Diane's father fell backward toward the earth—feet together, arms outstretched.

When his body thudded lifeless to the dirt, the sound was louder than the gunshot itself. The report blew through the clearing, bending the thick undergrowth and felling the sapling trees in a visible wave. A peel of thunder exploded like a cannon as a simultaneous arc of light tore the black fabric of the sky in two.

While Bryan Cockerton lay in the dirt, a halo of blood soaking into the ground around his head.

Recoiling, the demon shrieked, its seven heads yowling in a jarring cacophony. Releasing the girl, the beast rose high above the canopy of trees and disappeared, merging into the darkness that already lived there.

As Diane crumpled to the ground.

XIV

A thousand miles away, just beyond a rudimentary cabin nestled at the base of a dark Georgia mountain, a man abruptly stopped what he was doing. Like a sonic boom, a wave of dark energy resounded within him, filling every fiber of his being with a deep, bass vibration of intensely satisfying power. Jubilant, he fell to his knees in the moss and dirt.

"It is time!" he exclaimed as he raised his head to the night sky, certain that the darkness there had swallowed the stars.

And in his mind he was once again in the Little Woods.

XV

DeLaCroix Laveau made the sign of the cross over her chest and the head of the crying boy in her lap. *It is done. Nobiscum Deus.* "God be with us, my innocent one," she said to Andrew as she reached for the cell phone on the back seat and thumbed 9-1-1.

In the clearing, Ian lifted his niece into his arms and ran, taking them both as fast as he could from the darkness that was the Little Woods.

twenty-two
1977

A S THE NEIGHBORHOOD flashed in blue and red amid a storm of night sirens and rescue vehicles' blaring horns, the young brothers stumbled weak and confused from the crackling inferno of the Little Woods. Screaming when she saw them, Mrs. Cockerton raced ahead of her husband, scrambling headlong down the tractor trail in disregard of the thick mud that pulled at her ankles and enveloping smoke that pulled at her lungs. There she wrapped her sons in her deep, protective embrace as seemingly endless police cars and fire trucks roared past the three huddled together as one.

In the Sunday paper that morning (the presses literally grinding to a stop so the publisher could run a special edition) the broadsheet newspaper announced the devastation. The front page was emblazoned with an apocalyptic monochrome photo of the charred and smoking remains of the Little Woods. The headline above it, in huge block lettering across the entire page, read:

SIX MORE CHILDREN DEAD OR MISSING

And then on page three, the follow-up:

Woods of Death Claim Children in Cursed Neighborhood

An already grieving community is reeling this morning as six more children have been found dead, or missing feared dead, less than two weeks after the tragic death of Matthew Chauncey in the woods adjacent to the idyllic rural neighborhood. Craig Dalton (12) was found by his mother in their home late Friday night. Police are labeling the child's death as homicide as his father, Charles Dalton, was also found deceased. The father's death is currently listed as unknown cause. The gruesome discovery of three other children was made by police as they followed up on a report filed by Mrs. Patricia Raker, whose two sons went missing early Friday morning. The three bodies were located in remote woodland on the outskirts of the rural neighborhood in which the children lived. One of Patricia Raker's sons, Jimi (11), has been identified as among the three. A fifth body was discovered in the early hours this morning by Fire & Rescue when responding to a devastating overnight fire which officials have described as "an inferno" which has all but destroyed the same enclave of woods where young Chauncey was fatally injured in a much smaller fire just twelve days ago. The name of the child is yet to be released as significant trauma to the body is making identification difficult at this time. The Chief of Police has been willing to reveal, however, that he believes the injuries to be suspicious in nature and not resultant of the flames. He is unwilling to provide any further details at this time. The sixth child, Patricia Raker's eldest son, Jack Raker (15), remains missing and is now feared dead. The police have issued a BOLO for the boy's father.

The article made no mention of Bryan or Ian Cockerton. Neither did it report anything about Matt's father, Mr. Chauncey, to whom (though they would see him from time to time, puttering in his vegetable garden) the boys would never again speak.

II

Hare Cockerton placed the house on the market three days later. But with the media circus reveling for months in the public's unquenchable thirst for ever-more sensational headlines—each local outlet competing fiercely to capture the greatest number of readers or listeners or viewers with the latest, juiciest nuggets of pseudo-fact—the house sat for nearly a year without a single serious inquiry. Local TV segments featuring Woody's parents on the six o'clock news didn't help, only adding to the frenzy as they brayed for Mr. Raker to receive the death penalty for the murder of their son, Woody, even though Raker was yet to be convicted and any direct link to the boy's death was proving to be legally tenuous at best.

Seems their political leanings are significantly less to the Left, Hare Cockerton thought as he watched the interview repeated on every newscast for three days straight, *now that the repercussions of those tenets have a direct and very personal impact on their own lives.*

Hare didn't think that was very groovy of them.

So in short, while the 'Cursed Neighborhood' remained the delicious topic of everyone's coffee conversation, no one actually wanted to live in the place nestled so idyllically at the edge of the 'Woods of Death.'

Of course that didn't stop plenty of them from driving slowly through, brazenly pointing at the various split-level ranch homes in elated awe as they giddily speculated which must be the Chaunceys' or the Rakers' or the Daltons'. Weekends were particularly bad, and on more than one occasion Hare Cockerton had found himself chasing off a car which had pulled right up onto their lawn to confront Bryan and Ian for the explicit and personal details they were sure the two young boys must surely have.

The worst was four months later.

Normally an eagerly anticipated highlight of the community calendar, trick-or-treating invariably meant a neighborhood full of giggling ghouls and munchkin monsters begging for sugary candy as the sun went down.

But this year, the porch lights were all off.

Behind curtained windows, the neighborhood families mostly huddled in quiet mourning, embellished with a modicum of nervous shame, as countless teenagers from the surrounding communities drove incessantly up and down the street. Revving their engines while screaming and laughing, the adolescents threw penny candy out the windows of their beat-up cars to 'honor' the Cursed Kids, a new tradition they'd concocted . . . and which still takes place today.

That was also the last time anyone heard from Kathy Dalton.

She hadn't died, nor was her disappearance all that dramatic or mysterious. Mrs. Dalton simply slipped away one night in early November, leaving the house—and most of the belongings in it—to rot. Six months later, when the last snow of the winter finally melted, the bank auctioned off the entire property in a single Saturday sale. A childless, affluent couple from Vermont moved in three weeks later. Veronica Cockerton had run into the buyers at the grocery store once, and commented to Hare what a lovely young couple they were. Chayton was a big football fan and suggested Veronica extend Hare an invitation to come by and watch a game with him on any given Sunday. His wife, Ashlie, was more enthusiastic about the craft closet she was converting from the upstairs room which they may, or may not, have known had been the bedroom of Craig Dalton . . . and thereby the room where the twelve-year-old boy had been suffocated by his father, just moments before Charley Dalton himself had become a lifeless shell atop his dead son.

They did briefly mention, Veronica had added when relating the produce-aisle meeting to Hare later that day, something about hearing that the previous owner—Kathy Something-or-Other, they called her— was apparently living down south on the Gulf Coast somewhere. And did she know her very well?

To which Veronica politely had offered very little by way of an answer. And that was the last time Kathy Dalton's name ever came up again.

⚡⚡⚡

Though followed by the stigma of what had happened, Bryan and Ian eventually made new friends at school. At first they had been the focus of intensely morbid curiosity. Then, the objects of thinly-veiled sympathy. After a while this too slowly faded, and one day they simply woke to find that life had settled, as it also had for their parents and the majority of the families in the neighborhood, into beautiful, mundane normalcy.

By the the time Bryan stepped across the stage to accept his high school diploma (while his brother and parents beamed with pride from an audience of three hundred other hot and restless families) it was as though nothing had ever happened in the Little Woods at all. Indeed, the name itself—which had first elicited such feelings of joy and promise . . . and then invoked such vile and damnable horror—simply vanished from memory entirely. Like the remnant wisps of a bad dream on a rainy day.

And the Beast of the Woods never existed.

Twenty-Three

REBECCA'S INTENSE CONVULSIONS grew increasingly violent as the Pittsburgh medical team could do nothing but observe. With twelve minutes yet remaining for the hyperbaric chamber to safely depressurize, they stood by as the woman's limbs twisted and thrashed while her entire body stiffened.

When her back arched deeply one last time and then sharply recoiled, Rebecca's head was slammed against the chamber's canopy. Pressed against the viewing window, her facial features were savagely flattened.

A moment later her heart stopped.

One of the nurses turned away; the other's eyes became wet.

Outwardly, the specialist overseeing the treatment showed no emotion at all. On the inside, the doctor was drowning in helpless turmoil as she studied the second hand of her watch and silently began counting.

The last thing Rebecca heard was the static B-flat tone of the EKG as the spiking dot on the monitor fell and then moved across the screen in a flat, bright green horizontal line. The accompanying note trailed away as her body loosened and she moved toward an endless void.

The darkness is warm and welcoming.

It envelops her like a blanket on a cold, damp night, and Rebecca does not fight it. Voices seem to beckon her—soothing melodies of those she had held most close and dear. Her mother's voice rings above them all, though she cannot discern what the woman is saying. Others come more clearly: an uncle long since passed; her grandmother on her father's side who had always taken her and her cousins camping at the lake in the summer months between school years.

Then Veronica Cockerton.

Her mother-in-law's voice is clearest of them all, and it washes over her like sweet wine. "Come, dear," Veronica appeals. "Come to where the light is warm and filled with comfort and love. Come and be where you belong."

And Rebecca feels her grip on the world loosen as she moves toward the twinkling glow, far in the distance. The journey takes a million years, or maybe only a second, until the sparkling warmth is brilliant and big and filled with vibrant energy. Her husband is in that glow, and he opens his arms wide.

"It's okay, babe. It's your time . . . ."

Filled with safe shelter and all her heart had ever desired, Rebecca prepares to accept his embrace. Their bodies slowly entwine in a tender caress, and it feels more beautiful than anything she'd ever experienced in her lifetime. She nuzzles into Bryan's chest and the beat of his heart matches hers. Together, the light they create expands and flows in a powerful wave that fills her soul wi—

The pain in her abdomen struck like a spike.

It tugs her mercilessly backward as Bryan's arms give way and she is torn from his embrace.

It came again, a lightning bolt through her gut.

She is pulled further away; Bryan now a football field distant.

Then a third time, this the most excruciating, and Rebecca screamed as the searing torment clawed at her from the inside out.

Bryan—and the twinkling light—are no more than a speck in the abyss.

The solid B-flat tone returned to her ears and immediately separated into a series of crisp, distinct blips.

Rebecca gulped for breath; the doctor released hers and marked precisely forty-two seconds having passed on her wristwatch as the EKG rose to a peak, fell immediately to a trough roughly a third its size, then peaked again after two small inflections. Settling into smooth, even cycles it repeated this way as the pressure in the chamber continued to diminish for another eleven minutes which passed without incident as Rebecca fell into a deep, comforting sleep.

The wall of the forest flashed deeply purple as the red and blue emergency lights projected from the Twin Ponds as a single, synchronized pulse in the night. In the back of one of the newer box-style ambulances, two paramedics administered oxygen to Diane Cockerton while hastily checking her vitals.

The young girl's eyes were open.

But glazed and unblinking, they stared beyond the activity taking place in a flurry just inches from her. She did not answer when the paramedics asked her baseline questions, such as her name and if she knew where she was. Instead, the girl only turned her head to the side and stared intently through the ambulance wall—as if it did not exist—and she were watching an entirely different set of events taking place . . . far across the field and deep inside the forest.

Asleep on the front seat of Della's VW Thing, Andrew lay unaware of the bustle of activity taking place in the field all around them. His head nestled into the woman's lap, he slept as she lovingly stroked his hair. Periodically, he would make quiet, endearing child sounds, accentuated by simultaneously bunching himself into a tight ball to draw himself as close to the woman's warmth as possible.

Speaking to a pair of officers a dozen feet away, Ian fell to his knees in the mud and standing water as Bryan's body appeared through the wall of trees. Carried on a stretcher by three men and a woman in dark pants and crisp white shirts, a heavy white sheet covered his brother's body. Where the contours of the fabric loosely delineated the shape of Bryan's face, a growing stain had begun to soak dark red, almost black.

And Ian screamed.

Pleading with his arms outstretched to the black veil of night, he cried out as the tears flowed down his face and cleared the dirt of his cheeks in a maze of light, intersecting lines.

Della stayed at the house with Andrew the rest of that night while Ian slept in a light blue vinyl-cushioned chair next to his niece's hospital bed. After spending the night under observation, Diane was released into his care the following mid-morning. The attending physician provided a report containing little more than a note about the scratches on her neck, coupled with a prescription for an antibiotic cream which was to be applied twice daily.

"She's fine. At least that's what we can physically determine," the doctor told Ian as he gently pulled him aside as Diane stared emptily down the corridor. "Now, what's going on there, on the inside, that's a whole different story. And rather beyond my expertise, I'm afraid. I can't even begin to imagine being so young and witnessing my father committing suicide. In the woods. In the middle of the night. It's almost unfathomable."

He handed Ian a card with the name and number of a specialized child psychologist printed in Comic Sans font next to a goofy cartoon flower that had a big, smiling face and the slogan, 'We Make Young Minds Bloom.' Ian nodded and slid it into his back jeans pocket, agreeing to make the call as soon as possible.

They made their way home in silence and were greeted by an excited Andrew and a considerably more subdued Della who helped Diane from the car, taking the girl into her arms and squeezing her tight.

Her arms at her sides, Diane neither hugged Della back nor made an effort to withdraw from the embrace. She merely stood there, neither allowing nor disallowing it to happen.

On the third day, Rebecca rose to her feet of her own accord for the first time since passing out in the garage. Finally given the all-clear by her specialist, she anxiously prepared to be transported back to St. John's hospital by non-emergency ambulance the following morning.

Though her motor and neurological functioning had returned largely to their pre-incident performance (a 'miraculous recovery,' the specialist had informed her) Rebecca remembered nothing of how she had come to be in the hospital in the first place.

She certainly had no recollection of her husband's dead childhood friend looming over her, a leering grin splitting the charred skin of Matt Chauncey's face as the garage filled with choking exhaust fumes.

Nor did she remember anything but indistinct, nebulous images from the forty-two seconds during which she, herself, was biologically dead.

Rebecca did understand one thing with brutal clarity, however.

She knew that her husband was gone.

Having no direct knowledge of this fact, she could not begin to explain why she felt this way. It was something intangible, deep inside, which told her it was true: a dull, pervasive aching in her soul.

Of course no one at the hospital would confirm this feeling. Neither, however, would they deny it. Even Ian had artfully side-stepped her request to put Bryan on the phone.

Which is when she truly knew.

V

At the Major League, Tony Lamont cracked open a beer and was already handing it to Felipe before the photographer had pulled out a barstool. "When's your buddy come back?" Tony asked as he mopped out a dirty glass with a cloth that wasn't much cleaner.

Felipe took a swig before answering. "Yeah, I know. Like, I'm back at work a week already, Tone. And it's fucking boring there at the best of times . . . . So I hope he gets his ass back here, like soon."

Lamont nodded and turned up the TV. The Orioles were kicking some serious butt. It mattered little to him, since the Yankees weren't the other team. Which also meant it was no big deal when Menendez asked him to flick the station. So, just this once, the proprietor conceded to a customer's request. "We'll be educated adults and have the news on then, I think, my friend."

Menendez sighed but didn't argue, surprised that Tony had acceded to his request at all. He always had enough of news at work, and would prefer anything else. Literally anything. Reruns of the *Brady Bunch* would be awesome, for example.

Tony flicked the station and the TV crackled and flickered before settling upon a grainy picture of a primly tailored anchor reading a story about some alleged New York political wrongdoings.

Boring . . . . Felipe thought.

Followed by something about a city waste disposal strike.

Yup. What's new?

Then, "—And now this from the national wire. Mr. Bryan Cockerton, survived by his wife and two children, was found in the woods near his home this weekend by Mr. Ian Cockerton, an executive manager with our sister newspaper, the *Manhattan Bulletin*. News of the bizarre death has rocked the small western Pennsylvania town of . . . ."

Felipe teetered on his stool as the bar began to swim.

". . . Exact details have yet to be released, but the death by suicide has left the tight-knit community reeling as they search for a connection between this latest tragedy and a series of harrowing childhood deaths in or around the same woods eighteen years earlier in the summer of 1977. And now to Jim for the weather—"

For the first time in all his years, Tony Lamont dropped a glass.

As Felipe collapsed to the floor.

VI

Ian stood in the doorway of the bedroom and looked upon his niece sleeping uneasily on the bed. Every few moments Diane would jerk or thrash in brief, sporadic fits, her face tight and tense.

"Yes," he spoke quietly into the cordless phone as he backed into the corridor. "All is good here. We can't wait to see you tomorrow, too. Sleep well, Rebecca." He hung up and retracted the articulated metal antenna back into the handset with his palm. "I don't think she believed me," he whispered to Della who had quietly sidled beside him.

"You sound surprised."

Ian shrugged. "I don't know what to think, anymore."

"You have a gift Ian. An incredible gift of projection. As I said the other day to you and Br—" She hesitated as the name formed on her lips. "—You and Bryan, it's something I had to learn and, personally, have to work very hard at. For you, on the other hand, it comes naturally. And I don't think you realize just how powerful yours is, hun. I'm sure Rebecca picked up on what you are feeling."

"Well, I never asked for what you're calling a 'gift.' And I'm not sure I even want it any more. Hell, I forgot I even had it for nearly two decades. What's a few decades more of ignorant bliss?"

"Or, sugar . . ." Della countered, "now that you've rediscovered it, you hone it. Make it into something good. Something truly Good." She placed her hand on the small of his back and rubbed in small, gentle circles.

Ian shook his head but told her he'd have to think on it. He softly closed the door to Diane's room. "It's her I'm worried about right now, more than anything."

Della was worried too. The light seemed to have gone out behind Diane's eyes. Understandable, given what the girl had just experienced. After all, how in God's name does a twelve-year-old process anything at all about what she'd just been through? It was beyond the realm of any reasonable possibility.

Except that it wasn't.

"Maybe we just take it one step at a time, hun. Focus on Rebecca coming home tomorrow. I think you know that you two gotta put on your oxygen masks first. Y'know? Neither of you will be any good to her, or Andrew, if you're unable to find a way to cope with this yourself, first.'

Ian replied only by opening his arms. He didn't have to say anything at all. Della wrapped hers around him and they held each other until the tears had drained away.

VII

Neither could sleep, and Della found Ian downstairs in the TV room.

"You, neither?" she asked and Ian shook his head and shrugged.

"Not sure when that will be possible again, Della. I can't even fathom closing my eyes right now. I know what I'll see if I do."

Having not witnessed what he had, it was something she could scarcely begin to even imagine. But it was something she understood.

All too well.

They sat in silence across from each other until Ian rose and pulled a bottle and two glasses from the buffet behind the sofa.

"Sugar, can I ask you something?" she said with cautious apprehension as Ian poured them both a whiskey and settled on the couch next to her. "It's just . . . something's been on my mind since the hospital. Something Dr. Fieldhouse said to Bryan."

"Of course. I think you know you can talk to me about anything now."

"Sure—yeah, absolutely." Still, Della smiled shyly and cleared her throat. "It might be a sensitive topic. That's all."

She didn't know why she had become fixated upon the question she was about to ask, or why it was important to ask it. But she had learned long ago that when something persistently gnawed at her gut, there was always a reason why. Even if it made no sense to her at the time. She quaintly called this ambiguous nagging a 'God Nod.'

Ian took a gulp of whiskey, briefly closing his eyes and watched in his mind as the liquid ran down his throat and seared it like iced fire. He exhaled and the tension expelled with it. "Go ahead. Shoot."

"Is there a chance Rebecca could be pregnant?"

Ian coughed, thumping his glass roughly onto the coffee table.

"Pregnant?"

"Yes."

"Why? What on earth would make you think she's pregnant?"

Della paused before answering. She watched closely how he watched her back. "Something Fieldhouse said. When he was talking to your brother about the treatment plan for Rebecca. He said something that—at the time—seemed perfectly normal, all things considered."

"But . . . ?"

"But over the past few days it's struck me in a way I can't explain. I keep finding myself going back to it. And from experience, that usually means there's something left unturned."

Ian fidgeted in his seat then straightened the bottom of his shirt, smoothing it over his lap. "Exactly what did he say?"

"He said, 'Given her *condition*, we're placing Rebecca on a chopper.' At first I thought nothing of it. As I said, it seemed perfectly in line with what was happening. I'm certain we all assumed he meant her condition due to the hypoxia."

"I agree. So why the concern?"

"The more I thought of it, Ian, the more it seemed such a uniquely simple way to refer to something as complex as her medical prognosis. Her condition. Then I started hearing that phrase in my mind. Snippets of other people using it when they say things like, 'Hey, you shouldn't be carrying such a heavy box . . . in your condition.' Or, 'Should you really be drinking wine . . . given your condition?'"

Ian said nothing at first, then: "Sure. Or maybe that's just your mind focusing on it being used in the wrong way in this instance. Or maybe Fieldhouse using that phrase is just coincidental."

But Della knew there was no such thing.

"Maybe. But then—and this is the icing on the cake—then I remembered he said that, 'In just a few minutes they'll be medevacked to Pittsburgh.' *They'll,* Ian. *They'll.* He said *they'll* be medevacked."

Ian downed the rest of his drink and stood up. He turned away and paced the edge of the room. "He said that because he was referring to

Rebecca *and the paramedics*. That's why he used the plural."

Della shook her head. "Huh uh. I don't buy it, Ian. The paramedics were flying with her, sure. But to include them in that phrasing doesn't work, hun. The paramedics weren't being medevacked. Rebecca was. The medics were the support team. I just don't see—"

"DELLA ENOUGH!" Ian turned quickly, his face hard.

Della flinched, her mouth frozen mid-sentence.

After an unsettling moment, she rose from the couch. Eyes down, she apologized as she gathered her things.

"I've overstepped my bounds. I'm sorry. This has all been a tragic, terrifying ordeal and I'm harping over semantics." She made her way to the door leading into the garage and plucked her summer coat from the rack. "Maybe I should head home for the night. You know, give you some space. I think that would be a good thing right now. For us both."

She stepped into the garage and pressed the button to the automatic overhead door. It clunked and ground upward louder than ever. "Let me know how Rebecca is. After you pick her up tomorrow. Bye Ian."

Ian lowered his head.

"Fuck," he admonished himself and rubbed his palms over his face. He hadn't taken but a minute before going after her. "Della, wait!"

But she was already pulling out of the driveway.

He watched in disappointment as she accelerated down the top road of the neighborhood and pulled onto Route 60 without stopping.

VIII

The phone in Della's apartment above Dempsey's Tavern was already ringing before she stepped inside. She let it ring, tossing her keys in the drawer and hanging up her coat as it chimed away in the background.

Staring at it with disdain, she dropped her handbag on the rug beside the couch and made her way into the kitchen.

The ringing eventually cut off mid-peal, sometime during the process of her fishing a bottle buried at the bottom of the freezer.

She filled a tumbler with icy cold vodka and rocks. And just like that, the apartment became safe, blissful silence. The only sound was the vodka cascading over ice like a babbling brook over translucent, smoothly polished stones.

She plopped onto the tattered but comfortable sofa which fit so perfectly beneath the window that it was clearly meant to be nowhere else. It was the only substantial thing Della loved enough to make the effort of hauling it along with her all those miles, despite her necessarily hasty departure from the Big Easy. The sofa's pillows had long become threadbare at the edges; its seat cushions permanently depressed to her precise shape. Which also meant that, like the couch's position beneath the window, Della also fit so perfectly upon it that she was clearly meant to be nowhere else.

This was home.

This was where she belonged.

She took her first sip of vodka and the cool, thickened liquid slid smoothly down her throat, becoming instantly warm. Every cell of her being seemed to be soaking it up like a sponge as it immediately spread through her chest, her stomach, her extremities.

With this tingling sensation also came a calm, grounded stability; something she now realized had been largely absent since she first met Ian Cockerton.

Which had been just four days ago.

She stared absently out the window at the copse of trees at the rear of the Tavern. Previously, they had offered a welcoming oasis to which Della would surrender as she reestablished her center and replenished her soul. She would dedicate thirty minutes, just for herself, with the sole purpose being to absentmindedly stroll among the powerful, natural pillars and luxuriate in the rich, dark smells of the flora. In doing so, the dark noise in her head would quiet to a manageable background static, and all would become right in her world once again.

But tonight, cloaked by darkness, the copse offered only angst and intimidation. For DeLaCroix Laveau, what had once been her respite, even during the most challenging of times, was now a place where evil's presence lay in wait. The innocent splendor of the natural world had twisted and morphed to reveal a dark, uncertain and malevolent place where primeval demons played.

And this complete one-eighty in perspective had occurred in but a matter of days, beginning at the seemingly benign, random lunchtime meeting where she served Rebecca and the brothers steak hoagies in the bar—beneath the very spot where she now sat.

But it had been neither innocuous, nor a matter of chance. That meeting had been ordained to change her life.

Or perhaps more accurately, to clarify it.

How is any of this even possible? she asked herself as she took another sip and allowed herself the latitude to momentarily ignore her own question, instead savoring again the whole-body experience as the vodka quenched every pore. *And if it's finally over, truly over, why do I feel like I don't have one damn bit of closure? Bryan's suicide was the ultimate pronouncement of Good. A sacrifice borne of truest love. For his daughter, for his brother; his son, his wife . . . hell, even for me. It was the antithesis of the heinous scapegoat sacrifices. Bryan's death was not resultant of an act of hate, but an act of purest love. And it worked. Diane is back home. Rebecca will be home tomorrow. And the Darkness was finally expelled by Light. The cycle, at last, is broken.*

The cycle.

The seven.

These two things, more than any other, surfaced over and over. They rankled the intuitive side of her, disallowing the closure she sought.

Because if the Beast had fulfilled the seven sacrifices all those years ago, why had any of this come to take place now?

Better question, why *was it happening at all?*

While lost in this collage of images and mixed emotions, Della found herself increasingly being pinged by one specific memory in particular. Not from the past days, but a memory from many years before. It was the conversation she'd had with Dr. R. Bartholomew, immediately following his presentation at the university.

So with vodka glass balanced expertly in hand, Della dropped from the couch and scooted across the rug. Kneeling before the impressive collection of books she'd acquired over the years (which, like the sofa, she'd made the concerted effort to haul with her) she ran a finger over the array of colorful spines until it nervously came to a stop on *The New Apocrypha*.

The follow-up book to his originally published journal paper, Bartholomew had personally signed it as they spoke.

He'd also slid his business card into a random pair of early pages.

The hardback opened immediately to the spot, and Della lifted out the card which had been trimly awaiting her. She turned it over and grimaced at the sight of the information still scrawled across the back in red ink.

Written by Bartholomew's own hand, it was the name of his hotel, just down the road. And his room number. A big red X had been scratched beneath these, which she imagined was the expression of a kiss.

He hadn't jotted any of this info on the card as she'd spoken with him, so he must've prepared one (or perhaps several) before he'd even taken the stage . . . having one singular post-presentation goal in mind. Which explained why the author had spent so much time talking with her and answering Della's multitude of questions—probably mind-numbingly inane to him—while artlessly signing the other patrons' books and all but shooing those tiresome intellects and professors on their way.

Creep.

The experience had soured her instantly, so she'd tucked the book under her arm while making her meek apologies. Once home, she blindly slid the book into an empty slot on the shelf.

And there it sat, never to be opened again.

Until now.

She'd often wondered why she'd kept Bartholomew's book all these years, given what an unsavory experience it had devolved into. Sure, she'd made a point of bringing most of her library with her, as she counted the wisdom within those volumes as amongst her life's greatest treasures.

But normally she would've just dumped this book in the trash on the way out of the lecture hall, given what had happened. Especially when she'd kept so little else of personal significance from her former life, things that echoed with much more positive vibrations.

So much of that life had, after all, been abandoned in New Orleans exactly where it lay. Literally. Even her favorite mug, the one from which she had sipped chamomile as she first read Bartholomew's original journal paper, sat on the side table next to where the sofa had been. It was the last thing she'd seen as she closed the door to her apartment and locked away that part of her former life forever.

The image of that moment was still floating in her mind as the business card dropped from her fingers.

It wafted to the floor as she steeled her jangling nerves, preparing herself to absorb the words printed across the book's crisp, untouched page. Words she had been divinely led to read only now:

and the question ultimately asked, 'What significance is derived by a theorem proposing that the demonic beast prophesied in the Revelation of Saint John is the same demon of the Rabbinic Hebrew text of Enoch, written some three to five hundred years earlier?'

The answer to that is both sublime and simple: to have in our possession the key to understanding the ambiguous, dreamlike (often described as hallucinatory) version of the end of days according to Saint John.

In the ancient Book of Enoch, the angel Azazel is heralded as being amongst the most prominent leader of the Watchers, angels issued by God to protect Mankind. But angered by the love God bestows upon His greatest creation, Azazel refused to bow before Man. Thus cast from grace, the Watchers (Greek: Grigori) aligned with Satan and propagated their own creations, Nephilim, being the vile offspring of their copulation with humans. The Watchers then proactively engaged in eradicating the natural and Universal spiritual balance by enticing Mankind from the Light and towards violence and warfare; witchcraft, corruption and impurity.

"The whole earth has been corrupted through the works that were taught by Azazel: to him ascribe all sin." – The Book of Enoch, Chapter 10:8

An increasing number of fringe groups, the new Gnostic elite, one might say, therefore recognize Azazel as the right hand of Satan. And though the demonic leader of the Watchers was bound unto the wilderness by Archangel Raphael, Enoch warns us that the presence of Azazel will abide in that place in unfathomable darkness only until the time of Judgment.

The new Gnostics believe this time is the same prophesied by Saint John in his Book of Revelation.

Adhering to the belief that Azazel is the right hand of Satan, his Presence can then be recognized as the seven-headed beast which Saint John warns us will be summoned in the end of days.

Once unleashed from the dark wilderness in which it waits, the demon beast Azazel shall mock the seven archangels by feeding upon the innocence of seven sacrificial scapegoats, one for each of its blasphemous heads.

Then and only then can the demon Azazel fulfill its destiny, which is to prop-agate the most heinous Nephilim of all—an unholy 'virgin' birth of the Dragon Lamb of Satan. A blaspheme of both the Virgin Birth and the Sacred Trinity, the Dragon Lamb is the Satanic inverse of Jesus, our Holy Christ.

Being the great deceiver, this Dragon Lamb will possess the power to lead the world into Darkness as it ultimately extinguishes all Light.

"And I beheld another beast...and he had two horns like a lamb, and spake as a dragon. And he exerciseth all the power of the first beast before him, and causeth the earth and them which dwell therein to worship the first beast....He doeth great wonders...And deceiveth them." – Revelation, 13:11-14.

When viewed through this new Gnostic lens, the Apocalypse of John is no longer an absurd fairy tale. Instead, the Book of Revelation becomes a road map of Mankind's apocalyptic end; a leaked battle plan of Satan's final attempt to upset the spiritual balance forever.

The most critical mistake of Mankind is to view both the Book of Enoch and the Book of Revelation in terms of an ancient and irrelevant past, or an absurd-ly surreal prediction of the future. For in terms of pure mathematics, when past and future are offset, they cancel one another out and what we are left with is only the present day.

Make no mistake, Satan's strategy for the end of days is already underway and will be taking place in the least likely—

The phone next to Della clanged violently to life.

She winced so fiercely that the tumbler twitched from her hand, vodka sloshing over the rim and drenching her lap.

"*JESUS!*"

She jumped to her feet, two ice cubes dropping from her lap to the floor. Swiping the pool of liquid from her jeans, Della strutted awkwardly to the kitchen where she mopped the rest of it from her lap with a dish towel. Her hands trembling, she carefully poured another vodka.

The phone stopped ringing.

Echoes of its chimes were still fading into the corners of the small apartment, still finding resting places in myriad nooks and crannies, echoing hollowly down the empty wooden staircase to the bar, when it started ringing again.

She snatched it up.

"What do you want—!" She knew the greeting was gruff, but also knew without a shadow of a doubt that the only person who would be calling this time of night would be Ian, trying to make friends again. And quite frankly, her nerves were shot and she was in no mood to play this game with him right now.

The other end of the line crackled.

"Ian?"

Silence.

And then something barely audible, a small noise.

In the background.

As if the line had gotten crossed with another call. A sound that her mind was certain was . . .

. . . *a little boy's giggle.*

Her breath caught in her chest and Della recoiled, throwing the phone down so that it slammed hard in its cradle.

And just like that, the apartment's silence was no longer blissful safety.

The phone immediately rang again.

Her fingers trembling, Della warily lifted it from its base and placed it next to her ear. She had not been aware that she was still holding her breath until it escaped from her chest in a cascading rush when Ian's voice came to her from the other end of the receiver.

"Della? It's Ian. Can you hear me?"

"Ian! Jesus—"

"I could hear you but I guess you couldn't hear me. I wanted to say I'm sorry. Listen," he said, not allowing her to talk. *"Rebecca can't be pregnant. And it's nothing to do with what the doctor did or didn't say. It's because she can't get pregnant."*

Della breathed evenly, steadying her hand before taking a long sip of vodka. "She can't . . . ? Meaning?"

"She and Bryan were pregnant again less than a year after they had Diane." The line was silent until she could hear him nervously clear his throat, pulling the receiver away from his mouth. *"That second pregnancy was ectopic, Della."*

"The baby formed outside the uterus?"

"Yes. She miscarried early. Lost a great deal of blood. It was very scary. Bryan thought he might lose her too."

"Oh God, Ian. I'm so sorry. I didn't know."

"Yeah. But she was okay and after enough time had passed they tried again. Three more times, in fact. But she lost every one."

"But Andrew . . . ."

Ian wavered before replying. *"It's no longer biologically possible for Rebecca to carry a child."* The poignancy in his voice palpable, he allowed Della a moment to process that before adding: *"Andrew is adopted."*

She grabbed Bartholomew's book from the floor. The page and paragraph were dead center: *Only once the seven have been taken can the Beast fulfill its ultimate destiny. Before the Two Witnesses, Azazel shall propagate the most heinous Nephilim of all: an unholy virgin birth of the Dragon Lamb of Satan.*

And in a single moment, it all fell into place—why Dr. Fieldhouse had used the phrase he had; why Della had sensed such a deep, spiritual intuition in Diane and the pings of the young girl's uncultivated but powerful ability to project; why the Beast had shown no interest in Andrew.

Why they had been lured back to the woods.

Della felt her heart hammering in her chest. Her mouth dry, she slugged the vodka. She desperately wanted to sit but found herself only able to pace in concise, repeated circles around the room.

"I-Ian, um, hun—" She was certain he must be able to hear the pounding of her heart the phone line.

A moment of silence.

A brief crackling; a static hiss.

A distant, barely audible sound like a voice, but not quite a voice.

Then . . . . *"Yes?"* Ian's reply was small and tinny.

Della pursed her lips and held the phone away as she exhaled, long and slow, before breathing in again through her nose. Try as she might, the intake was jerky and stuttering at best. It was amplified back to her as she placed the phone to her cheek.

"I know this is going to sound off, somehow, and I don't mean it to . . . ."

Another moment of silence, which lasted an eternity.

"It's okay. Go on."

"Bryan said that seven friends had died. But . . . are you sure that's true? I guess . . . what I'm trying to say is—I guess—is . . . was Jack Raker's death ever confirmed? By the authorities?"

"No." Ian's reply was instant. *"They never found the body. But then again, Old Man Raker never admitted to having anything to do with Jimi's death either. Or Woody's. Or Big Dan's, for that matter. I remember my father shaking his head when he told us how Raker proclaimed his innocence all the way through the trial, right up to the moment they hauled him out in cuffs to see the county tailor for a stylish orange jumpsuit fitting."*

Della knew he was trying hard to lighten the mood, but she wasn't able to smile. "Listen, Ian. I need to speak with Rebecca. Tomorrow. In person . . . . Can you make that happen?"

Though her heart had settled to a less frenetic rhythm, Della had been unconsciously biting deeply into her lip. She realized it when she took a sip of the last of the diluted vodka in her tumbler and the liquid stung like a wasp.

"Rebecca? What in God's name for? I don't think that's a great idea—"

"You know I wouldn't ask if it wasn't desperately important."

"Sure," Ian begrudgingly agreed after an uncomfortably long silence. But truth be told, he was privately relieved at the excuse to see Della again. He'd hated parting the way they had tonight. *"Why don't I just stop by your place on my way back. As long as she's up to it, of course."*

"Of course," Della assured and placed the phone gently in its cradle. She paused there, in front of the side table, her eyes glazed and faraway, before the hefting her handbag off the floor rustling anxiously through its contents. It took a moment to comprehend that the semi-automatic was not going to suddenly materialize beneath the tissues and lip balm, wallet and hand wipes.

Because it had been bagged by the police and taken into evidence.

After Bryan shot himself.

She had so easily believed it had been the ultimate sacrifice, the most virtuous of acts to save his daughter and finally break the decades-long cycle of darkness.

Except believing that no longer made sense.

Because only six boys were confirmed dead. The realization of what that statement meant tolled in her mind so loudly that she grabbed her temples. *It may have taken almost twenty years to achieve it, but it was Bryan who had become the seventh. And there was only one way that could have happened.*

DeLaCroix Laveau threw the handbag down and screamed.

After a length of time of which she had no recollection, she retrieved the bottle of vodka from the freezer and settled numbly into her indent on the sofa, a cold plume wafting from the freezer door she'd left open.

This time, she drank straight from the bottle as the silent tears came.

IX

Ian chose instead to drop by Dempsey's before it opened the next morning, parking in the rear of the Tavern next to Della's VW Thing.

He was only there a brief time before dragging something out of the building and tossing it with indifference into the back of the Blazer.

He whistled to himself as he drove to the hospital where Rebecca was already waiting in the lobby, along with Dr. Fieldhouse.

X

Nearly a month passed. In that time, Della had not contacted Ian again. Even Dempsey's Tavern had gone dark, the steel workers and nine-to-fivers scratching their heads and complaining about the irresponsibility of it all, and how typical it was of a Southerner's work ethic, as they scrambled to find a new watering hole to satisfy their post-shift thirst.

In her own way, Diane had also disappeared, not speaking a single word since that night in the Little Woods; not even to comment on the size of her mother's belly . . . which had so quickly grown so considerably large that Rebecca would often her forearms atop it when she stood in any one place for very long. Andrew did comment, wondering why his mommy was getting so fat, and was delighted to find that a miracle was about to happen for their family. He wasn't sure what that meant, but it made him giddy with excitement anyway.

XI

Together, Rebecca, Ian and the kids all stayed in a small and inexpensive hotel suite near the town's modest center. It was safe there—amongst the buildings, and the people, and the concrete. Only once, at noon, and with he and Rebecca closely together for the duration, did the two adults return to the neighborhood to retrieve what they required from the house. The memories there, the vibrations, were simply too strong.

Too terrifying.

Although both would disguise their apprehension as grief.

It took little more than thirty minutes to clear the house of what they required most. Rebecca gathered a few of Diane's books; Andrew's action figures. She packed a few clothes and personal belongings, but mostly she filled her suitcase with shoe boxes full of photographs. Ian took only the cheap ivory Buddha from his old bookshelf. It was smooth. And comfortable. And when he closed his eyes, it made him think of his brother.

And then, like the Daniels' and so many other families in the neighborhood, they were gone.

Never to return.

XII

The plane's engines thrust in muted resonances outside the insulated oval windows. It was a comforting sound—a modern sound.

A safe sound.

The First Class cabin was almost empty, save a few businessmen making the evening journey to New York alongside them.

The plane rose from the ground and angled sharply above the glittering Pittsburgh skyline while the setting sun shone brilliantly on the multitude of shiny, silver buildings full of people doing their own thing. People busy getting on with life. And some people (fifty-nine thousand, give or take a hundred or so) shouting and cheering on the football game in Three Rivers Stadium, hoping for yet another Monday Night victory at the start of yet another glorious season.

Ian grinned, kissing the top of Rebecca's head as she bundled snugly against his shoulder. Across the aisle, Andrew giggled quietly to himself as he enthusiastically colored in the complimentary books provided by the nice stewardess. Every now and then he would press his face to the window, blow, and then draw something in the haze.

Diane only stared silently ahead until the gentle rumbling of the engines lulled her to fragile, uneasy sleep.

The journey took only a few hours as the clouds beneath the rumbling plane turned a magnificent purple, and then grey to black.

The stewardess lowered the cabin lights and smiled as she passed by one last time, nonchalantly pulling Diane's blanket a little higher under her chin before settling into her own small jump seat adjacent to the hatch in the front galley.

Ian reached up and turned off the overhead reading light, effortlessly closing his eyes and relishing the darkness it brought.

In her seat across the aisle, Diane grimaced and winced in her sleep. In her mind's eye she was back in the Little Woods.

She knows the color is draining from her face. She twitches and reaches for her father, her eyes pleading as the oxygen in her brain depletes. With one last effort, she weakly extends her arm, fingers spread wide . . .

. . . and the gun skates out from the brush.

As if drawn toward her open palm like a magnet, it spins from the clasp of tendrils and thorns and comes to a rest at her uncle's feet.

In that moment her eyes slowly close; her chin drops to her chest. A long hiss escapes from her parted lips as her arm falls limply to her side.

But in her mind she still sees the events, the vibrations painting them as clearly as if seen with her own eyes.

Perhaps more clearly.

Her father lunges for the pistol. But so does her uncle, who gets to it first. "IAN, GIVE ME THE GUN!" her father screams.

"NO!" Her uncle's response is vehement, almost venomous.

Her father seizes the semi-automatic but is unable to gain control of it. Her uncle's hands are wrapped firmly around the textured handle, his index finger squarely on the trigger.

Uncle Ian grins.

But it is a twisted, gnarled smile that is sour and bass and wrong.

Guess I was the cartoon ranger all along, *her father forlornly projects, realizing what is about to happen before crying out:* "LORD FORGIVE ME MY SINS AND DELIVER MY CHILD FROM EVIL!"

Satiated with delight, Uncle Ian's eyes are ablaze as he squeezes the gun's trigger. The high caliber shot takes off the back of her father's head—

As the gun's report exploded in her mind, Diane wrested from the vision with a violent, tremulous jolt. Tears gushed instantly down her cheeks, her mouth quivering uncontrollably.

"Mommy—!" she cried out, her first spoken word in over a month.

Rebecca did not hear.

The expectant mother was sound asleep, her head resting awkwardly against the window, her left hand embracing her belly.

But Ian was not asleep.

He reached across the aisle and placed a finger against his niece's trembling lips. "Shhhhh, babygirl," he whispered and kissed Diane's forehead, his eyes devoid of all warmth as she stiffened and shied away. "It's all going to be okay. You're with Uncle Ian now . . . ."

∞

2013

ONE

Martin Shade was a normal man. He lived a normal life. With a normal wife. And two normal kids. His house wasn't unlike so many others in that development: a single story stuccoed home in a small enclave of no more than thirty or forty others, all nestled neatly aside one another like cookies on a tray. He had a dog, two cats (which he abhorred) and drove a meringue colored Prius for its ecology and economy. Now, this isn't to say that Martin wasn't extraordinary in his own unique way, as are we all. He was quite adept at fixing electronic malfunctions in small and mid-sized appliances. And rather terrific at math, geography and politics. Also at taking out the garbage without being asked by wife Marlena.

And Marty was just superb at trivia facts.

The capital of Greece? Athens. The 1976 movie in which Robert Redford both starred and produced, and which dominated that year's Academy Awards? *All The President's Men.* The year Pac-Man was introduced to the American marketplace? *1980.*

So you see, he had a talent of sorts.

Now, I know how you're picturing Marty already: shortish, stout, round-faced with spectacles and a somewhat nerdish if jolly mannerism about him. But there you'd be wrong, for Martin Shade was also remarkable in another way: he was handsome. Beyond reproach. Not those catalog model looks, perhaps, but naturally charismatic enough in a respectably boyish manner to make more than the average woman turn her head, if only for the briefest moment. Martin sported a wry and naturally mischievous smile beneath bright blue eyes that glinted in the sun, and which too easily stole attention away from his fairly well-trained body for a forty-two year old. Tall and lean, but with plenty of lean tissue and neatly defined muscles, think Jimmy Stewart meets Mark Wahlberg, and you're getting close.

And of course, there's one final way in which Marty Shade was extraordinary, but we'll come to that a little later . . . .

On the day we met, I was already late for work. I'm supposed to be at the club and ready to go on stage at eleven sharp. It was already nearly midnight. One more time, Ambrus Ruud, the club's Hungarian proprietor had told me, and I might as well find somewhere else to dance. That was two weeks ago, and I'd made sure I hadn't been late since. Until tonight. When I'd experienced, let's say, something of a . . . difficulty . . . with a current beau.

It seems that ill-tempers and obscene amounts of alcohol don't make for good bedfellows after all.

Jackson was living proof of this as he came at me insanely fast— considering his near incomprehensible stupor—with my favorite eight-inch kitchen knife gleaming in star-like twinkles from each serrated edge beneath the stark, fluorescent overhead light. He thrust the knife at my face, missed, and struck the wall behind me instead.

The fact that I'd kicked him in the nuts may have had something to do with his poor aim.

Or then again, maybe it was the eleven beers.

Anyhoo . . . . It was a brief moment of comic relief as I watched him tug at the knife's handle, doing the best he could to loosen the blade which was now embedded in the freshly painted drywall. I especially liked when the clumsy attempt caused him to lose his grip and his hand slipped wonderfully easily down the edge of the blade, opening his palm with a thin, deep line that separated the thin webbing between thumb and index finger. Jackson held it up and stared with an odd mix of curiosity and numb misunderstanding.

I backed away, out of the kitchenette and toward the pantry, as the clean pink line grew wider, a crimson rivulet first oozing then pulsing from it. He followed me as the blood ran in a sheet down his outstretched hand and fell in great red raindrops onto my new beige Berber carpet. I think it was that, more than his act of intended violence, that pushed me to do what I did next. In fact I know it was. My landlady was a very pleasant woman, probably in her mid-sixties or early seventies (I always found it a little difficult to age people when theirs was so far from my own) who I was proud to say had become something of a friend, if a forty-plus year gap between us could allow the use of such an intimate term. She had been promising me for some time now that she would redecorate the six apartments above her sprawling home, with mine being first. She had begun to make good on it too, starting with my new carpet. 'Because you are just a sweetheart,' was her reason. I wasn't going to argue. At $750 a month the place wasn't bad. Not bad at all. But it sure as shit could use a refresher. And I'm sorry ladies, but that Martha Stewart stuff just ain't my cuppa tea, so I was happy to let her take the reins.

I reached behind me, through the partially open bi-fold louver doors of the pantry, and pulled out the first thing my left hand came upon. I'm still a little intrigued at just how easy it was to swing that four-foot fluorescent tube at Jackson's head. It just sort of came to me, like a matter of instinct. I guess if I were an animal, that's exactly what it would be called. But as I was in fact a twenty-nine year old blonde pole dancer, I'll say it was simply having a big pair of *cajones*.

So to speak.

The tube exploded against the side of Jackson's head in a satisfying way I hadn't expected, having never shattered one of these things before. Amid a powdery blast of glass and dust, I was left holding a six inch piece that remained intact as Jackson was left holding his temple—which, unfortunately, had also remained intact—with the good hand that wasn't ruining my carpet. Where I'd expected his head to crack open like a ripe guava, the result instead had been little more than an antagonism.

Ever poke your finger at a wasp you'd caught in a glass jelly jar? It was something like that.

"You bitch! You fucking *bitch*!"

Okay, I guess I deserved that one. This time, anyway. Lord knows Jackson had accused me of being a female dog at least seven (yes, seven, I'd been keeping track) times a day this past week. Which is precisely the total length of time I'd known this latest Prince Charming who, I'd been certain, was going to be different this time.

"I'm gonna rip you a new asshole like you never been ripped one before," he warned with an unsettlingly calm tone. I was quite sure he had every intent of following through with it as he lurched forward and lunged at me with that gross, bloodied fist which now looked as if it had been dipped in a vat of burgundy wax.

Now, let me take a moment to fill you in a little bit. Because Jackson may have been pretty, with that long dark hair and three day stubble that showed the world he didn't give a shit what they thought—he was living life his way, your opinion on the matter be damned. But he wasn't the sharpest tool in the shed. He was strong, though. And tough. He was also at least a good fifteen years my senior. (Okay, so I admit it. I may have some daddy issues. But what girl doesn't?) A motorcycle mechanic for a local custom chopper shop that put out some sick looking bikes that fetched twenty, thirty, even forty thousand bucks on a fairly regular basis, Jackson was kept busy from the time he strutted into work till the time he shuffled out, tired and worn and ready for a beer. Or ten. And the amount of labor he dedicated to those custom cycles through his great, big, grease-embedded mitts was evident now that one was coming at me. It seemed the size of a catcher's glove, and I had no intention of letting it make contact with my face, head or any other part of my body.

Not if I could help it. So I ducked to the left.

His fist slammed into the jamb of the pantry door. The wood crushed a little beneath his knuckles and I could see the white paint crinkle to bare, clean wood splinters. Much the same way as his sun-darkened skin split at the knuckles to reveal bare, clean bone.

"MotherFUCKER!" he howled as he shook the hand and blew on it in precisely the same way your mother used to do with a piece of meat straight from the oven that was still too hot for you to eat.

"Hurt much?" I asked with a glimmer of a smile and felt immediately remorseful for the comment. Not out of fear of further retaliation, but because of the boyish look that swept instantly into his face: bottom lip beginning to curl out and down into an adorable pout, eyes filling with that same deeply rooted sadness that had so attracted me to him in the first place when he'd stepped into Tangerine Dreams.

That night he had been alone, not with the usual group of drunken cronies that is so indicative of the usual crowd we get. (There's safety in numbers, you know.) And, unlike most of our clients, his reticence to come up to the stage with a fistful of dollar bills—ready to be shoved down my too-tight G-string in the hopes of brushing a certain Neverland reserved for a special few—was exactly what I needed to be attracted to him in illogical measures.

I'd approached him to solicit a private dance. Not once, not twice, but three separate and very dedicated times. Far more effort than I would invest in any other disinterested punter. After all, this is a numbers game, pure and simple. Approach them once—prefaced of course by that little smile, a cursory glance, a pole-slide or booty-shake, and then pulling your attention away as swiftly as you had bestowed it—and if the clown says no, he either: A) has no money, *not worth your time*; B) is interested in another girl, *again not worth your time*; or C) is one of the many voyeurs who milk a $9 beer for an hour and then disappear with not so much as a single Washington crossing their palms, *definitely not worth your time*.

So why I invested so much of my time, which in this biz truly is money, to attract Jackson is still a mystery to me. There was just something about him I guess. That boyish innocence behind a hugely powerful frame of a man. A rugged charm that smacked of Bad Boy . . . but not really bad, just Hollywood bad. Know where I'm coming from? So, the third time was lucky and we retired around the corner to a deliberately darkened area where Management turned a conveniently blinded eye—an eye that, despite being optically challenged, could still make out its twenty percent cut rather too clearly—and settled into one of the booths with no table before it. Jackson perched somewhat tentatively upon the torn and tattered red vinyl seat while I collected $50 in tens from his calloused hand and began to grind in his lap, tease his legs, stroke his chest through his tight cotton T-shirt, and whisper sweet everythings in his ear while Guns 'N Roses belted out *Sweet Child O' Mine* in thumping bass and distorted treble from tweeters long ago split from ridiculous volumes.

And that was all she wrote.

Now here I was, reaching into my kitchen junk drawer for a tidy little black number that happened to be a .38 semi-automatic made by some Dutch gun company whose name I can't remember, and don't really care to anyway; one which I was assured by a previous man-friend—who also happened to be an active duty Tampa cop—made the best handgun for your buck. So, I'd bought it with the proceeds of two nights' tips, filled the little cartridge thingy with bullets ("Rounds," the cop had corrected me at the time rather indignantly, and to which I had simply responded: "Which are bullets . . . right?") and with little further thought, dropped the lot into the kitchen drawer alongside a dozen colored paperclips, three old unpaid bills and about six dollars in loose change.

I slid the gun out now and gripped it far too tightly in my left hand, balancing my unsteady forearm with my right, just like the cop had shown me. I was shaking, and it was obvious. But Jackson took no steps closer, freezing pretty much in place like you see in the movies. I thought he was threatened by the show of force, but now have to wonder if he was merely frightened that if I didn't calm down I might just squeeze the trigger by mistake. Five pounds of pressure, they say is all it takes. And at this close range, even a child could drill a hole into a human head and turn it into a spaghetti squash. Sigs were that easy to shoot.

That was it. It was called a Sig . . . a Sig-something.

"Kandi . . ." Jackson pleaded so softly and unlike the ugly thing he had been only moments before. This Jackson was the Jackson I had fallen in love with a week ago. And by the way, you like the name? Kandi. As in, Kandi Kane. As in, I joined the Tangerine Dream around Christmas last year, and the rest is pretty obvious. And yes, I was at least smart enough to not give Jackson my real name. Not yet, anyway. But who knows, give it another day or two and I might've.

Well, I might've given him the legal name I've been known by for years now, which is Justine. No way I would ever be so dumb as to tell him the name I actually grew up with, which is Diane.

Never.

Not even as head-over-heels in love with him as I was.

"Just put it down. And we'll talk," Jackson pleaded quietly and was motioning downwards with the palms of his hands. More blood dripped onto my new rug, the drops now a little thicker, a little darker.

"Stop doing that, you useless asshole." Mine wasn't a plea but a dictate, and he knew it. Now his hands, like the rest of him, froze where they were, sort of outstretched and at waist level. He looked as though he was gonna get out his prayer mat and face East.

I laughed. And waggled the gun at him, telling him just to go, to get the fuck out and leave me alone. And if he ever came back I'd kill him.

And l would.

So now I was late for work.

And this is precisely where we started, right?

I looked out the bedroom window to make sure Jackson was in fact gone, even though the squeal of his motorcycle's wide rear tire had already confirmed it. I pulled the curtain aside and watched the chopper angle away from my building, across the parking lot (ignoring the painted lanes and lines) and with a deep lean to the left, bank out the exit and into the traffic in front of our small apartment complex.

The clock radio on my nightstand declared 11:38.

Shit shit shit shit SHIT. If I said it enough times it acted as a mantra to my getting ready, seeming to pulse me along, the way the beat of a great song just makes you hafta dance.

"Shit!" I declared one more time as I pulled on black stockings, lacy tanga briefs from VS, skirt, cotton blouse half buttoned, and slipped into my old beaten Nikes.

I scurried out my front door with purse, keys, and one of those big, sturdy paper bags, the kind with the wonderfully useful handles you get from the more upscale clothing boutiques—like at the International Plaza —and which was now unceremoniously stuffed with three different outfits, none of which I'd purchased there. It was only then that I realized I still had the .38 in my hand. How quickly I'd become accustomed to this thing which, while never frightening to me, at least had demanded a modicum of respect when I first held it. Now it seemed as natural a part of me as my watch. Or holding my car keys. Funny. I guess I could see how some folks, some men typically, might become so fanatical about them. There's a certain sense of satisfying power, having the authority of life or death held so effortlessly in your little hand.

But I had no time for this pondering, so simply tossed the gun into the big trendy bag with all my other stuff and raced out to the parking lot. In seconds I was on Madison and pushing my '92 Mustang convertible (aptly but unimaginatively named 'Sally') for all it was worth as I rocketed left, out onto the connector, and then right onto Dale Mabry Highway.

The Tangerine Dream wasn't much to look at, I'll admit. I cringed the very first time I walked into the place, and felt dirty and cheap as soon as I left. So, you are asking, why the hell would I take a job there?

And the answer is simple . . . . Money.

Lots of money.

For doing very little.

So, okay. I get it. It's a bit seedy. A little like legalized prostitution but without having to actually do anything to the guy, if you know what I mean. But for me, when I'm on stage I zone out, feeling the beat pulsating through me, the bass pumping loud and mad; guitars screaming and grinding. And just like that, there's no one else. It's just me and the music.

Now I'll grant you, it wasn't always like that. The first time, well, that was something to behold I'm quite sure. Some skinny little girl, all nerves and attitude, trying too hard and even harder to look at. But it's like that for every girl the first time, or two, or ten. Now l just go with it, and in a weird kinda way, I actually enjoy it. A little bit anyway. The customers are nice, and if you treat them right, they'll come back and treat you right, too. Then it becomes more like visiting with friends.

Except you're at work.

And half naked.

And your friends are stuffing dollar bills down your panties.

But other than that, it's just like hanging out.

Mustang Sally shot past the gleaming steel and glass of Raymond James Stadium—*Go Bucs*—and I knew I was just minutes away. Thank God. I'd be late, but I probably only missed one dance. And of course the All-Girl lineup. But I could work it out: do some extra special moves, hit the poles one or two times more, you know, basically make good so Ambrus wouldn't up and fire me on the spot. I was sure that's all I would need to do, tonight anyway. And by tomorrow he'd have cooled down, probably even forgotten about it, and be all-a-fluster about some other girl or some vendor giving him shit. Or some punter that owes him and hasn't coughed up. Yeah, Ambrus was running books on the side. But is there anyone in this business that isn't?

And then Sally veered for no apparent reason. At least that's what I thought until a sound like a large balloon popping told me one of my tires had burst and was now just a bunch of shredded rubber strips decorating the blacktop. We (Sally and me, of course) narrowly missed a black Malibu coming up on my left as we filled both lanes of Dale Mabry. Then we careened sideways as Sally's front end tilted off-center . . . and the concrete median strip apparently jumped up from the middle of the road and kicked Sally's front legs out from under her.

We skidded to a stop with her hood hanging over the center strip, forcing oncoming traffic in the passing lane to swerve to keep from spinning me like a bottle at a teenagers' party. Sally's ass-end obstructed the passing lane of my own side of the highway in equal measures, forcing cars over here to make the same maneuver.

So this just wasn't my night.

I leaned against the steering wheel and held my face in my hands, ignoring the obnoxious *bluuuuuurt* of the horn as my elbows pressed the center of the wheel. This was all a little too much, I'll admit. I'd been cool as a cucumber back at my apartment, unfazed by Jackson's drunken, violent rage. Pulling the gun had seemed so logical and simple at the time, in the heat of the confrontation. Now, the full realization of what might have gone down was bubbling to the surface and I began to cry, sobbing a strange tune that intermingled with those inadvertent sporadic pips from Sally's horn as I shifted weight from one elbow to another.

"Hey," the stranger said softly and with a calculated amount of caution, not wanting to startle me as he leaned down and peered through my open driver's side window. One shirt-sleeved forearm was braced atop my door, which I now realized had been jarred open. Great, I thought, or perhaps even mumbled aloud as I threw my hands up in surrender. Not only a crash, but fucking Sally was this close to bucking me clean out of her. Thanks Sal.

"Who's Sally?"' the man queried as he leaned lower and a little more into the car to get a better look at me.

"Never mind," I said. "Just fuck it."

I pushed open the door and swung my feet out, making sure to give Sally a good, swift kick in the dash in the process. I began to lift myself out of the bucket seat, but the man was blocking my egress.

"Uh, excuse me?" I said rather too pointedly, but didn't really give a shit at this stage.

He looked a little embarrassed and moved to one side. Not a lot, just enough to allow me to step out while still having to brush up against him to do so. "Hey, are you okay? I mean, are you hurt or anything?"

Even though I knew I hadn't been hurt, I still looked down at my body as if to make sure, as if this man who I'd never met somehow knew something about me I didn't. Like when someone tells you that you look a little under the weather. Even though you don't feel it, you'll look in a mirror the next chance you get . . . just to make sure. It's amazing how much of our well-being hinges upon others' perceptions of it. I always found that both vexing and more than a little sad. I was really irritated about it right now, mentally reprimanding myself for allowing him to pull me right down into that kind of socially dogmatic quagmire.

And I know what you're thinking: chill girl, he only asked if you were okay. He's only doing the right thing.

And you'd be right, but I wasn't in the mood to be all P.C.

"Just a bruised ego," I told him with a clinging attitude as I brushed myself down. Why was I brushing myself down? Lord knows. I wasn't dirty, there had been no glass breakage, no damage at all, quite frankly. So you tell me. That's just something you sorta do, right?

And then that irritated me too, so I kicked Sally's front quarter panel. It made a small Nike-shaped dent. Great. So *now* there was actual damage. I knew I would regret that later, but it sure as fuck felt good right now.

"Piece of shit. Sally. You piece of metal CRAP!"

"Whoa, okay. Listen," the man said, perplexed while slowly backing away, his hands gesturing innocence, all open and non-threatening, the way we naturally do when we're showing that we've no intention of poking the bear with a stick. "I just wanted to help. That's all. You're fine. That's good. And since you're alright, I guess I can go on my way."

He backed away fully now, turned, and started back towards his car.

Suddenly I felt like a real piece of garbage. This guy goes out of his way to stop for a stranger in need, and I basically treat him like he's the source of all my problems. Certainly like he was some serious nuisance I didn't need. I sighed, closed my eyes for a moment and resigned myself once again to the fact that I can be a real bitch.

Then I asked him to wait.

He stopped and turned, showing me for the first time that he was actually kinda cute . . . in a Good-Boy-Turned-Even-Better-Boy sort of way.

He smiled, the slightest I think a smile could be and yet still be considered a smile. "Bad day, huh?"

I shook my head. "You have no idea.."

He looked to Sally, back to me, then Sally once more. "Oh, I think I have some idea . . . ."

"Okay," I surrendered. "l guess you do."

I paused to consider what I was about to say next, and in hindsight, things would have turned out a lot different if I'd just let him go.

But I have this thing about lost dogs, and this guy seemed to fall square into that category. Something about him told me he might even be the poster child for that group. So I was hooked. Call it Superman syndrome, needing to be needed, or maybe just being way too soft.

No matter, I heard myself saying the next words before I'd even made a conscious decision to let them out.

"Listen, uh—?"

"Martin," he answered and extended his hand to be shook.

"Okay, Martin. Listen Marty, do you think you could get me out of this jam? I need to be someplace, like an hour ago. It really isn't far from here, about two minutes. Would you mind?"

As I said all of that, I found myself shaking his hand without even realizing it. It was smooth and gentle, but strong. And if I'm honest, I think I could've stood like that for hours, just my hand in his.

His smile broadened. "Of course. Wherever you need to go, I'll get you there, Miss, uh . . . ." He tilted his head and those eyes found mine in a way that was almost hypnotic.

"Justine," I found myself offering. And then just completely blurting out, "Justine. Justine Trattoria."

Wait. What? Oh God. Why the fuck did I just tell him my name.

He seemed utterly indifferent to what, for me, was such vulnerable if not dangerous honesty, and simply squeezed my right hand with one final pump. "Funny name. But okay then, Justine Justine Trattoria. Let's go . . . ."

A.G. MOCK *is a writer and publisher whose multi-decade career spans both the UK and the US. He currently lives on the Gulf Coast with his incredibly patient wife, two peculiarly challenging but adorable dogs, and a cheeky ghost who likes to clatter about in the guest bedroom and occasionally lock them all out. His wife and dogs he treasures wildly; the ghost he can take or leave.*

The Little Woods *is his debut novel.*

EPOCH

EpochThrillers.com
AGMock.com

Made in the USA
Columbia, SC
28 June 2021